MW01193976

ELM STREET

Memories of a Home

To my friend, Joan

amazing friends equal

great memories!

SCOTT DOUGLAS VAUGHAN

© 2016 Scott Douglas Vaughan

All rights reserved.

www.scottdvaughan.com / www.elmstreetmemories.com

This book was edited and proofread, with appreciation, by the editors of CreateSpace Independent Publishing; Patty Patterson of Lexington, SC; and Vicki Vaughan of Lexington, SC. A special word of appreciation to consultant, editor, and proofreader William D. Vaughan of Takoma Park, MD.

The cover photograph is of Cumming Elementary School, Elm Street, Cumming, GA, circa 1965.

Back cover photograph is of sixth-grade friends, from left: Keith Stone, Stan Harris, author Scott Vaughan, Richard Webb, and Steve Taylor. Photographs used with permission.

Grateful acknowledgment for permission to include the following copyrighted material:

"Joy to the World"
Words and Music by Hoyt Axton
Copyright (c) 1970 IRVING MUSIC, INC.
Copyright Renewed
All Rights Reserved Used by Permission
Reprinted by Permission of Hal Leonard Corporation

"Last Train To Clarksville"
Words and Music by Bobby Hart and Tommy Boyce
Copyright (c) 1966 Screen Gems-EMI Music Inc.
Copyright Renewed
All Rights Administered by Sony/ATV Music Publishing LLC, 424 Church Street, Suite 1200, Nashville, TN 37219
International Copyright Secured All Rights Reserved
Reprinted by Permission of Hal Leonard Corporation

"I Wish We'd All Been Ready"
Words and Music by Larry Norman
Copyright (c) 1969 Beechwood Music Corp. and J.C. Love Publishing Co.
Copyright Renewed
All Rights Administered by Sony/ATV Music Publishing LLC, 424 Church Street, Suite 1200, Nashville, TN 37219
International Copyright Secured All Rights Reserved
Reprinted by Permission of Hal Leonard Corporation

"Summertime Blues"
Words and Music by Eddie Cochran and Jerry Capehart
© 1958 (Renewed) Warner-Tamerlane Publishing Corp.
All Rights Reserved
Used by Permission of Alfred Music

Scripture references from the Holy Bible, King James Version.

Scott Vaughan's author photograph provided by Dawn Strawbridge, Lexington, SC. Photos by Dawn Strawbridge (www.dawnstrawbridge.com).

ISBN: 1535405015
ISBN 13: 9781535405010
Library of Congress Control Number: 2016912149
CreateSpace Independent Publishing Platform
North Charleston, South Carolina

I have tried to recreate events, locales, and conversations from my memories. In some instances, I have changed the names of individuals and places. I might also have changed some identifying characteristics and details such as physical properties, occupations, and places of residence. This book is a memoir inspired by people, places, and events.

Dedicated with love and respect to my first friend,
Richard Joel Webb

Some of these stories are true.
Some of these stories are based in truth.
Some of these stories should have been true.

Don't forget the broken window in the courthouse.
Don't forget anything we ever did ever!!!!
—Richard Webb

Written in Scott Vaughan's sixth-grade yearbook, 1971

Contents

Author's Note

For those who read my 2014 book, *Brookwood Road*, this book is not a sequel. On a historical timeline, both *Brookwood Road* and this book, *Elm Street*, are based on stories from my life, 1959–1973, or until I had completed eighth grade at age thirteen.

I had the great fortune of living two childhoods. *Brookwood Road* captures stories from my childhood on our family farm at the southern-most end of Forsyth County, Georgia. *Elm Street* captures stories from my childhood days in Cumming, Georgia, the county seat of Forsyth County, where I attended school and church and played around town while my mother worked there.

Blessings,
Scott Douglas Vaughan, 2016.

Sometimes, you will never know the value of a moment, until it becomes a memory.
—Dr. Seuss

To purchase *Brookwood Road*, please visit www.brookwoodroad.com or look for it in paperback and Kindle formats on www.amazon.com.

PROLOGUE

It was hot even for late May, and it was still hot at dusk on this particular Friday.

Outside the gymnasium of the Acorn Junior High School on Elm Street, 162 students gathered excitedly. Tonight they would graduate from eighth grade, meaning they would, in the fall, join other eighth graders from across Acorn County at the comprehensive high school. Ahead of them were high-school sports, dating, part-time jobs, proms, a nationally recognized marching band, driving to and from school, and extended weekend curfews at home. At the conclusion of tonight's ceremony, after principal Garland Shoemake had handed each of them a diploma, they would launch from being older children to young adults.

The ceremony was starting later because the old gymnasium, built in 1941, had no air conditioning. Any cooling came from big fans that attempted to circulate air but actually just circulated smells from decades of sweat-stained bleachers and old varnished wood from a basketball court that creaked and moaned with every dribble. The old gymnasium—and the junior high school—had been Acorn's county high school until 1955, when the new high school was built. That year, the junior high became home for the Acorn School District's sixth through eighth graders. The night had a nostalgic feel to it—many of the parents of this year's graduates had attended high school at the old school building; some had even played basketball in this very gymnasium.

The 162 students were dressed in their Sunday best. The girls wore knee-length white dresses with red or black ribbons in their hair; the boys wore black pants, white shirts, and red ties. The color scheme was no accident. The red, black, and white of the Acorn Junior High Bullpups matched appropriately with the red, black, and white of the Acorn County Bulldogs and the red, black, and white of the University of Georgia Bulldogs, who played in Athens, about an hour's drive to the east.

Organizing the students into alphabetized single-file lines fell to the eighth-grade teachers, and they were having quite a time bringing order to the excitement. There was the occasional push or shove or farting sound blown into a boy's crooked elbow. The girls, already acting more mature, stood with arms crossed, shaking heads and counting the days until they could be free of these goofy boys and date high-school juniors who could already drive.

Missing all this ceremony excitement was eighth grader Frank Wilcox. He stood backstage with the eighth-grade sponsor and English teacher Mrs. Mary Daniel, Principal Shoemake, and Superintendent of Schools Clarence Lambert. Roger Williams, the pastor of the First Baptist Church of Acorn, stood with the small ensemble. As the adults talked among themselves, Frank could feel his teeth chattering. It was a nervous tic that no one could see, and he was glad for that. Frank hated when his nerves led to chattering teeth, especially on a hot May evening.

Pastor Williams leaned toward him. "Are you ready?" he whispered. Frank hardly looked up and said that he was ready. "You'll do just fine," the pastor said, patting Frank on the back. Frank was glad Pastor Williams was on the graduation stage because Frank knew he needed the Lord's favor right now, and he figured his pastor had a direct hotline.

Superintendent Lambert, with his paunch and professorial manner, said, "You'll do fine, son. Your mama used to give fine talks in church about missions, and I'll bet you are just as good a speaker." Mr. Lambert had served as a deacon and Sunday School superintendent at the First Baptist Church.

Despite the encouragement, Frank wasn't altogether ready for this evening. And his teeth weren't chattering because he was the one student selected by Mrs. Daniel to speak on behalf of the other 162 students. His teeth were chattering because Frank had a secret.

Frank had two speeches. There was the one Mrs. Daniel had written for him, and it was the one he had given during the graduation rehearsal earlier that day. Then there was the speech he had written because, well, he was the one doing the speaking. The way he saw it, why did a rising high-school ninth grader need a teacher to write his speech for him? The problem was that everyone, including Tom and Janet Wilcox (his parents) and R. C. Wilcox (his beloved grandfather), all had heard Mrs. Daniel's speech and thought that would be the one he would give.

There was also the issue of his maternal grandmother, Carolyn Holmes, his Mema, who taught seventh-grade math and science at the school and was one of Mrs. Daniel's good friends. His Mema and Mary Daniel had served for years together in the local chapter of the Georgia Educators Association and the Acorn Garden Club. His Mema, too, had heard him rehearse Mrs. Daniel's speech.

But, to be honest, it was his Mema who planted the idea for the secret, second speech. Upon hearing his rehearsal one Wednesday after school, she had said, almost to herself but loud enough for Frank to hear, "I don't know why Mary couldn't let you write your own speech."

Now, as he stood surrounded by the small quartet of adults, he stared through a slit in the old stage curtain. There must have been four hundred people sitting in rows of metal chairs on the old gymnasium floor. A few other renegades, including the Piper clan, sat in the old bleachers. Frank reached into his left pocket and felt the folded speech written by Mrs. Daniel; he then reached into his right pocket and felt the folded speech that he had written.

He was going to stand up and give one of the speeches. However, even at this eleventh hour, he had not yet made up his mind about what to do. He looked at his sweet mama's face in the crowd and tried to imagine her reaction if he read the self-written speech. He might not live to attend Charlie Keller's sleepover following the graduation ceremony.

Mrs. Daniel touched him on the shoulder and motioned for him to take his seat on the stage. As he and the adults took their seats, the curtain opened, and the famous high-school band's ensemble, the Red

Peppers, began playing the familiar "Pomp and Circumstance." His classmates began marching in from the rear of the gymnasium.

Watching his friends enter the gymnasium, he felt a familiar pull on his emotions. About two dozen of these friends had been alongside him since kindergarten at the First Baptist Church; some of them had been friends before that through Sunday School at the church. He could still remember birthday parties when they were all very small children. Charlie Keller had always been his friend like the way a brother or sister has just always been there. Their friendship was born from the fact that their mothers, Janet Wilcox and Midge Keller, had been best friends growing up in Acorn. These people walking into the gymnasium weren't just friends; they were family, having all grown up together in this wonderful place called Acorn. Frank knew to his core that once they got to high school, things would be different as they fell in among 150 or so other rising ninth-graders from across the county.

As he watched his friends take their seats, Frank also did not feel particularly worthy to be on the stage delivering this short speech. He was here only because of an inexplicable string of events that had begun in the fourth grade, taken root in his seventh-grade English class, and culminated with his being chosen as editor of the school yearbook in the eighth grade. Mrs. Daniel, as the class sponsor, was also responsible for the yearbook.

Frank knew that had the class elected its speaker, he would not have been the one chosen. His lifelong friend Charlie was the most popular boy in his class, was a better-than-average athlete, was one of the top academic students, and was known for his sense of humor and fun-loving way of agitating the teachers. The agitation had led to him setting primary school records for hallway spankings, which only increased his celebrity. Charlie easily could have been chosen as the class speaker.

Lester Freemont could have been chosen on academics alone. There was no boy—not one—who had scored better than Lester Freemont when each semester's report cards were handed out. And it wasn't just one year. No, Lester Freemont had been king of academics from the day in first grade when students took their first spelling test.

Pete Yancey could have been chosen on friendliness and kindness alone. Pete was popular because he didn't care whether he was popular or not; Pete's mission every day of school was to be kind and helpful to everyone around him—no matter how much anyone had or didn't have. Pete was happy and content just being Pete. Students respected him.

Frank spotted Steve Dickson sitting near the front of the auditorium. Steve Dickson sure as hell wouldn't have been chosen to speak, Frank thought. Steve had left a trail of tears in second grade, announcing to everyone in Mrs. Edith Wright's class that there was no Santa Claus.

There was Van Piper, who was just mean as hell, and everyone knew it and everyone stayed away from him. It was a miracle that Van was even at this graduation, but there he was, sitting close to his smaller sidekick, Travis Jackson. Neither of those two would have been chosen to speak unless they had scared everyone into voting for them.

Any number of girls could have given this speech. There were so many bright, pretty, poised girls in Frank's class that any vote would have likely involved a dozen or so runoff elections to choose just one of them. Perhaps that was why none of them had been chosen. It would have been too complicated and stirred up too many angry mamas coming to the school on behalf of their daughters.

And then Frank spotted his friend Wendell Mann. That made him smile. He wasn't sure if Wendell would have been asked to give this speech, but he knew one thing: there was no better encourager or friend than Wendell Mann. And Wendell was the only one in the audience— the only one—who knew Frank's secret of the two speeches. As their eyes locked, a smile exploded on Wendell's happy-go-lucky face—a smile that caused Frank to smile back even as his teeth chattered so badly he bit his tongue.

Students seated, the Red Peppers concluded the musical introduction, and all eyes turned to the podium as Mrs. Mary Daniel stood to begin the ceremony.

Frank Wilcox closed his eyes and breathed deep.

Van Piper blew a fart into his elbow, creating muffled giggles as Mrs. Mary Daniel congratulated the graduates. The graduation ceremony had begun.

INTRODUCTION

Acorn County, located just forty miles due north of downtown Atlanta, was organized around 1830 from land earlier settled by the Cherokee Indians. The Cherokee were forcibly relocated to Oklahoma in 1838 and 1839, along with other "civilized" tribes, in a movement referred to as the Trail of Tears because of the weeping that occurred during the relocation.

Acorn County and the county seat of Acorn were not named for any one particular person. There was no General Acorn from the Revolutionary War, and neither was there a Governor Acorn who served well in the Georgia legislature. Rumor had it that one of the early Cherokee, certainly before being run out of the county, favorably said something about the land being a place where mighty people—like oak trees—would grow.

"Chief, you mean like growing up from an acorn?"

Something like that, allegedly. And whereas most Georgia counties were named differently than the county seat, Acorn was an exception. Acorn County had one incorporated town, and that was the town of Acorn, located just about at the geographic midpoint of the county. Acorn was the government, business, and educational center of the county.

In the years between the end of the Civil War, 1865, and 1950, Acorn County was largely a poor place to be. Reconstruction after the war had been hard on Atlanta—not to mention the town being burned to the ground by the infamous Yankee general William Tecumseh Sherman, also known as "Sherman" in an unflattering way.

By 1950, things took a turn in Acorn County. Acorn County was already a fertile agricultural area, and when the poultry industry was introduced, the economic upturn was significant. The county was soon dotted with chicken houses, and chickens became a significant part of the county's landscape. There was some discussion about changing the school's mascot from the Bulldogs to the Roosters, but brighter heads prevailed.

In the southern end of the county, just a mile from the Fulton County line, R. C. Wilcox had borrowed money from his father-in-law, William Perry McIntosh, to start his own poultry farm on Brookwood Road. Things went well until R. C. realized that everyone in Acorn County was getting into the chicken business, and that prompted him to shift over to raising, butchering, and processing hogs. In fact, when Frank, born in 1959, was a boy on the farm, R. C. and Kathryn Wilcox and their son Tom were operating a six-hundred-head hog farm, milling their own feed for the hogs, butchering the hogs, and packaging pork products under the Wilcox Sausage Company label for distribution all over north Georgia.

The poultry boon had an economic impact on the town of Acorn. Business flourished. In the center of town was the massive, old, two-story courthouse, where court and county business were conducted. And all around the courthouse square, hardware stores, furniture stores, five-and-dime stores, drugstores, grocery stores, and department stores opened and thrived. Just off the square, funeral homes built new buildings, churches made improvements, and banks grew and moved to new buildings. Even the faithful Dairy Queen was refurbished. What's more, everyone knew everyone, and everyone helped everyone—even if they all did gossip about one another at the same time. And Acorn was safe. Children could ride bicycles and visit one another in small neighborhoods that began to pop up around the town limits.

Despite the economic upturn, the Acorn County population in 1960 was 12,170—only about 1,600 more than the population surge of the 1870s at the end of Reconstruction. In 1960s Acorn County, children had simple pastimes. They went to school by day, and they helped and played on farms when they weren't in school. Some played on small community sports teams. Most of the county's children, even those living near Acorn, had experienced some kind of farm life—even if it wasn't chickens or hogs. Some had experience with cows, too.

Despite the nation's states each adopting a compulsory attendance law, children were often seen as free farm labor, and giving up that labor for schooling was sometimes a luxury. Those who attended school up until about 1950 often did so at small community schools, which might house grades one to eleven, were taught by part-time teachers and older students, and were within walking distance of students' homes. In Acorn County, these small, rural community schools sometimes met in independent structures but might have also met in barns or church meeting houses. By 1960, the nation's families had accepted the relationship between a lack of education and an increase in poverty, and most families wanted their children in school. This put pressure on the small community schools to be more structured and focus on the measurable results of education.

In Acorn County, smaller community schools, such as Brandywine, where Kathryn Wilcox attended, merged with other community schools to form regional schools. Students were able to travel further to the regional schools because of public school buses, which had grown in national popularity since World War II. The regional schools taught grades one through eight, though some grades might have been taught within one classroom. The county's high-school-age students were transported publicly or privately to Acorn and Acorn County High School.

By 1965, when Frank Wilcox became the next generation of Wilcox children entering school in Acorn County, students in the southern part of the county attended Big Creek Elementary before moving on to Acorn County High School. When Tom and Janet Wilcox married in 1958, Janet had agreed to move from town to the Brookwood Road farm provided that Tom agreed to two conditions. The first condition was that the family attend the First Baptist Church in Acorn. It was where Janet had grown up in church and where the couple had gotten married. The second condition was that their children would be educated at the Acorn town schools—a twenty-mile round trip from the farm. To aid the arrangement, Janet worked in Acorn, first as the town clerk and later as a small-business owner. The fact that her parents, including her mother, a schoolteacher, both lived and worked in Acorn helped the arrangement.

In Acorn, there was the Acorn Primary School for grades one through five, and the Acorn Junior High School for grades six through eight. Both were on Elm Street in the shadow of Acorn County High School, which served all the county's high school age students.

This was the Acorn educational environment in 1964 as Frank Wilcox and his closest childhood friends entered kindergarten at the nearby First Baptist Church, preparing them and nurturing them toward the start of public school on Elm Street in August 1965.

ONE

SCHOOL SPANKINGS

Frank Wilcox was starting school. It was late August, and most of the summer of 1965 was in the rearview mirror. Frank was nervous because he had always been safe and secure in the family environment of Brookwood Road and rarely went anywhere without someone in his family along with him. He had emotionally survived kindergarten because it was only a half day and was at a very familiar place. School was a venture into the unknown.

The family had all gathered on Sunday evening to celebrate Frank's start of school the next morning. Frank's daddy, Tom, had churned vanilla ice cream—the last churn of summer. Frank's beloved Granny, Kathryn Wilcox, had cradled him in her lap and said, "You are going to love school. You will learn to read, you will learn how to add and subtract numbers, and you will make lots of new friends."

His grandfather, R. C. Wilcox, had bought him a wallet and put two one-dollar bills inside. Frank had never had a wallet before, and he wasn't altogether sure he wanted to put it in the back pocket of his blue jeans and sit on it all day. But he did like the two dollars inside. "If you ever get left at school, maybe someone will bring you home for those two dollars," R. C. had said, chuckling to himself. He had said it more to get a rise out of Kathryn, because he was sure she was never going to let this grandson—or any grandchild—be absent-mindedly left anywhere.

Trying to ease any anxiety over starting school, Frank's mama, Janet, had produced a photograph of his kindergarten class from the First Baptist Church. She began reminding him of the friends who would also be at Acorn Primary School. But mostly she focused her assurances on the fact that Charlie Keller would be at the school, as Charlie was Frank's best friend. Frank could not remember when

1

Charlie had not been his friend, and in many ways, Charlie was his security blanket in all things uncertain.

"You and Charlie will even be in the same classroom together," she said. "And I'll bet you'll have a chance to sit together." He stared at the photograph, wondering if any of the other children from kindergarten would be in his class.

"It's all a gamble," Tom said, throwing dice from a game of Monopoly onto the kitchen table. "You don't know what numbers are going to show up, and you have to play the numbers you are given. You and Charlie could be in a room full of girls." Most boys might have cringed at that thought; Frank was generally indifferent. Through Sunday School and then kindergarten, he had friends who were girls, and if they were in his class, that would be just fine.

"You'll have to be on your best behavior," Tom said. "If you go to school and misbehave, the teachers can spank you."

R. C. laughed. "That's right. I used to get a spanking about once a week. My teachers never had a sense of humor. Mr. Martin would grab me by the shirt, run me outside, and take a hickory switch to my ass. I'd try to run away but ended up just going around in a circle while he held me with one arm and whipped me with the other."

"You deserved it," Kathryn said. "You were always trying to make people laugh when they should have been studying."

"Did you get a spanking at school, Daddy?" Frank asked Tom.

"No, he did not," Kathryn said. "Your daddy was shy and quiet and tried his best not to get his clothes dirty."

"Just do what you are told," Tom said, looking at R. C. "And don't be a jackass."

This was all new information. Frank could accept that he would be at school, away from his family, even though he was nervous about it. He did not like that the school dress code required him to wear blue jeans all day, even though the August heat prompted the wearing of shorts. He could accept that he would be eating food in a giant room full of children and that the food would be prepared by people he did not know. He could accept that he would have to ask permission to use the bathroom. He could accept that he had to trust that someone he loved would be there after school to make sure he got home, though he was glad to have two dollars just in case.

But this spanking business was unsettling. Strangers could now spank him whenever they wanted to spank him? Further, his parents and grandparents seemed to be comfortable with it.

"Daddy, do you mean that if I misbehave, they will slap me on the hand?" Frank asked, thinking about the time Charlie's mom, Midge, had spanked his hand for a slight indiscretion. She had heard him say "hell," as in, "It's hot as hell."

"No, I mean they will beat your ass if you act like a damned fool," Tom said, staring directly into his oldest son's face. "And if they do beat your ass, they will also call me. And when you get home, I will beat your ass, too."

Frank began to cry.

"Now look what you've done," Janet said.

"Just listen and obey the teacher, Miss Johnson," Janet said. "Be a good boy. You are a good boy. You aren't going to get a spanking." She gave him a bowl of vanilla ice cream with Hershey's chocolate syrup generously poured over it. Frank stared at the ice cream, tears rolling down his cheeks.

At bedtime, Janet sat on the edge of the bed he shared with his younger brother, Jack.

"I know you are nervous about going to school, but you don't have to be nervous," Janet said. "You will be surrounded by people who know you even if you don't know them."

Frank looked at his beautiful mama, and he really didn't want to leave her.

"Mrs. Wright, who teaches second grade, is one of your Granny's best friends—all the way back to when they were in school together. Mrs. Mize, in the library, was one of my teachers." Janet began to name, one by one, all the faculty and staff who attended church with the Wilcox family, including Mrs. Wolfe, who managed the cafeteria, and the principal, Mr. Pulliam. "I used to go to sleepovers at Mrs. Wolfe's house," she said.

"You are going to recognize Mrs. Housley from church," Janet continued. "You remember her from Sunday School last year. Mrs. Hicks, who teaches fourth grade, I believe, was a friend of mine in high school. Your Mema teaches at the junior high, and she knows all the teachers, and they know her, too. You will be surrounded by people who know you and will take care of you."

"And can spank me," Frank said.

"I ought to pinch your daddy's nose off," Janet said. "Do you what you are told, and you won't get a spanking."

Frank could not get over it. He got his fair share of whippings, mostly from Janet, but the thought of a stranger just suddenly pulling out a belt, or a whip, or a hickory switch, or a ruler, or a flyswatter, or a hairbrush (he had been spanked once with the back of a hairbrush) was just more than his imagination could handle.

It was a sleepless, restless night. The excitement over the black book satchel filled with brand-new school supplies was tempered by the thought of teachers going wild, whipping students for all kinds of infractions. If only he could talk to Charlie about all of this.

The next morning, Frank woke early. He put on his new school clothes; quietly ate his scrambled eggs, bacon, and grits; brushed his teeth and dressed; and then, with black book satchel in hand, climbed into the Galaxie 500. Janet drove him the ten miles on Highways 141 and 19 to Acorn Primary School, just a mile from the courthouse square in the center of town.

As they drove down Elm Street, the school came into view, and Frank was so nervous he was shaking. He wanted to vomit. He thought he might have diarrhea. He thought Janet might have to spank him to get him out of the car. There were too many people here and too many people he didn't know.

Janet parked the car. She sat quietly with him, staring at the bustling school building.

"Do you want me to pray for you?" she asked.

"Do you need to pray for me?" Frank asked her back, fighting back the tears. Why would she need to pray for him? He had seen an old episode of *Bonanza*, and someone had prayed for the Cartwrights before they went to fight the Paiutes.

Janet squeezed his hand and prayed, and she prayed for him to be at peace and to have a good, fun day at school. She even prayed for all the school days before him—twelve years' worth of days.

"Let's go," she said, and they got out of the car. Frank saw more children than he had ever seen before in one place, and most all of them looked older than him. He walked close to his mama, a half step behind her and clutched the black book satchel.

All the children had book satchels. These plastic-and-cloth satchels were a child's version of an adult attaché, attempting to turn small children into would-be adults going off for a day at the office. In truth, the satchels were oversized, created to carry several large textbooks and a full collection of school supplies. Frank's satchel contained one spelling book, a box of Crayola crayons, a handful of pencils from his grandfather's now-closed chicken hatchery, and a portable pencil sharpener. There was so little in the large book satchel that it would not sit upright, and it collapsed onto the floor. Teachers tired of stepping over the sad, drooping satchels and finally asked students to slide them under their seats.

Janet led Frank into the bustling school lobby and then down the long left corridor with first- and second-grade classrooms on either side of the hallway. There was a lot of noise and activity as parents delivered their babies to school for the first day, and teachers welcomed students into their rooms. Janet spoke to the teachers and parents as they walked down the hall.

Feelings of nausea gave way to a sudden urge to pee, and Frank thought he might pass out. It was the longest walk of his life, but finally Janet came to the last room on the right, and she stepped into the classroom with Frank hiding in her shadow.

Miss Jeannette Johnson peered around Janet and said, "You must be Frank. Welcome to first grade!"

It was Miss Johnson's first year of teaching, and the young teacher appeared kind. Frank began to feel better in the safety and security of this room that smelled fresh and new and clean. Miss Johnson smelled good, too. Even at six, Frank appreciated good-smelling people, especially women. Miss Johnson took him by the hand, gently moving him away from Janet, and led him to his seat.

Frank saw Charlie, and things were immediately better.

His friend pointed to the bathroom in the corner of the classroom. "That's the bathroom," he said. "I went in there. It smells bad."

Frank said, "Did you know that we can get a spanking at school?"

Charlie had received a similar warning from his parents, and now he pointed to the front wall and a blackboard that nearly covered its length. Frank saw the blackboard and then followed Charlie's finger pointing above it. Dangling from a hook on the wall was a giant board. It was the size of a paddle Frank had seen in his grandfather's fishing boat.

He looked at Charlie, and then he turned around to find Janet. She had gone, deciding to slip away without a lot of drama. Frank turned back to face the giant board, and something inside him told him that it was for beating students.

"Students, please take your seats," Miss Johnson said. Frank had never sat down so fast in all his life, believing it best to follow orders. Sitting also protected his backside from any possible spankings.

A voice came from nowhere, and Frank and the other students looked around, startled. Miss Johnson pointed to a box on the wall, and the voice coming from it was principal Pulliam. He welcomed the students and then invited them to stand for the Lord's Prayer and the Pledge of Allegiance to the US flag.

Our Father, which art in heaven, Hallowed be thy name.

Thy kingdom come. Thy will be done in earth, as *it is* in heaven.

Give us this day our daily bread.

And forgive us our debts, as we forgive our debtors.

And lead us not into temptation, but deliver us from evil: For thine is the kingdom, and the power, and the glory, for ever. Amen.

Frank knew the Lord's Prayer from the Bible and could recite it easily with a group.

For the Pledge of Allegiance, a girl named Debbie was asked to stand by the US flag, which was positioned on a pole almost touching the ceiling, and lead the class recitation.

Miss Johnson might have then talked about the day's schedule; she might have introduced herself; she might have talked about how much fun they would have in first grade, and she might have talked about basic rules of conduct within the class. Whatever she talked about, Frank Wilcox did not hear a word of it. He just sat focused on that board dangling from the wall, and it seemed to get larger and larger the more he looked at it. Then he imagined how a spanking looked. Did students bend over? Did they stand up? How in the world did Miss Johnson swing that paddle? She must be superhuman.

Frank thought it would be interesting to see someone get a spanking just to clear up any questions.

He got his wish. On the way to the cafeteria on that first day of school, walking down the long hallway toward the ramp leading to the cafeteria, Frank heard a *whap, whap* and saw a second-grade teacher spanking a girl he knew from church. The girl was bent over with her hands on her knees.

By the time Frank got to the scene of the spanking, it was over, and the girl was crying. She saw Frank and recognized him and said, "Please don't tell my daddy!"

Dear Lord, Frank thought, *Mama did not pray hard enough in the car this morning*. He was in a madhouse. Several of his classmates began to cry at the horror of the hallway spanking—on the first day of school! If it could happen to a girl from church, it could happen to any of them.

After lunch, assembled back in the classroom, Miss Johnson asked the students to place their heads quietly on their desks for a quick nap. Frank was happy to comply. He decided to keep one eye open just in case Miss Johnson got trigger happy. After a few minutes of rest, she said each student would be asked to tell a little about himself or herself and maybe ask a question that she could answer.

Miss Johnson was about to meet Van Piper. Hell, they were all about to meet Van Piper.

He was the youngest of the Pipers, who lived east of Acorn up on a hill known as The Ridge. The Pipers were not known as being criminal, but they were known for being troublesome. More than once, a fight had broken out at the Fourth of July street dance, and the fight sometimes involved more than one Piper. Sometimes it even involved their women. Fight one Piper, you fight them all—even Mama Erstline, who was the matriarch of the Pipers and known for chewing tobacco.

It was probably a bad idea to put Van Piper in the classroom of the newest and youngest teacher in the Acorn Primary School. It was probably a setup. First-grade teachers probably huddled around in the smoke-filled teachers' lounge, lubing and polishing their wooden paddles, and decided to give Van to Miss Johnson because she wouldn't know any better.

He was a big boy—not fat, but tall and broad. He was the biggest boy in the first grade—even bigger than Steve Dickson, whom Frank had met in kindergarten and was the biggest boy Frank had ever seen. Van Piper was bigger than that. He was a man among little first-grade boys. Standing next to Charlie, who was the slightest in the class, Van looked like a giant.

One by one each student stood, made a shy introduction, and then refused to ask a question. Neither Frank nor Charlie had a question. When the introductions got around to Van Piper, he had a question. "Can I use the bathroom?" Miss Johnson excused him to the bathroom.

The introductions continued. Once concluded, Miss Johnson asked the children to take out their reading books.

"I want to introduce you to Dick and Jane," she said, creating some muffled laughs from some of the boys who thought it was funny to call a boy Dick. Frank did not get the joke, but Charlie explained to him later that what he called a tallywacker, some other families called a dick or a peter.

Frank looked at his friend in horror. He was thankful that his name was Frank. He found out later that people up north sometimes called their hot dogs franks.

Miss Johnson was about to continue her introduction of Dick and Jane when she realized Van was still in the bathroom. She also heard what sounded like a kick to the inside of the bathroom door. She quickly put down her reader and walked back to the closed door of the bathroom.

"Van, are you OK?" she asked. There was no sound.

She partly opened the door and shrieked.

Van Piper was hanging halfway out the window of the bathroom, trying his best to escape school altogether. Unfortunately, he was stuck in the window because it only opened at a forty-five-degree angle, and he was too big to crawl through it.

"He's trying to escape," Charlie said, and he joined other students in gathering near the bathroom door to watch. Frank had his eyes on the growing two-by-six board hanging from the blackboard.

Inside the bathroom, Miss Johnson awkwardly grabbed Van by his belt and tried pulling him back inside the window, but Van had caught hold of a shrub and was hanging on for dear life. A boy named Roger was now practically inside the bathroom door and was relaying information back to the class.

"There's a turd in the toilet!" he shouted. Everyone crowded in as if they had lived six years on earth without ever seeing a turd.

Miss Johnson pushed Roger back out the door and shouted to the class, "Children! Please return to your seats right now!" It was a full-on first-grade jailbreak, and Dick had not even yet been properly introduced to Jane.

Mrs. Housley, who taught the class across the hallway, was a veteran among first-grade teachers in Acorn. Her husband was the Acorn postmaster, and they were cornerstones of the First Baptist Church. Leaving her well-mannered class, she walked into chaos across the hall.

Frank watched as the veteran teacher walked to the front of the classroom and took the ceiling beam off the wall. She turned it over in her hands, and Frank thought she was perhaps the strongest woman he had ever seen, twirling a fifty-foot board in her hands like that.

She walked to the bathroom and peered inside.

"Son, get back in this classroom right now," she said. "I'm going to count to three, and then I'm going to use this paddle."

Realizing his butt was an exposed target, Van released his grip on the shrubbery and allowed Miss Johnson to help him back inside the classroom. He stepped into the doorframe, and Miss Housley pounced, taking him by the arm and leading him toward the hallway. Miss Johnson, weary and frazzled, followed.

Miss Housley stood in the open door of Miss Johnson's classroom, completely capable of watching her own class through the open door across the hallway. Miss Johnson took Van to see principal Pulliam.

When Van returned, he sat down and quietly sat there for the rest of the day. Charlie heard through the playground grapevine that Van had been spanked by the mother of all paddles—Mr. Pulliam's electric paddle. The electric paddle was reserved for special cases that could not be solved by the telephone poles hanging from the classroom blackboards.

Frank wanted to approach Van and ask him about the spanking. He wanted firsthand knowledge and was not willing to ask the girl from the church for fear he might be next on that teacher's list. It was better, he figured, to stay around Miss Johnson, who was obviously not prone to spank anyone. But Frank did not ask Van about the spanking because he wasn't completely sure that Van wouldn't hit him.

Acorn Primary School was a veritable den of possible violence.

He was never more relieved by the bell at the end of the day. A teacher called his name when his ride home arrived, and Frank ran out of the school to see Papa R. C.'s black Cadillac. His Granny and Papa R. C. were in the front seat, and his daddy was in the backseat. He jumped in beside his daddy and threw his sagging book satchel on the floor.

"I survived," he said.

"You survived?" Tom asked.

"Yes, I didn't get my ass beat today, Daddy," Frank said proudly. Laughter filled the car.

TWO

MIKE

Mike Royston sat in the back of Miss Johnson's classroom. He was a tiny boy with blond hair combed neatly by someone who loved him deeply. He wore black-rimmed glasses that constantly needed a nudge back up on the bridge of his nose. He was quiet and shy. Like all the other boys, he wore jeans with colorful T-shirts or button-down shirts, depending on the day and the weather, and black leather shoes on feet that no longer walked.

There was no other person like Mike Royston in the Acorn Primary School. Mike was permanently confined to a wheelchair. He had been born to the wheelchair. Until now, he had only been surrounded by family and friends at one of Acorn County's smaller membership churches. Now, he was thrust into a spotlight held by strangers—children he did not know.

None of the students in Miss Johnson's first-grade class had ever been around a handicapped person, and most had never seen a wheelchair. So most kept a distance from Mike, not knowing exactly how to react or what to say. Mike was painfully aware of the outright stares, uncomfortable avoidance, and honest questions from a few bold classmates.

"What happened to you?"

"When will you get better?"

"Why can't you walk?"

Miss Johnson was quick to be Mike's champion. When she heard a question, she stepped in to help Mike answer it. She also pulled curious students aside and did her best to explain what it meant to be handicapped and how to respectfully ask questions. It was through all this education that Miss Johnson had a great idea. She decided that each day, a student would be assigned as Mike's "helper." In this role, each student would learn about acts of service. She located a desk beside Mike's wheelchair and issued one simple directive: "You will be Mike's legs today." That meant, specifically, pushing Mike, in his wheelchair, onto the playground, and to the cafeteria at lunchtime. It also meant pushing Mike's wheelchair to the soft-drink machines early in the afternoon when the class had its designated Coke break. During Coke break, students with a dime could walk to the school's vending machines and purchase a soft drink. Inside the classroom, the day's helper would ensure Mike's pencils were sharpened and help him pull books from his desk for study. If Mike needed to use the bathroom, the helper alerted Miss Johnson, who intervened.

As word of Miss Johnson's idea made its way to the supper tables of her students, the parental reaction was mixed. Some parents were happy for their student to help Mike, but others questioned whether this kind of assistance should fall to students.

A compromise was reached. Helpers would serve voluntarily and would only be expected to assist Mike to the playground, the cafeteria, and the drink machines during Coke break. A note was sent home so that parents and students could discuss the situation, and then parents could accept or reject their student's participation in serving Mike.

Tom and Janet Wilcox might have discussed what was going on in the first-grade classroom, but Frank was not privy to their adult conversations. When the compromise was reached, Janet approached Frank with the question: "Son, do you want to help this little boy?"

To be completely honest, Frank did not want to help. He had not stated this, but he did not want to help. It wasn't because Mike was in a wheelchair because Frank found it all more curious than repulsive. It was very simply because Frank was lazy. Frank's goal was to attend school and not get a spanking. That was his mission, and anything else was a distraction.

"I don't really want to help," he finally said one morning, sitting down at the kitchen table to a breakfast of fried eggs and bacon. Tom sat across from him and didn't look up. Janet had her back to him, standing at the kitchen counter. No one said anything. So he said it again. "I don't really want to help."

That was when Janet snapped. She wheeled around, took one step, and began a 7:00 a.m. sermon while waving a wooden spoon in the air. "There's absolutely no reason why you can't help this little boy," she said. "I'll declare, are you going to be that lazy of a person, that self-centered of a person who can't help someone? Are you going to just ignore another person who needs a little kindness?"

Tom looked up at his oldest son and closed his eyes. He slightly shook his head, acknowledging that Frank had stepped into a hole that he knew all too well and from which there was no easy climb out.

"Well, I'm making the decision for you," Janet said. "You *will* go to school and help this little boy, and if need be, you will help him every single day. I don't care if you are the only one who will help him." Her voice rose to a yell. "In fact, you had better be prepared to help him whether it's your day or not." And with that, she brought down the wooden spoon on the kitchen table. The spoon snapped, and the end of it began dancing around the table until it landed perfectly on Frank's plate between the eggs and bacon. Frank heard his mama, but he stared at his plate, amazed at the perfect landing of the spoon's broken end piece. He wondered if she could do that again, but now all he could say was, "OK, OK. I'll do it."

Janet's reaction was genuine. She knew what it felt like to be the odd one out. Her family had moved to Acorn from Covington, Georgia when she was twelve. She didn't know a single person when she began school; she was terribly homesick for the friends she had left behind. She remembered the awkward feeling of being in a classroom surrounded by people who did not know her and who all knew one another very well. She knew what it was like to be the unwanted center of attention, and her heart just broke wide open for this little boy experiencing all those emotions—from a wheelchair, no less. Fortunately for Janet, a girl named Midge Holbrook had approached her and invited her to a sleepover, and within a week Janet had forgotten all about the pain of moving. She had a new best friend who would be like a sister to her for the rest of her life, and Midge opened the door for her to make friends with many other girls in Acorn. Janet knew both the heartache of uncertainty and the power of another person's servant heart.

Six-year-old Frank just knew that he was going to school that day, willingly volunteering to serve as one of Mike's helpers. He wasn't the only one who must have received a parental lecture, because every child volunteered, and Miss Johnson could not have been happier.

Students began serving Mike that very day, learning to push the wheelchair and learning how to make turns that wouldn't crash Mike into a wall or clip a desk. Pushing the wheelchair off the sidewalks to the playground was a bit of a challenge, but each student mastered it well.

An unusual feature of the Acorn Primary School was the ramp extending down from the school's lobby to the cafeteria. The ramp was about ten yards long and wide enough for a car had someone been truly interested in driving from the cafeteria to the school office. Each day at lunch, Mike was pushed down the long hallway of classrooms to the ramp, and then each helper-of-the-day eased the wheelchair down the ramp to the cafeteria. Inside the cafeteria, Mike was parked at the table reserved for Miss Johnson. The helper then went to get Mike's lunch and bring it back to him. The helper then sat by Mike as both students ate lunch together.

Frank's first day pushing Mike in the wheelchair went well. He managed the playground, and he got Mike to the cafeteria, carefully pulling back on the wheelchair as it eased down the ramp. He parked Mike, got lunch for both himself and Mike, and then sat down beside him. Neither boy spoke until Mike quietly asked Frank to pass the salt.

Handing Mike the salt, Frank leaned in and whispered, "Does it hurt being in that chair all day?"

Mike shook his head no and then whispered, "I do wish I could ride the merry-go-round on the playground."

Frank tried to envision it but could not. "It's not that fun," he said. "If you don't have someone big pushing the merry-go-round, it's really kind of boring. It might be more fun just to ride really fast in your wheelchair. Do you ever get to ride fast?"

"No," Mike said quietly. "Everyone is too afraid I'll get hurt."

14

"That's too bad," Frank said. "You sort of have your own car."

Mike smiled, excusing Frank for not understanding that he was trapped in this wheelchair and desired more than anything the thrill of the playground like all the other children. After that encounter in the cafeteria, Frank watched each day at recess as Mike was parked at the side of the playground while all the other children played. On occasion, one of the custodians helped move Mike into a swing, where he was very gently pushed by one of the teachers. Mostly, Mike sat in his wheelchair, and Miss Johnson sometimes read him a book.

Frank began making it a practice to speak to Mike more often, and many of the other children had accepted him as one of their own and spoke to him as well. The girls in class really took to Mike, and Mike really took to them. They were always fluttering around him during class, offering to help him even when it wasn't their day to help. When recess came, however, Mike remained alone on the sidelines, which now made him sadder—longing even more to join these children who were becoming his friends.

Frank stood with Charlie at the merry-go-round, and both boys stared across the dirt playground full of screaming children. The little boy in the big wheelchair was parked as a spectator to all the fun.

"I wish we could get him on the merry-go-round," Charlie said. "I wish we could lift him out of the chair, put him on the merry-go-round, and then just push him around some."

Frank said, "He wants to do that. He told me so in the lunchroom. He wants to know what it's like to go fast."

As the two friends talked about Mike and how they felt sorry for him, Van Piper walked up behind them. He had heard them talking about Mike.

A few days later, it was Van Piper's turn to be Mike's helper. Mike didn't like these days because Van was reckless with the wheelchair. Most days, Van made revving engine sounds while pushing, tried to get the wheelchair to bank on two wheels, and sometimes crashed Mike into the wall. Today, however, Van was calmer in the way he pushed Mike to the playground and back. After recess, Van pushed Mike over to a sink, where the two boys carefully washed their hands for lunch.

Miss Johnson smiled. She had been worried about Van's days as Mike's helper, but today Van was going about his service in a kind, orderly fashion. She was pleased and complimented the big boy on his service. Van just smirked at her, obviously not used to being complimented. Miss Johnson called for the students to line up behind Van and Mike and to quietly walk down the hallway toward the cafeteria.

In single file, the quiet children followed Van, who was pushing Mike along in orderly fashion. Miss Johnson didn't notice when Van suddenly began intentionally taking longer strides. This, combined with his size and normal stride, began to put distance between Van and Mike and the remainder of the class. Van was almost to the cafeteria ramp when Miss Johnson noticed he had left her class behind. It was too late.

At the top of the ramp, Van leaned in to Mike's right ear.

"I'm not doing this to be mean," he said. Mike turned his head to look at Van, and their eyes locked. Mike Royston knew exactly what was about to happen. "Here you, go, my friend. Here...you...go!" Van Piper shoved that wheelchair down the center of the ramp toward the waiting, open doors of the cafeteria. He shoved that wheelchair with all the strength he could muster just as the rest of the class caught up with him.

Miss Johnson shrieked once again in horror, for this was one hell of a start to a teaching career.

Frank stared in disbelief as Mike flew down the ramp, wobbling a little until the wheelchair corrected itself and started sailing. He lifted his arms in the air over his head. Miss Johnson was running after Mike, but there was no way she could catch the wheelchair.

By no minor miracle, Mike cleared the doors of the cafeteria, barely missing the doorframe. Mrs. Samples's first-grade class scattered wildly, creating pandemonium as one of Miss Johnson's students shouted, "Look out! Runaway wheelchair!"

"Open the doors so he can get outside," Van Piper shouted as Mike now sailed toward the rear doors of the cafeteria.

Van's instructions did not come fast enough. Mike crashed into the doors, but the wheelchair did not overturn. Miss Johnson, a cafeteria worker, and a custodian all reached him at the same time, fearing the worst, fearing he had been injured somehow.

Mike Royston simply looked at the three adult faces, beaming with a smile on his face, and said, "Can I do that again?" Behind him, Miss Johnson's class cheered as if Mike Royston had just won the Olympics—downhill racing.

Van Piper got his second spanking of the first grade. Deep down, he felt this one was worth it.

THREE

CHARLIE KELLER

Frank stood in the corner of Miss Johnson's classroom, facing the concrete block wall. The US flag was beside him in its stand, and Frank was fearful that he was going to knock it over. He was being punished. He had cried over the embarrassment of being caught, confronted in front of the entire class, and then punished by standing in the corner. Now, he was relieved. He was relieved he had not gotten a spanking.

He looked back over his shoulder and saw his best friend, Charlie. Charlie stared at him, nervously bouncing in his desk and smiling. Frank closed his eyes and turned back to the wall. He saw a spider crawling on the window to his right and began watching it nervously.

Charles Keller, affectionately nicknamed Charlie by those who loved him, was born a handful of months after Frank. Their mothers had been the best of friends, and it was only natural that the girls' first-born sons would be best friends, too. It was these generations of friendships that further welded the Wilcox and Keller families together at all major holidays, birthdays, some summer vacations, church, Saturday-evening visits, and dinners out. As more children were born, the family weaving grew even stronger.

The Kellers lived in the center of Acorn and had a long and respectable history in farming, cotton ginning, merchandising, and construction. Everyone knew them, and they knew everyone. The Wilcox family lived ten miles to the south of Acorn on the Brookwood Road farm, but the distance along two-lane roads did nothing to stop the friendship. Moving his Acorn bride south to the farm, Tom had promised Janet that they would attend church in Acorn, and any future children would go to school in Acorn. That promise was about friendship and maintaining some semblance of proximity to the Kellers.

Frank could not remember a day without Charlie in his life, and there were family photographs to prove it. The earliest was the two of them as babies propped up side by side on the sofa at the Kellers' home. It was one of a hundred or so photographs that showed the two friends growing up together on the road to kindergarten at the First Baptist Church. There were photographs of them playing with new toys on Christmas Day, discovering Easter eggs, riding on steam engines in the Fourth of July parade, playing in the rare North Georgia snow, and dressed as cowboys, each holding a gun aimed at the photographer. They were each other's first overnight friend, and during summers they often spent entire weekends together. No birthday was planned without first ensuring the other could be in attendance.

Charlie was the younger and the smaller of the two. He was also the more athletic. As he got older, Charlie's reddish-brown hair became wavy, and he was one of Frank's first friends to wear glasses. Even though he should have picked other boys ahead of Frank during backyard competitions, Charlie always chose Frank with his first pick. There was never a question about it. As they got older, Charlie was the better student. The As just came naturally for him; Frank had to study and work to make Bs. Charlie was the class clown, the center of attention, and everyone loved him—even teachers aggravated by him loved him deeply.

Charlie was good for Frank because Charlie's successes pushed Frank to try harder, to work harder, and to be more outgoing. Frank wasn't jealous of Charlie; Frank was inspired by Charlie. Sensitive, moody, shy, nervous, and reserved, Frank could be happy in the shadows of popularity, but being Charlie's best friend made that impossible. It was good for Frank.

Frank was good for Charlie because Frank's reserved nature often pumped Charlie's brakes and caused him sometimes to think before he acted. If Charlie's personality was "let's give it a try," then Frank's personality was "let's think about it first." They met in the middle, and it was what galvanized their friendship even as they stepped into the public arena at the First Baptist Church Kindergarten.

The boys were inseparable during that year in kindergarten, sitting beside each other and in groups together. Miss Polly, their favorite teacher, gently tried to ease them apart, but the two friends kept migrating back to each other. They were even bathroom buddies when Miss Polly found it easier to take two boys at a time to the single bathroom in the old white house where the kindergarten met. It was in that bathroom that the friendship was first tested.

Charlie peed all over Frank one morning at the toilet.

Miss Polly began to rethink her strategy of having two boys standing together at a toilet, sword-fighting their streams of pee into the toilet basin. In his excitement over the sword fight, Charlie had peed all over Frank, and then when Miss Polly tried to stop him, he peed all over her black Naturalizers. He went on to pee all over everything, and when the flood was over, Frank stood still, shoulders slumped, crying because he was soaked from the waist down. Miss Polly wanted to join him.

Order was restored, and Frank was able to put on the extra clothes he had brought to school for such a time as this. Charlie went back to a box of Crayola crayons as if nothing had happened. Miss Polly wondered how in the world so much urine could be in one five-year-old boy. Frank never shared another toilet with Charlie, but aside from that, their friendship was unaffected.

Now together in Miss Johnson's first-grade class, their friendship had been tested again. It had landed Frank an hour of shame standing in the corner with his back to all his classmates.

The class had been introduced to Dick and Jane, and this introduction had led to reading skills. Reading skills had led to spelling simple words and some compound words. Spelling tests were a student's first introduction to testing and to grading.

"Class, I want you to take out your writing tablets," Miss Johnson said. "I will call out a word, and you write it down. Do your best to spell it correctly. I want you to sit straight in your desks and keep your eyes forward. Don't look on your neighbor's paper. That's cheating. Do your own work." Frank took out his tablet and numbered his paper 1–10. As

Miss Johnson called out words, he felt confident about spelling them correctly.

"*Everyone,*" Miss Johnson said. "*Everyone* will go on the picnic. The word is *everyone.*"

Frank panicked. He had no idea how to spell *everyone.* He looked up, and his eyes cleared Charlie's shorter, slumped shoulders. Charlie had spelled the word, and it was in full view. Frank did the only logical thing he could do at this moment of panic and crisis.

He cheated. He wrote what Charlie had written and finished the rest of the test with ease.

Then, he felt a wave of guilt. At recess, he stopped Charlie and confessed his transgression to his friend. Charlie said, "Next time, just tap me on the shoulder, and I'll let you see the whole thing. I don't care." Frank thought nothing else about it.

Everyone else was about to get involved, specifically Miss Johnson.

As Frank's eyes jumped Charlie's shoulders to see the word *everyone,* Donna Padgett, sitting to Frank's right, was looking at his paper to see how Frank had spelled the word *friend.* The spelling word for the day should have been *cheating.*

In her attempt to cheat from Frank's paper—a risky move for more than one reason—Donna had leaned too far from her desk to get a better view. Miss Johnson saw Donna and her cheating ways. As Frank was confessing to Charlie and Charlie was forgiving him, Miss Johnson had Donna Padgett in front of her desk. She scolded Donna and told her how wrong it was to cheat off another student's paper and that cheating was like stealing from another person. Miss Johnson's sermon was so strong that Donna thought for sure she was headed to Mr. Pulliam and his electric paddle.

That was when Donna Padgett became a snitch, hoping to plea-bargain. She folded like a cheap tent. If she was going down, she was taking down the whole corrupt system with her.

"Frank cheated too," she said. "He was looking at Charlie's paper."

When recess was over, and the children came back to class, Miss Johnson called Frank and Charlie to her desk. Frank noticed Donna standing in the corner farthest from the wall of exterior windows. She seemed to be crying.

"Charlie, did you let Frank copy from your spelling test?" Miss Johnson asked.

Charlie said he didn't let Frank, but that it was OK. He didn't care if Frank copied from his paper. He put his hand up on Frank's shoulder. That was when Frank noticed Donna slumped forward against the wall, and Frank felt his legs go weak. He imagined the series of spankings he was going to get, starting here with Miss Johnson and continuing through several generations at home. He was about to tell Miss Johnson that he most likely would not be at school the next day because he would be unable to sit down when she dropped the verdict.

"Frank, do you realize that you did something very wrong?" she asked.

Frank nodded that he understood. He was sent to the other corner at the front of the class. He stood facing the wall. Charlie returned to his seat.

It was a long hour for Frank Wilcox, standing in the corner of the room. When Miss Johnson told him to sit down, he walked to her desk and apologized. Tears welled up in his eyes.

Miss Johnson smiled. "Please don't do that again," she said.

Frank said he would not. Then Miss Johnson did something that was perfectly first grade and perfectly first class. She turned from the desk and invited Frank to give her a hug. He did. He was forgiven.

At the end of that day, when the final bell rang, dismissing school, Miss Johnson said, "Children, I hope *everyone* has a good afternoon and evening." She looked directly at Charlie and Frank, and she smiled.

FOUR

THE PENCIL KING

An objective of the Acorn Primary School was to teach children how to manage money. A local bank provided each child with a small rubber coin holder. One side of the coin holder had a slit from end to end, and squeezing the coin holder opened the slit. The pocket change could be stored inside, and releasing the squeeze closed the slit with the change inside. The coin holder easily fit inside pockets, book satchels, and purses. It even came with a small easy-open chain, allowing attachment to a variety of personal items. Of course, the backside reminded every student—and every student's parent—that the rubber coin holders were provided free of charge by the First Federal Bank of Acorn.

Like most students, Frank carried a dollar in nickels and dimes each day. His lunch in the school cafeteria cost twenty-five cents plus an additional five cents for a half pint of white milk. Additional cartons of milk—somewhat lukewarm at times—were available for another five cents each. Frank was sad when he learned that chocolate milk was not offered in the cafeteria.

Beyond the cafeteria, students could visit Mrs. Fagan, who was the school's secretary. Somehow, Mrs. Fagan's family was related to Frank's Papa R. C. It had been explained to Frank, but he got lost in the branches of the family tree and never fully understood the relational connection. Mrs. Fagan, in addition to normal secretarial duties in the main office, ran a school store that had pencils, writing tablets, cheap crayons, tissue, and erasers for sale.

Frank was hypnotized by the school store. More than once, when he needed a pencil, he visited Mrs. Fagan, who sold him three pencils for a nickel. He loved the exchange—that this coin with a man's face on it could be exchanged for something very useful.

Janet scolded him about buying pencils in the school office.

"Why did you do that?" she asked him. She held up a white pencil in front of him. "We have boxes and boxes of these pencils, and you can have as many as you want for free." It was true. Just as the First Federal Bank had purchased the rubber coin holders for students, R. C. Wilcox had purchased an endless supply of pencils with his name printed on them—R. C. Wilcox Poultry Company—and R. C. gave them away to all of his customers. The problem was that the Wilcox Poultry Company was now Wilcox Sausage Company, and the pencils were generally useless for advertising the farm.

Putting Frank's school-bought pencils on the kitchen table alongside the R. C. Wilcox Poultry Company pencil, Janet shook her head and mumbled to herself, "I wish we could take these white pencils to the school and *sell them*."

Frank heard his mama and thought it was a great idea.

The next day, Frank took one of the boxes of R. C. Wilcox Poultry Company pencils with him to school. Before the bell rang, calling the classrooms to order, he went down to the school store and held up a pencil in front of Mrs. Fagan. "Can you sell these pencils?" Mrs. Fagan chuckled to herself and said, "No, we can't sell your granddaddy's pencils at the school."

Frank decided to keep the box of pencils in his black book satchel and draw from the box as needed during the school year. From there, he had the charitable idea of giving every child in his class one of the pencils. Students began coming to him for a pencil instead of going to the school store. Frank was more than happy to share the pencils, and soon he had given away all of those in the box. At home, he put another box of pencils in his book satchel. After all, his Papa R. C. had lots of these pencils.

Frank became popular. On the playground one afternoon, a first grader from Mrs. Housley's class asked if he could have a pencil, and Frank gave him one because he now carried several in his jeans pocket at recess. This led to boys and girls he didn't know coming to him, each wanting a pencil, and he was happy to provide them.

Frank Wilcox was suddenly the Pencil King of Acorn Primary School.

It was bound to happen. A student pulled out his blue rubber coin holder and asked, "How much do these cost?" Frank stared at the student. He had planned just to use the pencils and was happy to give one away to someone in need. Yet here before him was a student offering him coins for pencils. All he knew was that Mrs. Fagan sold three pencils for a nickel.

"I will give you three pencils for a nickel and then give you one more for free," Frank said.

That was how the defunct R. C. Wilcox Poultry Company entered the pencil business.

* * *

Frank loved his Papa R. C. He loved the way his grandfather wore the Stetson hat and always had access to Coca-Cola products and a freezer in his home stocked with ice-cream novelties. He loved that his grandfather seemed to be in charge of everyone, and he loved that his Papa R. C. loved him. He especially loved crawling into the king-sized bed as his grandfather raised a leg and made a tent out of the bed covers. He rarely farted while Frank was under there, but when he did, it was funny.

Frank had recently gone through some real heartache over his Papa R. C. For a few weeks, during the afternoon Coke break, when students marched single file to the drink machines and purchased a late-afternoon soft drink, Frank had bought an RC Cola. He loved Coca-Cola, but upon learning of RC Cola, he thought it best to remain loyal to his grandfather. Janet found him crying in Stozier's Woods one afternoon and took him to see his grandfather, and R. C. explained that he did not own RC Cola or even ever drink them.

"Son, I drink Coca-Cola," R. C. said. "When have you ever seen me drink an RC Cola? You go to school and drink whatever you want during your Coke break."

* * *

R. C. Wilcox was having a great day when he was called to the telephone. It was springtime, with warm days and cool nights. It was his favorite time of the year because it meant nice temperatures for work and restful nights of sleep. It was also the start of fishing season, and R. C. loved to fish. On his property, he had built a fishing lake, and he loved nothing more than finishing his day, sitting on the bank of the lake, drinking one—or several—Budweisers, and casting a line in peaceful solitude. This was one of those days. He had stopped working early and was in the cellar collecting his fishing gear when he heard Kathryn call him to the telephone. He rolled his eyes, pushed his Stetson to the back of his head, and walked a few steps from the cellar door to the office he and Kathryn shared inside their home.

"It's Dwight Pulliam," Kathryn said, handing the telephone to R. C. He gave a long sigh, letting his shoulders slump, and wondered why the teacher from Acorn was calling him. They were casual acquaintances at best.

After a few minutes of listening, and even chuckling a little, he hung up the telephone and looked at his wife. He stared at her, unable to really do anything but chuckle.

"Well, what is it?" she asked him impatiently.

"Apparently, Frank's been giving out those old poultry-company pencils to every child at school, and now he's started selling them," R. C. said. "Dwight wondered if Frank was acting on his own or if I had given him permission to sell the pencils. I think some of them around there thought I was the criminal mastermind of underground office-supply sales."

Frank had started taking his book satchel to the playground and setting up shop near the jungle gym. He wasn't trying to sell the pencils, but as children offered to pay him money, he took the money and gave each one a handful of pencils. Most students came away with anywhere from six to ten pencils for a nickel. Frank's second-grade teacher, Mrs. Edith Wright, who was Kathryn Wilcox's oldest childhood friend, had stopped the pencil selling and reported it to the office.

After talking it over with Kathryn, R. C. picked up the telephone and called his son, Tom, who lived on the farm but across the pasture. Father told son about grandson's pencil enterprise at school.

"I know, Daddy. I just got off the telephone with Dwight Pulliam," Tom said. "I'll put a stop to it."

"All right," R. C. said. "Go easy on him. He's just a little boy."

Tom didn't hear that last bit of instruction. Hanging up the telephone, he turned to his oldest son and said, "You can't be selling damn pencils at school." Then he tried, exasperated, to explain how Frank was in competition with the entire Acorn County School System and was indeed hurting this tiny revenue stream used by one school. "Not only are you doing something wrong, but you are dragging the family into it. That is Papa R. C.'s name on those pencils; everyone thinks he's encouraging it."

Frank was crying. Janet stepped in. "How many pencils have you sold, son?" she asked calmly, putting her hand on his.

Frank opened his rubber coin holder and held it out in small hands. It was so full of coins that it was bulging open and coins were falling out. The bottom of his book satchel was covered in nickels and dimes.

"Oh, my goodness," Janet said. She thought Frank had maybe sold a few pencils, but clearly, he had created a small business and was in need of a business license.

"Mama," he said through teary eyes and snotty nose, "I need a larger coin holder."

"No!" Tom shouted. "You need to stop selling the pencils!"

Tom and Janet took all the pencils away from Frank, who by this time had stored several boxes under his bed. Tom fussed and fumed the entire time.

"He's only in the second grade, Tom," Janet said. "He doesn't understand all of this."

"All right," Tom said. "Tomorrow, Papa R. C. and I are taking you to school. You are going to give all your pencil money to Mrs. Fagan in the school office. You can't take any more pencils to school. If you want a pencil, ask your mama for a pencil, and she will give you one. But it's only for you to use."

The next morning, Frank emptied his rubber coin holder onto Mrs. Fagan's desk. The coin holder was so full that it took a few minutes to shake all the coins out of it. R. C. apologized, but fighting back laughter took some of the polish off his apology. Tom apologized, and then Frank apologized, though Frank really wasn't completely sure what he had done wrong.

Mrs. Fagan took all the money. Mr. Pulliam said all was forgiven, but he wanted Frank to stay in from recess so Mrs. Wright could perhaps explain the economics of pencil selling to him. Frank loved Mrs. Wright, and he was perfectly happy to sit with her at recess. She told him stories about his Granny's childhood and shared very little about pencils, money, and competition.

FIVE

THE MONKEES

Frank and his younger brothers, Jack and Wayne, did not spend a lot of time watching television. They were almost always playing outside, exploring the farm, and their family never ate in front of the television. If they watched television, it was usually limited to Saturday-morning cartoons until they got bored and went outside.

They also watched *The Popeye Club* each afternoon just before supper. Atlanta's NBC affiliate, Channel 2, produced *The Popeye Club*. It featured (host) Officer Don Kennedy, his friend Mr. Green Jeans, and several puppets. The show featured comedic bits involving a studio audience of children intertwined with cartoon episodes of *Popeye the Sailor Man*.

Charlie had introduced Frank to an afternoon replay of the one-hour *Daniel Boone* drama, featuring actor Fess Parker. The show had begun when Frank and Charlie were in kindergarten, and by the time they got to second grade, it was a show most boys watched and then re-enacted on the school playground. With Frank's eyes opened to Daniel Boone, he began to be interested in watching episodes of *Bonanza* and *Combat!* with his daddy, Tom.

Television began changing around 1966 when Frank was in first grade. Television networks began marketing directly to children in prime time. Batman, the caped crusader, aired on Wednesday, January 12, 1966, on Atlanta's Channel 11 (ABC). The thirty-minute colorful action drama featured a leotard-dressed Batman and his young crime-fighting sidekick, Robin. The two crime fighters spoke in a simple, dramatic way that spoke to children. Each Batman adventure was stretched over two weeks. In the first episode, the audience was introduced to a villain-of-the-week, who plotted major thefts in Gotham

City. By the end of the episode, Batman and Robin had found the criminal but had fallen into his—or her—trap. This cliffhanger set up the next week's episode when the superheroes escaped from the criminals—who amazingly always left the crime fighters unguarded. The remainder of the episode led to the capture of the criminals, following a fantastic fight scene complete with cartoonish words on the screen such as BAM and KA-POW, as if every fistfight included a punch that made a KA-POW sound.

Children went wild over *Batman* and other weeknight television. Merchandising followed, leading to an army of caped crusaders wandering the streets of Acorn on Halloween. Those children who opted out of the school lunches and brought their own lunch—Frank never was allowed to do that—suddenly had Batman lunch boxes. On the Acorn Primary School playground, a lucky boy was chosen as Batman, and he successfully took on every other boy in a make-believe Gotham City.

As successful as *Batman* might have been, what followed in the fall of 1966 was revolutionary. Across the United States, a cultural revolution was simmering among young people as the Selective Service draft raised questions about the country's involvement in the rising conflict between North and South Vietnam in Southeast Asia. Young people rebelled against the war effort by embracing trends completely foreign to their families' World War II cultural roots. Hair was starting to get longer. Fashions were starting to move past button-down shirts. With the rise of Elvis Presley and then the Beatles' 1964 arrival in the United States, music was moving toward rock and roll. Television programmers saw it happening and introduced, on the NBC network, *The Monkees*.

Frank Wilcox joined a legion of children in being mesmerized. The Monkees were young, twentysomething boys, living on their own, innocently chasing girls, playing around, and making music. The weekly thirty-minute program featured the boys—Mike, Micky, Davy, and Peter—in a slapstick episode with Davy falling in and out of love each week. During each episode, the four Monkees put aside silliness and performed two songs. Merchandising went wild. When the Monkees albums could be bought in record stores—even the small one in Acorn—children such as Frank didn't just bite the apple but ate the whole darn thing. Frank didn't just like lead guitarist Mike Nesmith; Frank wanted to *be* Mike Nesmith. He wanted to play the guitar, he wanted to be on a stage, and he wanted to be in a band. He also wanted to grow his hair longer.

Up until this time, Frank and most of the boys had military crew cuts. That was the haircut of their daddies and their granddaddies and may or may not have even included a little dab of Brylcreem styling gel.

"I want to grow my hair out, like Mike Nesmith," Frank said one evening at the supper table, launching a massive debate over hairstyles, the collapse of American culture, the Apocalypse, and Tom's continuing monologue about "those damn hippies in Atlanta." It was Janet who negotiated Frank's hair growing out with a compromise that it be above the ears.

In Frank's obsession with the Monkees, Janet also saw a window of opportunity for her oldest son. She loved music, having taken piano lessons for several years. Her younger brother, Buddy, had played trumpet in the high school band. She had always thought it would be wonderful if her children were musicians, performing one day in the famous Acorn County High School marching band. She thought about all of this while watching Frank as he pretended a broom was a guitar and performed along with the Monkees, who were singing away on the family record player. Janet told Tom to buy Frank a guitar.

"I will buy him a guitar, but I want him to play songs by Buck Owens and Marty Robbins," Tom mumbled. "I don't want any of that rock-and-roll music played around here." Tom did as he was told and bought Frank a simple child's guitar, complete with *The Bert Higgins Play-in-a-Month Guitar Chord Book*. The acoustic guitar even had colored strings to match up with Bert Higgins's book for easier learning. Frank stared in wonder at this gift.

Overnight, Frank Wilcox became Mike Nesmith. He ordained Jack as Monkees drummer Micky Dolenz, and R. C. Wilcox purchased Jack a simple set of drums that were promptly moved to the basement. Frank and Jack were perfectly content banging away on their instruments with the Monkees playing on the record player. Frank was not one bit interested in learning anything from Bert Higgins. Frank just wanted to put the Monkees' record on the player, push the needle to "Last Train to Clarksville," and bang and sing along with the four television stars. This, he reckoned, was guitar playing.

"He needs lessons," Janet said. "He's not going to do anything with that guitar book, and I'm tired of hearing him bang on that guitar."

"Let's make him learn from that book; that's why we bought the damn thing," Tom said, and he closed Frank in his room with Bert Higgins for thirty minutes each day. One afternoon, Janet did not hear any banging, opened the door, and found Frank standing on the bed with a towel draped around his neck. He was acting out a scene from *Batman*.

"He needs lessons," Janet said. "We can't make him learn the guitar."

Tom, aggravated that all of this had fallen to him, began calling around Acorn and talking to men he knew taught guitar lessons.

Some said they didn't start teaching until a child was ten—that was three years away.

Some said they thought it wise to begin music instruction on the piano.

Some recommended the boy begin with *The Bert Higgins Play-in-a-Month Guitar Chord Book*.

As a last resort, Tom turned to an old hermit of a man living along the bottom of Sawnee Mountain just outside of Acorn.

"Have you let that boy's hair grow out?" the old man asked. "I don't teach no long-haired boys."

Tom gave up, but Janet did not. She called the high-school band director, who said one of his musicians was interested in teaching Frank how to play the guitar. Lessons were scheduled in the fellowship hall of the First Baptist Church.

Weeks passed, and finally the young man called Janet and said, "Frank's a great boy, but he's not interested in practicing, and he's not learning how to play the guitar. I feel guilty taking your money." The guitar lessons ended and went the way of Bert Higgins. The guitar banging, however, did not end.

Frank continued to play along with the Monkees, gaining more and more confidence and seeing himself as a guitar player. After all, he figured, he had a guitar; he was indeed strumming with his right hand, though his left was simply holding the neck of the instrument; and, most importantly, a sound was coming from the guitar. This added up to playing the guitar.

Mrs. Edith Wright was generally regarded as one of the nicest, calmest, and most loving of all the teachers at the Acorn Primary School. Learning that Mrs. Wright would be his second-grade teacher, Frank's Granny was especially excited; she loved Edith. In her class, Frank found a great encourager and someone who loved her students and often told them so. If she ever spanked a child, she cried.

Mrs. Wright ended each day of school with show-and-tell, a wonderful way for students to share their interests with one another and get a taste of confidence by speaking in front of an audience. Mrs. Wright carefully sat near each presenting student and was prepared to help guide him or her with simple questions if stage fright presented itself. Students brought everything from old coins, Indian arrowheads found on their farms, toys their grandparents had played with, and even an occasional pet—such as the day Steve Dickson brought a pet snake in an aquarium. On days when there were no presenters, Mrs. Wright took a library book and passed it around so that every student had a chance to read aloud.

The more students came and shared, the more Frank wanted to share something. He had some old arrowheads—even a stone used in a primitive tomahawk—but every boy in class had brought arrowheads to school. There were only so many times Mrs. Wright could help a student talk about the Cherokee tribe, and it was increasingly awkward to tell about the Indians being driven west on the Trail of Tears.

"What is something that you enjoy doing? What is something that you look forward to doing when you get home from school?" Mrs. Wright challenged the students and their show-and-tell pursuits. That was all Frank needed. He enjoyed getting home, rushing through his homework, putting on the Monkees, and singing away with the four boys from California.

And if that was what Mrs. Wright wanted, well, that was what Mrs. Wright was going to get.

Janet looked at him with a frown, "But you don't play the guitar, son," she said gently.

"I can play the guitar. I can take the record player, strum along, and sing," he said. That was how he presented the idea to Mrs. Wright, but she was so desperate for anything other than arrowheads that all she heard Frank say was, "I'll play the guitar."

"That would be wonderful," she said to him as he stood in front of her desk. "Bring everything you need on Friday." Frank reported to Janet that Mrs. Wright was fine with him playing the guitar for his class during show-and-tell. Janet looked at him and said, "But son, you don't play the guitar."

Not true, Frank thought.

When Friday came, Janet appeared at the end of the school day with the record player, the Monkees album, and Frank's Bert Higgins guitar with the many-colored strings. She was nervous and embarrassed and had secretly hoped she might come down sick so Tom could do this parental duty.

As Mrs. Wright welcomed her into the classroom, she began to say, "Edith, I need to tell you..." but was cut off by the excited teacher.

"Students, today, Frank is going to play the guitar for us. When I asked you to think about what you enjoyed doing, Frank told me he wanted to play the guitar for you. I am so happy." And she clapped excitedly to herself. She was a little unsure about the record player and had not really processed why Janet had brought it. She was about to understand, perfectly.

Frank walked to the front of the class and sat on a stool. He looked at Janet, who stood by the record player, preparing to drop the needle on "The Last Train to Clarksville." As the beat of the music began, Frank Wilcox began strumming feverishly, and he started singing as loud as he could along with his friends the Monkees.

Take the last train to Clarksville
And I'll meet you at the station.
You can be there by four thirty

'Cause I've made your reservation.
Don't be slow,
Oh no no no, oh no no no.

'Cause I'm leaving in the morning,
And I must see you again.
We'll have one more night together
'Til the morning brings my train
And I must go.
Oh no no no, oh no no no.
And I don't know if I'm ever coming home.

The students didn't care if Frank could play or sing. They were just excited to hear the Monkees album. Frank appreciated that response as he strummed right through the song "This Just Doesn't Seem to Be My Day," which both Mrs. Wright and Janet were beginning to appreciate. When Frank began wailing out "Let's Dance On," one of his friends stood beside her desk and began dancing something that bordered on obscene, and that inspired another girl to climb on a table and start dancing. Mrs. Wright was watching rock-and-roll chaos swallow her classroom, and Janet Wilcox stepped in to help curb the dance-off, which would have surely spun the local Baptists into orbit. By the time the record got to the song "Sweet Young Thing," Mrs. Wright stopped the concert for fear of what might happen.

As the class was being dismissed for the day, a weary Mrs. Wright walked up to Janet and Frank, who were quickly trying to gather everything for a hasty retreat.

"Frank," Mrs. Wright said, kindly, "I thought you could play the guitar."

Frank looked at her innocently and said, "Mrs. Wright, I thought I was playing the guitar."

For the next few years, Tom worked to find a guitar teacher for his son. Frank went through several good teachers, each of whom stopped the lessons because the student refused to practice. None of them ever understood that in the mind of Frank Wilcox, he could already play the guitar perfectly well.

Six

Valori Rath

There she was, standing at the open door of Mrs. Wright's second-grade class. She only knew one person in the entire school, and his name was Frank Wilcox. Frank gave her a slight wave so no one could really see it. She saw the wave and gave him a slight smile of acknowledgment. Mrs. Wright invited her to take a seat—a vacant desk right behind Frank. Frank could feel all eyes on him, and it was uncomfortable.

Tom and Janet Wilcox were very involved in the Acorn Jaycees and Jaycettes.

For decades after the end of World War I, and especially after World War II, Acorn's men and women had joined civic and community organizations, from those targeted to young farmers to those, such as Kiwanis, that pulled together Acorn's business leaders. The Jaycees, for men, and the Jaycettes, for the Jaycees' wives, focused on young men and women between the ages of eighteen and forty, providing leadership and civic involvement around business development, management skills, individual training, and community service.

Many of Tom and Janet's close friends joined the Acorn Jaycee and Jaycette organizations, and the organizations became great opportunities for the couples to get involved in their community. Janet became a president of the Jaycettes, and Tom was eventually elected as a chapter vice-president. He also led a committee that brought the first fair to Acorn.

Most of the county fairs at the time featured an agricultural exhibit, a cooking exhibit, an arts-and-crafts show, and a midway with carnival rides and attractions. For this project, the Jaycees wanted a young farmer involved in the organization of the fair, and, having recently won an Acorn County Young Farmer of the Year Award, Tom Wilcox was a likely choice.

Tom put together a committee—as was the Jaycee way—and each member of the committee took responsibility for an area of the fair. The Jaycettes were brought in to help with the project. It was decided that the fair would be at the local Acorn Town Park, which, along with a swimming pool, had one large baseball field. The field became the perfect location for the fair's midway. With help from the local county extension service, temporary quarters were built for farmers to bring and show their prime livestock, which largely consisted of chickens, cattle, and hogs.

Through a friend in nearby Roswell, Tom contacted the Deep South Fair & Carnival Company out of northern Florida and secured a contract to bring the midway to the first Acorn County Fair. The carnival company's contract included some food trucks, but mostly the Jaycettes ran all the concessions as a fund-raising effort for their chapter. The Deep South Fair & Carnival Company provided a variety of rides and attractions, including a Ferris wheel; a merry-go-round; a Scrambler, which few in Acorn had ever experienced and which upset many stomachs; bumper cars; the Tilt-a-Whirl; small automobiles that ran on a figure eight; and a trackless train that provided rides around the entire circumference of the baseball field. There was a variety of games lined up along the home-to-first-base line on the ball field. These games gave would-be heroes the opportunity to shoot at targets, throw softballs at targets, have their weight guessed, and even swing a mallet to ring a bell at the top of a pole.

Last, the Deep South Fair & Carnival Company provided two tent shows—one was a magician who had a twenty-minute show that included a woman mysteriously sawed in half but completely healed and perfectly well by show's end. Some from the Pentecostal Holiness Church called it heresy and wanted their money back, saying a woman sawed in half should not magically be put back together.

The other tent show, which no one really protested, was located in the very rear of the ball field, down the right-field line, and featured two dancing girls—Kitty and Birdy. These two girls were just good old

South Alabama girls who dressed scantily as if they were belly dancers from faraway Egypt. Onstage, they reportedly could dance without moving their feet, and during the last show of the night, they reportedly did amazing things with Ping-Pong balls tucked into their gyrating bellies. The Acorn Sheriff's Department provided two deputies for fear two old boys from north Acorn County would come down, fall in love with Kitty or Birdy, and then want to fight for them as Ping-Pong balls flew all over the tent.

On Elm Street, at the Acorn Primary School, the Jaycees and Jaycettes had gone to great lengths to advertise the fair, distributing flyers and postcards to all the children and offering each child one free ride of his or her choice on any given night—with paid admission, of course.

The children in Mrs. Wright's second-grade class were beside themselves, talking about the fair and hearing live reports from children who had attended early in the fair's ten-day run. More than one child talked about being high above Acorn on the Ferris wheel or being almost sick on the Scrambler.

Frank, in Mrs. Wright's classroom, and Charlie, in Mrs. Roper's classroom, were resident fair experts. Their parents, as Jaycees and Jaycettes, were at the fair during the setup and had been there every night of the fair. Frank and Charlie had gone to the park directly from school, worked on their homework, and then went about playing throughout the park. They had visited Mr. Marvel, the magician, and he had taught them a magic trick involving pulling a quarter from behind someone's ear. The boys were oblivious to the "hoochie-coochie" show, though they were intrigued that Frank's brother Jack kept turning up with Ping-Pong balls he had found around the tent.

One evening, early in the fair's run, Frank went to the concession stand to get a drink and noticed his mama talking to another woman whom he did not know. Beside the woman was a girl about his age, taller than he was with jet-black hair down to her shoulders. Frank thought she was beautiful—the most beautiful girl he had ever seen, and that was saying a lot. Frank thought most of the girls in his grade were beautiful. With mixed reactions, he had told many of them.

"Frank," Janet said, calling him over. "This is Mrs. Rath. She and her husband work for the fair, traveling all over to towns just like Acorn. This is their daughter, Valori, and she's going to be attending your school while they are in our town." It was not unusual for some children of fair employees to attend local schools while in town, and as a deacon at the First Baptist Church, Mr. Pulliam thought it was his God-given duty to open the doors of the school to any child who wanted to attend.

Valori Rath smiled at Frank, and he nervously smiled back. It was a clumsy meeting.

Janet said, "I want you to be Valori's friend at school, Frank, and help her meet some of your friends."

Frank ran off to play, leaving the women and Valori to talk some more. He found Charlie and forgot all about the little girl from the fair, and he certainly didn't expect her to show up in the doorway of his classroom. Now, here she was, and she was about to sit right behind him.

Valori was no stranger to being a stranger. She had been in a dozen classrooms, just like this one, each for only a few days. She said hello to Frank as she sat down, and Frank felt every eye on him, his classmates wondering how in the world he knew this girl.

"Hello," Frank said, and he turned around to face forward in the classroom.

Mrs. Wright, always gracious, introduced Valori to the class and told everyone that she would be with them for just a few days while the fair was in town. Valori gave everyone a free ticket to ride one ride at the fair, and she was an instant celebrity because of it. She gave Frank two free tickets, and he soon learned why. Valori never left his side for the next eight days.

It struck him that he was the only person she knew. The only one. There may have been snickers about his friendship with Valori, but Frank didn't care or didn't notice. He walked with Valori to the cafeteria and even told her about Mike's ride down the ramp and how he had enjoyed it. During the daily Coke break, he pointed out the soft-drink machines, whispering, "Don't get the RC Cola." He introduced her to

Mrs. Mize in the library, and Mrs. Mize helped Valori find a book to check out. At recess, Frank introduced her to Charlie and some of the girls, such as Lynette, Macy, Carla, and Sandra. Lynette did her part to make Valori feel welcome among the girls in the classroom.

With his attention focused on Valori, Frank noticed that she had developed a twitch in her eye. It was bothersome because she seemed to be twitching all the time. He didn't want to ask her about it because he thought she might start crying. So he asked Janet, who burst into laughter.

"She likes you," Janet said. "Someone has probably told her that if you like a boy, you should wink at him. She's not got a twitch. She's trying to tell you that she likes you." Frank stared at his mama with a million questions, but he decided to ask just one. "Did you wink at Daddy?"

"No, I am fairly certain that I've never winked at very many people," she said, laughing. "If you like her, you can wink back at her."

Tom had overheard and walked up, smiling. "Don't wink at anybody. You'll look dumb. It is better just to ignore the winking and hope it goes away."

Valori had worked her way into quick friendships and had fun talking to the other children about the fair. The children were so caught up in the fair that they saw the school playground in a different light. Now the merry-go-round reminded them of the Scrambler, and many of the boys had doubled up pushing the merry-go-round to make its speed more menacing. Riding the merry-go-round now required a passenger to hang on for dear life while going round and round in dizzying circles that left more than one child sick. Frank had succeeded during his turn only by hooking both one leg and one arm around a pole and then balling up as best he could with his head tucked into his chest. One boy broke an arm when he fell inside the merry-go-round and was beaten up by it before the boys could stop pushing.

The boys so dominated the merry-go-round that many of the girls were left as spectators. Eventually, the girls found their thrills on the playground's long row of swings, which with enough pushing could get some pretty high altitude as if they were on the Ferris wheel.

This was no playground for sissies.

Valori Rath, she of the fair with its rides and magician and games, was not content to be left out of anything. She wanted to ride the merry-go-round, and one day at recess, she ran ahead of all the children to get on it. Frank met Charlie outside the buildings and walked toward the playground with his friend. That was when Frank saw the gathering storm at the merry-go-round.

"Get off, fair girl," a boy shouted. "We don't want you here, and you can't ride today." Frank heard the bully. He watched as the crowd of boys grew around Valori as she sat on the merry-go-round. He watched as his new winking friend began to cry. Other children were playing, and the teachers were lagging behind to ensure everyone got to the playground. Not one person was coming to Valori's rescue.

Shy, sensitive Frank Wilcox started running toward the merry-go-round. He wasn't completely sure what he was going to do once he got there, but he was not going to let Valori stand against these boys alone. As he got closer, his feet now moving as fast he could go, Frank tripped and went stumbling into the crowd of boys. The loudest of the boys fell into the merry-go-round and then rolled hard onto the ground. He looked up to see Frank standing over him.

Frank was about to apologize when the boy said, "OK, OK. She can ride. But we don't have to push her." The boys all stood back, folding their arms and refusing to push.

Frank shrugged and began to push the merry-go-round. There was an old donkey at the fair, and donkey rides were provided, around in a circle, for the very smallest of children attending the fair. With Frank pushing the merry-go-round, Valori Rath's ride was slower than that donkey ride.

Frank was exhausted. The boys started laughing, calling him names and telling him, "Take your girlfriend and go kiss somewhere." Frank fell down in the sandy trough around the merry-go-round, and sweat poured from his brow. He looked up at Valori, who looked down at him. He was just about to tell her that he was sorry and that he had to quit when the pushing got easier. He looked over his shoulder to see Charlie pushing behind him. Steve Dickson started pushing, too, and Steve Dickson could push for three boys. Mack Holloway walked up and started helping, too. The girls came over from the swings, and Lynnette and Macy began pushing. A few other girls jumped on for a ride. Order had been restored at the merry-go-round. Valori Rath, who could ride the Scrambler whenever she wanted, thoroughly enjoyed the Acorn Primary School merry-go-round.

When recess was over, and everyone had returned to their class-rooms, Mrs. Wright called Frank into the hallway. He was very nervous because getting pulled into the hallway was usually a hop, skip, and a jump from getting a spanking. But Mrs. Wright simply said, "I saw what you did out there for that little girl, and I want you to know how proud I am of you." Then she hugged him.

A hug from Mrs. Wright was nice enough, but Valori told her par-ents all about it, and for the last two nights of the fair, Frank was able to ride as much as he wanted to ride without payment. For most of those rides, he sat by his new, short-term friend, Valori Rath.

On the last night that Frank saw her, just before the Scrambler started to turn, Valori Rath leaned over and kissed him on the cheek. Frank turned his face toward hers. And winked.

SEVEN

THE LIBRARY

When Frank Wilcox took his first step into the Acorn Primary School library, he was gone baby gone. Since he could remember, his Granny had tapped her own library of children's books and read the books to him. His mama and daddy were both readers, and Janet had taken out a mail-order subscription to Dr. Seuss books that they took turns reading to him. Frank had a love for books before he ever even started school.

Now before him were shelves and shelves of books. All he had to do was pick one out, check it out with Mrs. Francis Mize, the school librarian, and read it. None of his other feelings about school mattered at all, because having a wealth of stories at his disposal, trumped all other feelings, positive and negative.

In second grade, Mrs. Wright's class, now young readers, made a one-hour visit to the library each week, but they were also free to go to the library on their own, given her permission. Frank sometimes even opted out of recess in order to roam the aisles of the library. Mrs. Mize, who knew Frank's family from church and had taught both Janet and Tom in school, did not mind when Frank came to the library during the recess time. There were other students who did that same thing. For Frank, the library was his safe haven, his sanctuary, and his hiding place.

Frank fell in love with the Childhood of Famous Americans series. These easy-to-read books, at the time published by the Bobbs-Merrill Company, were each two hundred pages of illustrated history written in a way that helped children understand people such as athlete Jim Thorpe, author Mark Twain, detective Alan Pinkerton, Georgia's discoverer James Oglethorpe, entertainers Annie Oakley and P. T. Barnum, explorers such as Daniel Boone and Kit Carson, and founding fathers such as Benjamin Franklin and Nathan Hale.

The most popular of all the books in the Childhood of Famous Americans series was the book written by Guernsey Van Riper Jr., titled *Babe Ruth, Baseball Boy*. The Milwaukee Braves had just relocated to Atlanta, creating a new and widespread interest in all things baseball. Baseball card collecting became popular, introducing players and stories to boys and girls. Among those stories was the legend of Babe Ruth, the Sultan of Swat. Mrs. Francis Mize had a waiting list for the Babe Ruth biography that extended for weeks. It might not have been a *New York Times* Best Seller, but it was an Acorn Primary School Most Popular. The book was so popular that each student knew who had the book at any one time, and each student knew his or her place on the waiting list.

Frank had his name on the waiting list for the Babe Ruth book, but he continued pouring himself into the lives of other famous Americans. He was particularly intrigued with Revolutionary War spy Nathan Hale. Frank and his friend Lynnette, whom he had known as long as he could remember through the First Baptist Church, enjoyed reading the biographies together, and it became a friendly competition between them to see who could read the most in a week.

When Frank began checking out three or four library books every week, Mrs. Mize thought he might be skimming them, so she began asking about the books he had read. Frank unpacked so much detail that Mrs. Mize finally stopped him and said, "You've told me so much I don't have to read the book. A good book reviewer knows when to stop talking."

Tom and Janet thought maybe they had created a monster. Frank used the twenty-minute round-trip drive to school for reading; he took his books to the doctor's office waiting room, and he sat under the big oak tree beside Stozier's Woods on the Brookwood Road farm and read. He read all the time.

Mrs. Mize taught Frank and Lynnette how to use the card catalog to find the books they wanted in the library, and it was a revelation that caused Frank to whisper "Hallelujah." The kind librarian also suggested the pair of students visit the Acorn County Library and get to know Mrs. Jean Potts, who was the county's first full-time librarian.

Frank begged Janet to take him to the public library until she did so one day after school. Mrs. Potts became a lifelong encourager while Frank was living in Acorn. In fact, as he grew up, Frank spent many summer days at the public library, reading and visiting with Mrs. Potts. Some days he walked to the nearby Dairy Queen and picked up lunch or milkshakes for the two of them. It was Mrs. Potts who challenged him to read books that were more and more difficult.

The Acorn County Health Department was located right next door to the public library. As much as Frank saw libraries as his sanctuary and peaceful treat, the county health department made him feel sick to his stomach. The county health department, with its frosty-covered doors and windows and its harsh antiseptic smell, was where Janet took her boys for their regular vaccinations.

Frank knew pain. He had dropped a concrete block on his bare foot. He had also put four stitches in his right index finger while playing around with Janet's sewing machine one afternoon. He had fallen down the basement steps, foolishly trying to go down them backward just for fun.

Vaccinations, at the health department or at the doctor's office, were a different kind of pain. They weren't accidental; they involved a weapon and the use of that weapon by someone else. If all that wasn't enough, it seemed Janet always interrupted a perfectly good week by taking him and his brothers to the health department for vaccinations.

Even a kind nurse's suggestion, "Don't hold your breath—it will just hurt worse," did not work. The health department made Frank so nervous that he had diarrhea. There was nothing more mind-warping or stomach churning in his young life than a vaccination.

Frank had tried to appeal to his daddy. "What will happen to me if I don't get shots?" Frank had asked.

"You'll get sick and die," Tom had said, barely looking up from the newspaper he was reading. "Or, you'll get sick and spread it around to all the rest of us, and then we'll all die."

As bad as Frank hated vaccinations, he hated the thought of dying worse. He had seen death when his Papa Paul had died. He had seen death around his Papa R. C.'s slaughterhouse. He had seen the death of dogs. Dead was dead. At least after a vaccination, he could walk next door to the library or get a chocolate shake from the Dairy Queen. Still, he hated vaccinations and the health department just as much as he loved reading and the library.

Frank was not thinking about vaccinations this one afternoon in Mrs. Wright's class. He was reading a biography on the childhood of Revolutionary War hero Paul Revere. He hardly noticed Mrs. Wright walking the columns of desks and the single sheet of paper she put on each child's desk. Frank frowned at the distraction, picked up the paper, and looked it over. There was a red cross at the top and a message from the state of Georgia. Frank was able to read enough to know that a measles vaccination was going to be offered to students in the school library.

Panic set upon him and then horror. His beloved library was going to be the scene of pain and embarrassment. Frank was almost completely sure that when he stepped up for his vaccination, in front of all his friends, Mrs. Mize, and Mrs. Wright, he would pass out or puke—he wasn't completely sure which way it would go.

He delivered the flyer to Janet after school and immediately began questioning the need for the vaccination because, after all, he received vaccinations at the health department. Was this vaccination a new one or one that they had just forgotten about?

"Stop being a baby," Janet said, and she signed a form permitting Frank to get the vaccination in the school library. "Make sure you give this to Mrs. Wright tomorrow. Don't lose it." Frank took the signed form from his mama, folded it, and put it inside his book satchel.

The forms piled up on Mrs. Wright's desk as students returned them. Frank had resigned himself that the measles vaccination was going to happen, but why did it have to happen in his beloved library? Why couldn't the vaccination occur in the school cafeteria, where his favorite meal was corn and a yeast roll? Why couldn't the vaccination occur in Mr. Pulliam's office or in the school lobby?

On the day of the vaccination, a nurse from the health department set up shop in the school library. She was administering shots at the front of the library right beside the desk of Mrs. Mize. Students filed into the library in single file, winding down between shelves of books before turning and coming back toward the front of the library. The nurse sat there, politely waiting for the students to approach her one by one.

Adding to the drama, and to Frank's wildly nervous stomach, was the playground talk; students called it "the long walk" from their classroom to the point of vaccination. It was a quiet, procedural walk. Some children cried and begged not to go. One girl in Mrs. Crane's class had apparently peed on herself out of nervousness. When one teacher whispered to another, "They think they are sheep to the slaughter," it caused a chuckle, though most of the children didn't understand what the teacher meant. Nervousness was like a deadly virus all its own. The more children who expressed fear and nervousness, the more it affected the calm of all the other students.

Mrs. Wright tried to help ease the nerves and the tension in her classroom. "Children, we are going to line up in the hallway just as if we were going to the Coca-Cola machines," she said. Frank moved to the doorway with his friends—all of whom looked a lot more solemn than they did when going to the Coca-Cola machines.

"Goodness gracious, children, this is not the end of the world," Mrs. Wright said. "When we get back, you can have your Coke break, and I've made brownies for all of you."

That got Frank's attention. First and foremost, Frank loved the Willingham family's Dairy Queen. A chocolate milkshake was his all-time favorite treat. It was followed by his Mema's chocolate layer cake and Mrs. Audrey Gravitt's chocolate pie. Brownies were at the top of the list, too, and Frank didn't care who made them—even if the nurse giving the vaccinations had made them. He might've even looked forward to the vaccination if the medicine were cooked into a brownie. Hell, he'd take two. He had once stepped into the kitchen as Janet cooked brownies and was rendered "paralyzed," he told his brother Jack, by the smell. Freshly baked brownies created the most wonderful smell in the world.

The children perked up a little at the thought of Mrs. Wright's brownies. She had made them once before as an incentive to be still and pay attention to a presentation about how to brush your teeth. As part of this presentation, the children had been given a nasty piece of red *something* to chew, and the red residue left on teeth was to show why they needed to be brushed. The children all brushed their teeth afterward under the watchful eye of a medical professional, and then they enjoyed Mrs. Wright's brownies. Not everything in second grade made sense—neither did it have to make sense.

Entering his beloved library, Frank caught wind of antiseptic and thought he was going to pass out. The line of children marched down between the shelves of books, and Frank reached out to touch them as if they were old friends watching his march toward death. The line stopped as one by one the children stepped forward to the nurse, were swabbed with an alcohol-soaked ball of cotton, and were then stabbed by a needle. Each vaccination took less than twenty seconds. It was no time at all before Frank was just a few feet away.

He could fully understand why the girl in Mrs. Crane's class had peed through her clothes and onto the library floor. His legs felt as if they had turned to jelly. He wanted to cry, honestly, and it was at that moment when he felt a hand on his shoulder. He turned to see Mrs. Mize standing there beside him.

"Have you read the book on Sitting Bull?" she quietly asked him.

Frank gave a nervous nod that he had read it.

"Tell me about it," she said, and Frank began telling her all about the legendary Sioux medicine man, about what it must have been like to grow up outside on the plains and how Sitting Bull had first learned to ride a horse. Frank went on and on, giving Mrs. Mize a complete breakdown of the biography.

Somewhere in that explanation, he offered his arm to the nurse, felt the cotton swab, and received the vaccination that would protect him from measles, but he surely didn't pay much attention to it. He was too focused on telling Mrs. Mize about Sitting Bull.

"Frank, you start talking about these books, telling stories, and then I don't even have to read the books," Mrs. Mize said, laughing to herself. "Now, go back to class." It was just then that Frank realized the vaccination was over, so he shrugged and followed his equally joyful friends back to Mrs. Wright's brownies.

EIGHT

THE FEAST OF THANKSGIVING

Mrs. Wright's classroom had survived Halloween, complete with syrup-filled wax candy in the shape of cola bottles, cupcakes with orange icing, and drinks from the Coca-Cola machines. Those children who didn't have a dime for a drink were treated to one by moms helping with the day's party. Children were allowed to dress in their favorite costumes and then stand in front of the class to introduce themselves.

Frank had come to school as a wolf man, a reoccurring Halloween character for him. Last year's wolf man costume still fit around the waist, even if the pants were short, and the shorter pants actually lent to the authenticity of the costume. Lon Chaney Jr., who played the Wolf Man onscreen, would have been proud.

When it came time for him to stand in front of the class, he pulled down the plastic wolf man mask with its tight string of elastic around his head. He peered at his classmates through the two eye holes of the mask and did what he thought any self-respecting wolf man might do—he turned his head toward the ceiling and howled. *Loudly.*

On cue, his classmates howled back. That caused Travis Jackson's dog, Fred, to howl outside the classroom. Travis walked to school on some pretty days, and Fred came along with him—sometimes sitting outside the classroom until one of the school custodians or Mr. Pulliam chased him away. Fred was fortunate to have been chased away. On another day, a stray dog wandered onto the school property and began growling at students. Mr. Pulliam called everyone into the buildings and then called the Acorn Police Department. That dog was not chased away; it was shot dead by one of Acorn's finest right there on the playground. After the body had been removed, the playground was reopened.

With Halloween in the rearview, Mrs. Wright now focused on Thanksgiving. There would be no Thanksgiving party, but she wanted to draw attention to the holiday—to help the students deeply appreciate the holiday beyond just a day off from school and turkey at Grandma's house. She found a book titled *The Feast of Thanksgiving*, and the children took turns reading it aloud to the class.

That was when Mrs. Wright had a glorious idea: the class would produce a Thanksgiving play based on the book *The Feast of Thanksgiving*. And because the class was studying early American settlers going west, the Thanksgiving play would have an interesting twist. Instead of English pilgrims and the Wampanoag tribe breaking bread together in seventeenth-century New England, her play would be about a wagon of settlers going west and coming upon the Cherokee. The Cherokee would befriend the settlers—despite the settlers having driven the tribe off their homes to vast Oklahoma nothingness—and provide the settlers with food and water at the brink of disaster. These were very forgiving Indians.

She was beyond excited.

Mrs. Wright had a handful of roles for the play. There were the settlers—two couples with no children on kind of a double date across miles of prairie. They traveled in a wagon that was four school desks put together, two by two, with large paper wheels attached to the outside of the desks. It resembled a 1960s Ford station wagon.

There was a proud Indian chief, proud because his wife was one of the prettiest girls in the universe, not just the second grade. This couple had two children who sat all the time in front of the camp tipi. There was the chief's brother, whose mama had gotten carried away with makeup, presenting him as a hop, skip, and a jump from the warpath. There were four tribal maidens who, as it turned out, had no real part in the play except to stand behind the chief. They were like backup singers.

And there was a dog.

Selecting children for the parts in the play was not a democratic process. The children did not vote. Mrs. Wright selected the children she wanted to be in the play, and those children agreed to give up a handful of afternoon recesses to practice the play. There were some bitter feelings among some students, but Mrs. Wright consoled them with the possibility of an Easter play—which never happened. Mrs. Wright depended on the short memory of second graders.

At the first rehearsal, Mrs. Wright attempted to give out parts for the play. Everyone wanted to be an Indian, but Mrs. Wright said it could not be that way, and she chose four of the children to be the settlers. There was some general pouting among those chosen to be settlers, but Mrs. Wright reminded them how important they were to the Thanksgiving story, and moods were lightened. Without starving settlers, there was no one for the forgiving Indians to save.

Frank was standing off to the side with his friend Carla when Mrs. Wright selected Carla to be an Indian maiden and sit in front of the tipi. Mrs. Wright looked around the room, shrugged, looked at Frank, and said, "Frank, I need you to be the dog."

The dog?

Frank had been down this road before. Two years back, at the First Baptist Kindergarten, all the boys in the class had gathered to play out a scene from their favorite television show, *Daniel Boone*. Charlie Keller seized the opportunity to be the famous wilderness explorer by wearing a fringed leather coat to school. All the other boys in the classroom had shouted out parts they wanted to play—some even agreeing to be British redcoats, just to have a meaningful part to play. Frank, who was not as assertive as the other boys, watched as roles were claimed. When it was all said and done, Charlie came to his rescue. Not wanting to desert his best friend, Charlie said to Frank, "You can be my dog. You know Daniel Boone had a dog."

For several mornings during kindergarten, while his friends clumsily acted out scenes from *Daniel Boone*, Frank crawled around on the floor alongside his friend Charlie, doing his best impersonation of man's best friend. He even tried to bite one British soldier on the ankle, which got him kicked in the side by a boy named Ricky.

Frank was disappointed that Mrs. Wright had chosen him to play the role of the Indians' dog, and although he didn't understand typecasting, it was becoming painfully clear that he was playing a lot of canine parts.

"That's what happens when you dress up like wolf man every year at Halloween and howl like a damn dog," Tom said, trying to push his sons to dress in easy costumes like those of a farmer.

"I don't want to be the dog in Mrs. Wright's play," Frank complained to Janet that afternoon on the long ride home to Brookwood Road. "I don't want to crawl around on the floor and bark at people."

"Can't you just lie by a campfire or something?" Janet asked. She did not fully understand that it wasn't the crawling and barking that offended Frank, but the playing of the dog part in the play. "I'm not calling Mrs. Wright to complain about it. If you don't want to be the dog, then you need to tell Mrs. Wright that you don't want to be the dog. Stand up for yourself."

So the next day, Frank went to school and waited on the rehearsal during afternoon recess. As Mrs. Wright assembled the students, Frank said, "I don't want to be the dog." At that, another child spoke up and said, "I don't want to be a settler." And another child spoke up and said, "I want to go outside for recess."

Mutiny broke out on the set of *The Feast of Thanksgiving*.

Mrs. Wright, in her perfectly calm and soothing way, eased the troubled spirit of her company. She allowed the boy who didn't want to be a settler to be an Indian, and one of the Indians volunteered to be one of the settlers. And then she told Frank that he could just be an Indian, too...

...he could be the water bearer.

As the water bearer, she explained, Frank would carry around a large empty Clorox jug with the label taken off of it. When the chief said, "I need some water," Frank would run over to a make-believe stream and get the chief some water. Frank had gone from being the Indians' dog to being the team's water boy. To fill the void of the missing dog, Indian maiden Carla brought a white stuffed dog, which Frank thought looked more like a pony.

With the cast reasonably satisfied and calmed down, Mrs. Wright went on to helping the students think about their costumes. Many of the girls had long, colorful dresses that, with a few beaded necklaces and headpieces, made them look like Indians, albeit Caucasian ones. The settlers wore buckskin shirts (to be like Daniel Boone), pants, and old farm hats. The Indians, like Frank, wore cut-apart bed sheets painted with acrylic paint and used as vests or ponchos. They wore headbands, brown pants, and bedroom shoes. Mrs. Wright somehow produced lots of colorful feathers that were fixed into headdresses.

Other children in the class were chosen to help build a tipi for the Indian camp, which Frank thought was pretty authentic looking. Others helped build the settlers' wagon. Someone brought a Giddy-Up Stick—a horse's head attached to the end of a pole for make-believe horse riding—and the stick was stuck on the front of the wagon. That was one beat-to-hell horse, having to pull that frontier station wagon with four settlers riding in it—especially with no legs.

The week before Thanksgiving break, the children performed *The Feast of Thanksgiving* for the other students in Mrs. Wright's class. It was a simple production.

The play opened with the Indians working around their tipi, some building a fire and some preparing food. Carla sat in front of the tipi, holding her stuffed dog while Travis Jackson sat beside her. Travis had suggested bringing his dog, Fred, into class to be in the play, but Mrs. Wright asked him to bring a stuffed toy dog. What he brought was most certainly a stuffed horse, and the play's animal cast grew by one.

The settlers parked their wagon a safe distance from the camp and then proceeded to walk into camp. They were met by the chief and his beautiful wife. The Indian who had on the war paint relished his role and stood behind the chief, arms folded, staring menacingly ahead. Clearly, he had not forgiven the move to Oklahoma. Frank didn't wait on the chief to ask for water; he went and got some and offered it up.

After some general small talk, the settlers admitted they were starving from the time on the trail. They were also tired. The chief offered them food and rest and sent Frank on three trips to the nearby stream to fetch water for everyone. If there was any action in this play, Frank the Water Bearer was pretty much the only one doing anything.

The satisfied and comfortable settlers thanked and thanked the Indians for saving their lives and remarked that—lo and behold—it was Thanksgiving! The Indians had a general idea of what that meant—to the settlers anyway—and a celebration ensued. There was awkward dancing that resembled something like a cross between square dancing and the twist. The play ended with everyone happy and everyone thankful. The sour Indian participated in the celebration but didn't seem to enjoy it.

The class clapped, the cast bowed, and everyone was happy. Mrs. Wright beamed. Mrs. Wright was so proud of the play that over the next week, she invited every first-grade class and every second-grade class to come into her classroom and see it. Her poor students who were not in the play had the privilege of seeing it nine times—including a special performance one morning for the parents of those in the cast.

All the children who saw the play seemed to enjoy it. Mrs. Roper, understandably, had the best-behaved class of them all. She carried her paddle.

For the last performance, Mrs. Wright took one step perhaps too far. She invited the local newspaper, the *Acorn County News*, to come to the school and take a photograph of the cast at the conclusion of the play. The ensuing photograph ran the next week in the newspaper with this caption: "Members of Mrs. Edith Wright's second-grade class dramatized a story, *The Feast of Thanksgiving*, which had been read in class. All the first- and second-year pupils were invited to see the dramatization. All the children enjoyed seeing the headdresses, beads, long dresses, and Indian dances, which were quite authentic. The play was colorful and informative, and the students enjoyed it."

There was no mention of the settlers.

And rightly so. Because after the final performance, and before the photograph, anarchy erupted among the cast. The four settlers didn't really want to be settlers; they were just, well, settling by being settlers. The settlers really wanted to be Indians. By the time the newspaper photographer snapped his photograph, all the settlers had donned Indian headdresses, and now the settlers sat in their wagon dressed as Indians. Never had a Thanksgiving feast had this kind of impact on its participants. The newspaper photograph showed nothing but a cast of Indians; the poor settlers were nowhere to be found and had lost their wagon. Revenge of the Cherokee.

Mrs. Wright didn't care. She cut the photograph from the newspaper and pinned it to a bulletin board. And, more than once, Frank and the other students saw her pause at the bulletin board, stare at the photograph, and smile.

NINE

THE DEATH OF SANTA CLAUS

It was just another Friday in Mrs. Wright's second-grade class, and it was time for show-and-tell. Steve Dickson raised his hand, and Mrs. Wright called him to the front of the class. The students had been fascinated when Steve brought a snake to class, and they sat up straight to see if he had returned with another captive reptile.

Mrs. Wright was working at her desk. Steve faced his friends. He had nothing to show on this day. He only had something to tell. The words that tumbled from his mouth would send Steve Dickson into Acorn County immortality, especially among those passing through second grade at the Acorn Primary School.

"There is no such person as Santa Claus," he said.

Mrs. Edith Wright, not having anticipated what was coming, lurched at her desk. Across the room, as Steve's words rolled out to waiting ears, a wave of horror rolled over every student in the class.

Steve Dickson had just killed off Santa Claus. And he wasn't finished.

"All the presents come from our parents," he said. "Santa Claus is not real."

The phrase "the calm before the storm" is a meteorological phenomenon where an approaching storm sometimes pulls air in from several directions, creating a spooky stillness before all hell breaks loose.

When Steve Dickson dropped his one-two punch on the unsuspecting students of Mrs. Wright's class, there was a stunned silence so still that Frank heard water dripping from a spigot on the outside of the building. Then the storm blew in.

Several students began crying. One girl ran inside the small bathroom in the corner of the classroom, slammed the door, and began banging on the door from the inside. Another student dramatically

61

collapsed on the floor, twitching and moaning that the news could not be true. Reactions begat reactions. Some children normally not given to cry began crying because they figured they should be crying if others were crying.

Frank was still in shock, and he watched Mrs. Wright. She made it to Steve's side in four steps and never stopped moving. She ushered him into the hallway, not knowing exactly what to do. He had not lied; he had simply taken advantage of a big stage to share big, important news. Steve had not intended to be mean in his announcement. He was the youngest of four children, and the reality of Santa had finally been a secret no longer contained. He felt obliged to share this information with his friends.

As the news settled on Frank, he felt betrayed and could not wait to ask Janet if all of this was true. He knew she would not lie to him.

Mrs. Wright returned to the classroom, and Steve took his seat. She calmly went to the bathroom and helped the distraught girl back to her seat. Mrs. Wright walked to the front of the classroom.

"Children," she said, "let me talk to you for a minute." She began a rambling monologue that attempted to clarify Steve's statements without calling him an out-and-out liar, which he was not. Frank heard something that she said about the spirit of Christmas being alive in everyone, and Santa Claus would be as alive as the child within them. She even mentioned that she would bring brownies to the classroom on Monday, but not even brownies could turn back the tide of this Friday-afternoon revelation. Not one child in the classroom heard anything Mrs. Wright said.

The bell rang, ending school for the day. Students poured out of Mrs. Wright's classroom anxious to share the news, search for comfort, and mourn more publicly. Word traveled fast, as one boy walked out of the classroom and shouted for all to hear, "Santa Claus is dead!" When other students saw the teary-eyed outpouring from Mrs. Wright's class, well, it had to be true information. Teachers, caught unaware, tried to pounce on the news, hoping to prevent a backwash into the first grade. Children staggered out of school, many in tears, climbing into waiting cars for the ride home. Students on buses had the news confirmed by older students from the upper hallway.

"You mean you thought Santa Claus really brought all those toys?" a fifth grader said to a second grader on Bus Number 39, serving the town of Acorn. Bus drivers now found themselves involved in pastoral ministry—something they had not bargained for and were not compensated to provide.

Frank caught Charlie coming out of Mrs. Roper's classroom across the hall.

"Did you know about this?" he asked his best friend.

Charlie said, shaking his head, "No."

Frank walked out of the school, saw Janet in the Ford Galaxie, and climbed into the car.

"Mama," he said, "is Santa Claus real?" Before Janet could answer, Frank continued. "Steve Dickson said Santa Claus is not real and that you and Daddy are really the ones who put all those presents under the Christmas tree. Is that true?"

Janet might have expected a lot of questions on this Friday after school, but she was not at all prepared for this one question. She was also not a person to mince a lot of words, so she said, "Yes, it's true."

Frank had held in the tears, waiting on this confirmation. Now he felt as if someone had kicked him the balls, and he began wailing. It was the betrayal that got to him the most, and he wasn't even sure what that meant. He just felt very, very sad.

"It's all a lie," he quietly said to himself. "Everyone has lied to me." He put his head against the passenger side door and cried. His sorrow intensified as he thought about the questions he had. Would there still be presents? Would his parents continue providing presents? What was going to happen now?

Janet drove away from the school, suddenly noticing that several other parents parked here at the lower wing were having similar conversations with their children. Further, she saw a general melancholy unfamiliar to a Friday afternoon as school let out. She cleared things up pretty quickly for Frank. "If you tell Jack that there isn't a Santa Claus, you are going to get a spanking. You won't get any more Christmas presents, either."

Welcome to the world of deceit and cover-up, Frank Wilcox.

Across Acorn, reactions were different. Many parents were relieved or indifferent at the news breaking at school that day. Those relieved were glad they didn't have to be the bad guys, informing their children of the reality of Santa Claus. Those indifferent just didn't care either way. Those such as Janet, however, whose second-grader was the oldest child in the home, weren't ready for the fantasy to be over. Santa Claus was fun business.

Janet told Tom about the revelation when she got Frank home, and Tom took Frank on a walk down the farm's lake road toward the fishing lake R. C. Wilcox had built.

"Daddy, if Santa Claus isn't real, does this mean the Tooth Fairy isn't real?" Frank asked his daddy through trembling lips.

"Son," Tom said, "the Tooth Fairy is not real, but as long as you keep the secret, you will still get money under your pillow." Frank had started losing his baby teeth in the first grade and was pretty marveled at the idea of a fairy taking his teeth and leaving money.

Tom continued walking with his son and asked, "Are you about to ask me if the Easter Bunny is real?"

There was a long pause before Frank said, "No, I don't think I can take any more news."

It was good the news broke on a Friday afternoon. The school was closed on Saturday and Sunday, and the contagion had been calmed by Monday morning. Mrs. Wright believed it best just to let things be and not mention anything about what had happened. She was relieved when Monday morning was uneventful with no mention of the Friday bomb.

When the class returned from lunch, Mrs. Wright began the afternoon math lesson. That was when Macy raised her hand and said, "My daddy says Santa Claus is as real as I want him to be. I want him to be real. So he is."

Mrs. Wright closed her eyes and breathed deeply. No one responded to this statement.

"Your daddy is exactly right, Macy," she said. "He is a wise man." For some, Mrs. Wright's validation of Macy's statement was good enough. Santa was back from the dead. But not for Frank. The cat was out of the bag, and it was not going back inside. His parents had seen to that.

That Christmas, right on cue, Santa Claus visited the Wilcox brothers. Frank had even dressed up with his brothers, traveled to Lenox Square Mall in Atlanta, and sat on Santa's lap for the annual photograph. He had wanted so badly to lean in and whisper, "You aren't really Santa," but he had been reminded that a Christmas spanking awaited any leak of information to his brothers. He told "Santa's helper" what he wanted for Christmas, making sure he said it loud and slow enough for Janet to write it all down.

Frank was thirteen when eight-year-old Wayne finally learned the truth about Santa Claus, putting the myth to rest until the boys' sister was born a few years later. Then things started all over again.

Though neither Frank nor anyone in second grade that year ever forgot Steve Dickson's announcement, Frank came to admire the big boy with the big voice and the big laugh. Steve Dickson: a boy who could hit a baseball a hundred miles. Steve Dickson: a boy who always told the truth—even if unpopular. Steve Dickson: the boy who had killed Santa Claus.

TEN

MABEL

On my honor I will do my best to do my duty to God and my country and to obey the Scout Law; to help other people at all times; to keep myself physically strong, mentally awake, and morally straight.
—The Boy Scout Oath

The old, vacant, two-story house just stood there, beckoning a group of third-grade boys to "come and see" what she offered or once had been long ago. The seven boys sat in Charlie Keller's yard, staring at it. They were dressed in their solid-blue Cub Scout uniforms, pants, and shirt with a blue elastic belt. Around their necks each wore a blue-and-gold Cub Scout neckerchief held in place by a gold metallic slide with a wolf's head on it.

The new scouts had just finished a program on exploration, learning about the Lewis and Clark Expedition of 1804–1806, and they were itching for their own adventure into the unknown.

"We can go and be back before anyone knows we are gone," Charlie said. "I've walked over there before but never really looked around."

"What's so special about it?" Jim Vinton asked. "It's just an old house."

"There's a skeleton in it," Charlie said. "I heard you can look in those back windows and see it. It's a real skeleton, standing up in a corner."

Frank's stomach was hurting. He knew his best friend. They could sit here in the grass for as long as they wanted, but Charlie was going to lead them over to the old house. It was Charlie's chance to see if the skeleton was indeed there and to do so bolstered by the courage of company.

Janet Wilcox and her best friend Midge Keller had volunteered to lead Cub Scout Den 8—one of the several small groups of third-grade boys organizing in Acorn County to support the Boy Scout movement. Acorn County was the home of legendary Boy Scout Troop 39, now led by scoutmaster above all scoutmasters Jim Scully. The troop was known throughout North Georgia for its size, its contributions to the community, its participation in regional and national Boy Scout events, and for those in its ranks reaching scouting's highest honor, the Eagle Scout Award. Eagle Scouts had their names on a special plaque hanging in the Acorn Town Hall. The few teenage boys who stayed with scouting long enough to earn the Eagle Scout award were treated to the plaque, a photograph in the *Acorn County News*, and a sacred ceremony with a reception at the Acorn United Methodist Church. It was the Methodists, the Acorn Kiwanis Club, and the local Veterans of Foreign Wars that undergirded the famous Acorn Boy Scout movement.

With the exception of Frank, who lived in the south end of Acorn County, and Pete Yancey, who lived at the northernmost end of the county, the Cub Scout Den 8 members lived in or very near the Acorn town limits. And most of the boys had roots in the First Baptist Church or had attended kindergarten together there.

Pete Yancey was the baby-faced, smiling boy who liked everyone and whom everyone liked. Built like a fullback, Pete knew he was naturally one of the strongest of the boys but never bullied anyone. He loved to joke and needle his friends but knew when it was time to stop. Soft-spoken and polite around adults, he often greeted his friends with a simple wave and a "Hey, ho, it's a great day," something he had picked up from his beloved grandfather.

Jim Vinton was tall and athletic. He was quiet and well mannered. He sang gospel music with his younger brother, and they sometimes were featured on the local AM radio station. Like Frank, Jim had a fascination and love for chocolate milk, and Jim had mastered a curious digestive trick—he could belch on command. It came in handy when the boys were in need of entertainment.

Emmett Morgan was a small, soft-spoken boy. You had to listen just right to realize that Emmett was talking to everyone, though it sounded as if he were only talking to himself. He and Charlie were the smallest of the boys, and Emmett was the calmer of the two of them. Emmett had a gift. Emmett could draw cartoons, and he was a genius at it.

Lester Freemont was big like Pete but taller. Lester was the smartest boy in the third grade and probably the entire school if aptitude tests were given. But Lester was not a know-it-all; he just had the gift of listening and learning and understanding, and his friends were amazed by it. Lester was the only one of the scouts who had not attended the First Baptist Church kindergarten. He had become friends with Pete, Charlie, and Jim through Mrs. Roper's second-grade class. His daddy was a revered educator at Acorn County High School. Lester's reserved, cautious attitudes were similar to those of Frank, and the two became good friends.

Travis Jackson was the thrill seeker of the group, and when Charlie planted the seed of visiting the old house to put eyes on a possible skeleton, that seed germinated in Travis Jackson. He was all in. There was nothing Travis wouldn't try and no dare he would turn down. Already, in the short tenure of Cub Scout Den 8, he had climbed to the top of a pine tree at Charlie's house and attempted to jump out of the top, hoping a wadded bed sheet used as a parachute would break his fall. He now wore a cast on his right arm, having whacked it on several branches coming down through the tree. Travis was the only one of the boys whose daddy had approved of his hair growing beyond a military buzz, and he kept blowing his hair from the side of his mouth.

Today's scout meeting had started like every other. The scouts met every Tuesday afternoon at Charlie's house in the center of Acorn, pledging allegiance to the flag, listening to a guest speaker on a variety of interesting topics, sometimes engaging a craft or art project, eating refreshments, and then pouring into Charlie's backyard to play until parents arrived at 5:00 p.m.

It was during this playtime that the boys generally got up a game of football, kickball, or baseball, and each of them at one time or another had noticed the old house with its old second-story roof peeking over a vacant lot full of weeds. Today, they sat staring across the lot, having finished off Kool-Aid and a package of Oreo cookies. The weather was still warm, but fall was coming.

"I don't know if we should do it," Lester said. "Maybe we should ask your mom if it is OK; maybe she and Mrs. Wilcox will walk over there with us."

Charlie shook his head, and Travis slid over beside him. The two were a united front.

"We need to go right now and hurry back," Charlie said, knowing the den mothers would not approve of the scouts going on private property and shuffling around an old vacant house.

"Why do you think there's a skeleton in there?" Lester said, hoping for anyone else who might stand up as a voice of reason.

"I heard that the man who lived there died, and he had no family, and so there was no one to get his skeleton," Charlie said. "It's supposed to be just standing in the corner of the back room."

"He died standing up?" Pete Yancey asked. "He just walked in that back room one day, died, and froze right there as a skeleton?"

"I don't know all the answers," Charlie said. "That's what we need to go find out."

"I'm going," Travis said, waving his cast in the air. "I'm going if I have to go by myself." He looked both ways and ran across Woodland Drive to the vacant lot. Charlie smiled, winked, and ran after him. The other boys followed, but Frank and Lester were the last to cross the road. They still weren't completely sure this would end well.

The old house had once been one of the proud, prominent homes in Acorn. It had been owned by the Thomas family, and Dr. Fred Thomas had once practiced medicine in the back of his home. He had also been a scientist and had made contributions to Emory University in Atlanta. He had never married and did not have a family, and upon his death, his estate had fallen into a settlement abyss. Everything was still in its place, having been in legal limbo for several years.

Dr. Thomas had named the skeleton Mabel. It was a teaching skeleton, the full size of a five-foot-ten man or woman, and it was hanging from a metal frame in the back room of the house he once used as an office to see patients and to teach some visiting students from Emory University.

The Cub Scouts walked across the vacant lot and were soon standing on the edge of an old lawn. The grass refused to grow because of huge water oaks that sucked the moisture out of the ground. The root systems of the old oak trees protruded above the soil.

"No trespassing," Lester said, reading a sign posted on one of the trees. "That means we should not be here."

Frank put a hand on his friend's back but didn't say anything. Lester looked at him and was thankful for the gesture of support.

"Lester," Charlie said. "You are the biggest. You lift me on your shoulders so I can see inside that window. Once I see if the skeleton is real or not, we can go. Just like that. We'll be back in my yard in no time."

Travis had first gone to Jim Vinton, believing the tallest boy was his best shot to see inside the windows, but Jim's shoulders were too narrow to support the thrill seeker. So Travis turned to Pete Yancey. Pete rolled his eyes and bent down to scoop up Travis.

"Make sure he doesn't pee on you, Pete," Jim said, knowing that Travis had a bad habit of waiting until the last minute to pee and often pissed uncontrollably from excitement.

"If you pee on me, Travis, the skeleton will be least of your problems," Pete said, cautiously sticking his head between Travis's legs and then lifting him up into the air. Travis balanced himself using Pete's head.

"Onward," Travis said, kicking his knees on Pete's shoulders.

With Lester and Pete staggering toward the windows, Travis and Charlie held each other's elbows to help keep things steady.

The rest of the boys followed closely, helping balance the two riding their way to the high windows of the first floor. Finally, Charlie and Travis were able to reach out and grab the windowsills to look inside the dirty windows of the old house. No one noticed that Emmett had climbed onto the back porch, found the back door unlocked, and easily opened it. He mumbled something, shrugged, and walked inside.

Before Charlie and Travis could slide off the shoulders of their transportation, Jim burped loudly and followed Emmett inside the house. Frank still held back and was the last of the boys to step inside.

Once inside, the boys, bunched together, started out slowly and then began to run through the bottom floor of the house until they all heard Travis say, "Here it is." They walked up behind him and read a sign on a closed door: "Doctor's Office." Charlie stepped in front of them, taking charge as it was his idea to be there in the first place, and opened the door.

"Dang," Emmett said, and he said it so understandably and so calmly that all the boys turned to face him in surprise. Then they saw the object of his exclamation—standing in a dark corner, fully upright, was indeed a human skeleton.

"Dang is right," Travis said, and he actually started toward the skeleton. "Anyone want to dare me to touch it?" No one did. In fact, Lester, Pete, and Frank were already backing out of the room. But Travis and Charlie were not to be denied, and they approached the skeleton in the corner.

"It's his real bones," Charlie said, touching the presumed Dr. Thomas staring open-jawed into the room. "We need to help him down off this rack. He probably got up on here and couldn't get down and just died hanging here."

The boys crowded in, the braver ones in the front. A decision was made to get the skeleton off the rack and make it more comfortable. Jim suggested they find a shovel and bury it in the backyard, and as Lester was known to bring a Bible to school, he could say a few words over the grave. Jim frowned at Frank upon the suggestion that the tall tenor sing "Amazing Grace" around the grave.

Travis found a stool and climbed up to eye level with the skeleton. He pushed up on the lower jaw so that the mouth was closed and then let it fall back open.

"I wonder if he was shouting when he died," Travis said. "I wonder if his last words were 'Help, help; I can't get down from here.'"

"It was probably more like 'How the hell did I get up here in the first place?'" Frank said, chuckling at himself.

They all stood quietly for a moment in a strange reverence, and Jim Vinton burped to break the silence. "I can get him off this rack, but you guys be ready to take him," Travis said. Pete and Lester stepped in and awkwardly held the skeleton around its midsection as Travis unhooked the alleged poor Dr. Thomas and lowered him down.

Emmett, laughing and talking to himself, had rolled up an old examination table, and the skeleton was placed on the table, facing upward. Charlie had seen a recent *Friday Night Frights* scary movie on television and thought it appropriate to cross Dr. Thomas's arms over his chest, saying, "This is how they buried people, or at least it's how they buried Count Dracula." Frank knew it wasn't so because his Papa Paul had died the year before, and he didn't recall his grandfather's arms being folded at any time during the proceedings.

All the boys stood around the skeleton. Travis had left the room and now returned, holding an old, dusty hat that Dr. Thomas had most likely worn with one of his finest Sunday suits. Travis put the hat over the skeleton's face, but then it was decided just to raise the head a bit and put the hat on the skeleton's head. They covered the skeleton up to the neck with an old blanket.

"Let's get out of here," Lester said, giving a tug on Frank's shirt. "We've been here long enough." Everyone agreed, and the boys started out of the office, feeling they had performed a good deed done daily, in the Boy Scout way, by freeing Dr. Thomas from the corner and giving him rest on a table—with his favorite hat on his head and covering the bones of his private areas.

They were starting out of the house when they heard an unfamiliar, ragged voice. "You boys ain't supposed to be here. This is private property. No trespassing is what that sign says." The old man known as Whistlin' Ben pointed with his only arm to the sign on the tree. Whistlin' Ben wasn't exactly a vagrant in Acorn, but he had little to do other than occasionally shoot courthouse pigeons, which were an ongoing nuisance. Charlie and Emmett had testified that the shootings did occur, having seen them, and that it was a sight to behold, watching Whistlin' Ben position a twelve-gauge shotgun with only one arm, blasting away at pigeons. It was a wonder indeed that no one around the courthouse had been gunned down.

"Mabel is what Doc Thomas used to call her. I suppose she was a woman. I'm not sure how you tell the difference when all the valuables fall off."

The boys didn't have a clue what this smelly old vagrant in the dirty overalls was talking about.

"Doc Thomas is buried over yonder in the town cemetery down from the Dairy Queen."

And then Whistlin' Ben started telling stories about Doc Thomas and how he never refused to see anyone sick and how people would come around and knock on the back door all the time, needing help. He told them about Doc Thomas delivering babies, going out to farm accidents, and even occasionally pulling a tooth that was bothering someone. Doc Thomas had held the hands of many dying folks in Acorn County and prayed with many of them, too.

The boys just looked up at him, unsure of what to say, some staring at the space where his right arm should have been.

"You boys shouldn't be coming around these old houses in town," Ben said. "And you shouldn't be trespassing on other people's property. You ought to know better."

The boys had been gone too long. They knew it. Without a good-bye to Ben, they started across the open field toward Charlie's house. Lester, Frank, and Pete were in the rear, and it was Lester who was the last to turn and look at the old house. He nudged Frank, who turned just in time to see Whistlin' Ben go inside.

ELEVEN

WENDELL MANN

There would be a day in the future of Acorn County when people poured into her boundaries from Atlanta and beyond. The opening of a major four-lane artery from the heart of Atlanta up through Acorn County would change Acorn County into one of the fastest-growing areas of the United States.

But that was decades away. Now, in 1967, newcomers to Acorn County were numbered in a dozen or so families each year, generally only replacing those who died or moved away. It was big news when a new family came to Acorn, especially when it meant new faces at public school or in the pews of churches.

Wendell Mann's family was one of those new families, and Frank first met Wendell in the boys' Sunday School class taught by Mr. Horace Bennett, deacon emeritus and finance chairman of the First Baptist Church. The class met on the second floor of the church's three-floor education building. A water fountain just outside the classroom door was what Mr. Bennett called "the watering hole" because so many folk congregated there, chatting and interrupting his lessons. Mr. Bennett also had to pause his lesson when a third-floor toilet flushed overhead, causing him to stop and say, "Thar she blows, boys. Thar she blows!"

While Mr. Bennett had a fun way about him, his Sunday School lessons were dry as sand. Frank and Charlie sometimes played rock, paper, scissors in Mr. Bennett's periphery. Sometimes the two friends got tickled and had to be separated, but that only caused them to stare at each other and laugh even more.

"I'm trying to teach you about Jesus, boys," Mr. Bennett would say to the laughter, and then he often laughed too.

Frank had a history of getting spankings at church. More than once, Tom had spanked him for giggling and restlessness during Preacher Acree's sermons. Janet knocked the fire out of him after Sunday School the year she taught him. He had asked an honest question during one lesson, and Janet thought he was being a smartass. He had barely got out of the room before she gave him two licks across the backside. Tom had also spanked him one morning after Sunday School. Tom was substitute teaching and was deep in a lesson from Mark, chapter 3, about the man with a withered hand. Tom looked up to see Frank staring at his hand in twisted-up fashion, trying to get a visual of what his daddy was talking about. Tom thought he was being a smartass and spanked him in the third-floor bathroom.

More than once, Tom had said to Mr. Bennett, "If he misbehaves, come get me."

"They are just boys, Tom. I don't see it as disrespect, and I don't think Jesus is offended either," Mr. Bennett said. "These are all good boys. They just have to be silly and stupid some of the time. I have to keep a straight face when I'm with them, but sometimes I laugh all the way home."

The faces in Mr. Bennett's class never changed because few people ever moved to Acorn. That was why it was big news when Frank walked into Mr. Bennett's classroom and saw a new face.

Wendell Mann was hefty in a big, thick way. His curly brown hair gave him a distinct look, but more than anything, it was his grin. It was a grin that went from ear to ear, and when he laughed, he laughed so hard that his eyes naturally squinted almost shut. He was always grinning. There was an open chair beside Wendell, and Frank sat down in it.

"My name is Wendell," he said to Frank. "I want people to call me Rock, but no one does." The two boys talked after Sunday School and from that day forward always sat together during Sunday School and the following worship service. Charlie sat with them, too. Frank and Wendell became close friends.

During a sleepover at the Brookwood Road farm, the two new friends slept in sleeping bags in the Wilcox family's front room.

"Do you miss your old home?" Frank asked Wendell.

"Not really," Wendell said. "I'm glad I've got new friends, like you."

"You are my friend, too, Wendell," Frank said.

This new friendship was why Frank felt sick at his stomach on the day he learned that Wendell planned to jump from the swing set on the school playground. He was certain his new friend was going to die in the third grade. He imagined all the third graders gathered around Wendell's body as Mr. Pulliam looked down at him and said, "He was a good boy, but not very smart. It was foolish to jump out of that swing set." Everyone was sad.

The playground's swing set included four swings hanging from a crossbeam attached to two inverted V legs. Each of the dangling swings was a wide strip of leather secured to the cross beam by two long, heavy chains. The length of the chains made it possible, with the right help pushing the swing, to go very, very high in the air—much higher than the normal backyard swing. These were professional-grade, thrill-seeking swings.

Van Piper liked to swing as high as he possibly could, jumping out of the swing at its highest point and seeing just how far he could jump. He challenged all comers to jump farther than he could.

Perhaps Wendell, as the new boy in school, was just trying to impress everyone, but for whatever reason, he accepted the challenge.

"Have you lost your mind?" Frank asked his friend. "You can be injured and break bones."

"You worry too much, Frank," Wendell said, laughing at him. He patted his thick belly and said, "I've got plenty of padding."

It was going to be a swing-off, with the winner being the one who could jump the farthest from the swing. Van and Wendell had agreed to meet at recess; swing side by side, going as high as their nerves allowed; and then jump from their respective swings. Whoever landed the farthest away would be the winner. The prize would be the satisfaction of winning.

Van Piper had never lost anything to anyone, ever. He was still a man among boys. There were rumors swirling that he was at least two years older than everyone else in third grade. Someone suggested he might have hair under his arms, but no one believed it because that would have made him a daddy. By comparison, Wendell was a big pillow.

"If you win, he might want to fight," Charlie said. "My recommendation is to kick him in the nuts as quickly as possible. Don't wait around on him. Just get up and kick him in the nuts. We'll help you hide." Frank and Wendell laughed out loud at the visual, especially with Charlie acting out the parts of both kicker and the one being kicked.

On the day of the swing-off, all the third-grade boys ran to the swing sets to watch. Most expected to see Van or Wendell—either one—die, but short of dying, most of the boys hoped to at least see a broken arm and maybe some blood. Charlie had prepared them to see a groin kick, too.

To everyone's surprise, including Van Piper's, Wendell crowed loudly, "I'm going to win." He threw his head back and laughed. "I'mmmmm going to winnnnnn!"

"What are you going to win?" Frank whispered to his new friend. "What are you going to win? There's no prize; you're just going to break a leg or an arm."

Wendell put a big arm around Frank. "Naw, now, I'm not going to get hurt. I'm going to beat Van Piper, and everyone is going to know about it. I'll be the king of the playground after this." And he laughed and laughed.

Van was growing weary of the fun-loving newcomer. Van decided that after he won, if Wendell was still living, he would beat up Wendell just to send a message to all the other little third graders on the playground. The message: don't laugh at Van Piper.

The boys each got inside one of the swings. It was determined that Steve Dickson and Pete Yancey were of equal strength and would be best suited to get the boys started in the swings. Steve went over to push Van, and Pete lined up behind Wendell. On the count of three, the pushing began and continued until pushing was impossible. Then it was up to the swingers.

Both boys were swinging on their own, pulling back hard and then thrusting forward. By this time Mrs. Baggs, who had third-grade playground duty, responded to the commotion and appeared at the top of a hill. She looked down at all the boys. All she saw was two boys swinging and a bunch of other knuckleheads standing around as if waiting their turn. No one was fighting, and if no one was fighting, then all was well.

The two boys were now swinging so high that the tension on the chains gave way a little, meaning they were just about at the peak of their swinging height. Wendell slid his hands up the chains, moving his hands so that they were on the inside of the chains. This was a classic prejump move that every boy knew was necessary to get all of your body inside the chains. Every single boy had jumped from a swing, even if it was on smaller models in their respective backyards.

"They are going to die," Frank said to Charlie, who was staring wide-eyed at the swingers, wishing he had thought to take Van's challenge.

When Wendell prepped his jump by repositioning his arms, Van Piper saw him and did the same thing. Van wanted to be the first to jump, and he heard Wendell singing, "I'm going to jump, I'm going jump in just a minute—next time through, here I go!" Several of the boys had moved around facing the swings from a distance so they could rush to see broken bones and blood.

Van's confidence was a little shaken by the singing confidence of the new boy. So on his next upswing, Van threw himself out of his swing and sailed. Van's arms and legs were spread, and he yelled out, "Oh, shit!" as he flew through the air. He later denied screaming, but everyone had heard it.

As Van sailed, Wendell did a very curious thing. He brought his arms back outside the chains and started slowing down. He had no intention of jumping.

Van hit the ground hard and began rolling, stirring up a cloud of dust. Mrs. Baggs had returned just in time to see the jump, and she was running down the small hill as fast as her short little frame would travel. "Stop it, boys. Stop it right now," she shouted and ran to where Van had come to rest on the hard playground. He was moaning, and his arms were skinned and bleeding. Nothing appeared broken.

Wendell's swing had slowed to a stop, and he sat there in it, twirling around as all the boys ran to see if Van was alive. Frank walked up to his friend.

"You never planned to jump, did you?" Frank said, lightly jabbing at his friend. "You never even planned to jump."

"And look," Wendell said, pointing to the injured Van, who was now being yelled at by Mrs. Baggs. "Looks like I won." Frank smiled and shook his head.

TWELVE

GOODBYE CRUEL WORLD

Dynamite comes in small packages.
—An American Proverb

Charlie Keller was funny and made everyone laugh. Sometimes it was the things he said, and sometimes it was the things he did, and sometimes it was the boundaries he pushed. Whatever the circumstance, Charlie had discovered that people thought he was funny, and he relished in it. But there was more to Charlie than just being funny. He had emerged as one of the best students in third grade, and he was always willing to help others. More than once he had helped Frank overcome a hurdle in math. He was also athletic and one of the fastest boys in the school. He was everyone's friend.

But Charlie had one big problem: the more his audience demanded of him, the more he felt compelled to give them.

Mrs. Roper had tried to put the brakes on Charlie in second grade. Frank, across the hall in Mrs. Wright's class, had heard the news that Mrs. Roper had spanked him with her wooden Bolo paddle minus the attached elastic and bouncing ball. She had spanked him on two different occasions. That might have been enough to stop the normal entertainer, but Charlie Keller was not the normal entertainer.

The spankings just endeared him more deeply to his audience, especially when he returned to the room smiling and giving a wink to his dear admirers. "All is well," he communicated with that grin, and "The show will go on." Even Mrs. Roper hid a chuckle at some of the things Charlie did. She only spanked him to prevent anarchy from breaking out among the other students.

Charlie Keller was emerging as the prince of Acorn Primary School.

Mrs. Maxine Baggs, unfortunately, was not going to be at the coronation.

Mrs. Maxine Baggs was serious about education. She stood in front of this new class of third graders and told them that they were now on the upper hallway, where grades, tests, and learning would really begin. She told them that there would be times to play and there would be times to learn. When they were inside, in her classroom, it was a time to learn.

She then invited each student to stand up and give a short introduction to the rest of the class. One by one, students gave these introductions, telling where they lived, what their parents did for a living, and a little about their hobbies. Mrs. Baggs asked a question or two when appropriate, smiled, and thanked each student after each introduction. Frank liked her. He liked her smile. He liked that there was order in the classroom.

When it was Charlie's turn for an introduction, he stood and coughed into his hands. He then sang his introduction as if he were Elvis Presley. As the classroom exploded with laughter, Charlie danced a little as part of his act. Frank was glad to be reunited with his best friend in third grade, but even he did not expect this bit of entertainment. Frank looked at Mrs. Baggs to see what her reaction was going to be.

Mrs. Baggs stared at Charlie. Her face was blank. She reminded Frank of a teller he had met at the First Federal Bank—all business. Mrs. Baggs thanked Charlie, never acknowledging his efforts, and went on to the next student. Frank thought he saw a flash of anger in her eyes and expression, and he tried to warn his friend at recess. Charlie didn't want to hear him.

The first time Mrs. Baggs spanked Charlie in the school hallway, she didn't lose her temper. She simply called him to go outside the classroom. She took her Bolo paddle from inside her desk, followed him into the hallway, shut the door, and proceeded. Students heard the *flap, flap, flap* as the paddle met Charlie's jeans-covered backside. Charlie returned, smiling and smirking, and Mrs. Baggs followed, winded but confident she had made an impression. Her short, solid stature provided a lot of torque behind that paddle swing.

Frank thought Mrs. Baggs did her best to avoid spanking Charlie. She tried a variety of punishments, including keeping him in for recess. She once made him sit in the hallway to do his homework, but Charlie wandered down to the cafeteria ramp and was entertaining second graders on their way to lunch. Mrs. Roper returned him to Mrs. Baggs, who spanked him with Mrs. Roper as a witness. Poor Mrs. Roper didn't know which one—Charlie or Mrs. Baggs—most deserved her sympathies.

It became at least a weekly event. Mrs. Baggs and Charlie quietly walked with each other to the hallway, where there was the *flap, flap, flap* of paddle hitting britches, and then they would return to class. Mrs. Baggs had a long, successful teaching career, and it would be hard to imagine she paddled any student more than she paddled Charlie Keller. He would have been in the Mrs. Baggs Hall of Fame.

"I don't know how you stand it," Frank asked him one day at lunch. "Doesn't it hurt?"

Charlie shook his head and said, "Not really. If I'm thinking ahead, I sometimes put a piece of cardboard in my pants before school starts." Genius.

There was no cardboard for Charlie's pants the day Mrs. Baggs reached her breaking point. Of all the people who might be tangled up in the ongoing struggle between Charlie and Mrs. Baggs, Frank Wilcox was the least likely to play a part in the unfolding drama. But it was Frank who served as the spark that inadvertently struck the match that lit the dynamite.

Mrs. Baggs had continued the tradition of show-and-tell on Friday afternoons. Frank had brought what he considered one of the best items ever, but he wasn't waiting around until show-and-tell to show and tell about it. R. C. and Kathryn Wilcox had been on a short vacation trip to Florida. On these trips, R. C. liked to visit Stuckey's roadside convenience stores, where he loaded up on pecan rolls, saltwater taffy, and driftwood signs with funny sayings imprinted on them. He also bought funny little novelties and occasionally small slide viewers that featured topless pinup girls. On this recent trip to Florida, R. C. had returned with a handheld novelty that tickled him to no end.

The novelty was a small wooden toilet. Opening the lid of the toilet revealed a man's head as the last part of him to go down. The poor man looked up to an imprint on the inside toilet seat that read, "Goodbye cruel world." Imprinted on the side of the toilet was the inscription:

Goodbye cruel world.

The moon may kiss the stars on high,

The stars may kiss the bright-blue sky,

The dewdrops may kiss the green, green grass.

But, you, my friend, can kiss my...

"Ass!" Frank shouted, and he and his grandfather laughed and laughed. Frank knew then he had to take this to school and show it to his friends. He hid it in his book satchel and carefully passed it around the classroom during the day. It didn't take long before Mrs. Baggs confiscated the little toilet. She didn't scold Frank; she just took the small toilet and returned it to him at the end of the day.

"Do you think this is appropriate for school?" she asked him, disappointed that the quiet little boy had brought this vulgar item to school. "Do you think this is something your family would be proud to know came to our school today?"

Frank apologized, and she released it to him, telling him to never bring items like that, even if his grandfather did purchase it and give it to him. Frank returned to his seat, preparing to pack the little toilet in his book satchel.

"Can I take it home with me?" Charlie whispered.

Frank shrugged and handed it to his friend. In a way, he was glad to be getting rid of the novelty because Mrs. Baggs's scolding had taken the fun right out of the funny little toilet. Charlie turned the toilet over in his hands, smiling, and put it in his own book satchel for the weekend. It was a big mistake.

Using the bathroom between Sunday School and church services on Sunday, Charlie pointed at the toilet and said to Frank, "Goodbye cruel world." He laughed to himself. Frank laughed with him.

On Monday, before Mrs. Baggs called the class to order, Charlie handed the toilet back to Frank, and Frank quickly hid it away in his book satchel. He knew he would probably get a spanking if Mrs. Baggs saw the toilet, especially after telling him not to bring it back to school. Charlie grinned. Frank knew something was swirling in his friend's head, but Frank was too caught up in hiding the toilet from Mrs. Baggs.

The morning continued without any kind of classroom incident, and then, just after returning from the cafeteria, Charlie asked for permission to leave the classroom and use the bathroom. Mrs. Baggs granted permission, and Charlie left the room for the boys' bathroom. It was located halfway down the upper hallway of the school.

Mrs. Baggs began teaching. Children began learning. All was well.

But Charlie did not return to class. After several minutes passed—long enough for him to have returned—Mrs. Baggs eyed his empty desk and stopped teaching. She asked Lester Freemont to go check the bathroom and ensure that Charlie was not sick. Mrs. Baggs specifically called on Lester because, given a task, Lester would perform the task efficiently and without delay. He had proven this time and again.

Lester left the class and in just minutes returned out of breath. He stood in the door of the classroom, breathing heavily, and finally said, "Charlie has flushed himself down the toilet!"

Chaos erupted. Frank dropped his head on his desk and closed his eyes. This would not end well, he thought.

Mrs. Baggs stood, which immediately called the class to order. She walked out of the classroom and shut the door behind her. Lester led her to the bathroom.

What happened next is the stuff of legend. Lester later reported that he had walked back down to the bathroom and that Mrs. Baggs had intercepted custodian Everett Poole on the way. Mrs. Baggs was not in a big rush because she was fairly confident that this grit in the oyster of her life had not really flushed himself down the toilet. That was impossible. Ensuring the bathroom was empty, Mrs. Baggs, Mr. Poole, and Lester went inside. They found Charlie sitting in a toilet, his pants soaking wet, his arms dangling on the side of the toilet.

Lester reported, directly to Frank, that Charlie had looked up at the three peering faces—two of which contained grins—and said, "Goodbye cruel world. Goodbye."

A lesser woman would have completely lost her mind, but not Mrs. Maxine Baggs.

Lester reported that Mr. Poole, now laughing along with Lester, took Charlie by the hand, saying, "What's wrong with you, boy? You sure are curious." He helped Charlie out of the toilet.

"I was laughing pretty hard," Lester told his classmates. "Mrs. Baggs just took Charlie by the hand and walked him out into the hallway. He was dripping all over the floor. I thought she was bringing him back to class, but she just kept on going toward Mr. Pulliam's office. She told me to come back to class and take my seat."

Hearing that Charlie was on his way to Mr. Pulliam's office sent a ripple of quiet fear through the third-grade class. It was one thing to goof around in class and get a spanking from Mrs. Baggs. It was something altogether different to be taken down to Mr. Pulliam's office. No one had ever seen his electric paddle, but the legend of it was widespread.

There was no electric paddle. The legend began in 1961 when the Acorn Primary School first opened. A troublemaker had been sent to the office by one of the school's teachers. A few of his friends saw him go into the office, and then they heard the *whap-whap-whap-whap* and electric whirring of the school's mimeograph duplicating machine. When the student emerged from the office, clearly having had his course corrected by Mr. Pulliam, someone had asked, "Were you spanked by a machine? I thought we heard a machine." The student, wanting to seize as much drama as possible, said that Mr. Pulliam had spanked him with an electric paddle. Neither Mr. Pulliam nor any other educator had confirmed or denied reports of the electric paddle, leaving it as a big mystery and deterrent to bad behavior.

Mr. Pulliam did not spank Charlie.

"Mrs. Baggs just opened the door and led me inside," Charlie reported that evening when Frank called him at home. "Mrs. Fagan called my mama because I needed dry pants and underwear."

Frank asked, "They didn't yell at you in the office?"

"They fussed at me, but by the time mama got there, we are all laughing about it," Charlie said. "I told them they could see the little toilet because you had it." Frank closed his eyes, thankful he had gotten away from school before anyone saw the little toilet.

"Did you ask them about the electric paddle?" he asked.

"I asked if I could see it, and Mr. Pulliam said it was being repaired because of too much usage," Charlie said. "I don't think there is an electric paddle. If there was one, Mrs. Baggs would have used it on me by now."

That school year ended with a class party on the last day of school. Class moms had refreshments for all the students, and Mrs. Baggs handed out final report cards. She praised the class for its good work during the year.

Frank invited Charlie to come home with him and spend the night. As the two boys met Mrs. Baggs at the door, she smiled at them. She looked at Charlie, and Frank thought there might have been tears in her eyes when she said, "Charlie Keller. You are one funny little boy, but I do love you." She had learned what the entire school was learning: it was impossible not to love the prince of Acorn Primary School.

Thirteen

Good Manners

Frank was dizzy. He sat on the emergency-room table as Dr. Jim Mashburn examined the back of his head. All Frank heard was the word "stitches," and he thought he might just go ahead and pass out.

He barely heard Janet telling Dr. Jim how the accident had happened outside her store, The Sewing Shop, just off the square in Acorn. When Tom and Janet married, Janet was working as the Acorn town clerk, but she had stopped working while she had her three sons. Now that Frank and Jack were in school and Wayne was a year away from kindergarten, she decided it was time to return to work.

Tom and Janet bought The Sewing Shop, which had been opened by a local attorney's wife and then changed hands once or twice. Purchasing the store made perfect sense to Janet. She could drive her sons to school in Acorn and manage her store, the boys could come to the store after school, and then they would all drive back home together at the end of the day. The small store sold everything anyone needed for sewing, including bolts and bolts of fabric, patterns, and notions such as buttons and zippers and lace. Janet was young enough to understand the needs of a younger audience as well as the sewing needs of traditional seamstresses in Acorn.

The downtown Acorn business community was a thriving place for small, locally owned, family businesses. Most businesses were open all day on Monday and Tuesday and also on Thursday through Saturday. Businesses closed at noon on Wednesdays, partly because it gave employees a break for working all or part of the day on Saturday. Closing on Wednesday also gave folks a chance to get ready for Wednesday-night church services, which occurred at most of the Baptist and Methodist churches. No business opened on Sunday except for maybe restaurants and gas stations, which both generally opened around noon and were closed by late afternoon. These were people who knew one another, sent their children to the same schools, turned out for high-school football games, lined the streets for the annual Fourth of July parade, attended churches together, and watched their children date and marry one another. The business owners cared for one another. If Janet had to run to the bank, the ladies next door at the dress shop stepped over to watch her store. It was not unusual for one storekeeper to go get lunch for several other neighboring store owners. There was no need for credit cards. If someone needed something on Tuesday but needed to pay for it from a Friday paycheck, handshake credit was given. People knew one another, and they knew families generationally.

Frank was amazed at his mama's ability to know people. He sometimes mentioned a boy or girl from school, and Janet would take out the county telephone book, scan the last names, find a familiar address, and finally point to the correct telephone number.

"I don't really know his family," she would say, "but I know of his mama and daddy." And she might even add a story about the family, recalling how she specifically knew them.

Janet loved Acorn in the same deep and emotional way that her hero, Scarlett O'Hara of Margaret Mitchell's novel *Gone with the Wind*, loved Tara. Janet had grown up in the middle of town, sometimes walking to the First Baptist Church. She rode her bicycle everywhere, including visiting her best friends. She was emotionally invested in this town—this community—that had easily adopted her when the Holmes family moved there. She was deeply grateful. She saw The Sewing Shop as providing a place from which her boys could explore her beloved town the way she had as a girl, and she encouraged them to walk around town. She even loaded their bicycles in the family station wagon so the boys could ride bikes around Acorn during the summers.

The Sewing Shop was also a good place for the boys to learn about customer service, kindness, and gratitude, and Janet made sure the boys got plenty of education. When they were at the store, she insisted they speak to adults when spoken to, look people in the eye, and talk with confidence. When someone complimented them, she insisted the boys respond with a confident thank-you while looking the person in the eye. When a customer had a lot to carry, one of the boys was expected to hurry ahead and open the door, saying, "Thank you for coming in." If necessary, the boys were expected to help carry purchases all the way to a customer's car. There was a back area to the store, and that was where the boys were required to stay—out of sight unless she needed them to help up front. Many afternoons were filled with Frank and later Jack working on homework in the back of The Sewing Shop. It was in that back room that Jack met with Roger Williams, who was the new pastor of the First Baptist Church, and Jack had prayed for Jesus to be his Savior.

Janet's lessons began to extend beyond The Sewing Shop. Frank loved walking or riding his bike to the library, where he spent after-school and summer hours reading under the care of librarian Jean Potts. The boys easily walked to the Dairy Queen; they bought comic books from Jackson's 5 & 10; and Frank loved the cheeseburgers with chili at Jack's Restaurant, which also sold Miss Audrey's homemade chocolate pie.

"When you go into someone else's store, always announce yourself," Janet said. "Make sure the manager of the store sees you and hears you say 'Hello.' That way they know who is in their store, and they know you aren't just in there sneaking around. Nobody wants a boy sneaking around in their store.

"And, for heaven's sake, be friendly," she preached. "Be the kind of boy that everyone is glad to see and looks forward to seeing when you walk into their store."

She even made sure the boys thanked Mr. Greene, who drove the school bus that dropped them at the store after school.

"Mama, he just mumbles whenever we thank him," Frank said.

"Thank him anyway," Janet said without looking up from the work she was doing.

It was a lot of pressure, but Frank listened carefully to his mama. He wanted to make a good impression on people.

That was why he thought it was a good idea to write in the front of *The Baptist Hymnal* "Greetings from Frank Wilcox"—as a way to be kind to those who picked up a hymnal for congregational singing at the First Baptist Church. He went on a "greeting spree," writing that greeting in as many copies of the hymnal as he could find.

When someone pointed it out to Janet, she forgot all about being friendly.

"Son, what would make you do something like this? You have damaged this property in God's house," she said, boiling to the point of spanking him. He knew exactly why he had written the message in the hymnals—he was saturated in conversations about being polite and friendly and was looking for a way to demonstrate all this new knowledge. Besides, Jesus would appreciate it.

One summer day, at lunchtime, Janet walked with Frank to Jack's Restaurant, which, outside of the Dairy Queen, was one of his favorite places. When the restaurant owner, who was a friend of Tom and Janet's, asked if Frank had enjoyed his lunch, he nodded yes.

Janet gave him the evil eye.

"When you are asked a question, I want you to answer it so people can understand what you are saying," she said. Then a light went on and she said, "From now on if you eat at someone's home, I want you to take your plate to the sink and tell the cook that you enjoyed your meal. If you eat in a restaurant, I want you to tell the waitress that you enjoyed your meal."

Frank was beginning to think his sweet, pretty mama had lost her mind.

But Frank complied, and Jack learned to do the same thing. More than once when the Wilcox family visited friends and enjoyed a meal, the boys awkwardly told the cook how much they had enjoyed their meal. The host family's children were glad to see the Wilcox boys go home.

All this politeness was what had led Frank Wilcox to an Acorn County Hospital emergency-room table while Dr. Jim stitched up his bleeding head. Frank's politeness had led to an after-school friendship with Tommy Hanks.

Tommy Hanks lived with his family in Acorn and sometimes got off the bus with the Wilcox brothers at The Sewing Shop. In the alley behind the store, the friends created competitions by bouncing tennis balls off a wall; they helped each other with homework, and they visited Jackson's 5 &10 for the latest comic books.

Tommy's mother had approved of this friendship when Frank had thanked her for a snack she offered one day after school. When she bought some fabric one day at the store, Frank had carried it all the way to her home and even carried some of her groceries, too. He refused any kind of compensation. A boy this polite had to be a friend worth having.

One afternoon, the Wilcox brothers got off the bus at The Sewing Shop, finished their homework, cleaned the store's bathroom, and carried out the trash. Janet had personally taught them how to clean a bathroom, vowing that none of her future daughters-in-law "will have to work as a household servant while my boys sit around like kings of the castle." Frank and Jack could clean a toilet as well as anyone on the planet.

When the boys finally emerged from the store, Tommy was waiting on them, and there wasn't much time left in the day for play.

"Let's just throw rocks at the building," Jack said, grabbing a few large pieces of gravel from The Sewing Shop parking lot. "We'll stand over here, away from any cars, and see who can throw the most rocks way up there on the roof."

Jack threw the first rock, and, not surprisingly, it went all the way to the roof.

"If you make one, you have to move back farther," Jack said, giving himself a challenge.

Frank threw a rock, and it, too, made it on top of the roof.

Tommy didn't really understand the game, largely because he didn't have a brother and competition wasn't a part of his every waking moment. Instead of standing where Jack and then Frank had stood for their first throws, Tommy just launched a rock from far behind where Frank was standing.

Tommy was a likable boy, and everyone in the third grade liked him. He was friendly and amiable and got along well with others. Tommy was a good student, and as he got older, he became a great musician in the renowned Acorn County High School band.

But Tommy Hanks could not throw a rock to save his life, and he most certainly could not throw a rock upward. It was unfortunate that he had both chosen the largest rock possible and stood behind Frank.

Frank never saw it coming.

Tommy reached back and launched the rock up toward the roof, but rather than arch toward the roof, the rock simply went straight up and came straight down like a bomb. It landed right on the crown of Frank's head.

Blood went everywhere.

"Well," Jack said, looking at Tommy, "you sure aren't going to win. You had better run home." And Tommy disappeared. Jack ran into the store, shouting, "Frank's bleeding to death!"

Janet dropped everything she was doing and ran into the alley behind the store. Frank was wobbling around, dizzy, clutching the back of his head, and covered in blood. Janet grabbed Frank, and his legs sank when she said, "Oh my soul. You've got to go to the hospital."

"Lord, this is Jack," Jack said, leaning on his recent conversion. "It was my idea to throw the rocks, and I'm sorry. Please don't let Frank die, because it would be embarrassing to die this way."

Frank wanted to laugh, but he was starting to see two of everything.

Into this chaos came Janet's mother, Carolyn Holmes, who was on her way home from school and thought she'd like to see her family before they left for the day. She ran into the store and came back with a wad of paper towels, hoping to slow the bleeding with some pressure.

"Can you take him to the hospital while I close up the store?" Janet asked, and the boys' Mema willingly agreed. The two women threw an old blanket into the back of Carolyn's car, and Frank wearily crawled into the backseat.

"Try not to bleed all over your Mema's car," Janet said. Frank looked at her with a blurred sense of disbelief.

"I don't think I can help where I'm bleeding, Mama," he said, blubbering because, at this point, he felt crying was about all he could do.

"Try not to die," Jack said, climbing in the car with his brother. This was just too much adventure to pass up. "I'm not sure you are going to make it, and if you don't, can I have all your baseball cards?"

Janet called the hospital to say her mama and sons were on their way. When Carolyn arrived at the hospital, Dr. Jim was waiting. He had walked up from his office next door and was waiting inside the small emergency-room doors. By the time Janet arrived, the tall, thin doctor had finished putting the sutures in Frank's head. Dr. Jim's brother, Dr. Mark Mashburn, had delivered Frank and his brothers into the world.

"He doesn't seem to have a concussion, but you need to watch him," Dr. Jim told Janet. "He's going to have quite a headache. I'd keep him home tomorrow to watch him." He then looked at Jack and asked, "Did you hit him in the head with the rock?"

"No sir," Jack said, looking the doctor in the eyes per Janet's coaching. "Tommy Hanks did it. He said something about hitting the moon when he threw the rock, but he missed the moon and hit Frank in the head." Dr. Jim chuckled to himself and gave each of the boys a Charms pop.

Because he was no longer bleeding, Frank already felt better. Janet and Carolyn were leading the boys out to the car, scolding them for throwing rocks when Frank stopped suddenly.

"I need to do something," he said, and then he turned and walked back inside the emergency room.

Dr. Jim, with his stethoscope around his neck, looked over his glasses and stared at Frank.

"That you, sir, for saving my life," Frank said. "I do appreciate all that you've done for me." He then staggered back outside to the waiting cars.

FOURTEEN

THE MYSTERIOUS NOTE

Frank noticed the folded note before he ever sat down at his desk. He had left his science book on his desk during recess, and now there was a folded note barely sticking out from the top of the book. He sat down, pulled the note from the book, and opened it.

His heart skipped a beat.

In bright blue ink pen, a girl had written a world-changing question. "Do you like me?" Below, there were three boxes. One box was labeled simply Yes, and another box was labeled simply No. A third box was curiously labeled Maybe. Frank turned the paper over, and nothing was written on the back. Whoever had given him this curious multiple-choice quiz had inexplicably forgotten to include her name, and without a name, Frank had no idea how to answer the question. He looked around the classroom, hoping to catch one of the girls watching him, but none of them appeared very interested.

Frank folded the paper and put it deep inside his science book—back deep in the geology section, where he never planned to go.

Despite not knowing who had left him the note, Frank was excited over the prospect that someone had left him a note. This was significant. Since kindergarten, Frank had not been shy around the girls. Frank saw girls as a reason to attend school. To have one of them—even anonymously—express interest in him was something to boast about.

At home that evening, Frank produced the note at the supper table.

"Who's it from?" Janet asked him, turning the paper over in her hands.

"I don't know," Frank said.

Tom took the paper from Janet. "Huh. I never thought Maybe would be a choice." He laughed to himself and handed the paper back to Frank.

"What do you think I should do?" Frank asked.

"I think you should ignore it," Tom said. "If you act like you don't care, she'll probably send you another one."

Janet frowned. "I don't think girls should pass notes to boys, just like I don't think girls should call boys on the telephone," she said. "I especially don't like the fact that she wouldn't give you her name."

"Maybe she's just shy," Frank said, understanding that as a reasonable answer. There were times when he was pretty shy himself.

"I think you should throw it away and pretend it didn't happen," Janet said.

Frank was not about to throw the note away. The note was a victory—a girl at Acorn Primary School apparently liked him and had left him a note. Frank put the folded note in his underwear drawer, which was where he put everything that was important to him: white Hanes briefs, an arrowhead, his Bible, a pocketknife, three marbles, an old glass bottle with a faded Wild Turkey label on it, and folded money he had gotten for his birthday.

The next day at school, Frank spent the entire day thinking about the girls in his classroom. Which one of them had left the note? Was she sending him other messages—such as things she said—that might be a clue? Were any of these girls being friendlier than usual toward him? Had anyone winked at him? When he went to recess, Frank left his science book on his desk, and this time he left it open, presenting it like bait to the mystery note writer. By the end of the day, there were no clues toward solving the mystery.

"Maybe you could flush her out," R. C. Wilcox said to his grandson, who lay beside him on the king-sized bed. "Make a list of all the girls you think left the note, and then give *them* a note. The one who checks the Yes box might be the one who left you a note."

"Papa R. C.," Frank said, eating an ice-cream sandwich in the bed, "what if more than one of the girls checks the Yes box?"

"Son," R. C. said, unwrapping his third ice-cream sandwich, "if that happens, you let me know. It will be a proud day in Wilcox family history."

Frank thought of five girls he liked well enough for a personal survey. Unlike the mysterious note he received, Frank decided to put his name on the notes. He also only gave two options: Yes or No to the question, Do you like me? There was no place for a gray area like Maybe.

Like the anonymous person who had violated his science book, Frank's plan was to rush in from recess and quickly place the notes on the desktops of the five girls he had chosen. He didn't mind his name being on the notes, but he wanted to avoid personal confrontation. During recess, however, Frank got involved in a game of tag and was unable to get back to class in time for private distribution.

Frustrated, Frank made a bold decision. He took the five notes out of his jeans pocket and walked around class placing them on the appropriate desks. Most of the girls had a look of stunned surprise on their faces. However, the bold move paid off. All five of the notes were returned—though more privately—with the Yes box checked. One of the returned notes did have a disclaimer: *I like you, but I am not in love with you. My daddy says I'm too young to have a boyfriend.* That was fair enough, Frank thought because he wasn't sure what he would do with a girlfriend if he had one. As far as he was concerned, this was all just an exercise in flirtation.

What happened next was an all-out love fest in Mrs. Maxine Baggs's third-grade class at the Acorn Primary School. Those five girls, each receiving Frank's note, decided they wanted to know which boys liked them. So they began passing notes. This triggered even more note passing. There wasn't a Maybe box on any of the notes, though a few recipients took the liberty of adding their own Maybe box as a write-in option.

It all became such a frenzy that students were passing and receiving multiple notes in a day, and all manner of secrecy was gone. Frank had barely sat down one morning when he received three notes just handed to him. What's more, notes started being passed between third-grade classrooms, using the playground and lunchroom as distribution points. Jim Vinton received two notes in the lunchroom—from fourth-grade girls. Pete Yancey even received a note from *another school*—from a girl he knew who attended the Midway School. The note had made its way to him through the girl's fifth-grade cousin who attended the Acorn school. Notes were flying fast and furious.

On top of everything, no student wanted to hurt another student's feelings, so everyone checked the Yes box on every note received. The note-passing chaos was driving the ever-logical Lester Freemont out of his mind. He decided to use his show-and-tell opportunity to talk about all the note passing.

Lester held up ten notes that he had received just that week. He tried to explain that he liked everyone in the class, and it was not necessary for him to put it in writing through all the notes. What's more, he said, "If you ask someone to like you, I think you are really asking that person to be *in love with you.*" A wave of horror made its way among the students as some realized they had passed notes to people with whom love didn't stand a snowball's chance in hell.

Lester's public clarification on this like and love business was a central theme at a Den 8 sleepover the following Friday night at Charlie's house. Each of the boys pledged a vow of secrecy, and then each boy shared the name of his third-grade love interest. Lester pretended to sleep through the pledges and revelations and then announced he knew all the boys' secrets without taking the pledge of secrecy.

Lester's public clarification also put a gradual end to the note passing at the Acorn Primary School. Frank had not received or given a note in more than two weeks when he walked into Mrs. Baggs's classroom from lunch one day and saw a note in the seat of his desk. He sat down, opened it, and read: "I still want to know if you like me. Do you?" Again, there were three options, Yes, No, and Maybe. Frank swung around in his seat to see if any of the girls were looking at him, but they were not. The note, just like the original, didn't have a sender's name with it. It was maddening. How in the world could he answer? How in the world could he respond if he didn't know who had sent the note?

He put the note in his back pocket but smiled at the mystery of it all. This note, he reckoned, meant the writer actually loved him because he had received it well after Lester's show-and-tell clarification. Frank was nervous about who was behind the note writing but could not help but also feel a little flattered.

A week or so later, he received a clue. Mrs. Baggs called on Frank to collect English essays written by his classmates. As Frank made his way around the room, he came to Mayvin Stewart's desk in the rear of the classroom. Mayvin handed her essay to Frank, and he placed it on the stack. Turning, Frank looked down, and the handwriting was unmistakable. What's more, the bright-blue pen used to write Mayvin's essay was a perfect match for the bright-blue ink used on the notes he had received.

Frank felt his heart beat three times faster. Frank had felt Mayvin was the prettiest girl in Miss Johnson's first-grade class, and she had not gotten over it during the past two years. He had even held Mayvin's hand in the first grade, though to be completely honest, it was during a playground game of Red Rover.

Red Rover, Red Rover!

Send Frank right over!

In every succeeding game of Red Rover, Frank had made sure he stood by Mayvin so that he could hold her hand. She was always willing, though probably because it was a rule of the game.

After suspecting Mayvin's bright-blue pen behind the note writing, Frank smiled at Mayvin, and she smiled back. That was a good sign. She had long brown hair always pulled back in a ponytail. A ribbon matching the fabric of her dress always held the ponytail in place. She had pretty eyes and a prettier smile.

"I think Mayvin Stewart is the one who wrote me the notes," Frank told Tom and Janet. "She uses that same ink pen in class."

"You should just ask her," Tom said.

"Ask her what?" Frank asked, looking seriously at Tom, waiting on expert advice from his daddy.

"Walk up to her and say, 'Hey, baby, are you the one writing these notes to me?'" Tom said. "And she'll say, 'Yes, I am, you sweet thing.' Then you can say, 'Well, give me some sugar.'" Tom laughed so hard he was shaking, and he then had trouble catching his breath.

Janet looked at her oldest son and said, "Don't do that. Do you think your daddy was ever that brave around girls? He wasn't. I know."

Frank knew that he had to know once and for all if Mayvin had written the notes. The next day, he took the two notes with him to school, and before class began, he walked up to her desk. She sat there, looking through a girls' magazine she had brought from home.

Frank cleared his throat and said, "Mayvin, did you write these notes to me?"

Mayvin Stewart looked at the two notes but did not look up. "I wrote them," she said. "But not for you."

Frank sat down in an empty desk beside her. "Well, they were both on my desk. One of them was in my science book. I thought maybe they were from you."

She shook her head no.

Frank said, "We held hands a lot during first grade, so I thought maybe they were for me."

Mayvin Stewart closed the magazine and leaned close to Frank. "They are for Charlie," she said.

Frank stared into her face, trying to absorb the words.

"Why did you leave them on *my desk*?" Frank asked, feeling as if he had been kicked in the stomach.

Mayvin shrugged. "I guess I thought that was Charlie's desk. Will you give them to him?" Frank was now the third-grade mailman.

Frank continued staring at Mayvin Stewart. No more Red Rover for you, sweetheart.

Frank stood, turned, and walked toward the front of the classroom. He sat down at his desk and looked across the aisle at his closest friend, Charlie Keller. He handed the notes to Charlie.

"These are for you," he said, and then, raising his voice as loud as he could, finished with, "They are from Mayvin Stewart."

FIFTEEN

SHOOTING BASKETS

As Frank entered the fourth grade, boys and girls were beginning to show an interest in athletics. Many of the boys were playing baseball, collecting baseball cards, and Frank was right in the thick of it. Boys and girls were learning the art of shooting a basketball, some with an eye toward one day playing for the successful Acorn County High School Bulldogs and Lady Bulldogs. There was no formal physical education class at the Acorn Primary School, but there was Mrs. Carolyn Hicks.

If there was an all-star teacher at the Acorn Primary School, it was Mrs. Hicks. She was full of life and energy, was creative and funny, and a student had hit the jackpot of the teacher pool if he or she landed in Mrs. Hicks's fourth-grade class. She had been a standout basketball player on a state championship Acorn County High School team. She was just a handful of years younger than most of her students' parents. Janet Wilcox considered her a friend from both church and school; Carolyn Hicks was also the daughter of Principal Dwight Pulliam.

Not only did Mrs. Hicks bring creativity to the classroom, finding new and engaging ways to interact with her students, but she also brought organization to recess. No longer did a few athletic boys dominate the playing field for a game of football or softball; she introduced the idea that every child could play—and every child *would* play. She introduced the idea of having team captains who selected teams, and the last person chosen was the next day's team captain. She served as the umpire or referee of games, and she knew which players to encourage and which players to chide.

Frank loved organization; he despised chaos, so he quickly fell in love with Mrs. Hicks. He also loved the way she just said what was on her mind, laughed loudly, and kept everyone well-behaved. Even

Charlie Keller sat in amazement. He had met his match, and she rarely had to spank him.

One day, Mrs. Hicks brought a basketball into the classroom and began dribbling in front of all the boys and girls. Some had played around with a basketball at home—perhaps their moms and dads had been Acorn ballplayers—but none of them had ever had a teacher bounce a basketball in class.

"Today," she said, "we are going to learn how to shoot free throws." She began diagramming a basketball court on the blackboard, explaining the difference in a jump shot, a layup, and a free throw. "We are going to learn how to shoot all these shots, but first we're going to learn how to shoot free throws."

She then dismissed the class to walk single file down the hallway, down the ramp to the cafeteria, and outside to the playground. A lone basketball goal stood at the edge of the playground like an intimidating giant beckoning one and all to "come on; give it a try." Mrs. Hicks had ensured that custodians had put a fresh, new cotton net on the goal. She wanted her students to hear the "swish" of the ball sinking in the net.

"It's not even recess," Charlie whispered to Frank. "We're going outside to play, and it's not even recess." Frank was just as amazed.

Mrs. Hicks lined the boys and girls up behind a line that she noted was the foul line.

"When you get fouled in a basketball game, you sometimes get to come stand behind this line and shoot a free basket called a foul shot or free throw," she said, handing the ball to Mack Holloway, who was generally considered the best athlete in the class. Mack had a basketball goal at home—his mama had played basketball for Acorn County High School—and he easily sank the foul shot.

Mrs. Hicks then told him to go stand under the goal and rebound the ball for the next shooter. After shooting, whether the shot was made or not, the shooter became the rebounder for the next person and then went to the rear of the line.

Frank had never in his life touched a basketball, so he got near the back of the line. He was the last person in line and watched those in front of him take their shots. He watched how they positioned their feet. Some bent their knees; some did not. Some brought the ball to their left or right shoulder and pushed from there. Those who knew what they were doing put the ball in front of their faces and shot from there. Frank was amazed that almost everyone in his class could make the foul shot—even Charlie and Emmett, who were considerably smaller than everyone. Swish, swish, swish.

Clank. That was the sound Frank's shot made when it battered against the backboard, completely missing the goal. He felt his face flush with embarrassment, especially considering most of his friends had easily made the shot and had obviously been practicing at some unknown location without him for a long, long time. He moved under the goal to rebound for the next shooter, who bent at the waist, brought the ball between his legs, and prepared to toss it in underhanded.

"Try not to shoot a granny shot," Mrs. Hicks said as she laughed out loud.

"Why is it called a granny shot?" someone asked.

Mrs. Hicks said, "'Cause that's the only way Old Granny could get the ball up that high. She had to reach down and throw it up from between her legs."

The next time Frank came up to shoot, he fired the ball away, trying to mimic Mack Holloway. The ball missed the goal and the net and bounced down through the playground. Mrs. Hicks sent him to fetch it, shouting "Stink shot" while holding her nose and laughing. Even Frank laughed along with the other children because Mrs. Hicks had that kind of magic—helping you laugh at yourself without feeling humiliated.

The line rotated around several times, and Frank missed every shot he took. When Wendell Mann patted him on the back, offering him comfort, he felt sick at his stomach. Frank was the only boy who had missed every shot. Wendell's comforting pat sent the message that all had noticed and all felt sorry for him.

From that day forward, during every recess period, Mrs. Hicks's class was at the basketball goal. Once children mastered the shot, they were free to go and play as normal. Every day the class returned to the goal, Frank found himself with a smaller and smaller group of girls.

Mrs. Hicks became a cheerleader for those remaining. She even took to coaching them one-on-one, helping students master the shot. Frank's shooting had improved. He was getting the ball up near the rim, but it just wasn't going in the basket.

To help his practice, his daddy, Tom, put up a basketball goal in the backyard of the house on Brookwood Road. Tom, along with farmhands Ernest and Leroy, positioned a large, sawed-off electric power pole into the ground. At the top of it, Tom fastened a basketball goal. All of this happened on a Saturday morning, and Frank could hardly wait to practice sinking the new basketball his daddy had purchased at the hardware store in Acorn. Frank's Granny, Kathryn Wilcox, came out to see the inaugural goal. She stood from a distance in her blue, striped seersucker dress with arms crossed.

Janet, too, had come outside, holding Wayne by the hand. Jack stood cautiously watching the goal construction and was eager to take his turn shooting a basket.

"It will be OK if you miss," Frank whispered to Jack. "I miss a lot at school when we practice, and we've practiced more than you have." Jack just stared at him.

The goal in place, Frank stood where the *World Book Encyclopedia* had indicated the foul line should be located. He positioned the ball in front of his face as Mrs. Hicks had shown him and fired it up toward the hoop. The ball hit the plywood backboard and went flying toward a muscadine vine. Jack chased it down.

"Jack, let me have the ball," the boys' Granny said, opening her hands to catch the ball. Frank was amazed—how in the world had she caught the ball, and how in the world did she expect to shoot it toward the basket? Clearly, this would be a granny shot because she was a granny.

Kathryn Wilcox had played basketball as a girl, even if it was just sometimes shooting a ball at an orchard basket with the bottom punched out. She walked to the foul line, threw the ball up to herself, caught it, looked at the basket, pulled the ball to her face, and launched it. The ball flicked off the backboard and dropped through the hoop. No granny shot required.

Jack hollered, "My turn," and he chased down the ball.

Frank simply stared at his grandmother. How in the world had she done that? And how horrifying that she had made a basket when he had failed so miserably to do so. But for Frank, this freak show was not over.

Jack awkwardly bounced the basketball on the grass, pulled up to the foul line, and with every fiber of his small being, launched a shot that lifted both his feet off the ground. Swish. The ball dropped easily through the hoop. Jack began dancing around the yard, thrusting his hips and waving his hands over his head, whooping and hollering. If it had not poured insult into injury, Frank would have laughed at his younger brother. But instead, he just lowered his head and walked away.

"Come back here, Frank," his beloved Granny yelled after him, but he just continued walking. He could not swallow the fact that both his Granny and his younger brother had easily made the basket while he had missed.

His grandmother chased him down. "I want you to practice," she said. "I want you to try twenty times a day, and I want you to take your time. More than anything, keep your eye on the goal and don't take your eyes off it. Watch the ball go to the basket, and see if it doesn't drop in." He nodded that he understood, but he was still was in no mood to be around Jack, who was chasing down his own rebounds and throwing the ball up toward the hoop.

Frank began practicing, and Tom and Janet helped him by keeping Jack and Wayne away. It did not help. The more Frank practiced, the most he lost his patience; and the more he lost his patience, the more reckless his shooting became; and the more reckless his shooting, the more he missed the basket. Occasionally Janet painfully looked out a bedroom window, saw her son's frustration, and said to Tom, "He's going to have a nervous breakdown."

Whether it was just desperation or whether it was frustration or whether it was just exhaustion, one afternoon Frank picked up the basketball and heaved up an underhanded granny shot that gracefully floated through the air and sank in his backyard goal. He stared in shocked amazement as the basketball bounced around on the ground before rolling toward the grape vines. Granny shot or not, he had just made a basket.

He picked up the basketball and from an angle hoisted another granny shot. The ball flicked through the air and dropped through the net. He ran to the ball and picked it up, staring at it as if it had become magical. He went to the side of the basket and made another granny shot. He got farther from the goal and launched another successful shot. He couldn't miss. It felt good, so he just kept shooting successful granny shots.

While he continued to miss the traditional shots at school, he practiced the granny shots at home and successfully made them. He even tried some one-handed and made them. He tried some one-handed, left-handed shots and made them. He even tried a shot with the side of his body facing the goal, tossing an underhanded granny shot from the side, and he made it.

He was king of the granny shots. His confidence soaring, he called all of his family out to watch an exhibition. They chuckled at his odd shooting style—and mastery of it—but seeing him happy made them all happy, and everyone took shots at the goal in their own way.

At school, Mrs. Hicks was growing impatient because she wanted to move the class on to learning a jump shot and a layup, and she wanted Frank to master the foul shot so she could move the class forward. She called everyone back to the foul line and announced it would be the last day of foul shooting.

One by one, the boys and girls took their shots, and most of the shots slipped through the net with ease. Frank was the last in line. He took his shot, and as it clanged against the backboard. Mrs. Hicks shook her head.

"I can make it," he said under his breath.

"What was that?" Mrs. Hicks asked him.

"I can make a foul shot," he said as all eyes were on him. Frank did not like being the center of attention, and he had just thrust himself into the white-hot spotlight of attention.

"Well, we would sure like to see you make one," Mrs. Hicks said. She took the ball from Mack Holloway and tossed it back to Frank.

Frank Wilcox then took two steps to the side of the foul line. He held the ball underhanded. He closed his right eye and lifted his left foot slightly off the ground. He then tossed the ball underhanded up toward the basket, and the entire class watched as it sailed up and through the hoop.

Charlie hollered, "What in the world was that?" He fell to the ground laughing.

Mrs. Hicks's face lit up like a child's on Christmas morning, and she threw her head back and laughed as loud as she could—not making fun of her student but celebrating whatever in the world had just happened.

Frank wasn't finished. He jogged up, took the ball from Mack Holloway, and began putting on a granny shot clinic, shooting the underhanded shots at various angles and all to the amazement of his classmates. Finally, Mrs. Hicks called an end to it.

On the walk to class, Mrs. Hicks came up behind him and said, "I've never seen anyone make that many shots in a row." He turned and smiled at her as she laughed and messed up his hair.

Sixteen

Fractured Follies

In 1969, when Frank was in the fourth grade, American television culture was in transition, responding to the culture at large. While a few years from reaching deep into the South, a countercultural revolution driven by the Vietnam War was building around free expression, though some of it had turned violent and self-destructive. The counterculture was spreading across the United States, largely through television programming, including one-hour television variety shows incorporating the music, style, and language of the day. Among the top twenty television shows, seven were variety shows, including the number-one show on NBC—*Rowan and Martin's Laugh-In.*

The popularity of these variety shows caused Mrs. Hicks to have a wonderful idea. She decided that her class would stage its own variety show, *Fractured Follies.* Her vision for the show was simple—in a fifty-minute program, there would be a series of short skits and music, with every student participating in at least one of the "acts." There would be costumes and staging, and every student would come away with a level of confidence, having "performed" onstage in front of others.

Some of the students had obvious talent—like Jim Vinton, who could sing, or like Carla and Sandra, who had taken dance lessons and could actually dance. Everyone recognized Charlie as being the funniest kid in the school, so Mrs. Hicks knew she had to have him in some kind of a comedic skit. Some students were bunched into a barbershop quartet. Some of the girls put together a short puppet show. Some students could play the piano or the guitar. In between each act, Mrs. Hicks had some students reenact popular television commercials of the day.

Granddaughter: Grandma, can I help you make your special fried chicken?

Grandma: If you can keep a secret, I use Shake 'n Bake now.

Granddaughter: You do?

Grandma: Sure, I'll show you. First, we shake; then we bake.

Daughter (at the dinner table): Mother, why isn't my fried chicken as crispy and juicy? I want your recipe.

Granddaughter: Grandma didn't fry it.

Son-in-law: But it's crispy like fried.

Granddaughter: Can I tell? It's Shake 'n Bake, and I helped!

Grandma, looking at the camera: Shake 'n Bake coating mix; it's better than frying.

Charlie had been paired with another boy, Steve, and the two put on a ventriloquist act that was the hit of the entire show. With Charlie costumed as the "dummy," he sat on Steve's lap while Steve asked Charlie several questions. Charlie responded in ways that had everyone laughing.

As all the acts were coming together, Frank had nothing to do. Someone had already told Mrs. Hicks that Frank could not really play the guitar, despite his illusions to the contrary. With all the excitement surrounding the skits, Frank watched from the outside. He had no particular skill and could not take the entire audience outside to watch him shoot granny shots. As it turned out, there were four girls in a similar situation: *talent poor*. During one class period, as students worked on their acts and practiced their lines, Mrs. Hicks called Frank and the four girls to her desk.

"Let's have a skit called 'Fairy Tale Theater,' and while one of you reads the story of the Three Little Pigs, the others act out the story. Frank can be the wolf, three of you girls can be the pigs, and one of you can read the story," she said, giving each of the five children an assignment.

Frank wanted to protest being the Big Bad Wolf. Though it was true that he was the Wolf Man every Halloween, it was only because the costume got more realistic the less it fit him. But Mrs. Hicks had made up her mind.

"OK, great. That's what you are doing. Now, go over there in that corner and start practicing," she said, handing them a book with the story, and then she walked away.

As one of the girls read the story, Frank and the other three girls began talking about what they would be doing during the skit. These classroom rehearsals continued for a few weeks until Mrs. Hicks decided a stage rehearsal was necessary.

On the stage, Mrs. Hicks watched as the students began acting out the story.

As the pigs' mother—who was the narrator—prepared to send her three piglets into the "big wide world," she warned them to "beware of the big bad wolf." Frank stood there, not particularly big or bad and certainly not intimidating anyone.

"Frank," Mrs. Hicks said with a deep sigh. "You have to act this out. When she says 'Beware of the big bad wolf,' I want to see you stomping around, looking scary. I want little children in the audience to be afraid. I want old women in the audience to wet their pants."

Everyone laughed, so on the next try, Frank got more into character, being more ferocious until Mrs. Hicks said, "That's better, but don't be the big, bad bear. Just be a wolf."

Now Frank was confused. What was the difference between a bear and a wolf?

When it came time for the big bad wolf to knock on a pig's door and say "Little pig, little pig, can I come in?" Frank did so, looking as scary as possible, and he was starting to get into his part. He stomped around on stage, taking big deep breaths and then blowing as hard as he could toward the pig's house of straw, sticks, or bricks. He stomped around so much that the poor narrator had to stop reading and let all this stomping and heavy breathing continue for what seemed a full minute.

Mrs. Hicks was about to tell Frank to rush things along, but then she thought better of it. Instead, she just waited and had the narrator begin reading again.

When the story got around to its climactic scene, Frank could not blow down the last pig's brick house, and he could not persuade the pig to let him in. As the wolf, Frank climbed up a ladder, pretending to be on top of the pig's house, and jumped a safe distance down a makeshift chimney into the last pig's fireplace.

"Frank," Mrs. Hicks said, "I want you to imagine what it would be like to fall into a pot of boiling-hot water."

"I would probably die just from falling down this chimney," he shouted from inside the house of bricks.

"Well, the wolf has too much hair and skin to die in this version," Mrs. Hicks shouted back. "When you jump and land in the fireplace, I want you to come flying out of there, running around, screaming, holding your fanny, and then run off the stage, never to be seen again."

Frank did as he was told, taking an unusually long time to run completely around the stage, hands on his backside, before running off the stage, howling.

The girls, as the Three Little Pigs, then sang a chorus as they danced arm in arm in a circle.

Who's afraid of the Big Bad Wolf, Big Bad Wolf, Big Bad Wolf?
Who's afraid of the Big Bad Wolf?

Frank stood in the backstage shadows, watching the girls sing and dance. Technically, he thought, the Big Bad Wolf was not dead, and the scalding of his backside would have probably begun to feel better by now. All this dancing around would surely get on the wolf's nerves.

Mrs. Hicks applauded, told the children to keep practicing, and moved on to coach another skit in the *Fractured Follies* lineup.

Fractured Follies might have started as just a small student play put together by a fourth-grade class, but it was becoming much, much more. Mrs. Hicks was so proud of the way the show was coming together, and the students were having so fun with it, that she decided to have a series of performances for the school and two separate evening performances for family and friends. She even designed a printed program for distribution during the performance.

It was the evening performances that made it necessary for Frank to tell his family about the production.

"That sounds like fun," Janet said around the supper table. "What are you going to be doing?"

"I'm in a skit about the Three Little Pigs," he said, looking across the table at his daddy, who was eating and not appearing to pay much attention. "I'm going to be the Big, Bad Wolf."

Tom looked up and began shaking his head, a sly smirk cast across his face. "I'll be kiss my ass," he said. "Well, at least I guess you've got the costume for it."

Jack asked, "What are you going to do? Is there going to be a chimney for you to jump down?"

Frank began telling his family about the skit, and then he went into a larger description of the entire show, especially Charlie's ventriloquist act and how funny it was.

"Let me get this straight," Jack said. "You have to dress up like a wolf and chase girls around the stage while everyone else does something like sing or dance or make people laugh?"

Jack then turned to Janet and asked, "Do I really have to go to this?"

Janet said that yes, the entire family, including grandparents, was going to see the *Fractured Follies*. Everyone was going to support Frank as the Big Bad Wolf. As it turned out, wearing his now-very-small, tattered Halloween costume, Frank was more of a wolf man in the spirit of Lon Chaney Jr. than he was the Big Bad Wolf in the spirit of James Orchard Halliwell-Phillips and later of Walt Disney.

Showtime came, and the first groups to see it were other students at the school. There was a show for the first and second graders, and then two shows to reach the third-, fourth-, and fifth-grade classes. Mrs. Hicks's students heard the clapping and the laughter of the audience, and that only encouraged them to be better. As confidence grew, each show seemed to improve on the one before it.

So when the first Thursday-night show came around for family and friends, *Fractured Follies* had taken on a life of its own. It had gone from a little classroom project to a community show unlike anything that regularly ever happened in Acorn County. That first night, emcee Jim Vinton stood out front and welcomed everyone and then came backstage to report, "The lunchroom is packed with people."

There was a buzz of excitement among the cast.

And right on cue, one act followed another. The audience applauded along with Carla and Sandra as they danced the Charleston side by side; it laughed along with Lisa and Jane and their puppet show; it followed right along with the commercial skits from television; and it thundered with laughter as Charlie's head swiveled as Steve's dummy in the ventriloquist act. Skit after skit featured every child in the classroom, and every child was applauded.

Frank and the girls went through the story of the Three Little Pigs as they had rehearsed it. Frank ran offstage, howling from his scalded backside. He turned to watch the Three Little Pigs dance around the stage singing "Who's Afraid of the Big Bad Wolf?"

That was when Frank decided that no self-respecting Big Bad Wolf would let this happen. The Big Bad Wolf would not tolerate this taunting by three little pigs. The applauding audience had just given Frank more confidence than he had ever had during any of the rehearsals. He figured it was time for the Big Bad Wolf to have the last say in this classic story.

As the girls held hands, danced, and sang, they suddenly faced the Wolf Man, who had returned from backstage and now stood menacingly in front of them. Frank raised his arms above his head and howled as loudly as any werewolf had ever howled at a full moon. The girls screamed, having never practiced this part of the show, and they were genuinely frightened by the werewolf in front of them. One of the girls jumped from the stage. Frank chased the other two into the curtain, got tangled up in it, almost fell down, and then stumbled behind the curtain.

Initially, there was nervous laughing from the audience, but that gave way to a full ovation.

Jack Wilcox slipped down into his chair, hoping no one recognized him as Frank's brother. He looked to his left and was pretty sure Tom was sliding down into his chair as well.

SEVENTEEN

FINDING A VOICE

For all of his shortcomings athletically, musically, and on the stage, Frank Wilcox had a secret. He loved to write short stories. It came out of his love for reading and his love of television, watching an episode of *Bonanza* or the *Wild, Wild West* unfold. His Granny had taught him the alphabet before he ever started school, and Tom and Janet had invested in a Dr. Seuss book-of-the-month club when he was in first grade. Each Thursday when one of the books arrived in the mail, Tom or Janet would sit with him on the sofa and read it to him. He naturally fell in love with the library.

Since the second grade, he had written stories in secret, writing them first in print and then in the cursive taught by Mrs. Baggs in the third grade. The stories were generally Western by nature, focusing on a sheriff in a lawless town. Occasionally, he wrote about a make-believe sports hero winning a game against staggering odds. Sometimes he wrote about Civil War characters. It got to a place where Frank checked out a book from the library, read the book, and wrote a story. If he read a book about a high-school football team, he turned around and wrote a story about a football team. He read and wrote all the time.

But only one person knew about the stories, and that was Charlie Keller.

When Charlie came to visit, Frank pulled out his latest stories and invited Charlie to read them out loud. Frank wanted to hear his words read by someone else, and he wanted to see the reaction. Did Charlie laugh at something funny? Did he pause when Frank wanted him to pause? Charlie always obliged because he thought Frank's stories were always funny. Even when Frank tried to write seriously, Charlie thought it was funny.

"And Billy goes out for a long pass," Charlie read aloud, "and—oh, wait—the ball hit him in the head!" Charlie laughed so hard that he cried. Sure, while he was laughing at Frank, Frank was learning from it. And he laughed, too, because it was just so much fun to watch Charlie laugh out loud.

After Charlie had read the stories, Frank rewrote some of them, taking out what Charlie had thought was funny but wasn't supposed to be and rewriting others to include what he thought Charlie might like to read. Frank sometimes wrote imagining Charlie reading and trying to guess how his friend might respond to it.

"Don't tell anyone about my stories," he asked of Charlie. "I just write them for me and you."

As much as Frank loved to write his stories, he equally hated math. This was a family concern, especially as Frank's Mema was a math teacher at Acorn Junior High. Each time he received a report card, his Mema called to check on his math grade, and it was always his lowest grade. At times he thought she took offense to it. Janet became so concerned that she had Frank spend the night with his grandmother each Wednesday so that she could tutor him in math.

"Let's sit down here at the kitchen table and do your homework," his Mema said calmly. And Frank would begin, and she would correct. He would start over, and she would correct him. If she taught him anything, it was always to have two sharpened pencils and several erasers before starting math work.

"Math requires us to be able to stop and start over," she said, pressing the need for using pencils rather than ink pens. Frank applied that logic to his writing and always made sure he had two sharpened No. 2 Black Warrior pencils when he started writing. He found that Parson's Department Store, on the courthouse square, sold the Black Warrior pencils.

The tutoring sessions under Frank's Mema usually ended up in a cycle of frustration for both teacher and pupil. Rather than show her frustration, Carolyn Holmes would suddenly say, "I need to start supper," calling an end to the session as Frank fumbled around with a Black

Warrior pencil. As his Mema left the table, Frank followed, escaping to read or to open his spiral notebook and continue writing a story.

In Mrs. Hicks's fourth-grade classroom, students were beginning to learn long division. Even if slightly behind, Frank had been able to keep up with the class until long division was introduced. He stared at the blackboard with its dividends and quotients. He was stumped about the concept of being able to check a problem for accuracy by multiplying two of three numbers in the problem. Frank turned to his friend Lester Freemont, who was kind enough to help him with long division, but there wasn't enough time for Lester to be Frank's full-time tutor. Finally, Frank just pretended to listen to Mrs. Hicks while continuing to write one of his stories.

"I don't know what we are going to do," Janet said in dramatic frustration, waving his long division test with its F grade wildly in the air. "I never one time failed a test in all my years of school. I hope you know that it's possible you will have to stay another year in the fourth grade."

Frank didn't say it for fear his mama might whack him, but he thought, *Another year with Mrs. Hicks would be wonderful.*

"And they won't let you stay in the class with Mrs. Hicks," his mama, now a mind reader, said. "No, sir. You will be in the class taught by Mrs. Ascot." The dreaded Mrs. Ascot was notoriously strict and mean; rumor had it she twirled her paddle—in a windup—after each swat. She also taught the best-behaved Sunday School class in Acorn County.

"Spare the rod; spoil the child," Mrs. Ascot always said, ordering a student to lean over and put hands on knees. Tom had even seen her walking down the streets of Acorn one afternoon and said, "There goes Mrs. Ascot; makes my damn stomach hurt to see her."

Janet continued her rant. "I don't know what your Mema is going to say when you tell her that you got an F on this test." The truth was that his Mema just sighed, generally happy that Frank was her grandson and not her son at this particular time.

"Well, get them next time," she said, and Frank thought that was pretty funny. The family's greatest mathematician sounded strangely like his first baseball coach, who told Frank the exact same thing when he struck out for the twelfth time in four games. Frank was surrounded by optimists.

Perhaps someone—his mama or maybe his Mema; Frank never knew—called Mrs. Hicks. But soon after, she stopped teaching early one day and gave students time to work on their math homework. And she took that time to walk around the classroom, checking on each student. When she came to Frank, she stopped, leaned over, and whispered, "I'm going to help you understand long division."

Mrs. Hicks quietly worked with Frank, showing him as simply as possible how to do long division. And, just like that, Frank understood it. The light in the cupboard went on, and he understood it. Mrs. Hicks patted him on the back and was about to move on to another student when she noticed Frank's spiral notebook underneath his math papers.

"You have a lot of clutter on your desk, Frank," she said, and she removed the notebook. "If you will keep your desktop neater, it will be easier to do your work." The open page on the notebook caught her attention, and she read it. Then she looked at him.

"Why are you writing this?" she asked him, quietly. "This isn't an assignment."

He whispered as softly as possible, "I like to write stories," hoping no one else around him could hear and hoping that no one was really paying attention.

"Do you mind if I borrow this and read it tonight?" she asked him, and Frank had no choice but to agree. What was he going to do? Say "No, you can't read what I've obviously been working on during your class time"? She tucked the notebook under her arm and continued moving among the students.

That night he called Charlie and told him that Mrs. Hicks had taken his notebook full of stories, and he was not really sure what she was going to do with it. He feared she would be mad that he was writing instead of listening to her math lessons. He also feared she might call his parents.

"She will think they are funny," Charlie said. "Oh, wait. Billy got hit in the head by the ball." He laughed loudly into the telephone. "Don't worry about it. She's not going to spank you over it." That was apparently Charlie's new bar on school-related mischief: to spank or not to spank.

Frank walked into the classroom the next day more than a little anxious. Mrs. Hicks sat at her desk and did not look up as he took his seat in the row next to the windows. He looked at the clock over the blackboard, and he could hear it—tick, tock, tick, tock. *Why doesn't she say something?* he wondered.

The day began like any other. There was the Pledge of Allegiance and the Lord's Prayer said over the intercom system by Mr. Pulliam. Mrs. Fagan read a few announcements, and the students were wished a good day.

Mrs. Hicks began teaching the day's work.

Frank was bewildered. She had not spoken to him. She had not even looked in his direction, giving him a message or a sign that she had read his stories. He had no idea what she was thinking. Frank was beyond nervous. It was maddening.

The class went about its day, and by the time the class returned from lunch in the cafeteria, Frank was pretty certain Mrs. Hicks had not read his stories. He decided not to trouble her about it. He put his head on his desk, as he generally did after lunch, and waited on Mrs. Hicks to call everyone to begin the day's social studies lesson.

"Class," she said. "We have a treat today. Frank..."

Frank jerked his head off the desk and turned red as a beet. He held his breath, not sure what was about to happen. He stared at his teacher, gently shaking his head and wanting to stop whatever she was about to say but not sure how he could possibly stop her.

"...is going to read one of the stories he has written. Come up here, Frank," she said.

Frank was pretty sure he was going to puke. There were thirty-one other children in that classroom, and, including Mrs. Hicks, there were now sixty-three eyes looking directly at him. One of the boys had a patch over his eye, protecting everyone else from pinkeye. Charlie began applauding as Frank walked to the front of the room.

"Come on, Frank," Mrs. Hicks said. He got up and began walking toward the front of the class. Later, talking to Charlie, he compared it to walking the aisle of the First Baptist Church to confess Jesus as his savior.

"My legs were moving, but I wasn't telling them to move," he said.

He took the notebook from Mrs. Hicks, and she turned him to face the class. Then she walked to his desk and stood beside it, blocking any possible attempt to run for the desk and jump back in it for safety. He looked at the classroom door, wondering what kind of spanking he would get if he just fled the room and the school right now. Could he make the woods behind the school's playground before anyone caught him?

He made eye contact with Charlie, who had a grin from ear to ear. Frank knew he was praying to hear the football story read aloud so he could shout out "Oh, wait. Billy got hit in the head by the ball." But Frank was in no mood for humor right now. He flipped through the notebook until he reached a story he had written about his favorite Western character, US Marshal Joshua Randall.

"Frank," Mrs. Hicks said. "I still need to teach some this afternoon, so please get on with it."

He nodded and began to read. It was strange, reading his own words to a live audience. He had only heard Charlie read his stories. He read, "A man crashed out of Bessie Phillips's saloon, followed by another. Gunshots followed next. Marshal Joshua Randall tore out of his office."

Frank looked up. Everyone was listening. He finished the story, adding some animated movements as his confidence grew. When he finished, Mrs. Hicks walked up to him and leaned against the front of her desk right beside him.

"Will you read another one tomorrow?" she asked him. He nodded that he would. She gave a friendly point to his seat—her way of telling him to sit back down. "OK, having just learned of Deputy Palo's death and the wounded Marshal Randall, I think it's a good time to talk about our history lesson."

Frank cautiously looked around to see if any of his friends were prepared to make fun of him. All eyes were on the teacher, and for that he was thankful. Occasionally, Frank continued to read his stories to the class after lunch. But Mrs. Hicks was not finished with him. She had a bigger vision for Frank's stories and for his self-confidence. She also had the benefit of her daddy being the school's principal.

That was how Frank came to stand in the school office, staring into an intercom microphone that was about to carry the adventures of US Marshal Joshua Randall to every student at the Acorn Primary School.

He was not the first student to stand here in front of the unseen school. For a few years, Jim Vinton had sung Southern gospel songs every month or so. Macy had taken turns with other students to read a daily devotion from the *Open Windows* devotion book provided by the First Baptist Church. It wasn't unusual for Mr. Pulliam to interrupt everyone's day with a special announcement regarding a "guest student's" presentation. It was just unusual for the interruption to come from Frank Wilcox.

Frank cleared his throat and began reading. "El Managua was the meanest bandit of the West. Marshal Randall was forced to postpone his wedding to Julie Tompkins and set out after the outlaw. He found tracks, followed the river, and went up into the mountains." El Managua had killed the marshal's deputy, Bert Palo, and left a teasing note that read, "Come and get me. Your friend, El Managua."

When Frank finished reading and returned to Mrs. Hicks's class, Charlie Keller exploded with laughter. "Come and get me. Your friend, El Managua," Charlie crowed. "They were friends?" And then Charlie acted out what it must have been like for poor Deputy Bert being shot and left for dead with a friendly note attached to him.

Frank laughed at his friend and went over and took his seat. Mrs. Hicks began teaching the next subject, and during the day she passed by him and said, "Great job today." It was all the encouragement Frank needed to keep on writing. Someone else could worry about the math.

Eighteen

The Duck Walk

Mrs. Hicks stared at the two boys in front of her desk.

"I told you all to be quiet while I was away from the room," she said. "Tomorrow, I will see you after school—tell your parents that you will be staying about thirty minutes late."

Frank and Charlie were sent back to their seats.

Lester had sold them out. Actually, Lester had sold Frank out, and Frank had sold Charlie out.

Mrs. Hicks loved her class, and the students loved her. However, like most teachers, there were times when she had to briefly leave the class, trusting the students to behave and not call attention from neighboring classrooms. This was pretty standard procedure up and down the hallways of the school—teachers had to go to the bathroom just like everyone else. Some even took time out in the fabled teacher's lounge, which sounded far more glorious than it was. The teacher's lounge was a nook of a room featuring a table, a sofa, and several chairs. It also featured ashtrays because more than one teacher needed a Camel or a Marlboro to get through the day. It was even rumored that there was an ice-cream freezer in there and that the freezer was stocked with treats such as ice-cream sandwiches.

Frank's own Mema, whom he visited at the Junior High School, sometimes appeared from the teacher's lounge, followed by a cloud of therapeutic smoke thick enough to choke a horse. Frank knew his Mema smoked; he was pretty confident Mrs. Hicks did not. He had asked his Mema about the availability of ice-cream sandwiches in the teacher's lounge, and she had assured him that no ice cream was in the lounge.

When Mrs. Hicks left her room, she always appointed a student to take names. This was popular in that it gave a student a measure of power, but it was risky power because the name taker was never popular among those whose names were taken for punishment. Frank never wanted to be chosen as the person to take names; as the boy from the farthest end of the county, he needed all the friends he could get. The one day he was chosen to take names, Mrs. Hicks returned to a sea of pandemonium and chaos, and Frank had not recorded a single name.

"You let me down," she said, looking at the blank page. "Everyone misbehaved because they knew you would not take down their names." Frank wasn't going to take down their names—he didn't care if they set fire to the school and danced around it like wild Indians.

Lester, on the other hand, stepped into the name-taking power with gusto.

"Lester, I want you to take names while I'm out of the room," Mrs. Hicks said, knowing she could trust her best student to be a detailed follower of instructions. "If anyone talks or gets out of their seat, I want you to write their name down." Lester was more than happy. Everyone knew Lester was more than happy. Whether Lester had the respect of the class or not, when he took names, *he took names.*

Once he even wrote down Steve Dickson's name for sneezing, counting it as making a noise.

On this day, Lester lorded over a quiet classroom. He sat on a stool, in front of the blackboard, staring down every student, watching for any and every reason to take down a name. He waited for any sign of weakness—a snicker, a whisper—and even kept an eye on Jim Vinton, hoping above all that Jim would belch for no other reason than that he could belch on command.

Unless the crime was outright disrespectful and hateful disobedience, Mrs. Hicks rarely spanked anyone. She was much more creative. She assigned guilty students to help the custodians during recess, and sometimes she sent students to the office to help out there. She one day punished three of the girls by having them collect everyone's used lunch trays and return them to the dishwasher. The girls pulled that duty for an entire week.

But on occasion, she turned to her favorite form of punishment: the Duck Walk.

Famed guitarist Chuck Berry used a duck walk during his stage performances. When he got to a certain riff in his hit "Johnny B. Goode," Berry would stand on one foot, arching his other leg into the air, give a slight squat, and then hop across the stage playing his guitar.

This was not Mrs. Hicks's form of the duck walk.

No, Mrs. Hicks's form of the duck walk was more of an exercise. Students were instructed to get down into a baseball catcher's position and, while in that position, waddle forward without hands touching the floor.

For the average nine-year-old, this was simply exercise and not a particularly difficult exercise.

Mrs. Hicks wasn't finished. Students were taken to the ramp leading from the school's foyer down to the school's cafeteria. The duck walking took place up and down that ramp. Going down the ramp wasn't so tough, but coming up was hard. Mrs. Hicks expected students to do this for thirty minutes with only the occasional break.

Lester sat before a well-behaved class on this day, and he wasn't happy about it. His friends weren't perfect, and he was going to be damned sure and point it out to Mrs. Hicks. Someone was going to mess up, and someone's name was going on this list. He had a reputation to uphold.

Frank was struggling through his math assignment, which then led to some random doodling on the paper, which then led to practicing his signature, which he was trying to perfect in the cursive writing style. And then the lead of his pencil broke, making a snap that also snapped the silence.

He held up his pencil to Lester and motioned to the pencil sharpener, asking without asking if the warden would allow him to use the sharpener. They were good friends, after all.

Lester inexplicably shook his head no. Mrs. Hicks had told everyone to stay in their seats. Frank shook his head in disgust and waited until Lester looked in another direction. Frank leaned to his left, where Charlie sat across a narrow aisle. Frank whispered from the corner of his mouth, asking if he could borrow a sharpened pencil.

Charlie whispered back, "Sure," reached into his book satchel, and handed his best friend a sharpened pencil. Frank returned to his doodling, which was masquerading as classwork. But Lester had heard Frank whisper to Charlie, and now Lester was writing, too. He was writing Frank's name on a piece of paper, and beside his name wrote the word "talking." Frank was unaware he had been caught and convicted.

Mrs. Hicks soon returned to the classroom, and Lester approached her with his piece of paper. There was only one name on the paper. "Frank—talking." Mrs. Hicks stared at it, and she was surprised.

"Frank," she asked, "were you talking while I was away?"

Frank was fighting back anger because he hadn't really been talking to be talking; he had just been borrowing a pencil. Frank told Mrs. Hicks that his pencil lead had broken and he needed to borrow a pencil, so he had asked Charlie to lend him a pencil and Charlie had obliged him.

Mrs. Hicks said, "Did Charlie do all this quietly?"

Frank said, "Well when I asked if I could borrow a pencil, he said that I could, and he gave me one."

"So Charlie was talking, too?" she asked, fighting back a smile.

Charlie could stand it no longer. "I was just trying to be helpful! Why am I involved in this?" He stared at Frank, who was still glaring at Lester. The class was starting to laugh at the comedy of it all.

That was when Mrs. Hicks called both Frank and Charlie to stand in front of her desk. She told them they couldn't talk when she was away, and, despite their protests of Lester's intolerance, she handed down the sentence: the boys would duck walk for thirty minutes after school the next day.

Frank felt sick at his stomach. If his daddy found out he had been misbehaving—and apparently that was a pretty low bar in the eyes of Lester and Mrs. Hicks—Tom would spank him. Tom had no tolerance for poor behavior at the Acorn Primary School. To his surprise, and probably because he explained the situation first to Janet and his mama ran interference for him, Tom never said anything about the incident.

The next day was an especially tough day for Mrs. Hicks. So tough, in fact, that she forgot all about the two boys needing to duck walk after school. She did not mention it throughout the day, and as the day came to a close, Frank and Charlie were pretty confident she had forgotten all about it. The bell rang to end the day, and she bid the class farewell and began packing to leave the classroom. Charlie saw the window of opportunity and whispered, "She's forgotten; let's get out of here. We'll just slip out with everyone else."

As Charlie quickly shoved everything into his book satchel, Frank said aloud, "Mrs. Hicks, aren't Charlie and I supposed to duck walk today after school?"

Charlie Keller almost had a nervous breakdown. He began to shake uncontrollably. He was in this mess simply for being helpful, and now, on the verge of escaping altogether, he had been sucked back down the wormhole.

"What are you doing?" he practically shrieked at Frank before collapsing on his desk, slowly beating his head on the desk. "What in the world are you doing?"

Mrs. Hicks paused and said, "You're right, Frank. Let's go down to the cafeteria." She motioned for the two boys to follow her out the classroom door. As they walked toward the cafeteria ramp, Charlie kept mumbling to himself, "Why, why is this happening to me?" Then he gave Frank a shove behind Mrs. Hicks's back.

At the cafeteria ramp, Mrs. Hicks demonstrated how to duck walk, and then she told the two boys to duck walk up and down the ramp until she returned for them. She was going to the teacher's lounge, which caused Frank to raise an eyebrow. He wanted to warn her about going in there; he wanted to warn her about the clouds of cigarette smoke. When she had left, Charlie turned to Frank, shoulders slumped. "I don't need help getting in trouble," he said. "Why didn't you just keep your mouth shut?"

Frank started laughing and couldn't stop. Even aggravated, Charlie was funny.

The boys began the duck walk ascent of the ramp, chuckling as they remembered Mike's wheelchair ride down the ramp. Then Charlie farted, and they both collapsed onto the ramp, laughing until their sides hurt. As they started duck walking again, Frank farted, and that caused them to collapse all over again. Apparently, duck walking made farting pretty easy, and the fun of it led them to try to fart as they waddled up and down the ramp.

At one point, they decided to race up and down the ramp, and Frank was able to win one of two races—a significant feat considering his more athletic friend was his competition. As the half hour wore on, their legs became more and more tired, and they stopped to rest more and more often. Even the occasional fart was no longer funny.

They looked up to see Mrs. Hicks standing at the top of the ramp.

"OK, that's it. You can go home," she said, laughing at them. "I've never seen worse duck walking in my whole life, and I'm tired of watching it." The two boys stood, scrambled to her, and picked up their book satchels. She shook her head at them, started back toward the teacher's lounge, paused, turned, and said, "Would you boys like an ice-cream sandwich?"

Nineteen

The Honor Roll

Frank stared at the two-page math test in front of him. This test, he thought, could change his life, giving him an A on his math report card and launching him onto the school's honor roll for the first time in his life.

The honor roll at the Acorn Primary School was a big deal.

To make the honor roll, during a nine-week grading cycle, a student had to make an A grade in every subject. An A was a grade point between 90 and 100. Except for a handful of students, with Lester at the top of the list, the honor roll was not consistently easy.

Students who made the honor roll were treated like royalty. They were excused from class to the cafeteria for an honor-roll party one afternoon at the close of the school day. At the party, each student received a goodie bag that included a coupon for the local Dairy Queen. A photograph was taken at the party, and it was submitted to the *Acorn County News* for publication. Parents and grandparents cut the photograph from the newspaper and put it on display as a tribute to their offspring's cerebral prowess.

On a student's report card, a teacher might write "Good student; always does his best," but on an honor roll report card, the note might read, "Great student; could be president one day."

Frank was surrounded by honor-roll students. Lester's report card could have been completed before the nine weeks even began. Charlie always made the honor roll. Pete Yancey? Honor roll. Steve Dickson? Jim Vinton? Honor roll. Most of the girls? Honor roll. Honor roll, honor roll, honor roll. For Frank, it was just maddening.

"Just one time, I would like to go to that party in the cafeteria, eat ice cream, and have my photograph taken," Frank lamented one afternoon to his daddy on the after-school drive from Acorn to Brookwood Road.

"Well, study harder," his daddy said. "They can't just cut your brain open and pour the information in there. You've got to study." Tom continued to ramble, but Frank didn't hear anything after "cut your brain open," because he was trying to imagine what that might look like and how he might fit it into a future story for the class. *A Mad scientist opens a brain and pours knowledge inside. Student makes the honor roll.*

Closing in on the third nine weeks of his fourth-grade year, Frank thought the stars might be lining up for him, literally. He always did well in reading, spelling, English, and social studies. He counted on those as As. Science and math were often stumbling blocks, but this grading period, the class had studied astronomy, and Frank loved studying about constellations, planets, and space. He was confident of an A. In math, since mastering long division in time to salvage his grades, he had been doing pretty well. He had also learned to seek out help from Mrs. Hicks when he didn't understand something.

"I might make honor roll this nine weeks," he told Janet. "I feel good about it."

"Well," Janet said, "just do your best." Janet had been a consistent honor-roll student. Tom had always done well in school, too, but he didn't care as much. For Tom, grades at school didn't make you a better hunter or fisherman. "You're a smart boy, Frank, but, like your daddy, you just don't always do well on tests."

If Tom heard her say this, he always looked at her, half-smiling while he said, "What the hell is that supposed to mean?"

"You know exactly what it means," Janet said. "You didn't try when you were in school." Tom had, however, won a schoolwide typing contest when he was in high school. As the story went, he was sitting in a typing class when the teacher announced a timed typing test was going to be administered, and the winner would represent the school at a regional competition for business students. For all his life, Tom was a tinkerer, and he loved machines. He loved "messing around" with machines. On the day of the timed typing test, Tom was playing around with his typewriter and wasn't paying attention to the teacher. He started typing before the actual timed test began. When the teacher collected the papers, with his unnoticed head start, Tom shocked the business school world by typing the most words per minute. It was an academic miracle, administrators thought.

Tom was really oblivious to what was happening around him. He just knew that he was being celebrated, and far be it from him to end everyone's fun and celebration. The school gave him a small award and then sent him to nearby Gainesville for the regional typing competition. He came in last place, which also shocked his teachers back at the Acorn County High School.

"I told them I was having a bad day," Tom said, retelling the story for his boys.

"What did they say to you?" Frank asked, laughing to himself.

"They said they wished I had been having a better day before they went to all that trouble to get me over to Gainesville," Tom said.

Frank was still thinking about his mama's encouragement to do "just do your best" as he stared at the math test in front of him. He took a deep breath. The test focused on fractions. His Mema had helped him prepare for the test, and fractions somehow came easy for him. He knew he could get through this test successfully if he just didn't get distracted and, from there, get careless. Distraction was always his worst enemy, and it didn't help that his desk was right beside the windows.

Outside, the school custodians were working on a drain pipe extending from the side of the school cafeteria. Frank was fascinated with what they were doing. He momentarily forgot about the test in front of him. Mrs. Hicks drew his attention back by standing by his desk, staring at him.

"Do you long to go help them with that drain pipe?" she whispered, and Frank snapped back to the fractions test. He was finishing it when he saw Lester stand, walk to the front of the classroom, and place his paper face down on Mrs. Hicks's desk. This was a good sign. Finishing an assignment before Lester finished usually meant Frank had hurried and not done well. If Lester finished ahead of him, it was a sign that things were in their natural order. Lester should have finished ahead of Frank.

Frank wrapped up his test, took it forward, placed it face down, and returned to his seat. He could now watch the custodians tackle the drain pipe problem for the rest of the class time.

The next day, when Mrs. Hicks passed out the graded math tests, Frank was delighted to see that he had made a 92 on the test. He was beside himself with confidence that he had made the honor roll and looked forward to report cards coming out the next week.

"I do believe I'm going to make the honor roll," Frank said over a Monday-morning breakfast that included something new called a Pop-Tart. "I do believe I am."

"I wouldn't count my chickens before they hatch," Janet said. "You might have forgotten about a bad grade here or there. No matter what you make on your report card, I'm sure we'll be proud of you."

Proud was well and good, but it was not the ticket into the cafeteria's honor-roll party and a photograph in the *Acorn County News*. His parents' contentment would not get Frank that coupon to the Dairy Queen and the chance to brag to everyone he knew that he had made the honor roll. He was sure that his Mema would even give him some money as a prize.

All through the day on the following Monday, Frank sat waiting on report cards to be given out. Mrs. Hicks intentionally waited until the very end of the school day, prolonging the madness but also working to ensure students didn't compare report cards throughout the day. At long last, the moment came.

"I'm going to give out report cards," she said. "You are such wonderful students." She started calling out names, and students one by one went forward for the green-sleeved report card—the green sleeve imprinted with the First Federal Bank of Acorn logo. Member FDIC.

Frank's name was called, and he went forward. She gave him no indication; she just smiled and handed him the report card. He returned to his seat and took a deep sigh. He pulled the report card from the sleeve, and his eyes went to the line that read Math.

It was an A. The beast that was math had been slain. The way was paved for the honor roll.

"I did it!" Frank practically yelled, thrusting his arms into the air and letting the report card fall to his desk. He looked at Mrs. Hicks, who was giving him an awkward smile as if she was unsure why this interruption was necessary and completely unsure what he meant by it.

Frank, still with his arms in the air, glanced down at the report card in front of him. He was beaming and was just about to scream out the words "honor roll" when his eyes fell on the line marked English.

It was a B.

Frank's heart sank. He slowly lowered his arms. He put his head on his desk. His report card had an A by every subject line except that one—English. It was a B. Somehow, early during that nine weeks, he had been tripped up in English and had forgotten all about it. He never made a B in English. Never. Embarrassment washed over him, and then despair. He had gotten so close to making the honor roll, only to fall painfully short.

Finished with the report cards, Mrs. Hicks made her way around the room and stopped by Frank's desk. "Did you think you had made the honor roll?" she asked him.

He was determined not to cry. He shook his head in the affirmative. She told him to come to her desk, and there she showed him her grade book. Sure enough, in the first few weeks of the term, he had stumbled out of the gate in English. It was Death by Adverbs.

"I'm sorry," she said, trying to fight back emotion. "You know I can't change your grade. You wouldn't want a grade that you didn't deserve." Frank nodded his head through watery eyes that he agreed with her, but he sure did hate feeling so left out of the fun his honor-roll friends had.

Back at his desk, Frank put the green-sleeved report card in his book satchel and tried to imagine his parents' reaction to the fact that he had fallen so very short of making the honor roll and making them all so proud of him.

"I don't give a damn about the honor roll," Tom said, shaking his head. His statement was designed to make his oldest son feel better. "I care a lot more about you cutting that grass out there on Saturday."

He pointed outside. Tom really didn't care about grades so long as they were passing grades and so long as there was an *S* for Satisfactory on the Conduct line of the report card. Tom might have had a nervous breakdown had Frank come home with a *U* for Unsatisfactory in Conduct.

As Janet signed the back of the report card for Frank to return the next day, she said, "Look at it this way, son. It's the best report card you've ever had. If you keep up the good work, you might make all As on the last report card of the year. You might even make the honor roll in the future. You've got lots of report cards to get before you are finished with school."

Frank felt as if he were receiving a consolation prize when Janet let him walk from The Sewing Shop to the Dairy Queen the next day after school.

None of them could see into the future, but that near miss of a report card would be the closest Frank Wilcox came to making straight As for the rest of his years in school, including college. He never made the honor roll. But the grass was always cut.

TWENTY

GREEN BEANS

The scouting report on Mrs. Elizabeth Smith was that she loved art and music. She also loved athletics and had been a great basketball player in her younger years. Frank was excited to find that his close friends were again in his class, having moved steadily together from third grade to fourth grade and now on to fifth grade.

It was going to be a great year if somehow Van Piper could be controlled.

Van Piper had not been seen around Acorn Primary School since the start of Frank's third-grade year and the swinging challenge with Wendell Mann. There had been rumors of Van moving to Texas. There had also been rumors of him moving to the state prison at Alto, Georgia, where mean-ass boys were sent. And Van Piper qualified all around as a mean-ass boy. When last seen in the third grade, Van had been larger than most of the boys. He was now returning to the Acorn Primary School even larger—and heavier—and was now a first-class, gold-star bully. Steve Dickson, the home-run-hitting legend of Coal Mountain, and Lester were larger than most of the other boys, but even they looked small beside Van Piper.

Wherever Van Piper had been for the past two years, he was coming back mean as hell. He had been considered a general pest before, but now he had taken up smoking cigarettes, and that was no rumor—Pete Yancey had seen Van smoking outside a barbershop in Acorn. Pete had reported that when the barber told Van to move along, Van had pointed his middle finger in the air and waved it in front of the barber.

"What does it mean when you stick your finger up in the air like that?" Frank asked, demonstrating this mysterious sign language in the face of his daddy.

"It means you are about to get your ass beat," Tom said. "Don't do that to anyone. I promise that things won't end well for you."

Just as the class had gotten a scouting report on Mrs. Smith, surely Mrs. Smith had gotten a scouting report on her class. Why she allowed Van Piper to sit in the back of the class was a true mystery. That far removed from her desk, he was disruptive, throwing paper balls at other students, belching loudly, and annoying those around him. Finally, Mrs. Smith moved him closer to the front of the room. Out of the thirty desk possibilities in that classroom, Mrs. Smith chose to relocate Van Piper directly behind Frank in the first column closest to the classroom door.

Frank immediately had the sympathy of every boy in the class. They stood around him on the playground and shook their heads, a few patting him on the shoulder for comfort. It was going to be a long, long year.

If things were bad, they were about to get much worse. Van had picked up a sidekick, and worse than that, he had pilfered one of the original Cub Scout Den 8 boys—Travis Jackson. Travis had been with the Cub Scouts during third grade but had dropped out during the fourth grade. Struggling to fit in somewhere, Travis was an easy target for Van Piper, who always kept to himself and rarely played sports with the other boys.

Van and Travis became inseparable, and Mrs. Smith's boys saw a change in Travis. He had taken on the smart-aleck, annoying, bullying habits of his much larger mentor, Van. And being in Van's shadow gave him a measure of power. If anyone tried to come after Travis, that person had to get through Van. Van could use Travis to do some of his bullying for him. Travis enjoyed the thrill of it all; it was a partnership made in a dark corner of hell.

Sitting behind Frank, Van found an easy target. Up until this year, Frank had enjoyed his seat in the classrooms—usually surrounded by at least one or two of the prettier girls in the school. Charlie was almost always nearby, too. Now he had the oversized Van Piper whispering in his ear, "Slide over so I can see your paper." When Frank would not do it, Van punched him in the back or shoved his knees into Frank's lower back. The back of the desk's seat had wooden slats providing just enough space for Van's big knees to press hard into Frank's back.

It was not unusual for Van to get up to sharpen his pencil and intentionally clear Frank's desk by knocking everything on the floor. Frank just picked up everything and went about his business. The lack of reaction drove Van crazy for more. Several of Frank's classmates suggested he talk to Mrs. Smith, but he would not. He did not want to be labeled a tattletale, and he wasn't completely sure Van would let him live. Frank enjoyed living.

Frank should have known something was in the works when Van suddenly stopped bothering him and turned his sights on Ned Fletcher. Ned was an inconspicuous student who was a pretty good second baseman despite glasses so thick they made his eyes look the size of quarters. Ned also farted every day about three in the afternoon, which became a signal that the school day was drawing to a close. Charlie had playfully nicknamed Ned Old Faithful because of his daily flatulence. Ned laughed about it; Charlie was laughing with him more than laughing at him. Van Piper had moved on to torment Ned, providing Frank with a well-deserved break.

"Keep an eye on your lunch tray," Ned warned the other boys in the class, showing his lunch tray with a soggy napkin dropped in the middle of it. Van had done that. No one was completely sure what caused the napkin to be soggy. Lunch—and sometimes recess—was fertile ground for Van and Travis to exercise their bullying.

Tom and Janet Wilcox didn't believe in packing a lunch for school. It was a lot less expensive to eat in the school cafeteria, and it was certainly a lot less trouble. And a hot school lunch was always going to trump a sandwich in the eyes of the Wilcox clan. Despite the warm greeting he received from Mrs. Wolfe in the cafeteria line, Frank was not a big fan of the school lunches. He loved the warm, homemade yeast rolls but was not a big fan of vegetables from large cans, and neither was he a fan of some of the entrees—such as fried fish.

"Why do we have fried fish every single Friday?" he asked Charlie one Friday on the way to the cafeteria.

Charlie replied, "I've heard it's because Catholics eat fish every Friday."

"What's a Catholic?" Frank asked. And what was behind their fishy power over the school lunchroom? Catholics were about a decade away from a public presence in Acorn—even a small group of Presbyterians met quietly out near the lake and didn't draw much attention to themselves. Acorn was Baptist, Methodist, and Church of God country.

Each day's processional to the school cafeteria was the same for each classroom, regardless of grade. Each class, at its appropriate lunchtime, lined up in single file for a long walk down the hall, down the cafeteria ramp, and into the cafeteria. The cafeteria smelled the same way all the time, regardless of whether lunch was being served or not. It had a sour-milk smell that came from mixing food scents with the scent of childhood sweat. That smell had leached into the concrete walls for all time.

This day, Frank quietly followed his classmates through the line, spoke to Mrs. Wolfe, and got his tray with lunch for the day. It wasn't bad. Country-fried steak, mashed potatoes, green beans that had been stewed a little too long, a yeast roll, and the big prize—peanut butter cake. Peanut butter cake was little more than a sweetened peanut butter icing layered thickly over yellow sheet cake. It was delicious and was so popular that it had become a trading commodity. A piece of peanut butter cake equaled a yeast roll and half the country-fried steak on the cafeteria trading market. Frank got his carton of lukewarm white milk and followed in line to a row of chairs along long tables in the cafeteria.

This day, Frank could not wait to put his tray on the table because his pants were driving him crazy. Trying to manage every possible dollar, Janet was determined to patch, hem, and let out her sons' pants to see if they could last an entire school year, or maybe two. Today Frank was wearing the "green" pants, as opposed to the "brown" or "blue" pants that he also owned. The green pants gave him lots of problems because there weren't enough belt loops, so when he sat down, the pants gaped in the back rather than fit snug around his waist. It was uncomfortable, and he felt his pants were always on the verge of falling down. He constantly had to stop and give them a yank up around his waist. The green pants were not as bad as the brown pants, which were made of a wool and perhaps burlap blend that scratched his legs unmercifully all day long. They also had been patched at the knees, and the patches were also uncomfortable against his bare knees. The blue pants fit wonderfully. As much as he tried to wear the blue pants every day, Janet caught on and made him wear the green and brown pants. Today he wore the green pants.

Sitting a few seats down from Frank was Travis Jackson, a wicked disciple of Van Piper, who had noticed Frank struggling with his green pants during class that morning. A plan was hatched for the institution's chow hall.

Frank sat quietly at lunch, rarely talking to anyone. He had just finished his lunch and turned his tray so that the peanut butter cake was directly in front him. It was a good day because he had gotten a larger piece from the middle of the pan. He stared at it, wanting to eat it slowly and savor the deliciousness. He was about to take his first bite when Travis Jackson stood up, walked quickly down the line of chairs, and in one quick motion dumped his green beans down into the back of Frank's green pants. Frank immediately felt the warm green bean puree in his pants and wasn't completely sure what was happening. He was concerned that he had experienced an unexpected blow of diarrhea. He stood up, trying to be inconspicuous, and walked toward Mrs. Smith. He asked for and received permission to use the restroom in the corner of the cafeteria. He noticed Travis Jackson laughing like a hyena and Van Piper laughing too.

It wasn't until Frank got into the bathroom and pulled his pants down that he completely realized what had happened. His pants were full of mushy green beans, and the mush had even soaked into his underwear. He did the only thing he could do in the face of such outright meanness—he cried. He quietly cried while removing his pants. He then used paper towels to get the green beans out of his pants. But he could do nothing about the wet underwear and the wet spot on the seat of his pants. It looked just as if he had peed all over himself.

Sitting on the toilet, Frank used paper towels to rub his pants, trying to dry them out. He was still doing this when Pete Yancey walked into the bathroom and saw him sitting there in his underwear. Pete began to laugh but quickly stopped when he saw how genuinely upset Frank was over his circumstances.

"What happened?" Pete asked sympathetically.

"Travis put green beans down my pants," Frank said. It sounded so funny he couldn't help but laugh through his tears, and that seemed to give Pete permission to laugh, too.

"What are you going to do?" Pete asked.

"I don't know," Frank said. "I'm not telling Mrs. Smith. I don't want anyone to know."

Pete removed his watch and put it on the edge of the sink.

"What are doing?" Frank asked him.

"I'll stand guard outside the door so you don't have to worry about someone barging in," Pete said. "I took my watch off in case I have to fight someone. I don't want to damage my watch." He went outside to stand guard.

Frank may not have wanted to tell Mrs. Smith, but someone else had told her all about the incident. She found Pete standing guard and relayed a message for Frank to take his time and return to class when he felt better. She told Pete to stay on guard duty. Travis got the spanking of spankings. He learned—as did everyone else—that having an athletic teacher such as Mrs. Smith allowed for a different kind of hallway spanking. Mrs. Smith could well wield her paddle, and she could bring the pain with it.

When Frank and Pete returned to class, Travis had his head on his desk. It was hollow justice for Frank because he knew that Van Piper had been the mastermind. Travis had not sold out his mentor, and Van had gone unpunished. Frank still had to bear the humiliation of having a big wet stain on the backside of his green pants. While it may have been his imagination, Frank felt he could smell green beans the rest of the day. Word spread quickly, and not everyone was kind in their reaction to Frank's plight or the stains. It was an embarrassing day.

Frank didn't feel like playing softball with his friends during recess that afternoon. He walked over to an empty bench and sat down, watching his friends. He didn't even feel like bringing his library book outside with him. He just sat there, feeling more than a little sorry for himself. His friends left him alone in his misery.

"I was looking for you," Mrs. Smith said, surprising him a little and sitting down on the bench beside him. "In all the excitement at lunch-time, I don't think you had a chance to eat your dessert." She gave him the largest piece of peanut butter cake he had ever seen. It was on a napkin, and she had brought him a fork, too. He smiled at her, and she patted him on the knee.

Twenty-One

Everyone Loves Baseball

Monday, October 6, 1969

Mrs. Elizabeth Smith stared at her students. A slight smile formed on her mouth, and she gently shook her head. They were supposed to be working on a social studies worksheet, but she could tell the boys were not. Every so often she saw a note passed from one boy to another, followed by a nod of the head. She had watched Jim Vinton walk over to the pencil sharpener, pretend to yawn by lifting his arms above his head and allow a copy of *The Sporting News* to drop onto the desk of Steve Dickson.

On the previous Friday, the class had celebrated winning a playground softball championship against a team from Mrs. Tribble's class across the hall. Mrs. Smith had provided the entire class with ice-cream cups to celebrate the championship and sent them home, yelling and cheering as they poured out of the school. This morning, they had returned from a tough weekend.

Over the weekend, the beloved Atlanta Braves had lost two games to the New York Mets in the new best-of-three National League Championship playoff series. The students were somber and dejected and certainly in no mood for class on this Monday. Since lunchtime, she had watched their moods return to normal, she thought, smiling, though little schoolwork was going to happen with the Braves and Mets scheduled to play game three of the championship series early this afternoon.

She laughed to herself, biting her lip before speaking so that she would appear stern.

"All right," she said, standing and dropping a heavy book on her desk. Every student jerked to face her, hands on their desks, eyes staring straight ahead. "I'm going to the office. While I'm away, you can trade baseball cards, talk about baseball, whatever you want or need to do. But when I return, we are going to focus on school. Is that a deal?"

"Deal!" shouted Charlie Keller as he spun out of his desk, baseball card in hand, and made a run directly toward Mack Holloway, who was willing to make a trade.

Mrs. Smith stepped to the door and then turned to face the class. "Wendell," she said, and he looked up nervously. "Don't trade Brooks Robinson. He's going to be a Hall of Famer, son." She laughed and left the room.

In 1966, the Milwaukee Braves had moved to Atlanta, bringing with them home-run-hitting legend Henry "Hammerin' Hank" Aaron. Only forty miles away from Acorn, practically every boy had been to Atlanta Stadium to see the Braves play live baseball. Tom Wilcox had taken his family to the stadium several times, always sitting in the 401 section of the upper deck behind home plate. The Wilcox brothers loved it when a Brave hit a home run and Chief Noc-A-Homa emerged from his left-field pavilion tipi and did a war dance.

As children were able to see their heroes play live games, all things baseball were on the rise in Acorn County. Boys and girls played for community baseball and softball teams; there was the collecting and trading of baseball cards; Friday-night sleepovers were held over through Saturday's televised *Game of the Week* on NBC; and every boy had a transistor AM radio under his bedcovers, listening to Milo Hamilton call the Braves' games on Atlanta's WSB 750. If you were a child in Acorn, it was impossible not to bump into something related to baseball.

The baseball frenzy had only intensified when Frank and his friends reached the fifth grade and the fall of the 1969 season. This year, Major League Baseball had split its National and American leagues so that each league had two divisions—an East Division and a West Division. The Atlanta Braves had won the National League's West Division, earning a spot in the new best-of-three National League Champion Series against the East Division winner, the New York Mets.

The Braves had finished 1969 with a 93–69 record, three games ahead of superstar Willie Mays and the San Francisco Giants and four games ahead of the Cincinnati Reds, who, in a handful of years, would be a dynasty known as the Big Red Machine. The Mets were in their eighth season as a Major League Baseball team. They had never had a winning season and had never finished higher than ninth place in the ten-team National League. In five of their first seven seasons, the Mets lost at least a hundred games, but this year they had won a hundred games. As the Chicago Cubs collapsed, the Mets overtook them and won the National League East Division with the nickname of Amazin' Mets.

Mrs. Smith's class was full of great baseball players. Several members of the Coal Mountain team were in the class, and Coal Mountain was generally regarded as the best in the county. Mack Holloway and Steve Dickson were among the Coal Mountain boys; Steve Dickson led the entire county in home runs. Frank thought his friend Lester had Babe Ruth's facial features, but there was no question that Steve Dickson was the Sultan of Swat of Acorn Primary School.

When the boys weren't trading baseball cards, they were on the school's upper playground, where teams were chosen and games were played, substituting a softball for a baseball. All interested fifth graders could participate, and some of the girls, such as Macy, were better than many of the boys, including Frank. Teams were chosen in pickup fashion, with far too many players on each team. Where a normal baseball team had nine players, a fifth-grade pickup team might have sixteen. Every player ran out on defense, and every player had a spot in the batting order.

Though Frank played first base for the Big Creek community team, he was not the best first baseman on the playground and often found himself standing with ten other outfielders, waiting to chase down a softball hit in their direction. Charlie almost always played shortstop or second base because of his athleticism, and Frank tried to line up behind him so they could talk back and forth during the games.

The competition driving these playground softball games did become problematic and led to an odd practice called "last strikes." Under this rule, hitters with two strikes could allow one of their team's better hitters—such as Steve Dickson—to finish the at-bat. If Steve hit the ball, the original batter got to run the bases, which wasn't very exciting if Steve launched the ball down near the Tastee Freez for a home run. The home-run trot felt like welfare.

The outfield, crowded with too many players, became more of a social event. Frank had become quite the storyteller, and he migrated toward a group of friends who were of like mind. They stood around visiting with one another, retelling funny stories and jokes until three outs were made by the better players in the infield. If a ball was hit to the outfield, one of the social club ran it down and threw it in to the infield. Sometimes, good-naturedly, the outfield social club heckled their own teammates, especially if an error led to a ball rolling into the outfield, causing someone to stop telling a story.

Eventually, the surplus outfielders would migrate in and out of the game altogether. One afternoon, Frank became fascinated by a game of mumblety-peg occurring between Van Piper and Travis Jackson. Mumblety-peg was an odd knife-throwing game. Most boys—and a few girls—had pocketknives. Standing face-to-face, two boys would flip their open knives off their shoulders, attempting to stick them in the ground between the opponent's feet. Frank was fascinated by the game and secretly hoped Van or Travis would stab one another in the feet. Charlie had to yell at him to come take his turn hitting in the softball game.

Mrs. Smith watched as the softball games involved fewer and fewer interested children, and it disturbed her that so few children were playing. The mumblety-peg contests also began reminding her of something that might happen in a prison yard. She decided to form a playground softball league, organizing her class into two separate teams to challenge teams from other fifth-grade classrooms. Frank celebrated that he was on the same team with Charlie, Mack, and Steve Dickson, and he also celebrated that there were only three outfielders, which gave him a chance to make a play. Frank's outfield play eventually helped him with the confidence necessary to score a roster spot on a softball team at 4-H camp that summer.

Frank's team eventually won the best-of-three playground championship, which ended on the Friday before the weekend start of the National League Championship Series between the Braves and the Mets.

That Friday's ice-cream cup celebration was doused over the weekend when the Mets beat the Braves in both weekend games. Henry Aaron homered in both games, but it was a bitter consolation prize. Returning to school on Monday, students had fallen back into card trading to ease their nerves over the Braves' precarious playoff position.

"Hurry up," Lester said as he stood beside Frank, debating a trade. "She'll be back in just a minute, and then we'll have to stop." Mrs. Smith had been gone for at least fifteen minutes, and that was a long time for a teacher to be away. She had not even designated someone to take names. She had just left them to finish up baseball business.

Frank had two Mickey Mantle cards, and Lester wanted one of them even though The Mick had retired from the Yankees the year before.

"OK, here you go," Frank said, handing over the Mickey Mantle card, and in exchange he got both a Maury Wills and a Willie Davis from the Dodgers. Mack Holloway had called it a dumb trade on Frank's part, but Frank had doubles of Mantle and needed Wills and Davis to finish out his collection of the Dodgers' starting lineup.

The classroom door opened, and they all quickly finished their trades and scurried back to their desks. Mrs. Smith walked into her classroom, pushing a television perched high on top of a rolling cart. Television days were usually reserved for programs on Georgia Educational Television or to watch news reports on space exploration or the funeral of someone important.

Mrs. Smith plugged in the television, turned the wire antenna, and ignored Charlie Keller's chirping question, "Who died in Washington, DC?" She turned on the television, and as it warmed up, she moved her teacher's chair out among the students—right in the middle of the classroom—and sat down.

A friendly face with a friendly voice appeared on the television.

Curt Gowdy of NBC Sports was just announcing the starting lineups for the Mets and Braves in game three of the championship series. An electric buzz went through the classroom, and Charlie said, "Mrs. Smith, I'd vote for you for president."

Mrs. Smith just smiled and said, "Come on, Braves."

TWENTY-TWO

Travis Jackson's Big Jump

Travis Jackson had stapled his fingers together while sitting under a classroom table. He had stapled his fingers together on a dare, with Charlie Keller suggesting he do it for a small ice-cream cup at lunch.

"Dear Lord, Travis," Mrs. Smith exclaimed, pulling the blond ragamuffin from underneath the table. She wrapped his hand in a paper towel and sent him to the school office. It was one of those fortunate times when the amount of blood was not indicative of the size of the wound.

Lester was assigned to walk with Travis to the office, and it was on that walk that Travis confided a plan that he was hatching.

"I am going to jump from a moving car," Travis said. "I just need a parachute."

Lester didn't look at the smaller boy. "You broke your arm in Cub Scouts trying to jump out of a tree. You might want to stick with playing around with staplers."

* * *

Travis's renewed fascination for parachutes had begun with a simple science lesson on wind resistance and gravity. As with any good science lesson, it became necessary to have a science experiment. Mrs. Smith wanted each of her students to construct a parachute that would be attached to an uncooked egg. The eggs would then be dropped from the top of the cafeteria, which was the tallest building on the school campus. The idea was that the parachute should protect the falling egg from breaking upon impact with the ground.

151

Frank and most of his friends didn't care one bit about the science behind this experiment. It was going to be just fantastic to make a parachute and drop an egg from the top of the school cafeteria to see what would happen—regardless of what happened.

Students were instructed to build their own parachutes at home, and Frank assembled the necessary plastic sandwich bags, trash bag, string, scissors, and raw eggs. It had not been easy.

"What are you doing with those eggs?" Janet asked him as he took a carton of eggs, acquired from Hershel's store up the road, from the refrigerator.

"I'm going to make a parachute for them, climb up in the tree house at Granny's, and let them drop to the ground," he said. "If this works, the parachute will protect the eggs, and they will land safely."

"I don't want you wasting all the eggs," she said.

"Mama, this is for a science experiment at school," Frank said. "If the eggs land safely, you can have them back."

"I don't want the eggs back after you have thrown them around on the ground," she said, though Frank wondered if she thought that was really any worse than where the eggs had come from in the first place. "Don't use more than three eggs for your practicing."

Following Mrs. Smith's directions, Frank put one of the eggs in one of the plastic sandwich bags, also acquired from the store. He had been fascinated by the sandwich bags since his first school field trip to the Grant Park Zoo in downtown Atlanta. As Janet prepared his sack lunch for the trip, he had been fascinated with the way she tucked a ham sandwich into each of the sandwich bags and then folded it in a way that secured the sandwich inside the bag.

More than once on the trip to the zoo, he had removed a sandwich just to turn it over in his hands and study the bag and the way it held a sandwich. Now he was equally fascinated to place a raw egg inside one of the bags and secure it within.

To make the parachute, Frank took the larger trash bag and punched holes in each corner. He then followed the directions and secured the corners of the trash bag to the sandwich bag using string. Next came properly folding the parachute in a way that ensured it would open correctly as it fell.

"This will never work," Frank's brother Jack said as he stared at the project on the kitchen table. "That egg is going to bust."

The two brothers rode their bicycles to their grandparents' house and climbed into the tree house they had built with the help of Ernest Moore, who worked for their Papa R. C. At the top of the tree house, Frank dropped his egg, and it crashed to the ground before the parachute had time to open.

"Told you," Jack said. "I told you this was a dumb idea."

"I can't help it," Frank said. "We have to do this for school." Frank tried the experiment two other times, with equally poor results. Both eggs splattered inside the sandwich bags.

He complained to his daddy, and Tom tried to make his oldest son feel better. "If you are going to drop these from the top of the school, it will probably work," he said. "The parachute will have more time to open, and that's the secret of protecting the eggs. In the tree house, you aren't high enough off the ground."

Frank shared this insight at school as the boys gathered on the playground to talk about their failed attempts at home. Jim Vinton reported using a small, plastic G. I. Joe parachute instead of the garbage bag, and his eggs had also broken. In all of this, the boys were learning exactly what Mrs. Smith wanted them to learn about wind resistance and gravity. Parachuting was damned difficult.

On the day of the actual school experiment, each student had his or her name written on his or her sandwich bag as a way to identify whose eggs survived and whose eggs did not. Because it was unsafe for students to climb to the roof of the cafeteria, custodian Everett Poole was drafted to take all the eggs to the roof and drop them. Before he dropped each egg, he called out the name of the student written on the sandwich bag. He added a measure of suspense, sometimes pausing before dropping an egg. Sometimes he even added sound effects to the drop, simulating the whistle of a bomb falling to earth.

Most of the parachutes opened as planned, and most of the eggs survived the fall. Some parachutes didn't open because Mr. Poole mishandled them upon launch. It was later discovered that Travis Jackson had used boiled eggs in an attempt to cheat the experiment. Mrs. Smith punished the cheater by having him clean up the entire mess of eggs and parachutes under the watch of Custodian Poole.

***

As Lester delivered Travis to the school office, the bleeding of his stapled fingers beginning to clot. Travis stared at Lester and said, "I bet I can parachute out of my daddy's car and survive it. I bet I can."

"You will need a lot of padding," Lester said. "You don't want to rupture your spleen." A few months earlier, Frank had reported that his uncle had ruptured his spleen, which was now considered the worst thing that could happen to anyone. No one knew much about a spleen or what it was or what function it had inside of a body, but imagining a ruptured spleen—whatever that meant—was horrible.

Later that day, on the playground, Lester reported his conversation with Travis, and none of the boys thought it wise to tell an adult or to talk sense into Travis. Instead, the boys thought of all the possibilities for harm and raised questions that Travis might want to consider. How much padding would be needed to absorb a jump from a moving car? Would you even need a parachute? Would a parachute have time to open? Would you bounce?

Pete Yancey stared at his friends in disbelief. "I believe we are ignoring the biggest question of them all. Would you die if you jumped from a moving vehicle?" Shrugged shoulders and nodding heads affirmed that it was a very valid question. Death would not be good.

"What would Evel Knievel do?" Charlie asked.

Robert Craig Knievel, also known to the world as Evel Knievel, was the nation's greatest daredevil. For a few years, Evel Knievel had been using a motorcycle to jump a variety of obstacles, including rattlesnakes, mountain lions, and as many as nineteen cars, and he had suffered a few broken bones when some of the jumps resulted in a crash.

But for the most part, Evel Knievel had been successful at his jumping. As he became nationally famous, Evel caught the attention of boys all over the United States.

"I can do this," Travis said with a bit of a snarl. He had separated himself from the Den 8 boys and was now under the wing of Van Piper. "Anyone dare me to do it?" He held up his two bandaged fingers.

Lester said, "If the fall doesn't kill you, your daddy will kill you. Or you might be sent away to Milledgeville." Milledgeville, Georgia's capital city before Atlanta, was now associated with the state's mental hospital, located there. When someone was going to Milledgeville, fair or not, the implication was that that person was going to "the nut house."

"At least he's not drinking gasoline," Steve Dickson whispered to Frank, recalling a recent sleepover when the boys had dared one another to drink gasoline for a dollar. "I'm glad Travis wasn't invited."

"I know for a fact there's a room at Milledgeville reserved for people who drink gasoline," Lester said. He never explained how he knew that factually.

Travis was not to be denied. He was going to jump from his daddy's moving vehicle because his classmates didn't think he should and they didn't think he would.

Pete Yancey said, "What kind of parachute would you need to survive jumping from a car?"

A new underground class project was suddenly on the table for consideration. If Travis was going to jump from his daddy's car, how could his classmates prepare him for survival? It was true that Travis was now more outside the friendship circle than inside, but he was still their classmate, and this notion of jumping from a car was certainly fascinating. Lester still wasn't sure this was a good idea, and, to his horror, a few of the boys even said they would pay their lunch money to see Travis jump from his father's Chevy one morning before school.

That was how Mrs. Smith's simple egg-in-a-parachute experiment escalated into a Vegas-style attraction.

Travis first considered making his historic jump from the car at the Tastee Freez located just below the school, at the end of Elm Street. He told the boys that his daddy's wide turn from Elm Street onto State

Highway 20 would provide plenty of room for him to jump out and clear the car. And, if things went as planned, he would bounce or roll right up to the dairy window at the Tastee Freez, where he could order a chocolate shake.

"There's too much traffic," Pete said. "You might get run over."

"It sure would be bad to survive the jump and then get run over by a truck," Jim Vinton said.

It was decided by committee, and with Travis's approval, that he would jump from his daddy's moving car in front of the school one morning. That way, there could be witnesses to ensure it happened, especially as money was now on the table. More than five dollars had been collected as an offering.

Many of the school's students arrived by school bus each morning, and the yellow buses turned off Elm Street and stopped in front of the school, allowing students to exit under a large portico protecting them from bad weather. Students not arriving by bus were dropped off by parents, who also used the front of the school and had to weave in and out of the school-bus traffic. Travis Jackson's daddy, Marvin, was one of those parents.

Marvin Jackson was no timid man in his own right. The apple of his eye—Travis—had not fallen very far from the tree. It was rumored that in his younger years, Marvin had wrestled a carnival bear, floated down part of the Chattahoochee River in a garbage can, run buck naked down Acorn's Main Street, and was a crazed stock-car driver on dirt tracks around North Georgia. Now, assigned to deliver his ten-year-old son to school each morning, Marvin saw it as a challenge to weave in and among the school buses just ahead of the morning bell that began the school day. It was not unusual, as children took their seats, to see Marvin swing his Chevy into the school parking lot—sometimes screeching on two wheels—and then gas the car toward the portico to drop off Travis.

Knowing this made Travis's decision to jump from his daddy's speeding car even more exciting.

It was decided that Travis would jump on a Friday morning in front of the school as his daddy jerked the old Chevy into the parking lot. If things went wrong, Travis would have the entire weekend to get better or for surgery on his spleen. Frank had suggested that Travis's funeral could be on a Sunday when all the students would be dressed for church anyway.

In the days leading up to Travis's jump, great planning went into easing Travis's impact with the ground. Steve Dickson donated his older brother's winter coat, saying that his brother had a new football letter jacket and no longer needed the old coat.

"I've seen pictures of my uncle's parachute," Emmett Morgan said before describing the parachute his uncle had used to jump into Vietnam. "I'm pretty sure a worn bedsheet tied to a winter coat isn't going to work very well." He went on to coach Travis in how to fold the bed sheet so that it would unfold perfectly as he jumped from the vehicle. His uncle had shown him how to fold a parachute, though when Emmett finished the folding, it looked more like a wadded washcloth after a Saturday-night ear washing.

Lester shook his head and said to Frank, "He's going to die."

Frank didn't even look at his good friend before saying, "He's not going to be high enough for the parachute to open. He's going to fall out of that car and roll." Frank was as interested in Travis's jump as every other boy, but he didn't care what happened to Travis. In Frank's mind, there was the lingering association between Travis, Frank's pants, and green beans.

Travis was done taking advice. He announced his plans to wear Steve's donated winter coat, adding two layers of extra clothing underneath. He also planned to wear baseball shin guards, strapping them on while sitting in the backseat on the way to school. He also had plans to wear a football helmet, though it wasn't completely confirmed where he would get the helmet.

"My cousin has one of those hats they wear in the marching band," Jim Vinton said, but it was quickly decided that the hat would be more ornamental than functional in the case of a student jumping from a car.

On the morning of the jump, all the boys had made plans for an early school arrival. After arriving, Frank hurriedly walked down the long hallway to Mrs. Smith's classroom, where he was joined by many of the other boys who had arrived early. They gathered near the large windows, looking out on Elm Street and waiting for Marvin Jackson's black Chevy to wheel into the parking lot directly in front of them. They fully expected to see the door fly open and for Travis to leap or jump or fall out of the car, throwing the parachute and sailing safely to the ground in front of them.

No one really knew what was happening that morning at the Jackson house, but one thing for sure was happening—Marvin Jackson knew it wasn't necessary for his ten-year-old son to wear a full winter coat on this warm morning. Marvin also knew his son didn't need catcher's shin guards at school. And Travis had been unable to procure a football helmet. Sitting in the backseat of his daddy's car, Travis had nothing to protect him but a queen-size bed sheet neatly folded as a parachute. Without the heavy coat, however, it was attached to nothing.

Inside the classroom, Mrs. Smith thought it curious that all these boys had gotten to school so early and were now eagerly looking out the front windows to the parking lot. She smiled. There was a bird feeder and a birdbath outside her window, and she thought perhaps the boys were watching birds this morning.

The black Chevy turned abruptly from Elm Street into the school parking lot just in front of Mrs. Smith's window, and the boys could see Travis's blond head inside the car. He wasn't wearing a football helmet. Just at the spot where they expected Travis to jump from the car, Marvin Jackson did something completely unexpected—he slowed down. He slowed down to a near stop because, in front of him, the car driven by another parent had come to a complete stop. A science project was being unloaded.

When Travis Jackson opened the passenger door of his father's car and jumped from it, throwing the bedsheet into the air for no apparent purpose, the car was almost at a complete stop. Rather than a thrill-seeking, parachuting sail from the car, the boys watched as Travis flopped out onto the pavement and then weakly rolled twice in the school grass as the bedsheet wrapped completely around him. He sat up in the grass like a mummy sitting up in a tomb. The boys roared with laughter.

Mrs. Smith shrieked and ran from the room, taking a nearby side door to get to where Travis sat in the grass. Marvin had shifted his transmission into park and jumped from the car to see about his son. Realizing the boy was OK, Mrs. Smith and Marvin Jackson took turns yelling at him from both sides. The boys inside the classroom howled at the show before them.

Evel Knievel would have been pretty embarrassed at how things had turned out.

A full investigation was made, and every boy was questioned about his role in Travis's failed jump. At the end of it all, Travis reported getting two spankings from his daddy, and the school made him help the custodians for a full week after school. Mrs. Smith made all the boys stay inside from recess that Friday, and she lectured them about safety and peer pressure. She called each one of them by name, shook her head, and said, "I'm disappointed in you. Do you know what happens to people who do things like jump out of cars?" she asked.

It was Charlie Keller who answered her by saying, "They go to Milledgeville." She did not find the humor in it.

As for Travis Jackson, his thrill-seeking continued. The very next week, in the cafeteria, he asked if anyone would pay him to suck a piece of spaghetti up one side of his nose and pull it out of his mouth.

Twenty-Three

My Country, 'Tis of Thee

In Flanders fields the poppies blow
Between the crosses, row on row,
That mark our place; and in the sky
The larks, still bravely singing, fly
Scarce heard amid the guns below.
—John McCrae, May 1915

Frank sat down in front of the new color television with his newly acquired green baseball card locker and took out all of his cards that represented the current Detroit Tigers club. The team's starting lineup was carefully organized on the top of the stack, and Frank dealt each player to a make-believe spot on the floor's make-believe baseball diamond, where they would play defense.

"More Americans dead" were the words that caught his attention. He turned to look into the eyes of a solemn, nicely dressed television news announcer he had heard many times before but to whom he never paid much attention. He stared at television images of young men carrying the lifeless bodies of other young men as the announcer reported the number of American tragedies in a far-off placed called Vietnam. He put the Detroit Tigers on the floor and turned, sitting Indian style, to face the television. The news was bad.

Janet stepped around him and turned off the television. "You shouldn't be watching that," she said. "Supper will be ready soon."

"Am I going to have to go there and die?" he blurted out.

"I pray not," she said. "But it's a long time before you will be old enough to join the army, and we aren't going to worry about it right now. Right now we are going to worry about eating these salmon patties before they get cold."

Frank was still thinking of the television images when he went to bed, and Janet sat beside him on the double bed he shared with Jack.

"Mama," he said, "tell me what's happening."

Janet did not know a lot about the Vietnam War and certainly didn't know a lot to tell a fifth-grade boy wrestling with adult images on television. "We are there to help people who can't help themselves against an army that wants to destroy them. And with war, young men go and fight, and some of them die. Not every soldier comes home. That's why war is terrible. But you can't worry about it. God is in control, even when we question His presence in times like these."

Her words didn't make Frank feel better. He only heard, "Young men go and fight, and some of them die."

"We live in a great country," his mama said. "We live in the land of the free and the home of the brave, and free and brave people want everyone in the world to live free and brave. So we go and help and put ourselves at risk to be injured or to die. That's what it means to be an American."

Frank did not sleep a wink that night, tossing and turning even as Jack nudged him and kicked him to be still.

The next day, sleepy and worried, he sat in Mrs. Smith's class and watched a patriotic film featuring singer Glen Campbell singing "America, the Beautiful" while an eagle soared over scenic spots in the American landscape.

Tears filled Frank's eyes, and the emotion surprised him. There was something that gripped him deep within his soul, watching that eagle soar over amber waves of grain, purple mountain majesties, and even the fruited plain. He was so overcome by the film that he slid his hand over his heart and thought about the men dying in far-off Vietnam. He even appreciated Glen Campbell, though he had failed miserably as a would-be guitarist to learn Campbell's "Gentle on My Mind."

As tender as Frank might have been, Mrs. Smith was that tender and much, much more. She actually stood with her hand over her heart. And somewhere in that Glen Campbell performance with that eagle sailing over the wilderness, a country church, and the monuments of Washington, DC, Mrs. Smith had an idea.

Mrs. Smith, like everyone watching the news and talking in hallways, was concerned about the United States and its involvement in Vietnam. As a younger generation unleashed a counterculture of antiwar demonstrations; radical clothing; and messages of peace, love, and rock and roll, she stood with a World War I and II generation that pushed back against it. The United States of America was proud and willing to fight and was willing to take the fight of freedom anywhere. But now the messages and images of young men dying and using mind-numbing drugs in battle were more than she could stand. The United States was in trouble in two places—Vietnam and at home. She concluded that her students needed a counter message to all of it: a message of patriotism.

There was nothing quite as friendly to teachers as a school with a cafeteria that came with a stage. It was an instant auditorium, and Mrs. Smith decided her class would offer a Veterans Day program for the entire school. It would be a star-spangled event with patriotic poems being read and a choir of fifth graders singing a tribute to all the veterans of all the wars, living and dead, who had served the United States of America.

The majority of her students were fully prepared for this presentation. They had been onstage for Mrs. Hicks's *Fractured Follies* one year before, but Mrs. Smith's stage vision was different. There would be no humor, no parodies of prime-time commercials, and no Big Bad Wolf chasing three little pigs around on a stage. No, there would be thirty students on choir risers, singing a patriotic tribute for all to hear. There would be the occasional reading of a poem such as John McCrae's "In Flanders Fields," there would be the Pledge of Allegiance to the US flag, and there would be the reciting of the Lord's Prayer. Mostly, there would be singing.

To prepare her class, Mrs. Smith transformed the hour allotted for the arts into an hour of daily patriotism. Normally, during this time of the day, children worked on art projects, or wrote short stories to read in front of the class, or learned about music. Frank especially loved writing his short stories during arts hour. He had been working on a story that exposed all the fifth-grade romances and the associated playground drama. The story earned him a round of applause from the boys, especially those falling victim to the manipulations of the girls.

But all of this, including Emmett Morgan's instructions for how to draw the Roadrunner from the Looney Tunes series of cartoons, was now put aside for an hour of concentrated patriotism and loyalty to the United States of America.

Along with marching her students to the cafeteria each day for rehearsal, Mrs. Smith also invited guest speakers to her class. One girl's grandfather had been awarded a Purple Heart in World War II, and the medal was brought to class, and the soldier's heroic endeavors were explained. On another day, a Methodist pastor came and talked about his work as a chaplain near an army fort in Virginia. Veterans lined up to come and speak to the class, and several brought items they had used as soldiers. The message was clear that the United States of America was strong, stronger than any evil in the world, and the nation would always persevere. The message was also clear that the people of Acorn didn't just sit back and watch other people go and fight.

When Frank and his classmates stood on those risers in the Acorn Primary School cafeteria and sang those patriotic songs, there wasn't one of the children who didn't understand the deep significance of war and patriotism and courage under fire. Many of the children had experience singing because many of them had been or were in children's choirs at church. But the Veterans Day program was different—this was war-effort singing.

None of the children realized what was happening, but Mrs. Smith realized it. In the early days of the program's preparation, the children had fidgeted while learning the songs. There had been horseplay in the hallways and on the risers. There had been giggling at someone forgetting the words of a song or singing the wrong chorus. Van Piper had even whispered, "Why in the hell are we doing this?" to the giggles of nearby students. But as they practiced and as they heard the classroom presentations, a patriotic fire was lit within these little patriots. They began singing as if they were marching to war, singing out of a love for a country they were just beginning to know, and singing so loudly that Mrs. Smith sometimes said they were shouting instead of singing.

At the end of the hour one day, Mrs. Smith announced that not only would they perform the program (over the course of a few days) for all the students at the school, but they would also have an evening performance for family and friends. A patriotic revival was breaking out in Mrs. Smith's class, and it was coming to a full-blown altar call when she gave each child a copy of a printed program she had prepared.

America the Beautiful
America (My Country, 'Tis of Thee)
You're a Grand Old Flag
When Johnny Comes Marching Home Again
I'm a Yankee Doodle Dandy
The Star-Spangled Banner
Stars and Stripes Forever
This Is My Country
This Land Is Your Land
The Battle Hymn of the Republic
God Bless America

And last, "Dixie," which really wasn't so much a patriotic song but was necessary because these were Southern children and many of them had family buried in small church cemeteries around Acorn. Frank's own great-great-great-grandfather, Andrew, had fought with the Thirty-Sixth Georgia Infantry at Vicksburg, Mississippi.

"Mama, did you know some of these songs are in the Baptist hymn book?" Frank asked Janet one evening over her homemade chicken pie and English peas. "Was Jesus an American? Did he die making people free and brave?"

Janet explained that Americans loved the Lord, and that was why money had the words "In God We Trust" printed on it. It was completely appropriate for the Baptist hymnbook to include patriotic songs. And "Yes, faith in Jesus does make us free from sin, and we can draw some bravery through faith in Him."

Her room now decorated in red, white, and blue, Mrs. Smith was getting her own questions from the class.

One afternoon, as the choir took a break, Pete Yancey asked, "Mrs. Smith, who is Johnny?"

Mrs. Smith loved these questions because it gave her an opportunity to teach. She explained that the song titled "When Johnny Comes Marching Home" honored the longing people had to see their loved ones safely return home from the American Civil War.

And Frank noticed tears welling up in her eyes. "It's something every family still longs for when loved ones go off to war. They want their loved ones to come home. Johnny was probably someone's boyfriend or husband, and the girl was praying he would be safe and come back home to her."

As serious as the mood had turned in the rehearsals, there were the occasional hurdles to overcome. The boys were having a difficult time singing "I'm A Yankee Doodle Dandy" without chuckling. "Doodle" was just a funny word to say and sing, and identifying oneself as a Doodle Dandy was just funny.

Mrs. Smith finally got so frustrated she stopped and asked Charlie to explain what he thought was so funny.

"I'm not a Yankee Doodle," Charlie said, fighting back laughter on behalf of his compatriots. "I don't really think any of us are Yankee Doodles." There were snickers throughout the crowd, leading Mrs. Smith to stomp her foot and regain control.

"This is a very important patriotic song," she said, pointing out a lyric that went:

I'm a Yankee Doodle Dandy,
A Yankee Doodle, do or die,
A real live nephew of my Uncle Sam
Born on the Fourth of July

"I guess if it's good enough for Uncle Sam to be a Yankee Doodle Dandy, it is good enough for you to be a Yankee Doodle Dandy, too, Charlie Keller," she said, apparently more than eager to defend Yankee Doodles everywhere.

Mrs. Smith was not finished.

"Of all the children in this classroom, Charlie, you should appreciate a song about the Fourth of July," Mrs. Smith preached on, apparently not having the best of days. It was true enough that Charlie's great grandfather had single-handedly started Acorn's Fourth of July celebration in the center of town—a Fourth of July celebration that had expanded into an event for just about all of northern Georgia.

Charlie just stared at the frustrated teacher and then said, "I'm sorry, Mrs. Smith. I'll be a Yankee Doodle Dandy for you." As he said it, the children went completely silent, waiting to see Mrs. Smith's reaction. When she gave a slight smile, they erupted in laughter.

The choir electrified the students who attended the school-day performances, and more than one teacher applauded Mrs. Smith's patriotic ensemble and the spirit that she had instilled in them toward love of God and country. Frank was still moved to misty eyes when he sang some of the songs, especially "America the Beautiful." And he noticed that Mrs. Smith's eyes were wet with tears throughout the program and that she was singing right along with her choir.

On the night of the performance for parents and friends, Mrs. Smith wore a navy-blue dress with a red-and-white scarf, and the students had all been encouraged to wear red, white, or blue. All but Van had complied; Van wore green for a reason no one understood except that he was just contrary to everything. Mrs. Smith made him change into an old white T-shirt reserved for water-color painting and a red felt vest held over from a Christmas program. It didn't even matter that it had a snowflake on it.

Behind the curtain, the children could hear the murmur of people in the cafeteria. The students were excited about their program, and all eyes were fixed on their fearless leader, their general, Mrs. Elizabeth Smith.

"We live in a great country," Mrs. Smith said. "A lot of people in our country are upset because of the war and because our soldiers are there. But many, many good men have gone to past wars and served our country and our world, and we are honoring them tonight. Do your best to honor them, and know that I am so proud of you." She wiped her eyes with a white handkerchief she held as she directed the program.

The curtain came back and the program began. The children sang, and Mrs. Smith sang.

The show ended with "God Bless America," and as the voices rose from the risers, something sacred happened that night in the Acorn Primary School cafeteria. As the children sang, the entire audience stood and began to sing with them. Frank turned to Charlie in astonishment.

God bless America, land that I love
Stand beside her and guide her
Through the night with the light from above

From the mountains to the prairies
To the oceans white with foam
God bless America, my home sweet home

Frank's eyes filled with so many tears he could no longer see his family. He understood patriotism. He understood the love of country and love of community. As the number concluded, there was an eruption of applause as choir and audience celebrated as one. Mrs. Smith dabbed her eyes with the handkerchief and slightly bowed as she applauded her choir's performance.

No one wanted to go home. As the children walked off the risers to join with family and friends, the pianist continued to play through some of the songs, and a community event continued for another half hour. Tom and Janet had offered to help clean up the cafeteria following the performance, so the Wilcox family was among the last to leave. Mrs. Smith had already gone back to her classroom to get things in order for class the next morning.

Tom turned off the cafeteria lights as the last of the audience walked up the cafeteria ramp toward the front of the school. At the top of the ramp, Frank remembered his coat was still in the classroom, and Tom told him to run down and get it. November's cool nights were upon them, and it was a twenty-minute drive down to the farm on Brookwood Road.

The hallway was dark, but the light was on in Mrs. Smith's classroom. As he approached the half-open door, he heard her. She was singing softly to herself, and, as he stepped toward the door, he also realized she was sobbing. He stood frozen in the doorway. She had her face in her hands. These weren't the tears of pity or regret, but the tears of sorrow—of loss. Perhaps she was crying for the current state of her country, Frank thought. Perhaps she was crying because she had lost someone dear in a battle somewhere faraway. Frank did not interrupt her. He stepped into the room, grabbed his coat off his desk, and left her to tears of patriotism.

TWENTY-FOUR

SACRIFICES

The Wilcox brothers were preoccupied with playing cowboys and Indians and watching Western television dramas such as *Bonanza*. Jack always played the popular role of Little Joe Cartwright because, like Little Joe, Jack was a lefty.

"I want a gun for Christmas," Jack said as the brothers pretended to sit around a campfire at the edge of the Brookwood Road yard. "I'm tired of using sticks as rifles. I want a gun—even if it's just a rifle that shoots exploding caps. We need guns." He tossed his make-believe rifle into the make-believe campfire. "You see, my rifle can also be wood for the fire. This is stupid."

Frank wanted a vest. He liked the vests that the men wore on *Bonanza* and in other Western shows, and he thought Janet might just sew him a vest for Christmas this year. Even before owning The Sewing Shop, Janet had sewn everything from curtains to tablecloths and from dresses to blouses. She had sewn a dress for her mother-in-law's birthday one year, and while Kathryn had been gracious in receiving it, Janet never saw her mother-in-law actually wear the dress. Frank decided to ask his mama if she would sew him a vest in time for his school Christmas party.

"I don't know if I will have the time or not," she said. "I've never made a boy's vest, and Christmas is a very busy time of year." But she promised to try. "I will try to have it finished in time for your school Christmas party, and you can also wear it to the Sunday School Christmas party."

This all aggravated Jack, who whined, "Can someone just buy me a toy gun? I'm tired of putting a stick in my pocket and pretending it's a gun." No one paid him much attention. Out of aggravation, Jack spat on the ground.

In what little spare time Janet had during the Christmas season, she went to work on Frank's vest, finding a pattern in her store and proceeding to find brown fabric that would hold up to the wear and tear of a ten-year-old boy. Frank had called her in to watch an episode of *Bonanza*, pointing out that he wanted a vest more like the saloon gunfighters rather than that of a cowhand.

Every day during that holiday season, Jack approached his mama after school and inquired about progress on the new brown vest with its shiny buttons. Every day, Janet reported the same news. "I'm doing the best that I can, Frank." That was the hopeful message until the week of the class party when Janet begged out of the assignment.

"I just don't think I can finish the vest by Friday," she said. "I am so busy at the store, I've got a Jaycette Christmas party this week, and I'm just running out of time. Can I finish it after Christmas when things are slower?"

"It's OK, Mama," Frank said. "You don't have to make it for me." The words sounded gracious, but Frank's disappointment filled him. He had so wanted the vest for the class Christmas party and had looked so forward to wearing it. It was impossible for Frank to hide anything from his mama, and she saw the disappointment on his face. She walked to the kitchen and gave a big sigh as she stood at the kitchen sink, looking out the small window at the pasture.

Janet finished the vest in time for the Christmas parties. It wasn't easy, but she did it. Each night after Frank and his brothers went to bed, she worked on the vest, hiding the progress from her oldest son. On the Thursday night before the party, she worked until almost midnight to finish the vest. She folded it and put it in Frank's chair for him to find at breakfast the next morning.

Stumbling to the kitchen for a bowl of oatmeal and a Pop Tart, Frank discovered the new vest in his chair. He woke up completely, hollered out loud, jumped around, hugged his mama, and thanked her for this special Christmas gift.

Jack sat at the table, his blond, tousled hair going in several directions, and mumbled, "Well, I looked around here and couldn't find a gun. All I want is a gun—not even a real gun. I'll just pray for a Christmas

172

miracle." He bowed his head, and Janet told him to stop because he was being sacrilegious.

At school, the vest came with its problems, which Frank had never considered when he requested it. No other child in the entire school population was wearing a vest—of any kind. This naturally drew attention to Frank, and it drew a lot of questions.

"Why in the world are you wearing that vest?" Charlie asked him, laughing and shaking his head. "No one really understands, and I don't know what to tell them." Beyond the questions came the snickering.

"I think we finally understand what a Yankee Doodle Dandy really is," Pete Yancey said, laughing. "Don't get me wrong; your mama did a good job making the vest, but no one really understands why you wanted a vest. Did she make you wear it?"

Frank just laughed along with his friends. He loved the vest, and he loved wearing it. He loved it so much that he wore it to Sunday School two days later and planned to wear it again that Sunday afternoon to the children's Christmas party at the First Baptist Church.

After lunch that Friday, Frank and his classmates were excused to the playground for recess while a handful of moms decorated the classroom, prepared punch, put out cupcakes and other treats, and prepared to welcome the students back into the classroom. The Christmas party did not include a gift exchange, but some of the boys and girls exchanged gifts, especially those who had a childhood love interest. Frank had purchased a small jewelry box that he planned to give a pretty girl named Denise. For two years, he had had a schoolboy crush on Denise, purchasing her Valentine's candy and Christmas gifts. Inside the jewelry box, he had written her a Merry Christmas note.

He was quite sure that the vest and the jewelry box would finally win Denise's heart, but it was not meant to be. She accepted the jewelry box and thanked him. With his vest, Frank might have looked the part of the poker player in an Old West saloon, but Denise had the true poker face down pat—she gave Frank no indication that there was any hope of a relationship. Frank got the message and by Valentine's Day had moved on.

Aside from the Christmas party at school, the First Baptist Church's annual children's Christmas party was the largest social event of the year for many of Frank's friends. All the primary-school children, including first- through fifth-grade children, were invited to the party in the church's fellowship hall. Frank loved this large room because it was in the church's basement and was always cool, especially during Vacation Bible School, when June temperatures were much warmer.

For the Christmas party, every child was to bring a gift to exchange. Each boy was to bring a gift for a boy; each girl was to bring a gift for a girl. Each gift had a tag designating the appropriate gender and age range so there would be no confusion when the gifts were distributed. Each gift was to cost no more than two or three dollars. Prior to the gift exchange, the children had refreshments; sang Christmas carols; and heard Mrs. Housley, who taught both Sunday School and first grade at Acorn Primary School, read the Christmas story from the Bible. Mrs. Housley commanded such respect that there was complete silence in the room as she read from scripture. The children also played games, including pin the tail on the donkey. Charlie always tried stabbing the poor donkey in the groin, much to the delight of the other boys.

All this activity fed the excitement of the gift distribution at the close of the party. From a doorway at the end of the fellowship hall, a skinny version of Santa Claus appeared and made his way to the Christmas tree, where all the wrapped gifts were arranged. There was great speculation as to who played the role of Santa Claus for the party, and those still believing in Santa Claus were told it was "one of Santa's helpers" who apparently was excused this year from being overweight and jolly. Besides being too skinny, the church Santa Claus was also somewhat aggravated by having to play the part.

As the gifts were distributed, the children went into a paper-ripping frenzy, almost as if they had never received a gift before. There were shouts as little girls opened dolls and boys opened bags of plastic army soldiers. For Frank, this was his last of the Christmas parties, and while he was excited about receiving a gift, the gift actually meant very little to him. The vest, made by his mama, was already the highlight of his Christmas season.

Standing with Charlie at the back of the crowd of children, Frank spotted his brother Jack, who was closer to the skinny Santa and clearly caught up in the frenzy of gift giving. Watching Jack made him smile because he loved his brothers more than anyone on Earth—they were his best friends, his roommates, and Jack was a bedfellow, sharing the double bed in the blue-painted room.

Jack had his hands reaching out toward Santa, and Santa was receiving gifts from all the Sunday School teachers not named Mrs. Housley. Mrs. Housley was around frenzied children all the time and, after reading the Bible story, had retreated to the refreshment table and a large piece of chocolate cake. Santa would review the tag and then hand the gift to an appropriate child. The teachers watched him carefully to make sure he gave the correct gift to the appropriate child—there was no trust in this aggravated Santa.

On the way to the party, Jack had held his wrapped gift to be given to another child. It was a G. I. Joe doll, complete with artillery launcher. Jack was hoping—praying—for a toy gun with a box of exploding caps inside. With these cap guns, the roll of caps was looped into the gun's barrel and then fed up through the hammer so that pulling the trigger dropped the hammer on a cap and created a pop, simulating a fired gun.

"I sure do want a gun," Jack said on the way from Brookwood Road to the church. "I sure do want a gun." Frank chuckled at his funny middle brother, who expressed his desire for cap guns, chocolate milk, and Dixie cup dispensers with the same passion. Jack even gave a little shudder for effect and gave Frank a wink. "It will be so much fun, Frank."

Now, at the party, standing before Santa, Jack had his eyes on a gift that resembled the packaging of a cap gun, a rifle, and he wanted that gift badly. He was trying to point Santa's attention to it, but Santa was just trying to finish as quickly as possible. The chocolate cake was looking better and better. Santa grabbed a gift in the shape of a jewelry box, looked at the tag, and pitched it to Jack. Frank watched as Jack tore into the gift's wrapping paper.

Frank took his eyes off Jack long enough for someone to hand him a gift. One of the teachers had stepped in to help pass out gifts to the older students in the back of the room. She smiled at Frank and said, "I love your vest, Frank. I wonder if your mama would make one for my husband." Frank smiled, soaking in the compliment, and thanked the kind woman for the Christmas gift. He tore the paper off the box.

Frank stared in stunned silence. In his hands was a Ben Cartwright action figure complete with a tiny rifle, holster and gun, hat, and lasso. Between this gift and the vest on Friday, this weekend was becoming its own bonanza for Frank Wilcox. He was really too old for the action figure, but he thought it would look good on the bookshelf in his room.

He looked up to see Jack coming toward him and was just about to say "Look what I got!" when he saw the look on Jack's face. Jack was fighting back the tears. He held up his gift. Frank stared in disbelief. In Jack's small hand was a round plastic container twice as big as a silver dollar. The top was clear, and inside a tiny ball rolled around and occasionally fell into small divots marked with 1, 2, or 3, for points collected. The game, probably from a gumball machine, could not have been worth more than a nickel. It was far below the average cost of a two-to-three-dollar gift.

Jack was crushed.

"You should have just kept the damn G. I. Joe," Frank whispered, feeling his anger rising at the injustice of the gift giving.

"I'm ready to go home," Jack said quietly.

That was when Frank noticed, across the sea of children, that one of the fourth-grade boys had opened a gift containing a black-handled, silver cap pistol. Frank moved quickly, taking the small toy from Jack's hand and making his way to the fourth-grader.

It wasn't easy, but Frank was an experienced baseball card haggler, and he knew the fourth grader was no match for him. He offered the boy his Ben Cartwright action figure and the small gumball toy in exchange for the cap pistol. To seal the deal, Frank also put in a quarter and said, "It's really three gifts for one gift."

Frank made his way back to where he had left Jack and found his brother sitting alone against the wall. He sat down beside him and gave his brother the toy gun. Jack stared at it and then stared at his older brother.

"You take the gun, Jack," Frank said. "I've got this vest that Mama made me."

Jack smiled at the gun. "I'll share it with you," he said.

"I don't mind using sticks." Frank laughed. "Now, let's go get some chocolate cake before Charlie eats all of it." And the two brothers rejoined the Christmas party.

Twenty-Five

The Reckoning

Reckoning: Settlement of a bill or of an account.

Van Piper had been on a five-alarm reign of terror.

And his favorite target—above all other targets—was Frank Wilcox. No one really understood why, except perhaps Van hated the attention Frank received from writing his fictional stories and reading them to the class. There was no other reason to dislike or torment Frank, because generally, Frank minded his own business, was friendly to everyone, and did as he was told by those in authority.

For whatever reason, Van Piper had targeted the smaller Frank Wilcox. And the bullying was relentless. Whenever the class walked in single file to the cafeteria, Van found a way to "accidentally" bump Frank into the wall, sometimes causing him to trip and nearly fall. It was not unusual to find that Van had hurried back to the classroom ahead of Frank and dumped the contents of Frank's book satchel on the floor. One day Frank stepped into the hallway bathroom to find his name written on a lavatory mirror: "Frank Wilcox sucks." Frank used an entire roll of toilet paper to smear the black shoe polish so his name was unreadable.

Van took it further. He wrote love letters to girls and signed Frank's name to them. The more Van tormented him, the more Frank felt alone. It was as if every other boy in the classroom was waiting to see if and when he might respond to the bullying, and they certainly didn't want to draw Van's attention in their direction. For a time, Van had focused on another boy or two, but he always came back to Frank. To make it worse, Travis Jackson constantly chirped about how "Van is going to get you!" It made Frank sorry that Travis hadn't broken a leg in his jump from the Chevy.

Charlie Keller had found a book in the library on sign language used by American spies in the Revolutionary War against the British. Charlie mastered the sign language, learning twenty-six different signs—one for each letter of the alphabet. He then went about teaching all the boys and girls who wanted to learn it. The sign language became important in warning one another about Van Piper and his intentions to wreak havoc in the fifth grade.

For all his methods of torment, nothing compared to Van's knees. Van easily weighed fifty pounds more than any other boy in the classroom, and he had a difficult time sitting in the small schoolroom desks. The desks were metal chairs, each with a curved wooden seat and two wooden slats across the back for support. The wooden slats across the back of the desk chair left the student's back exposed to the person behind him or her. Underneath the seat of the desk was a large opening for books and storage. Attached to the front of the seat, by a vertical arm on the right side, was a desktop. The only way to enter the seat was from the left—the opposite side from the vertical desktop arm.

For most children, the desks were easy to use, easy to slip in and out of, and practical. But a much larger student, such as Van, struggled to wedge his or her body into the desk, comfortably work, and then wedge out of the desk when necessary. Van's knees, big and meaty, naturally extended forward under his desktop.

It was unfortunate that Mrs. Smith had relocated Van Piper to sit behind Frank. Frank's back, exposed through the slats of the desk, was an easy target for Van's big, meaty knees. Van quickly realized that he could slam or push his knees into Frank's back in a motion that drew no attention to himself and hid the torment he was administering.

Van knew he was hurting Frank. He would drive his knees hard enough that it made Frank flinch and sometimes jump. Van whispered, "Let me see your paper," wanting Frank to slide just enough to his right so that Van could cheat off Frank's test papers. This practice demonstrated that Van was not exceptionally smart because Frank had already made a 36 on an important science test and was struggling with his math grades, too. Copying anything Frank did academically was not Van's best decision. Still, Frank refused to help him, and this always meant a day's worth of abuse: Van's knees slamming into Frank's back.

It was all getting the best of Frank, emotionally taking a toll. He dreaded going to school, and that was a shame because he loved school. He was too embarrassed to tell his friends, though most of them knew what was happening. None of them really wanted to get involved anyway, and Frank understood why. Frank blamed no one.

Mrs. Smith happened to see an incident at the end of school one day. Frank had gathered up his books and prepared to leave the classroom when Van reached up and knocked everything to the floor. Mrs. Smith pounced and forced Van to pick up all of Frank's belongings, neatly pack them in his book satchel, and apologize. Van did it, but he was seething as he did. And, right on cue, the very next day, Van hammered his knees into poor Frank's back all day long.

Frank could take it no more. In front of his mama, his daddy, and the Lord Jesus too, Frank completely melted down that night at the supper table. Tears flowed, and he wailed about the bullying. It was such an intense relief of raw emotion that Frank's brothers, Jack and Wayne, ran from the supper table to their bedroom. They were later found under the double bed that Frank shared with Jack.

"Son, sit down," Tom finally said, pointing at the chair just opposite him at the table. "We can't understand a damn word you are saying. I hear something about knees and your back hurts. You are going to have stop this crying and tell us what's going on."

Frank gathered his composure and, still trembling, told every detail of the abuse. He told about the books being knocked to the floor, he told them about being shoved in the hallway, he told them about the shoe polish on the bathroom mirror, and he told them all about the knees being shoved in his back.

There is an expression called "blowing the lid off," which relates to bringing something secret into the full light of day. The origin of the expression comes from the days of oil wells under intense pressure. If not properly monitored, the lids of the wells would be blown off by the pressure. The expression also had roots in steam building in a pot or a generator and blowing the lid off.

Frank had blown the lid off Van Piper's bullying, but it did not hold a candle to the blowing that was happening that night in the Wilcox kitchen. Janet was moving for the telephone, preparing to call everyone from school principal Dwight Pulliam to teacher Elizabeth Smith and even Van Piper's parents if she could find them. She was not afraid of the Pipers.

Tom was now yelling, too. "This shit is about to come to a screeching-ass halt!"

Frank did not like to see his small, wiry, rooster-like daddy get upset. He drank down his milk, ran out of the kitchen, jumped on his green bicycle, and took off down the dirt road along the adjacent Stozier's Woods—a narrow forest of pine trees. He hid there until he heard Janet's voice calling him back home.

"Did I do something wrong?" he asked his mama, who shook her head no.

"You should have told us as soon as this kind of thing started," she said. "You shouldn't have waited so long to say something. We don't send you to school so you can be miserable." Obviously, he thought, she had not considered the brown pants she sometimes made him wear.

"Did you call Mrs. Smith?" Frank asked her.

"Yes, and she's going to talk to Van," his mama said. "She promised me that she would be watching, and she's probably going to move you, too." Frank cringed. This was going to draw a lot of unwanted attention in his direction.

Nothing was said or done the next day at school. He did notice that Van was not in the classroom for part of the morning, but he returned for lunch and then took his seat behind Frank. He leaned forward and whispered, "You are a baby, Frank. You ran home and cried to your mama." And then Van slammed his knees into Frank's back perhaps harder than he had ever done so in the past. And, for good measure, he did it several more times that afternoon.

Janet picked him up from school, and she wasted no time. "Tell me the truth, Frank. Tell me the truth. What happened at school today?" Frank told her that neither he nor Van had been moved. He told her that Van had not been in class for part of the morning but returned and had jammed his knees in his back all afternoon. Janet stewed for the entire twenty-minute drive home to the farm.

At home, she told Frank, "I want you to ride your bike to your Granny's house and tell her that you want to borrow one of her hatpins. I'll call her and tell her you are coming."

In ladies' fashion, many women of Kathryn Wilcox's generation still wore hats in formal settings such as church, funeral homes, or society gatherings. Because her husband was a successful farmer and was a leader in agricultural organizations, Kathryn was a reluctant attendee at dinners and business meetings alongside R. C. Wilcox. She didn't enjoy the attention the way her husband did. Kathryn was a beautiful woman— even more beautiful when she was dressed with a fashionable hat pinned to her silky black hair. The long pins had replaced bonnet laces, which had been used to secure hats onto a woman's head. The pins, often with a decorative rhinestone attached to the top, were safely pushed through the hat at an angle and through the ladies' hair to secure hat to head.

Kathryn had received Janet's telephone call and was waiting for Frank to ride up on his bicycle. He walked up the brick steps to her kitchen door, and she embraced him, rubbing his back. He followed her to her bedroom, where she opened a large closet, revealing several hat-boxes on the top shelf. She removed one, opened it, and withdrew the longest pin Frank had ever seen in his life. And on top of the pin was a pearl.

"Wow," he said. "That's pretty."

"You be careful with that," his Granny said. "It's sharp, and it can hurt you." She carefully pinned it to his shirt so he could ride his bike home without getting stuck. Frank had faced pins and needles before, especially when Tom or Janet removed splinters from his hands or feet. He certainly didn't want to be stuck by this hatpin.

Under the carport, he was getting on his bicycle for the return home when his Papa R. C. appeared, walking up from the meat house, where Wilcox Sausage Company pork products were processed.

"There's an important lesson to be learned," R. C. said to him, re-moving the stub of an unsmoked Tampa Nugget cigar from his mouth. "Don't mess with the Wilcox women. As long as you live, son, don't mess with the Wilcox women." Frank was about to learn exactly what that meant, but even more importantly, so was Van Piper.

The next morning, at the breakfast table, Janet went back over the instructions.

"The first time this boy jams his knees into your back, I want you to turn around and politely ask him to stop and not to do it again," she said. "Do you understand?" Frank nodded that he did understand.

"When you ask him to stop, he's probably going to do it again," she said. "I want you to turn around and ask him a second time. Say, 'Please stop, and please don't do that again.' Do you understand?" Frank nodded that he did understand. "It's important that you politely ask him to stop bothering you."

Frank went to school, praying that through some overnight divine revelation, Van Piper had found Jesus, turned his life around, and was now the best boy in the entire school. Despite everything, Frank could be Van's friend if he would just let him.

Frank's prayers were not answered, but Janet's prayers definitely were answered. She was hoping her oldest son would have the courage to stand up for himself in the face of relentless bullying.

It did not take long that morning before Van asked Frank for a pencil, and Frank did not have a spare to give. Aggravated, Van slammed his knees into Frank's back, causing him to flinch.

"Please don't do that again," Frank turned and said to his tormentor. "I don't like it, and I want you to stop doing it." Van stared at him in disbelief. No one stood up to him. No one ever asked him to stop doing anything. He was in shock. His minion, Travis Jackson, was in shock, too, overhearing Frank speak to Van. Travis reacted first, coughing out a laugh, which inflamed Van.

Frank turned back around. No sooner had he done so than Van slammed his big knees into Frank's back again.

Frank turned again, whispering so only Van could hear him. "Please don't do that again. Please, please don't do that again. I'm tired of it. Please don't."

So much of what human beings say and do is left up to interpretation. Van heard Frank's whispered request as a pitiful, begging attempt to get him to stop doing something he generally enjoyed having the complete power to do. But that wasn't what Frank meant by his request. Frank was actually saying, "Please don't do that again because there are going to be consequences to your actions, and I'm ready for all this to be over."

Frank turned around and faced forward. He knew what was coming. He reached down along the bottom of his blue jeans and slipped into his hand the long hatpin with the pearl tip. Under his desk, he rolled the pearl tip between his thumb and index finger, and he waited.

It didn't take long. Van waited until Mrs. Smith had turned to face the blackboard, and he slid his desk so that it was as close to Frank's as possible. Then Van slid forward as hard as he could, driving knees into Frank's back. Frank shifted his weight to his left hip, exposing Van's right knee sticking through the back slats of the desk.

And Frank buried that hatpin in Van's leg.

All hell broke loose. *The lid had been blown off.*

Van Piper thought his leg had been amputated. Blood soaked his blue jeans, and the pain tore through his leg. He tried to jump out of the desk, but he was too big and lifted the desk off the ground as he screamed in pain.

Mrs. Smith wheeled around and rushed over.

"He stabbed me!" Van shouted as Mrs. Smith helped him from the desk. He grabbed the pearl head of the pin and started to pull it out but collapsed on the floor, screaming in pain. Mrs. Smith bent over him and pulled it straight out. Blood was now on the floor, and Van tossed on the floor like a dying rattlesnake. Travis Jackson stared down at Van and then looked at Frank, who, surprisingly, was staring right at him with cold, unblinking eyes. And Travis was pretty sure he read Frank's lips that day—lips that mouthed the warning, "You are next."

Mrs. Smith sent Van to the principal's office, with Lester walking with him to make sure he didn't pass out along the way. She sent Frank into the hallway and told him to sit on the floor outside the door and not to move.

As long as he lived, Frank never fully understood what happened next. Mrs. Smith eventually returned to him, where he was sitting on the floor, and said, "I want you to stay out here for a while longer. I'll come get you when you can return to class." Frank was sure he was going to get a spanking from either Mrs. Smith or Mr. Pulliam, but he got neither. And, to his knowledge, no further punishment came to Van, either. It was as if everyone had known what was happening, and everyone had been waiting on Frank to take the stand that only he could take.

For the rest of his life, Frank Wilcox had no problems with Van Piper or with Travis Jackson, and he didn't notice any other children having a problem with the two bullies, either.

But just in case, Frank had two other hatpins secure within his book satchel.

Twenty-Six

Twin Lakes

Frank had never been more excited about a bathing suit. At the start of the summer, he and Jack had gone shopping with Janet at Lenox Square Shopping Mall in Atlanta. Frank enjoyed these trips because Janet let him visit a bookstore, where he could buy one book. Today, he had chosen *Great Catchers of the Major Leagues*—a hardback—and he was excited about starting it.

Janet had also announced that he and Jack needed new bathing suits, so they ended up in Rich's Department Store. Frank immediately spotted the bathing suit that he wanted. It was white, but more what his mama called "dirty white," and the printed design featured large black spiders crawling on black spider webs. It was about the most modern, hip, cool bathing suit Frank had ever seen, and he wanted it.

"You will look stupid," Jack said, grabbing a solid-red bathing suit off a rack and pitching it to his mama. "I don't care what I wear."

"If we get this bathing suit, you will have to wear it all summer," Janet warned, looking at her oldest son. "If people laugh at you, you will still have to wear it."

Frank said, "I don't care if people laugh at me."

"That's for sure, mama," Jack said. "If he cared about people laughing at him, things would already be a lot different. He wouldn't be wearing that straw hat to church on Sundays." Frank loved hats and had found a straw hat to wear on days when he wore the brown vest.

She double-checked the sizes of the two bathing suits and put them in her shopping cart.

Frank was beyond excited. Jack just shook his head. "This has got bad written all over it," he said to himself.

There were lots of places to swim in and around Acorn County. The largest and best opportunity was Lake Sidney Lanier, whose banks were less than three miles from the center of Acorn. Several Corps of Engineers parks were on the Acorn County side of the lake, and many of those parks offered crude beaches from which people could swim and boat.

The town of Acorn had built a public swimming pool in the middle of town. It joined the old baseball field that was home to the county fair, family picnics, and an occasional go-cart race. Political conversations were already underway to tear away the old park and rebuild a new, much-improved town park, complete with new swimming pool, new ball fields, a shaded picnic area, and lighted tennis courts.

Then there was Twin Lakes, south of Acorn. Twin Lakes was a privately owned campground that included a swimming pool, two lakes for fishing, and a small store that provided camping supplies, bait and tackle, and hand-scooped ice-cream cones. Twin Lakes was the closest swimming pool to the Brookwood Road farm, and Janet often announced a "swim day" during the summer. These surprise outings to the pool often included a picnic lunch, two hours of swimming, and an ice-cream cone for the ride home.

It was at the Twin Lakes pool that Frank and Jack had once endured swimming lessons. Jack had taken to it right away, jumping into deep water, floundering around, and fearlessly climbing up the ladder of the pool's high diving board for a jump into the really deep water.

Frank was entranced by the teenage teacher, who was one of the most beautiful girls he had ever seen. Aside from the teacher, he did not like being in water over his head. He was perfectly content to splash around in water up to his neckline, conversing with his teacher, and he saw no added value in being in water so deep his feet could not touch the bottom.

Despite the pleadings of the pretty teacher, Frank held his ground, sitting on the edge of the pool, shivering, defiant, and unwilling to move. Janet threatened him, but he held his ground. Finally, both the teacher and Janet left him alone to float, swim, and play in the safer part of the pool. Later in life, Frank became a good swimmer, but it was only when he was ready to learn.

"Aren't you embarrassed that you can't swim?" Janet asked Frank on the drive home from Twin Lakes one afternoon. "All your friends can swim. Doesn't that bother you?"

Frank took another lick of the chocolate ice cream cone and stared at his mama in the rearview mirror. "I love chocolate ice cream, mama," he said.

Janet was now hoping the new bathing suit would push Frank to a place where he would be braver in the pool's waters. She had read in a grocery-store magazine that little things such as clothes could boost a child's confidence, and that boost in confidence could help the child overcome life's little obstacles. Already she could see how proud Frank was of the spider-covered bathing suit.

"You can wear your new bathing suit to the class swimming party," she told Frank on the ride home from Lenox Square. "All your friends will enjoy seeing it."

Frank had already thought about that. Fifth grade was over, and Mrs. Smith's class had decided on a swimming party to celebrate the unofficial graduation to the junior high school that fall. Like the pride he had had in wearing the vest to the class Christmas party, now he would try to impress his friends by wearing the new spider bathing suit to the year-end class party at Twin Lakes.

That last week of school was a frenzy of excitement. Mrs. Smith had invited the junior high–school principal, Mr. Garland Shoemake, to visit her class and talk to the students about how school was different for grades six through eight. She and the other fifth-grade teachers also extended the recess time each day, and some of the parents grilled hamburgers one afternoon as an alternative to the lunchroom fare. Mostly, the talk was of the swimming party, which would be the Saturday afternoon following Friday's last day of school.

Classroom moms were organizing lists of things to bring, and each student was assigned items to bring for a big class picnic that was open to the students' families. Frank had forgotten to show the sign-up list to

Janet, so in a hurry he signed up his family to bring Vienna sausages—the small processed wieners packed inside a can of gelatin.

Janet stared at him in shock upon realizing she was to bring Vienna sausages to the class picnic.

Jack howled with laughter.

"Why in the world did you sign us up to bring Vienna sausages?" Janet asked, exasperated.

"I like Vienna sausages," Frank said. "It was either that, potato chips, or sardines."

"Sardines!" Jack hollered. "Who brings Vienna sausages and sardines to a fifth-grade picnic?" He had collapsed onto the floor.

"I'll buy *you* a can of Vienna sausages, Frank, but I'm not taking a hundred Vienna sausages to this picnic," Janet said. "I'll call the class mom."

When the school bell rang on that Friday afternoon, students swarmed out of the school, free for the summer. The fifth-graders were moving on to the older junior high school building in the fall. As all his classmates dispersed, excited over the swimming party the next day at Twin Lakes, Frank's stomach began to hurt.

It occurred to him that he might well be the only fifth grader who could not swim. Even the thought of a new, wildly printed bathing suit could not shine over the thought that he might be stuck in the shallow end of the pool while all his friends jumped from the high diving board.

On Saturday, before he could even tell his mama that he didn't feel good and perhaps should miss the swimming party, Janet spoke. "Don't tell me you don't feel good. You are going to this party. You should have learned how to swim. Go put on the bathing suit."

Frank dropped his head and retreated, not knowing how in the world his mama had these supernatural powers to know what he was thinking and plotting before he could even open his mouth. When he emerged wearing the bathing suit, clutching a faded green bath towel, Jack admired his older brother and said, "Don't worry, Frank. It won't matter that you can't swim. Everyone will be in shock over that bathing suit."

Janet packed the new Ford station wagon, and she and the boys began the short six-mile drive to the swimming pool. She gave Frank a can of Vienna sausages, which he opened and began to nervously eat or eat nervously because he was a bundle of nerves about this swimming party. His stomach hurt so bad he thought he was going to be sick.

"You are getting Vienna sausage all over you," Jack said. "What's wrong with you?"

"Just nervous," Frank said.

"Look, just have fun," Jack said. "If someone asks you to jump off the diving board, just tell them you have diarrhea. No one will bother you for the rest of the day."

"These Vienna sausages may give me diarrhea," Frank said, popping another one in his mouth. "That would be a good excuse not to get in the pool."

At Twin Lakes, the crowd was swelling. Mrs. Smith's class and all the families were gathered at the picnic area of the campground. The campground itself was full of people, and the swimming pool was bursting with people on this hot Saturday in late May.

Frank forgot about his nervousness when he saw his friends Charlie, Pete, Lester, and Wendell.

"What in the world are you wearing?" Charlie asked him, and Frank's friends laughed out loud. "Did you go to New York City to get that bathing suit?"

Frank just ignored him. While most of his friends were wearing single-colored bathing suits like Jack, a few were branching out into Hawaiian patterns and other exotic prints. Frank was the only one wearing spiders on his bathing suit.

Immediately the suggestion was made to go to the pool, and the boys took off at a run for it. Frank had little time for resistance or to discuss diarrhea; he was caught up in the surge of his friends toward the water.

The boys jumped into the shallow water, which came up to their waists. All around them classmates were already in the pool. Frank forgot about his worries and enjoyed the game of water tag that broke out there in the four-foot depths.

"Let's go the diving board," Charlie said, and he expertly swam to the side of the pool, climbed out, and started a half-run to the board as the lifeguard blew a whistle and told him to stop running. Watching the other boys hurriedly follow Charlie's lead, Frank thought he might just puke. And he stood in the water—frozen.

Pete Yancey looked back over his shoulder and went back to Frank.

"Let's jump off the diving board," he said.

"I can't swim," Frank whispered, not wanting anyone to hear him. He was unaware that Lester had moved behind him in the water.

"Jump off to the side, and you'll have just a little ways to go to that ladder," Pete said, nodding his head toward the ladder.

Frank took a big deep breath and shook his head that he didn't want to do it. Just at that moment, Charlie stood on the edge of the diving board, screamed like Tarzan, and jumped into the water, making a big splash.

"I don't swim so well either," Lester said. "But I'll go with you, Frank. We can do it together."

Pete said, "I'll jump before you guys. I'll be over at the ladder. If you get in trouble, I'll jump in and save you. I swim pretty well."

"Maybe you could just call the lifeguard," Frank said, smiling nervously. The lifeguard was the beautiful teenaged girl who had attempted to teach him swimming lessons.

Frank knew deep within himself that he was going to get out of the pool and dive off the diving board. It was going to happen whether he could swim or not. It was time, and there were no more excuses. He had to do it. He had to conquer it.

But he felt sick.

He followed Pete and Lester toward the tall ladder of the high dive. Jack, who had already jumped from the diving board, ran out of the pool area to find his mama at the picnic grounds. She had to see Frank jump from the diving board or perhaps drown.

The boys got to the diving board, and Pete started climbing up the ladder of the high dive. When he was halfway up, Lester nudged Frank, who began climbing the ladder.

Frank had watched enough old Westerns to know what a hanging looked like. He had often imagined what those men thought as they climbed up the steps to the gallows. Well, now he knew what they were thinking – fear and panic. He was weak in the knees, felt his head spinning, and thought he was going to be sick. Lester had held back, remembering whispered conversations about diarrhea.

Frank reached the top of the diving board and held on for dear life. Pete walked out to the end, turned around, and said, "Watch me. Jump where I jump, and then just dog-paddle over to the ladder. You'll be fine. I'll be watching."

Pete was gone. Frank heard a splash. He peeked over to see Pete swimming to the ladder close by. Lester gave him a nudge in the back, and Frank started forward, sliding his hands along the diving board's rail and shuffling his feet as if he were marching toward the end of his life. He got to the end of the diving board and looked to the side to see Pete sitting on the edge of the pool. Jack sat down beside Pete to watch.

Frank noticed a strange look on Jack's face.

Jack then shouted, "You have Vienna sausage on your bathing suit!" Pete began laughing, too, as Jack leaned in, telling Pete about Frank eating a whole can of Vienna sausages on the way to the party.

Frank looked down to brush the Vienna sausage off his bathing suit.

But there was no Vienna sausage on Frank's bathing suit.

The designers of Frank's new "dirty white" bathing suit had apparently never put the fabric in water to test the fabric's transparency. While those designers had ensured the fabric's print included black spiders, not one of those black spiders was in the prime location on a boy's bathing suit.

Frank stared down in horror. His tallywacker was on display through the fabric of his bathing suit. For just a moment he was amazed at how much it looked like a Vienna sausage.

As Frank stood in frozen horror, looking at the crotch of his suit, Jack realized that he had mistaken Frank's pecker for a Vienna sausage. An explosion of laughter came as Jack Wilcox threw himself back on the concrete and laughed so hard his feet were kicking.

"Jump!" Pete shouted, laughing now himself. "For goodness' sake, jump!"

Frank had no choice. He had to jump because all heads were now turning toward the diving board. He jumped and crashed into the water, flailing at the air before he reached the surface. As he bobbed to the top of the water, he made out Pete at the ladder, floundered to it, and felt his strong friend grab him by the hand.

"Got you!" Pete said.

Frank grabbed the ladder and said, "I can't get out of the pool. Will you get me a towel?"

"You're right; you can't get out of the pool," Pete said, and he handed his friend a towel that belonged to someone else but was the closest available.

Frank climbed up the ladder and wrapped the towel around himself before running to the bathroom. He completely ignored the lifeguard's whistle and command to stop running. He wasn't stopping. She might have been pretty, but he was in a crisis.

Lester crashed into the water as Frank climbed out of it, and Lester's size caused a splash so big that attention was distracted from Frank's bathing suit. Pete and Lester followed their friend to the bathroom, finding Frank working feverishly to dry himself with the towel so that his bathing suit was again opaque.

Frank looked at his two friends and began to chuckle, giving Lester and Pete the freedom to laugh out loud, and within minutes they were all laughing. Jack had appeared in the bathroom, too, and he was laughing so hard there were tears in his eyes.

As the four boys walked out of the cinder-block bathroom, Frank's bathing suit had dried so that it was no longer transparent. Frank was relieved that he had escaped *everyone* at the pool seeing his exposure at the top of the high dive. He and his friends were starting toward Janet when she called them over to where she was sitting.

As the boys walked toward Janet, they heard a voice from the lifeguard stand. It was the beautiful instructor. "You did it, Frank! You swam in the deep end!"

Frank's face turned as red as Jack's bathing suit.

TWENTY-SEVEN

THE GEORGIA BULLDOGS

Charlie had disappeared for a week over the summer, attending a football camp sponsored by the University of Georgia Bulldogs in nearby Athens. Frank was glad no one had suggested he go off to summer camp. He had been to 4-H camp the year before, enjoyed it, satisfied his camp-going experience, and did not feel the need to attend another summer camp. He was perfectly content visiting the Acorn County Library, checking out a book or five, and sitting under one of the large oak trees on the farm. That was summer camp enough.

When Charlie returned home from the camp, he was wearing a Georgia Bulldogs camp T-shirt and told Frank all that had happened at the camp, day-by-day. Frank was glad for his friend but was equally glad Tom and Janet had not suggested he go slog around at a football camp during the middle of the summer. Frank was happy to read about football and let everyone else do the sweating.

Charlie had more information from his visit to Athens. "Did you know the Boy Scouts work at all the Georgia football games?" he asked Frank.

"What do you mean by work?" Frank asked him.

"One day, we were all in this meeting," Charlie said. "Someone came in and asked if any of us were in scouts. They said Boy Scouts are invited to come to the games and help out. They said you get in the games for free, and you get a free sandwich for lunch."

"We haven't joined Boy Scouts yet," Frank said. "You have to be in seventh grade."

Charlie shook his head. "I think you just need to have a uniform and look like you are in the seventh grade."

"All that trouble for a sandwich?" Frank asked him.

Frank didn't think much more about his conversation with Charlie until the telephone rang one night on Brookwood Road, and Janet called him to the telephone.

The caller was Mr. Ed Otwell, who owned and operated a small appliance-repair shop just off the courthouse square in Acorn. Besides repairing small appliances, Mr. Otwell also repaired bicycles, lawnmowers, and other small engines. But Mr. Otwell was more than the local fix-it man. He was the revered former scoutmaster of Boy Scout Troop 39. It was he who had built the successful troop and turned it over to Mr. Jim Scully, who had gone on to make the troop legendary throughout North Georgia. Mr. Otwell had been the scoutmaster when Charlie's daddy was in scouts.

Frank, like every other Cub Scout in Acorn, knew Mr. Otwell, if not personally then by legend. Frank also knew the Otwells from church.

"Now that you and Charlie Keller are becoming Boy Scouts, I'd like for you to go with me to Athens on Saturdays to the Georgia games," Mr. Otwell said through the telephone. "You will need to wear your scout uniform, and you will serve as an usher at Sanford Stadium until halftime. Then you can sit and watch the rest of the game."

Janet knew why Mr. Otwell was calling, and she was watching to see the excitement on Frank's face when he learned of the invitation.

"I don't think I want to go," Frank said.

"Are you sure?" Mr. Otwell asked him, surprised.

"I'm sure," Frank said. "Thank you for calling me." He hung up the telephone and looked up to see his mama. Janet's eyes appeared to be on fire, and Frank knew he had not done what she expected him to do. Frank did not possess his mama's mind-reading capabilities.

"You may be the laziest boy on the face of this earth," she said. "You pick up that telephone, call Mr. Otwell, and tell him that you will be happy to go work at the Georgia games."

Frank held up a book he was reading about the Green Bay Packers and pointed to it, indicating that his Saturday-morning plans included reading and not traveling to Athens at 6:30 a.m. to work at a football game.

Janet was about to unload on him when the telephone rang, and Frank picked it up.

It was Charlie.

"You told him that you didn't want to go?" Charlie shouted. "Are you crazy? Call him back before he invites one of the Wehunt brothers and I'm stuck with them for the entire day. Call him back!"

Beaten up on two fronts, Frank called Mr. Otwell and told the former scoutmaster that he had experienced a change of heart and would be glad to go help out at the Georgia football games.

There was only one significant problem, however. Neither Frank nor Charlie was in Boy Scouts officially. They were Webelos, which was a two-year scouting program between Cub Scouts and Boy Scouts. Tom called it "Boy Scout training," where would-be Boy Scouts camped and hiked with their dads so that when they became Boy Scouts, they would know what to do.

Janet had to call around and find a Boy Scout uniform that Frank could both borrow and fit into for these Saturday trips to Athens during the fall.

"I think this is all illegal," Frank said, staring at himself in the full-length bathroom mirror. On the left sleeve, written in black marker, was the name of the uniform's previous owner, Bob. "What if we have to show some kind of Boy Scout identification and we don't have it? Who is Bob?"

"I honestly don't think anyone will care, but you will let Mr. Otwell worry about any lying that needs to be done," she said. "He is in charge, and if he thought this was wrong, he wouldn't have invited you to go." Frank stared at his mama. He was pretty sure deceit wasn't the Boy Scout way.

Charlie had no reservations about borrowing an illicit Boy Scout uniform and going to the games. He had tasted Georgia football, and Athens, Georgia, was calling his name to return however he could get to her.

On the morning of that first game, Frank spent the night with Charlie in Acorn so they could get up, get dressed, and easily meet Mr. Otwell at the repair store in town. When they arrived, Mr. Otwell was already there with another assistant scoutmaster. There were no other boys—not even a Wehunt. It was just Charlie and Frank.

Riding through Buford, on the way to Athens, Frank nudged Charlie and pointed to the golden arches of a brand-new McDonald's restaurant. Both of the boys had seen all the McDonald's commercials on television, but neither of them had ever visited one of the restaurants. It was a new mistress, beckoning the boys away from the tried-and-true, and always dependable, Dairy Queen.

"I would love to go there," Frank said of the McDonald's. "The people on the McDonald's commercials seem so friendly. I would like to see if the chocolate shakes are as good as Dairy Queen's shakes."

Charlie said he had heard that McDonald's food was not as good as the Dairy Queen, but he agreed that it would be nice to try it and find out.

Hearing the boys discuss food, Mr. Otwell said over his shoulder, "We'll stop on the way home at the Dairy Queen in Winder." From Acorn to Buford to Winder, by way of Hog Mountain Road, Mr. Otwell drove to Athens; and, to the boys' surprise, he drove into a neighborhood and stopped in front of an older, but quite nice, brick home.

"This is where my daughter lives," he said. "We are going to go inside for a cup of coffee. You boys stay here in the car and wait on us." Charlie and Frank watched the two scoutmasters walk up a sidewalk and go into the house.

"Do you suppose she's pretty?" Frank asked Charlie. "His daughter, I mean. Do you suppose she's pretty?"

"I don't know," Charlie said. "Why do think he made us stay out here?"

"Probably because we are fake Boy Scouts and he doesn't want us exposed," Frank said, chuckling. "I guess my name for the day is going to be Bob."

They waited for as long as they could in the hot car, and then they finally got out and stood around the car. It was a quiet little neighborhood except for the neighbor's dog that barked at them without stopping. They found fun in throwing acorns at the dog, who saw this as a game and only barked louder.

"Hey now, what are you boys doing?" Mr. Otwell asked, walking outside his daughter's house. "Stop aggravating that dog." He went back inside, and the two boys waited some more.

Frank was getting aggravated at this waiting. This was time he could have been playing on a Saturday morning.

When they all loaded back in the car, Mr. Otwell drove to the university campus and parallel parked along Baxter Street within sight of the football stadium. It was not difficult to parallel park before the games, but more than once Mr. Otwell struggled to free his car from the parking spaces after the game. He might bump a car in front or back before finally getting his car out in traffic. If he did bump a car, he would always give a moan or a sigh, but it never stopped him.

After parking, Mr. Otwell took Charlie and Frank to Memorial Hall, just beside Sanford Stadium in the heart of campus. Inside this large student center was the Bulldog Room, which was a small student café. Frank had two chocolate-covered donuts and two cartons of milk for breakfast. Charlie had his own breakfast, and the two boys sat together while Mr. Otwell and his assistant scoutmaster sat at another table reading the morning's *Atlanta Constitution*.

When a pretty coed smiled at Frank and gave him a wink, Frank nudged Charlie and said, "That girl winked at me. That means she likes us."

Charlie laughed. "Bob, she probably thinks we look funny in these uniforms."

"I don't care what she thinks," Frank said. "A wink and a smile is a wink and a smile."

By 10:00 a.m. it was time to go inside the stadium. Through a special entrance underneath the Sanford Drive Bridge, the boys joined with other scouts from all across north Georgia and went inside the stadium. They walked alongside the famous hedges that separated the seating from the field and then took seats in the south section of the stands. An important scout leader from the North Georgia Council led them in the Pledge of Allegiance and a prayer and then gave directions on what and what not to do while serving as an usher.

Frank was paying close attention because he wanted to know the details of the instructions. Charlie leaned against his shoulder and went to sleep, mumbling, "Just tell me what to do when it's time to do it." He burped, and Frank frowned at the sour smell of Charlie's breakfast.

The scouting official said, "Now, boys, this is important. Some of the fans will be drinking alcohol and might sit in someone's seat. If an argument or a fight breaks out, Boy Scouts should not get involved—they should hurry to the top of the section and find a police officer like Mr. Warner here." An Athens police officer waved his hand.

Frank stared at the Boy Scout leader in stunned silence. Drinking? Fighting? Police? Frank hated to break the news to this important Boy Scout leader from Commerce, Georgia, but he had absolutely no intention of getting involved in anyone else's fight. As far as he was concerned, people could sit where they wanted, drink what they wanted, and fight when they wanted, and if the police got involved, that was their business. Frank might have been the worst possible usher in the history of Georgia football.

After the awkward speech about fan violence, the scouts were served a box lunch that included potato chips, a cookie, and a sandwich referred to as a Georgia Bulldog Sandwich. It was two pieces of white bread, a thin layer of mayonnaise on one slice and a thin layer of mustard on the other slice. Between the two slices of bread were a piece of ham and a piece of yellow cheese. That was it. Frank loved it and made his own Georgia Bulldog Sandwiches for the rest of his life.

Charlie and Frank were not the worst ushers in the history of Georgia football. Once the fans started coming into the stadium, Frank and Charlie enjoyed serving as ushers. It was fun. Most of the fans knew where they were sitting, but occasionally the boys were able to help someone find a seat. They also helped older people manage the steps of the stadium.

Then there was the man with the purple face.

Frank tried to hide his shock and then tried not to turn away when he was approached by an older man leading a younger man who wore sunglasses. The younger man also had a purple face—as violet as any purple Easter egg Frank had ever seen. The younger man also had no hair on his head but wore a baseball camp awkwardly turned at an angle.

"Son, can you help us find our seats?" the older man asked, and Frank took his two tickets. With the pair behind him, Frank led the two men down the steep steps of the stadium aisle. Frank found the row, and then he counted off the seats. Two younger men were already in the seats. Frank double-checked the tickets he was holding as the older man and his ward stood behind him in the aisle.

It was hot as hell in the September sun of this late summer day in Athens, and Frank was sweating inside Bob's Boy Scout uniform. He took a big breath and stepped into the row where the two trespassers were sitting.

"Excuse me; you may be sitting in the wrong seats," he said. "Can I see your tickets?"

One of them whipped around to face Frank. "Get the hell out of here, kid. Go do a good turn daily." He laughed, his friend laughed, and two cute girls laughed, too.

Frank stood his ground. "I think you are in their seats," he said, pointing over his shoulder at the men behind him.

"I don't give a damn," the young man said. "There are plenty of seats around here. Go find them another one."

Frank turned to the two men he was escorting. "Wait right here," he said. "I'll go get someone to help us."

The older of the two men being escorted said, "Hey, buddy, just check your tickets, and we will get this all worked out."

"Go to hell," the trespassing man said.

The older man and the young trespasser began yelling at each other as other fans around them tried to serve as peacemakers. Frank ran up the stairs, found an Athens police officer, and said, "I need you."

The police officer followed Frank down the aisle to the escalating altercation.

"All right, son," the officer said. "Go back up and help some others. I'll get this straightened out."

Within minutes, the police officer had restored order, the hateful fans had been moved, and the older man and his ward had been seated. As the officer walked back up to where Frank stood, he said, "Good job, son."

At the end of the game's halftime, the scouts were released from duty and could sit wherever there was a vacant seat for the remainder of the game. Charlie was disappointed that year because the Georgia Bulldogs finished 5–5. The next year, behind quarterback Andy Johnson and running back Jimmy Poulos, the Bulldogs were 11–1, beating Georgia Tech in Atlanta and then winning the Gator Bowl. Frank wasn't as crazy about the Bulldogs as Charlie, but he was sure becoming a fan of the red and black.

With five minutes left in the game, Mr. Otwell came to find the boys. This was their disappointing cue to leave the stadium in advance of the crowd, get to their car, and easily get out of Athens for the ride home. They listened to the remainder of the game on WSB Radio 750 out of Atlanta.

As they left Athens and signs of Winder, Georgia came into view, Mr. Otwell said, "I believe we'll stop at the Dairy Queen up here and eat supper before we go on home."

Frank had experienced enough for one day. He had reached his limit. He was wearing a borrowed Scout uniform worn by someone named Bob, he had gotten up at 6:00 a.m. on a Saturday, he had been forced to sit in a hot car and wait around a stranger's home, he had only eaten two chocolate-covered donuts and a single ham-and-cheese sandwich, he had been caught in the middle between two fans fussing over the same set of seats, and he had been forced to leave the football game five minutes before it was over. On top of all of that, his underwear was soaked with sweat and beginning to rub his ass raw.

"Mr. Otwell," he said, "I either want to stop at the McDonald's in Buford, or I want to go home. I don't want to stop at the Dairy Queen in Winder. We can eat at Dairy Queen in Acorn."

Charlie, who was drinking from a can of Coca-Cola, gagged and spat at the same time in the backseat of Mr. Otwell's car. He began chuckling to himself and punched Frank in the side. Approaching the Dairy Queen, Mr. Otwell punched the gas a little and sped on past it, aggravated at the interruption in plans.

In an hour, Frank was sitting across from Charlie in a booth at the new McDonald's restaurant in Buford, Georgia. They each had two cheeseburgers, French fries, a fried apple pie, and a chocolate shake.

When Frank attended his first University of Georgia game as a student in the fall of 1977, he walked over to the south stands and stood for a few minutes at the top of the section where he and Charlie had served for three years as Boy Scout ushers, following Mr. Otwell's itinerary every Saturday. Well, they had followed his itinerary except for one part—every Saturday they stopped at the McDonald's in Buford. Standing there, Frank smiled at the memories and thought for a minute that he could taste one of those Georgia Bulldog sandwiches.

Twenty-Eight

Strange Brew

Having successfully launched the annual Acorn County Fair, the local Jaycees and Jaycettes organizations turned their attention to other projects that helped the general Acorn County area. One of those projects was sponsoring the county's Junior Miss Pageant for twelfth-grade girls at Acorn County High School. Another project was the Acorn County Talent Show, which promised to bring together area talent to compete for a recording session at Lefevre Sound Studios in Atlanta.

Because their parents were actively involved in the Jaycees and Jaycettes, Frank and Charlie—and their siblings—were in constant tow for all the organization's community events. During the fair week, the children went after school, did their homework together, and then played throughout the fairgrounds until it was time to go home. During the last week's rehearsals and stage prep for the Junior Miss Pageant, the Wilcox and Keller children were right in the thick of things at the Acorn County High School gymnasium. Frank and Charlie loved the Junior Miss Pageant and had to be run off more than once for hanging around too closely with the contestants. When it came time for the countywide talent show, Frank and Charlie were also in the shadows as their parents made preparations and assisted with the setup.

The night of the talent show, neither Frank nor Charlie was particularly interested in any of the acts, which included a variety of Gospel-singing quartets, a musical juggling act by a World War II veteran, a banjo band with all six members playing the banjo, a dour man dressed in all black and playing songs about prison, a small ensemble from the award-winning high-school band, a dance band from nearby Gainesville, cloggers and square dancers, and a woman attempting to be the Grand Ole Opry's Minnie Pearl. For sure, there was a lot of toe tapping that Saturday night in the Acorn County High School gymnasium, but Frank and Charlie weren't having any of it. They were too busy sneaking popcorn and Cokes from the concession stands when their mamas weren't watching, and they had attached themselves to some girls they knew from school. Sitting in dark corners of the bleachers, the farthest point from the noisy stage, was the perfect spot for sixth-grade boys and girls trying to figure out the delicate art of flirting while eating stolen popcorn.

As the show reached its final few acts, Tom Wilcox found his wayward oldest son and called him from his group of peers. He gave Frank quiet instructions to begin walking around the gymnasium, picking up trash so that cleanup after the show would be much easier. Charlie's daddy was with Tom, calling his Charlie to trash duty as well.

Nothing could kill a flirtatious rendezvous in the school gymnasium like being called to janitorial duty. No sooner had Charlie and Frank said "We'll be right back" than the girls had gone and found another group of boys to flirt with. Frank and Charlie began picking up trash and putting it in large trash buckets given to them by their daddies.

"Swing low, sweet chariot," Charlie began quietly singing the spiritual learned through Scouts. The scouts often sang together while working outdoors on conservation projects. "Comin' for to carry me home, swing low, sweet chariot, coming for to carry me home." Frank laughed at his friend, who was trudging along behind him. They had worked themselves around to a corner nearest the stage.

Frank sat down on the bleachers, and Charlie sat beside him. They stared at the stage.

Guy Sharpe, the weatherman at WAGA Channel 5 television in Atlanta, was the celebrity master of ceremonies for the show. He was winding down the evening before introducing the show's last act, thanking the Jaycees for having him up for the evening and complimenting the crowd on being hospitable and supportive of all the acts. Then he introduced the last act—three local brothers from Acorn County.

Strange Brew.

Just the name alone caught Charlie and Frank's attention, and both boys sat up as the curtain opened on the three brothers. The stage exploded with a cover of Eddie Cochran's "Summertime Blues."

I'm gonna raise a fuss, I'm gonna raise a holler

About a-workin' all summer just to try to earn a dollar.

Every time I call my baby, and ask to get a date,

My boss says, "No dice, son; you gotta work late."

Sometimes I wonder what I'm a gonna do,

But there ain't no cure for the summertime blues.

Frank and Charlie stared at the scene before them. People on the back rows were up dancing, and many others stood while clapping and cheering. Frank and Charlie had never seen anything like this in their entire lives—all eleven years of them.

When Strange Brew finished playing, the gym erupted in applause. The dance band from Gainesville—one of the best-known dance bands in north Georgia—had been the odds-on favorite to win the competition. But that was before the judges heard the local boys from down in the south end of Acorn County. It took only a few minutes for the judges to report a tie between the Gainesville band and Strange Brew. Both bands would get a recording session in Atlanta.

The gym erupted again. Guy Sharpe was getting nervous and was glad he had thanked the crowd before Strange Brew closed the show. He made a hasty retreat from the gymnasium back to safety in Atlanta.

Frank turned to Charlie and said, "We need to start our own band."

Charlie, recalling Frank's second-grade attempt at playing guitar, looked at Frank to see if his friend was serious and then, realizing he was, said, "That's fine, Frank, but we don't play instruments."

"I don't care," Frank said. "We need to start our own band."

Frank still thought of himself as a guitar player on the sole basis that he owned one. He was still in and out of guitar lessons, never practicing and not especially caring how he sounded. He just liked to strum and sing away without a care. Tom and Janet still had the slimmest of hopes he would be a musician, but Frank was moving on to a different instrument altogether—the Royal Arrow Typewriter.

As soon as Frank could invite Charlie to Brookwood Road to play, he did so, and along with Jack, the boys went into the basement, where Frank planned to hatch his own rock-and-roll band. In the basement, Frank had his guitar and the drum kit that R. C. Wilcox had purchased for the boys. The drum kit had a bass, a snare drum, and a crash cymbal.

Charlie stared in disbelief and then collapsed on the basement's concrete floor, laughing so hard his glasses came off his head.

"Frank, you are insane," he screamed out. "You don't play the guitar, and Jack doesn't play the drums. And, in this band, what do you think I'm going to do? Dance?" Frank and Jack were laughing, too.

"I thought you could play the drums," Frank said to Charlie, "and Jack here can play the bottles."

Charlie was laughing so hard he began crawling to the basement door, hoping he could get outside to gulp in fresh air before he passed out from laughing.

"What are the bottles?" he screamed.

Frank pointed to a line of glass Coca-Cola bottles he had retrieved from his grandfather's meat-packing plant. He had filled them with water at varying levels so that they made different musical notes.

"I saw these at the fair," he said. "A man was playing 'Dixie' on them." Frank took one of the drumsticks and began tapping out a tune that wasn't really a tune at all.

"I'm not playing the bottles," Jack said. "I'm playing the drums. They are *my drums*."

Most bands had internal problems within the first year. Frank's band was having problems before instruments were even assigned—before it even had a name.

It was finally settled that Charlie would be the band's drummer on most songs, with Jack getting to be the drummer for at least one song. Whoever wasn't playing the drums would tap away on the bottles.

Charlie sat in amazement of Frank's confidence that indeed this would ever, ever be any kind of musical band. He smiled on the verge of laughing when he asked, "Frank, what songs are we going to play?"

"I was thinking," Frank began as Charlie began chuckling to himself, "that we would take basic nursery rhymes and speed them up like rock-and-roll songs."

Jack dropped his head. "Like 'Mary Had a Little Lamb'?"

"Right," Frank said. "We could also take some of those old patriotic songs we learned in fifth grade and speed them up."

Tears were coming to Charlie's eyes. "Like 'When Johnny Comes Marching Home Again'?"

"Right," Frank said.

Charlie ran out of the basement and fell into the grass of the backyard. Jack followed him. The two boys laughed so loud that one of the Wilcox cocker spaniels began howling.

Frank rubbed his eyes as he walked toward the open basement door. Leadership was hell.

Janet Wilcox had eavesdropped on what was happening in the basement, and while she thought Frank's band plans were indeed ridiculous, she was excited that he was thinking about music. She told Tom about it, and the two of them hatched a plan to take Frank to a concert at the Atlanta Civic Center. If he had been wowed by the brothers of Strange Brew, he would be even more impressed at a live concert at the civic center.

When she broke the news to Frank, he was indeed enthusiastic, and even more so when Janet told him he could invite his best friend, Charlie.

"Do you want to go to a concert?" Frank asked his friend, and Charlie, thinking as Frank did, that this would be a concert with musicians similar to Strange Brew, eagerly agreed to go. It was going to be their first rock-and-roll concert.

Except that what Tom and Janet had planned was not a rock-and-roll concert.

It was a concert featuring guitar legend Chet Akins, age forty-seven; piano legend Floyd Cramer, age thirty-seven; and saxophone legend Boots Randolph, age forty-four. All three members of the very popular "Nashville Sound" wore suits. Strange to two eleven-year-olds, yes, but Strange Brew they were not.

Just after an intermission, both Frank and Charlie were asleep, leaning against each other in the middle section of the Atlanta Civic Center. They woke toward the end of the concert to hear Boots Randolph play his famous song "Yakety Sax." Tom and Janet stopped by the Varsity Drive-In near Georgia Tech University on the way home.

Over a chili cheeseburger and a frosted orange, Charlie put a hand on his friend's shoulder and said, "Seriously, Frank, we are never going to have a rock-and-roll band. Never. But we can still enjoy the music."

Frank nodded in agreement. Janet was already pitching the idea of a concert by Herb Alpert and the Tijuana Brass.

In five years, Frank and Charlie, as students at Acorn County High School, attended regular Friday-night dances in the school cafeteria. More often than not, the live band at those dances was a familiar one. Strange Brew had changed its name to simply The Estes Brothers, reflecting the last name of the three brothers, and the expanded band became the hometown rock-and-roll heroes to a generation of young people growing up in Acorn County.

Later, as a student at the University of Georgia, Frank was president of his dormitory and on two occasions hired The Estes Brothers to play at outdoor university dances. As friends and fellow students fell in love with the band from Acorn County, Frank stood back and smiled, fondly remembering the night these brothers introduced Charlie and him to rock and roll.

Twenty-Nine

The Wolf Man

Acorn Junior High School had long held one of the most popular Halloween carnivals in Acorn County. Located in the center of the county, the old school building—once the high school—was easily accessed from all the county's borders. The property itself—with a gymnasium, wide hallways, and larger classrooms—was an easy venue for creating a Halloween carnival.

The Wilcox brothers were no strangers to the Halloween carnival; they often attended because their Mema was on a forced march to work the carnival with all other faculty. Tom and Janet usually piled their boys into the Ford Galaxie 500, and now the Ford station wagon, and drove the ten miles to Acorn. The small-town atmosphere of the carnival was so safe that children could gather with friends, disappear from parents, and enjoy the games and activities as traveling packs around the school property.

In the old gymnasium, there was usually a live band such as The Sawnee Mountain Quartet or The Shakerag Boys from down near Brookwood Road. It was not unusual for people to break into square dancing or a quick box step in the middle of the gym. One of the gym's basketball goals provided opportunity to shoot baskets for prizes; making three of four shots earned a small bag of candy corn. There was usually a parade of costumes as children—and a few adults—walked around the perimeter of the gym floor as Principal Garland Shoemake, Librarian Eunice Bright, and Custodian Junefly Adams chose a handful of winners. The prize was a homemade cake or pecan pie—nothing store bought.

In the school cafeteria, the lunchroom ladies sold and served a hotdog supper with slaw, potato chips, and Coca-Cola products. Each of the ladies was dressed in her own variation of a wicked-witch costume, though occasionally the theme of the year might be clowns. Some years, there was confusion, with some ladies dressed as witches and others dressed as clowns—and sometimes the clown costumes were scarier.

Then there were the classrooms, where patrons could drop a dime or a quarter and participate in activities such as a movie room, featuring old Three Stooges movie shorts; a fishing room, where patrons dropped a fishing line behind a curtain and pulled back a prize such as a baseball card; and a cakewalk room, where the prize was a homemade cake. Frank loved the cakewalk room and always made his way there for a chance at his Mema's chocolate layer cake.

Carolyn Holmes often managed the cakewalk room, and she ran a pretty standard cakewalk, which worked a lot like musical chairs. Chairs were put in a circle. Music was played as contestants walked around behind the chairs. When the music stopped, players jumped in a chair. Unfortunately, there was always one fewer chair than there were players. Whoever didn't have a seat was out of the game. A chair was removed for the next round. With each walk around the circle, the circle grew smaller until there were two contestants and one chair. Whoever got to the chair first when the music stopped won a homemade cake.

Frank so desperately wanted to win his grandmother's cake that she began making two of them, giving him one just to stay away from the cakewalk and have fun with his friends and family.

As new sixth graders at the junior high school, Frank and his friends had been privileged to watch as the Halloween carnival plans came together. This year, there was going to be a new addition to the festivities—one borrowed from some of the churches around the county. The Halloween carnival was going to feature a haunted house.

Mrs. Eunice Bright almost had a nervous breakdown when she first learned her precious library was going to be the scene of a haunted-house attraction. The Baptists and Methodists had been offering haunted houses as fundraisers for youth ministry for quite some time, but her Pentecostal Holiness roots saw anything glorifying ghosts and goblins as a direct portal straight to hell. Being required to work at the Halloween carnival was bad enough, but now she saw her library violated by it. As a judge for the costume contest, over in the gymnasium, she never voted for a child dressed as a monster, but if a child came dressed as Moses or the giant slayer David, that child had a good shot of getting Mrs. Bright's vote.

Inside the library, tables and chairs were removed, opening up the large room. Large refrigerator boxes were taped together, creating a crawl-through tunnel that occasionally opened into a dimly lit space where costumed monsters might be at work or play. Eerie music was played on a record player, and teachers moaned and groaned in the darkness for effect.

Frank had agreed to meet his friends Charlie, Pete Yancey, and Wendell Mann at the Halloween carnival. The foursome met in the gymnasium, which was already loud and chaotic as families poured inside for music, dancing, and the costume contest. It was easy for parents to sit in the bleachers and visit while their children played together on the hardwood basketball court.

Charlie had dressed as a farmer, which meant he had on the overalls and red bandana he wore each year during the Fourth of July parade. Pete had dressed as a football player, borrowing the high-school uniform of his older sister's boyfriend. Wendell had dressed as a soldier, calling himself Sergeant Rock, after the DC Comics hero. Wendell still wanted the boys to call him Rock, but it was a nickname that just never stuck.

Frank had finally shed his Wolf Man costume, dressing as a pirate. He had torn up some old clothes, tied one of his mama's red scarves around his head, and put on some of her older jewelry. In a bathrobe belt tied around his waist, he stuck the cap gun Jack had gotten at the Christmas party the year before.

"Are you a pirate or a gypsy woman?" Wendell asked, shaking as he laughed and that caused Pete Yancey to laugh even louder. Wendell began calling Frank Captain, and that was a nickname that never stuck either.

"Frank," a voice came from the bleachers. It was Tom. "Be back here in two hours, and don't make me come looking for you." Frank nodded that he understood, and he knew better than to test his daddy, who truthfully did not want to be there with all the crowd and its noise.

The four friends looked around the noisy gym, and Frank suggested they go to the cafeteria for food. They bolted out the front door of the gym and ran across the front parking lot to the school's entrance. Each of them had a pocket of quarters to fund his hot-dog supper and the different games set up in the classrooms.

In the hot-dog supper line, Pete Yancey flirted with some of the cafeteria ladies he knew from church. One of them, dressed as a clown this year, came from the serving line to give Pete a hug, and Frank started moving as fast as he could through the line, fearful that he might be next.

The boys sat down at a table together, and Pete waved at a friend, Nancy, whose daddy was a Shriner with Pete's daddy. Seeing Nancy brought up memories of another Halloween when the boys from Den 8 had trick-or-treated in Nancy's neighborhood.

"Her sister scared the daylights out of us," Charlie said. "I had to run across the street to Mrs. Curtis's house and use the bathroom so I wouldn't pee all over myself."

"I think you peed in their shrubbery," Pete said, laughing, and Charlie thought for a moment and agreed with him.

* * *

That Halloween night, Nancy's house had been dark and quiet. All the houses around it were lit, as neighbors expected children to come trick-or-treating. It was Frank who led the scouts up to Nancy's house and knocked on the door.

"No one is home," Charlie said, moving up to stand beside Frank. "Let's go. They must be away." But no sooner had Charlie said those words than the front door mysteriously began to open, and what stood before them was the scariest witch in all of Acorn, shrieking at the boys in her yard.

Frank turned and jumped on Lester Freemont, hoping his larger friend could protect him. Travis Jackson was so surprised by the shrieking that he dumped his candy on the sidewalk. As Cub Scout anarchy unfolded, a porch light came on, and Nancy's entire family poured out, laughing and handing out candy to the terrified scouts.

Later, at Charlie's house, the boys of Den 8 laughed over the neighborhood prank, but all felt it a shame that Nancy's older sister, one of the prettiest girls in all of Acorn, had to dress up like an ugly witch. It was just a shame.

* * *

"Are you going to the haunted house?" Nancy asked her friends, and the boys said it was part of their plans for enjoying the Halloween carnival.

"I saw the line all the way down the hallway," Pete said. "It must be pretty popular."

Frank wasn't paying much attention to the conversation. He was staring across the cafeteria, watching a boy sitting all alone. The boy wasn't wearing a costume unless you called an old black leather jacket a costume. This was no ordinary boy. This was Van Piper.

Since the start of this sixth-grade year, Frank had rarely seen Van and wasn't completely sure Van was attending school. He had a heard rumor that Van was sent back to Alto Correctional Institute for stealing; there was also a rumor he had been sent to Vietnam. There was another rumor he was dead or had killed someone, depending on who told the story.

Frank got up to empty his tray in a trash can. He then walked over to where Van was sitting. He sat down, safely, across the table from his fifth-grade nemesis. Van looked up.

"Hey," he said. "You want something? Did you come over here to stab me?"

"I just haven't seen you around and wondered if you were in school," Frank said.

"Yep," he said. "Your grandmother is one of my teachers. She's a nice woman." He kept eating a plate full of hot dogs. There was no question; Van was hitting puberty far ahead of his classmates. Frank swore he could see a beard starting to grow—unusual for any sixth grader.

"Are you here by yourself?" Frank asked him.

"Drove myself here," Van said. "I drove my daddy's old motorcycle."

"Do you have a license?" Frank asked him.

"No," Van said, now staring at Frank. "What the hell are you supposed to be? A woman?"

"I'm a pirate," Frank said, suddenly ashamed he had dressed up at all. He got up, started walking away, and then turned back.

"Me and my friends are about to go visit the haunted house, if you want to hang around with us," Frank said.

Van seemed to be using his tongue to work a piece of hot dog from between his back teeth. He looked past Frank to see the other boys, shook his head OK, and stood up from the table. Van walked away from his tray, leaving it for someone else to clean up. He followed Frank back over to where Charlie, Pete, and Wendell sat. Their eyes were wide, and Wendell was mouthing something that looked like "What are you doing?"

"Van is going to go with us to the haunted house," Frank said. Pete rolled his eyes.

Wendell, who was now standing behind Frank, whispered in his ear, "You have just invited a known felon to crawl through refrigerator boxes with us. What if he decides to take out revenge on you in those boxes? You'll be trapped. He'll kill you."

Frank figured it much differently. If Van wanted him dead, he was pretty sure he would already be dead, and if Van wanted to kill him, it would probably not be at the school's Halloween carnival. Van would just ride the old motorcycle to The Sewing Shop, call Frank out on Main Street, and kill him right there in grand fashion.

The five boys joined the line forming to the library. Frank kept up the small talk with Van while his three friends sometimes looked over a shoulder to make sure Frank was still among the living.

At the library doorway, each boy dropped a quarter in an old coffee can and entered through a slit in a dark curtain covering the doorway. A vampire, which resembled Mr. Williams, a sixth-grade teacher, pointed to the refrigerator-box entrance. Charlie, Pete, Wendell, Van, and Frank entered in that order. They had crawled just a little ways when Charlie stopped and shouted, "I got some bad news for you boys. I just farted, and it was a good one." Fumes filled the refrigerator box.

216

The boys kept crawling through the boxes down the length of the library. Wendell kept slapping Pete on the ass, telling him, "Hurry up; crawl faster," while Charlie kept shouting back, "Sorry about that one, boys."

They exited the boxes in a far corner of the library. A bright light came on that blinded them, and a ghost, obviously an adult underneath a sheet, hopped around and motioned for them to enter another refrigerator box.

It was then that Frank saw Van's face in the moonlight, eerily shining through the library windows.

Van Piper, the fearless conqueror of the Acorn school system, was very nervous—on the brink of terror. He was sweating across the forehead and breathing heavily.

"Van, are you OK?" Frank asked him, quietly, as Charlie and Pete crawled into the tunnel.

"I'm not crazy about all this crawling around in the dark," Van said. "It makes me jumpy."

Van climbed into the box, and Wendell turned to Frank.

"Now you have a nervous felon on your hands," Wendell said. He and Frank followed Van into the tunnel.

At the next opening, the five boys stepped into another corner of the library. They stood there not knowing what to do or what to say. Frank reached out and found Pete, who jumped.

"What are you doing?" Pete said.

"Trying to get my bearings," Frank said, hanging on to Pete.

That was when the light of a big flashlight came on, flooding the darkness and blinding the boys.

Then, from behind a bookshelf, a wolf man jumped out, hands up above his head, and growled at the five boys. Van Piper was closest to the wolf man, who had just made a serious tactical error. The wolf man had bumped into a night-blinded, nervous, once-incarcerated Van Piper.

With a single punch, Van Piper knocked the wolf man unconscious. He was out cold.

Poor Mr. Simmonds had been excited about being the wolf man in the haunted house. It was his first year teaching, and he was honored to be asked to serve. He had even gone to Atlanta and rented an adult-size wolf man costume from a theater company. He wanted to make a good impression. He had started out rather timid in the haunted house, afraid he might scare smaller children. But as the night wore on, Mr. Simmonds got into his character and realized he could be frightful without being scary. Jumping out from behind a bookcase, surprising students, and a few adults, and then laughing with them was a lot of fun. And the night had been going great. He thought he was the star of the haunted house.

He was watching the five boys crawl out of the tunnel because his eyes were adjusted to the darkness. He watched them stumble around and watched the one dressed like a gypsy or a pirate or a woman grab the football player's arm. *Time to get them moving along.* He flipped on a bright flashlight and jumped out as he had done more than two dozen times already. He threw his arms over his head and growled—almost howled—at the boys.

Mr. Simmonds realized at once that he was too close to the big boy—or was it a man—with the leather jacket. Before he could back away, the overgrown boy gave a shudder, took a step, and Mr. Simmons woke up several minutes later on the floor of the library with all the lights on and several faculty members standing over him.

When Van punched Mr. Simmonds, it was a beauty of a punch. Frank saw the whole thing. He couldn't have imagined a sweeter, more perfect punch than the one Van had thrown. It was prettier than any punch he'd ever seen any Western actor give on television. And as soon as he threw the punch, Van said, "To hell with this shit" and tore his way toward the library door. One of the teachers, dressed as a mummy, started toward him but immediately thought better of it as Van stopped, balanced his weight on both legs, and prepared to punch again. The mummy threw up its hands, surrendering, and Van continued running for the door. The boys took off after him, partly feeling they were accessories to the crime, but outside the library, they stopped. Van was running down the hallway toward the school's exit.

The lights were all on in the library, and teachers were running inside. Frank's Mema had walked away from her cakewalk duties, saw him, and said, "What happened, Frank?"

Wendell spoke first. "Mrs. Holmes, you won't believe it. Van Piper knocked out the wolf man." Carolyn Holmes went inside the library.

Charlie Keller was on the floor, laughing so hard his face was beet red. Pete Yancey was sitting beside him, shaking his head. Wendell looked at Frank and said, "Well, congratulations, Frank. You ruined Halloween. You invited a felon into the haunted house, and now it's closed. You've ruined Halloween for hundreds of children. Poor Mr. Simmonds may have to go to the hospital and explain all this to Dr. Jim."

In the aftermath, Frank and the boys were questioned, but it was obvious they had done nothing wrong. Frank even testified that Van was getting pretty scared before Mr. Simmonds had startled him. Mr. Simmonds had a swollen jaw, but it wasn't broken. A pretty, young teacher—dressed as a witch—took him to the emergency room, and later it was reported they had started dating. Frank thought things had worked out pretty well for Mr. Simmonds.

Van Piper did not return to school that year or the next. He came back when the boys were all in the eighth grade. When he returned, Van was driving a car and parking across the street at the Golden Pantry. He had a tattoo of a raven on his arm. Frank saw him from time to time around Acorn, and although they made eye contact, the two of them never spoke again.

THIRTY

RAFFLE TICKETS

Tom Wilcox was not happy. Not one little bit happy.

"Turning my boy into a damn salesman," he mumbled as Frank presented him with the opportunity to buy a ticket for a chance to win a turkey for Thanksgiving. Frank immediately regretted asking his daddy for support.

"What's the money going to be used to buy?" Tom asked, more tired and aggravated from his day's work than he was over the turkey ticket.

"It's to help our sixth grade go on trips," Frank said. "We are going to Fernbank Science Center, the Atlanta Museum of Art, and the circus."

Tom stared at his oldest son, not sure he actually had heard the word *circus*.

"I can understand the science center and the museum, but why is it the school's job to take every child in the sixth grade to the circus?" he asked. Frank got tickled when his daddy got this way, particularly if the wrath wasn't directed at him. He knew his daddy wasn't mad at him but was frustrated at the world. Tom sat in his brown recliner, his dirty work clothes still on, his feet propped up on the recliner's footrest.

"It's not funny, dammit," Tom said, and Frank started laughing even harder.

"I'm sorry, Daddy," Frank said. Tom tried to fight back laughing, too. He took a big sigh and closed his eyes. It was only a fifty-cent ticket and wasn't worth losing his temper over.

"So, Daddy, do you want to buy a ticket or not?" Frank asked carefully.

"Go see your mama," Tom said and either drifted off to sleep or pretended he was going to sleep.

Janet was cooking supper when Frank asked her about the tickets.

"We'll buy twenty tickets if you will set the table," she said, nodding her head toward the cabinet where the dishes were stacked. "And fill the glasses with ice."

"Do you think it's OK for me to sell tickets around here?" Frank asked, thinking about his family that lived up and down Brookwood Road.

Janet didn't see a problem with it and told him he could ride his bike up and down Brookwood Road the next day, selling tickets.

That was exactly what he did. He sold tickets to his grandparents, his aunt Delores, and his great-uncle Coy. At Hershel's store, his grandfather's cousins Arlene Anderson and her sister Elnora Wilcox both bought tickets. Arlene slapped her thigh and hollered, "I hope to win that turkey. I'll cook him up for Thanksgiving and then have turkey sandwiches till Christmas."

Frank was on a roll. He had sold almost 120 tickets just among family on Brookwood Road. When Janet offered to take him to nearby Jeannie's Beauty Barn on Highway 141, he jumped at the chance. He sold another fifty tickets to the ladies getting their hair fixed for the weekend.

He told Charlie, "I've sold almost two hundred tickets," and he learned that Charlie had sold about that same number. They felt pretty good about their sales until their sixth-grade teacher, Mrs. Carrie Tallant, told the class that anyone selling five hundred tickets would get his or her choice of prizes. This information created a frenzy of turkey-ticket selling.

Frank and Charlie decided to canvass the entire downtown Acorn business district, selling tickets in every store. They planned to go on this mission together and decided that at the end of it all, they would divide the tickets equally among themselves. Or, as it turned out, they could pool all their tickets together and get one larger prize to share.

Charlie walked with Frank, after school, to The Sewing Shop, where they left their books and began walking store to store throughout downtown Acorn.

That first day around town, they sold one hundred tickets. They could have sold more on that first day but chose to visit the jail, where they understandably couldn't sell to everyone in the building. Charlie asked if the boys could see one of the cells, but his request was declined because the cells were already occupied. Frank and Charlie received a stern warning from one of the deputies—a giant of a man who commanded their attention.

"You boys be respectful when you walk around town selling tickets," he said. "Don't interrupt business that's going on, and if a store is crowded, then you need to leave and come back to that store at another time. People are trying to make a living, and you don't want to get in their way."

The boys had gotten a similar warning from their mamas.

"You see these friendly men and women at church, but when they are in their stores, they have to focus on business and customers," Janet said. "They don't want boys getting in the way or distracting them from doing business."

As the ticket selling continued, day by day, the boys made pretty good time around the courthouse square. As Frank walked into one store, Charlie walked into another. At the larger stores, such as Parson's Department Store, they went inside together. In the stores, they approached the store owner and employees, choosing to approach customers on the sidewalks outside the stores. This had been a suggestion from Mr. Jackson at Jackson's 5 & 10, and it proved to be a good one. Mr. Jackson had also demonstrated how to look someone in the eye and firmly shake that person's hand.

Dr. Marcinko, at the Rexall Drugstore, where Frank had bought Valentine's candy for girls at the primary school, not only bought tickets but also gave each of the boys a pack of M&M's. He promised to buy a few more tickets if the boys came up short after visiting all the stores around the square.

Everyone—even those who didn't buy the tickets—was polite to the boys. Mrs. Goodson at Goodson's Drugs asked the boys to come back when she wasn't so busy with customers, and when the boys returned, she bought a handful of tickets. It was understandable that the boys were in high spirits about selling the tickets. Everyone in town loved them, most everyone in town knew them, and many in the town even went to church with them. It was fun just walking around town and visiting with people; selling the tickets was a bonus. At the hardware store, Mr. Martin showed them the newest sports equipment before buying a few tickets.

After working around the square, Frank and Charlie had seven hundred tickets between them. Next, the two excited salesmen ventured off the courthouse square to the businesses scattered around Acorn for a mile or more.

That was when they were introduced to Calvin James, owner and operator of the Acorn Feed and Mercantile. Acorn County was an agricultural community, and the Acorn Feed and Mercantile was one of the several suppliers to the farming community around the county. In addition to the store off the square, the Feed and Mercantile had three delivery trucks that delivered to the various farms.

Calvin James was a notorious grouch, but he had built a very successful business. R. C. and Tom Wilcox had done business with Calvin for years, and always found him to be extremely fair in deed and brutally honest in word. There was never a doubt as to how Calvin James felt about politics, religion, the weather, the time of day, the laziness of people, the value of a dollar, and, as it turned out, *raffle tickets*.

The boys opened the door of the Feed and Mercantile, setting a ringing bell in motion over the door. The store was old, dark, and dreary, with fluorescent shop lights hanging from the ceiling. It smelled of farm life—the smell of seeds and fertilizer and perhaps even some manure. The boys looked around the store, which was empty of customers this afternoon. They walked toward the cash register, looking around for Mr. James, who was hard to miss. Mr. James was a giant of a man—tall and heavyset. Frank thought that if Mr. James had been a grizzly bear, he would have been a good one. Adding to his somber countenance, Mr. James wore a black eye patch to cover an eye lost in a farming mishap on his own farm, and he always wore old lace-up work boots and leather gloves.

"Hello?" Charlie called out. "Anyone home?" The bell over the door had stopped ringing.

They heard movement from the rear of the store. His footsteps were heavy, and Frank saw Mr. James looking in their direction over the tops of merchandise in the store.

"Get away from that cash register," he bellowed, and the boys jumped back. They were several feet from the cash register and had no intention of touching it. "Can I help you with something?"

Frank cleared his throat, stuck his hand out, and looked Mr. James in the eye. He quickly drew his hand back when he realized Mr. James was not going to shake it. Mr. James had not had Mr. Jackson's course on handshaking at the 5&10.

"We are selling raffle tickets for our school to raise money for educational school trips this year," Frank said. "Charlie and I wondered if you wanted to buy some of the tickets."

"People all over town are buying the tickets to support the school," Charlie said, acting on the advice of Mr. King at the furniture store. Mr. King had told them that people would buy if they thought their friends and neighbors were also buying tickets. He called it the "power of the testimonial."

The boys had made their pitch. Now there was silence. Dead silence.

Mr. James then had a nervous breakdown, or at least Frank thought it resembled what his Granny had called a nervous breakdown describing the reaction of a woman who found rats in her pantry.

After Frank and Charlie had made their pitch about the tickets, Mr. James ordered—shouted—for both boys to sit down in chairs he had there by the counter and the cash register.

"I know who you boys are, and what you are doing is against the law," he bellowed. "Selling raffle tickets is gambling, and I'm calling the sheriff. He'll be around to see your parents; you better believe that. We'll put an end to this illegal activity." His voice was booming. Had Charlie not been with him, Frank would have cried. As it turned out, Charlie confessed that had Frank not been with him, he might have wet his pants.

"Now, leave those tickets right here so I can show them to the sheriff, and you two get out of here," Mr. James continued.

Charlie raised a finger, and Frank knew what he was going to say. Frank knew Charlie was about to tell Mr. James that they had already sold tickets to the sheriff and several of his deputies. Frank put his hand over Charlie's mouth.

"Go on. Get out of here, and don't come back," Mr. James said in a calmer but still unsteady voice.

The boys ran out of the front door of the Feed and Mercantile, slamming the door behind them. They ran back toward downtown Acorn and didn't stop until they collapsed in a grassy spot on the courthouse lawn.

"I have to tell my mama," Frank said. "Do you think he'll call the sheriff?"

Charlie admitted that he didn't know if Mr. James would call the sheriff or not, but it seemed unlikely. It seemed that if he was going to call the sheriff, he wouldn't have given them a chance to run away. The boys split up. Charlie went toward his house; Frank walked up the square to The Sewing Shop. Both boys gushed out the story to their parents.

What happened over the next twenty-four hours was always unclear to Frank and Charlie, but whatever happened, a lot of telephone calls were made. When Janet later told Tom about the incident, Tom began shouting at Frank.

"I told you this was a bad idea!" he said. "You shouldn't be going around town, bothering hard working people! Why in the world is the school taking you to the circus, anyway?"

"Daddy, we're not just going to the circus," Frank said. "We're trying to raise money for several trips, and one of the trips is to the circus."

Tom sensed Janet's rising anger and quickly realized he should not be yelling at his son. He redirected his anger, launching into a tirade about Mr. James.

"Tom, would you be quiet?" Janet said. "We just need to talk to Mr. James and straighten things out like adults. It's just a misunderstanding." Not much else was said that night, though Frank was pretty sure the handful of telephone conversations were more about the incident than about exchanging recipes for chicken pie.

The next day at school, Frank and Charlie told Mrs. Tallant that they had lost the unsold tickets—that Mr. James had taken them—and they needed some more tickets. She obliged them, and they set out that afternoon to sell more tickets, but now something was very different. Now the boys were scared. The joy of ticket selling was gone. They walked from school to the Dairy Queen, where they bought chocolate shakes, and then made their way to The Sewing Shop.

"You boys need to go back, right now, and see Mr. James," Janet said. "You need to apologize for trying to sell him the tickets, and you need to promise that you will only come in his store as a customer from now on." Apparently, Janet was speaking on behalf of all the adults now involved in this mess.

"Mama, I don't want to go back in there," Frank said. "He's mean and crazy."

Janet explained that his Mema had called Mr. and Mrs. James. As a teacher at the junior high, she was able to explain that this was a legitimate school project. It might be considered an illegal lottery in the state of Georgia, but it wasn't appropriate to scare two eleven-year-old boys out having fun together. She was able to explain exactly how the money was going to be used and may or may not have mentioned the circus.

It was the longest walk Frank or Charlie had taken in their lives, and certainly in their friendship. Frank and Charlie didn't speak until they reached the front doors of the Feed and Mercantile. They walked in together, flinching as the bell above the door signaled their arrival.

Mr. James was busy with a customer, but he looked over and saw the two boys standing there. Once noticed, they froze and did not move a step. When the customer had left the store, the giant of a man walked to them and stood there. He put one hand on the handle of a pitchfork, which was in a display of farm tools.

Frank spoke first. "Mr. James, I'm sorry that we came in your store yesterday and bothered you with the raffle tickets. We won't come in here again unless we are customers."

Charlie apologized, too, adding, "I've always liked your store, Mr. James. I like the smell of feed."

For a second, Frank thought he saw the big man smile, but he could have been imagining it. Frank also focused in on the pitchfork, which now looked as if it could be a weapon. Hearing their apologies, Mr. James turned and walked over to his desk beside the cash register. He came back with the raffle tickets and gave them to the boys.

"I don't buy raffle tickets," he said calmly. "I give a donation to the Boy Scouts every year, I buy an advertisement in the high-school annual and the football program, and I give my tithe to the church. That's enough. I appreciate you boys coming in today." He turned his back to them and went back to work. Frank and Charlie eased out of the store. Outside, Frank was trembling.

"Really, Charlie," he said. "You enjoy the smell of feed."

"I thought he might appreciate a compliment," Charlie said as the two friends walked back toward the center of town. They agreed to stop selling tickets, and they had enough tickets to get one good prize and share it.

The prize turned out to be a kite, which they flew in a vacant lot near the courthouse square. It was blue, yellow, and white with a royal blue tail. One afternoon they were flying the kite when a gust of wind jerked on it, breaking the twine and providing the kite its freedom from the world's restraints. Charlie and Frank ran after it, watching as it dove and rose over Acorn.

It was then they noticed the kite drop onto the roof of the Feed and Mercantile. They looked at each other and decided to forget about it. There would be other raffles, other prizes, and other kites.

THIRTY-ONE

THE COURTHOUSE CUBS

Thanks to the Atlanta Braves and their star, Henry Aaron, and baseball-card collecting, baseball was king. And wherever two or more gathered, a baseball game might just break out, taking advantage of imaginary base runners; outfield targets, such as a shrub, that determined bases allowed on a hit; and makeshift bases, such as an old tree standing in for first base. Baseball juiced the creativity of every child in Acorn.

It was out of this spirit that the Courthouse Cubs were born.

The Acorn County Courthouse was the centerpiece of Acorn. Built in the 1920s, it was a large, two-story, rectangular brick building featuring a massive clock tower that spiked high into the air. Big entrances, often left completely open as summertime breezeways, led into the building's first floor. To help with lighting, the windows were large, floor to ceiling in places. On the second floor, which was reached by wide wooden staircases, the windows gave a cathedral look to the building and the Acorn County Superior Court rooms. It was an imposing centerpiece of government in the center of town. The courthouse was the largest building in Acorn County.

Frank and Charlie had attended one murder trial in the courthouse, slipping into Judge Cain's courtroom after school and sitting under the glaring eye of a bailiff until they got restless. They had hoped to see a jury foreman yell out a verdict but became bored with a lot of talk between attorneys and the judge.

The courthouse property was dotted with large, majestic oak trees that provided lots of shade for the courthouse and for those gathering on the property during trials. The annual Fourth of July parade wound around the courthouse square, and the local Lions Club cooked and sold barbecue chicken quarters for those interested in a picnic lunch.

Occasionally, there was a Saturday-evening dance or gospel singing around a white gazebo in the northeast corner of the courthouse lawn. Acorn business folk often used the courthouse grounds for outdoor lunches, and young couples sometimes strolled around the crisscrossing sidewalks under the watchful eyes of a dozen chaperones managing businesses around the square.

"Why don't you boys go down to the courthouse square and throw a baseball?" Janet suggested one afternoon as Frank and Jack wrestled in the back of The Sewing Shop. "You are driving me crazy, and I've got a business to run."

It seemed like a great idea, and the boys had their baseball gloves with them. There was always a baseball lying around the store. Frank called Charlie, who lived a few blocks off the square, and told him to grab his glove and meet them at the courthouse. Charlie jumped at the chance.

On the courthouse lawn, the three boys formed a triangle and began throwing the baseball between them. Avery King was one of Jack's best friends, and his family operated the Acorn Furniture, Appliance & Electronics Store along the south side of the square. Tom and Janet bought lots of furniture from the Kings, and Tom had bought his family's first color television there, too. Avery spotted Jack on the courthouse lawn and grabbed his glove, and the trio became a quartet.

Greg Martin's grandfather lived off the courthouse square on the west side. Because his parents both worked, Greg often stayed with his grandfather after school each day. On this day, he and his grandfather were walking to town to the Martin Hardware Store, owned by their relatives. Greg was a schoolmate of Jack and Avery, and he saw the four boys playing catch in the courthouse yard. He borrowed a glove from a cousin in the hardware store and came across the street to play. The quartet became a quintet.

Jimmy West was an eighth grader at the junior high—he was two years older than Frank and Charlie. Rather than ride the bus home from school, Jimmy sometimes walked to town and caught a ride home with his mama after work. He was walking to Goodson's Drugs for a Coca-Cola when he spotted the five boys throwing a baseball at the courthouse. He had his glove in his mama's car and quickly joined the boys.

Six baseball players were enough for a game, especially if you employed a lot of imaginary runners and forced fair balls to be hit within a narrow zone where defenders had a chance to make a play. Balls outside the zone were foul balls. The boys decided they would meet the next afternoon and bring baseball bats.

It was Jack who first suggested the boys have a team name, and he even floated the name Courthouse Cubs. Jimmy didn't see the need to have a formal name, as they never had any intentions of playing against another team and didn't even have enough players to field a nine-position team. But he gave in to Jack because he didn't have a younger brother, and he thought Jack was funny.

The Courthouse Cubs were born with little fanfare.

Every afternoon, the six boys split into teams of three. Charlie and Frank were usually on a team together with Greg; Jack, Avery, and Jimmy were often on a team together. A patch of dirt was home plate. Two big oak trees with whitewashed trunks served as first and third base. Second base was generally a mystery. It was a crack on a sidewalk about where second base ought to be on a baseball field.

Each team had a pitcher, but oftentimes the boys just threw the ball up and hit it. This allowed for the pitcher to slide back and play more defense. Right-handed hitters had to pull their balls left of second; lefties had to pull right of second. Going to the opposite field was a foul ball simply because there weren't enough defensive players to cover the spacious courthouse grounds.

After-school traffic around the Acorn Courthouse square was generally light, and there were always vacant parking spaces to be found. This sleepy time of the day was the perfect opportunity for six boys to gather and play baseball in a very public setting. Foul balls might bounce into the traffic, sometimes landing with a thud on a car's hood or a truck's side panel, but never once did an angry motorist stop to yell at the boys. If anyone had a right to fear balls coming out of the courthouse yard, it would have been Mr. King at the furniture store. The large display windows of the furniture store faced the boys' home plate, meaning any foul balls directly behind the hitter were but three to four yards from the store's windows. The Kings never complained about the boys playing baseball, and Mr. King often sent Avery to the Martins' hardware store to purchase new baseballs.

By the time the boys got to the square each afternoon, they had about an hour to play. Stores closed at 5:00 p.m., including The Sewing Shop, and four of the players were closely tied to the downtown stores.

One afternoon, as the boys gathered, they noticed a lot of extra traffic around the courthouse. This usually meant a trial in Judge Cain's courtroom. Whistlin' Ben was often sitting around the breezeway of the courthouse when the boys gathered to play, and this day he called the boys over before they started playing.

"You might want to keep quiet this afternoon. There's a big trial going on—*arson*." He pointed up to the courtroom windows above them and then noticed a confused look on Charlie's face. "Someone burned down somebody's house. They tried to kill everyone in it, but no one was home."

For a few minutes, the boys considered going up to the courtroom and watching the trial, but the weather was just too nice. They walked to the rear of the courthouse building, which was the location of their large playing field. They chose up teams, and it was one of the rare days that Frank and Charlie were on opposite teams. In a very scientific game of rock, paper, scissors, it was determined that Charlie's team would bat first. Frank went to play first base.

As the leadoff hitter, Charlie decided to bat from the left side of the plate. Charlie could bat from the left or right sides with equal skill, and right now he wanted to bat as a lefty. Seeing this, Greg shifted to the right side of the field, knowing Charlie had to pull his hit to that direction for it to be considered a fair ball. Jack, also a lefty, was pitching. There was nothing unusual about all of this—it was just another after-school Courthouse Cubs game on the Acorn courthouse square.

In the courtroom, on the top floor of the courthouse, Judge Cain was fighting to stay awake. The trial was grinding down in legal talk between attorneys, motions here and there, and arguments about what was admissible in court. The judge had enjoyed a big lunch at Jack's

Restaurant just off the square and regretted not getting a cup of coffee to go.

At the baseball game, Jack wound up and threw the ball toward Charlie, who turned on it with the wooden, twenty-nine-inch Louisville Slugger "autographed" by St. Louis Cardinals' outfielder Lou Brock. Charlie's swing was picture perfect, connecting the sweet spot of the bat's barrel with the center of the baseball. With just enough of an up-swing, the ball sailed off Charlie's bat. Frank whipped around to watch it disappear into the limbs of a big oak tree next to the courthouse. The oak tree was so old that its roots had damaged the sidewalk.

Judge Cain's first thought was that someone had brought a gun into the courtroom and fired a shot. Before the judge could get to a .38-caliber pistol he kept in his desk, a bailiff pulled him down to the floor. Attorneys, clerks, and a few witnesses fell to the floor as a white Spalding baseball with 108 red stitches bounced around the courtroom, smacking the front wall of the room and hitting Bailiff Sam Bennett in the head before settling quietly in the middle of the floor.

It was the best hit of Charlie Keller's life.

When things settled down, Bailiff Bennett held the baseball up for all to see. Judge Cain called a thirty-minute recess. Bailiff Bennett said something about the boys playing ball in the yard as he rushed from the courtroom with the ball in his hand.

As soon as Charlie turned on Jack's pitch, Frank knew. Even as the ball disappeared into the big oak tree, he just knew. The crash of the large glass window was unmistakable. Frank whipped around to look at his friends. They rushed together and had a quick team meeting; the agenda item was simple—run or stay? The decision was made for them.

Bailiff Bennett ran toward them, shouting, "Stay right there. Do not move. I see every one of you." He was waving the Spalding baseball. "You boys are in a lot of trouble."

A sermon began, with Bailiff Bennett reminding the boys several times how much trouble they were in, and then he said, "I want your names and your telephone numbers. Your parents will have to replace that window. It's going to cost about three hundred dollars."

And that was when Jimmy West asked the legendary question every member of the Cubs would remember for the rest of his life. Jimmy, standing tall among his younger Cubs, asked of the $300 window, "What's it made of, platinum?"

The boys stared at Jimmy in awe. If he had not been their hero before, he was their hero now. Jack began laughing to himself and then whispered to Frank, "Hey, what is platinum, anyway?" Bailiff Sam Bennett, incensed now, collected names and telephone numbers.

"Tomorrow, you boys go directly after school and see Mr. Monday at his office over there," the bailiff said, pointing to a small brick building off the square near the county health department and library buildings. "He will tell you how much you've got to pay for that window. If you don't show up, I'm going to send the sheriff to visit you at home."

Frank thought back to Mr. James's threat to call the sheriff over the selling of raffle tickets; people sure did like to call the sheriff. Wasn't he busy with arsons? But Frank kept his mouth shut because he thought Bailiff Bennett might have a nervous breakdown if he received another question.

Frank might not have been a math whiz, but he had done the math and concluded that each boy would have to pay $50 if the window cost $300—that meant he and Jack would have to come up with $100 together. That was a lot of money, especially since he had only $14.62 from winning the treasure-chest giveaway at the new bank opening.

The Cubs decided to meet at home plate on the courthouse lawn after school the next day and walk to Mr. Monday's office together. Most of the boys had told their parents, and the parents had agreed to let the boys handle this problem themselves. Frank was more than nervous, but the company of the other boys made it all feel better.

The next day they walked into the county office building, and Frank noted the smell of paper. Where the library smelled of much-handled books and the health department smelled of antiseptic, the county office smelled of business. It had a clean, professional smell to it. It smelled of office paper, much like his Granny's office on the farm.

A door in front of them was stenciled COUNTY MANAGER, and they knocked on the door.

"Come in," a firm voice boomed. The boys opened the door and piled into the room.

Frank saw it immediately. The Spalding baseball was on Mr. Monday's desk as a reminder.

"Can I help you, boys?" Mr. Monday asked.

"We broke the window in the courthouse and came down to see you about it," Jimmy said, taking charge as the oldest. Frank was still intrigued by the smell of the office.

Mr. Monday looked across his desk at the six faces in front of him. He knew every one of these boys and their families, but they didn't know that. He leaned back in his chair.

"Who hit the baseball?" he asked. Charlie raised his hand.

"Son, that was a great hit," he said. "Not just the distance, but the fact that you got it up that high and through those trees so quickly." Charlie smiled, and the tension left the room. Jack even sat down in one of the chairs across from Mr. Monday. He took a Tootsie Roll from a candy dish.

"I was the pitcher," Jack said. "Threw it inside to him." Mr. Monday smiled at the blond boy making himself at home. "I guess you couldn't finish the game. Who was winning?"

Frank explained that the game had just started and that Charlie was the first batter.

"I guess that hit counts as a home run," Mr. Monday said.

The boys nodded. He reached for the baseball and pitched it to Jimmy.

"I'll take care of the window this time; you boys go play ball and have fun," he said.

Jimmy said, "We don't have to pay anything?"

"No," Mr. Monday said. "I'll have it replaced. If you see Judge Cain around, you might want to apologize to him. He doesn't expect an apology, but it would be a nice gesture."

The boys thanked him and were beginning to back out of the office when they heard the manager say without looking up from his desk, "It's just glass, boys. It's not platinum." He smiled, and the Cubs did, too.

Thirty-Two

Cubs versus the Garden Club

Thomas Jefferson, third president of the United States, said, "The greatest service which can be rendered [any country] is to add a useful plant to its culture." Jefferson believed what he said, explaining why he told eighteenth-century explorers Meriwether Lewis and William Clark to record plant life as they explored lands west of St. Louis to the Oregon coast.

The Acorn Garden Club would have loved Thomas Jefferson, and the third president would have loved the Acorn Garden Club. Unfortunately, the Courthouse Cubs did not share this affection with the garden club ladies.

The post–World War I men of Acorn County, like men all across the United States, had organized in service clubs such as the Jaycees, Kiwanis, and Lions Club. The women of the county joined church circles, the Jaycettes, and garden clubs. Most garden clubs could trace their history back to the 1920s and women's right to vote. This giant step of independence drew small-community women to organize socially and politically and to improve their communities. Local garden clubs charged themselves with making communities beautiful.

Acorn had two garden clubs—the Acorn Garden Club and the Azalea Garden Club. Frank's Mema was a member of the Acorn Garden Club, which met monthly at the Acorn First Baptist Church. Any woman who loved flower gardening could join. Many of the women married to Acorn's most influential men were members of the Acorn Garden Club, making it a powerful force to reckon with.

"Women have all the power," R. C. Wilcox told his oldest grandson while driving to Acorn one day. "They have all the power. Men think they have it, and most men are liars." He said this on the cusp of

Kathryn ordering him to town on an errand. "One day you will understand what happens to men who don't listen to their wives."

"What happens?" Frank asked.

"They freeze to damn death on a cold winter's night," R. C. said. Frank looked at him, puzzled. "Let's just say a mad wife isn't a wife that wants to snuggle." He winked at his grandson.

How the Courthouse Cubs came to be at odds with the powerful Acorn Garden Club was due to a series of unfortunate events.

The boys were playing baseball one afternoon, after school, when Whistlin' Ben walked up, asked them about their day, and then said, "Looks like you may have to find somewhere else to play. I hear the garden club is going to make flower beds all out through here." He waved a wide hand over the entire area where the boys played baseball. "I hear it's going to be real pretty."

Frank felt as if someone had just slapped him. Charlie's mouth hung open, and the boys griped and complained and generally said ugly things about the garden club, its members, its plants, and its plans. War was declared that afternoon against the Acorn Garden Club. These women, whoever they were, weren't just going to come in and destroy baseball without a fight.

Avery spoke to his daddy, Mr. King, who was one of the leading merchants around the courthouse square, and while Mr. King was the boys' biggest fan, he wasn't willing to take on the garden club. Most of them—if not all of them—were his customers at the furniture store.

Frank went to Janet and complained, and then he learned the most gut-wrenching news of all. His own Mema, Carolyn Holmes, was a member of the Acorn Garden Club. If she was a member, then most likely she had voted on the courthouse-yard gardening project.

"I'll bet your Mema doesn't even know you boys play up there," Janet said. "In fact, I'll bet those ladies didn't think about you all one single time. They just see those old barren spots where grass won't grow, and they want it to be prettier. You won't be able to stop them."

Frank tried anyway. He called his Mema and begged her to stop the garden club plans. As he spoke, he fought back angry tears at the injustice. The courthouse yard was a meaningful place for the Cubs.

Not only did they play baseball there, but they sometimes traded baseball cards, and it was a good meeting place in the center of town. These women were now trying to steal their childhood, and it wasn't fair.

"Honey," she said, "I'm afraid there's nothing I can do. I didn't recommend this project, and it was voted on and approved by the club. I think the ladies have already met with the county manager and with the town mayor, and everything has been approved. I'll be happy to speak up for you, but I don't expect it to do very much good."

Like every grandmother, Carolyn Holmes loved her grandsons, and especially Frank because he was the firstborn. He had opened the door to grandmothering, and he had a special place in her heart. Just four years earlier, when her husband, Paul, died, it was Frank who had spent some of those first nights with her as a new widow. She also had a friend in Frank because he loved nothing more than to hear her tell stories of her childhood.

True to her word, Carolyn went to the next garden club meeting and talked about her grandsons and friends playing baseball on the courthouse lawn and how the project was going to interrupt their after-school fun. As predicted, no one cared. It was full steam ahead—an avalanche of shrubs, azaleas, and camellias had been ordered. When those plants were delivered, they would be planted on the courthouse square, destroying most of the playing area between the first- and third-base trees.

Frank dug in and decided that he wanted to attend a garden club meeting and confront these women who hated baseball and, obviously, America, and perhaps even Jesus because surely God was a fan of boys playing baseball whenever and wherever they could play. He stopped short of declaring that God loved baseball more than he loved azaleas, but he was confident that God loved the Courthouse Cubs more than he loved azaleas.

"Stop it," Janet said. "Just stop it. You boys can find somewhere else to play baseball. You aren't going to go to a garden club meeting and cry and yell at those women. We would be run out of the church, and I would probably have to close The Sewing Shop."

Frank understood, but he was on a crusade. He was going to be the boy who saved baseball.

"You are about to get a whipping," Tom told him. "There are things you don't understand. This is bigger and more tangled up than just a handful boys playing ball after school. Go play on that old field over at the town park."

"That won't work, Daddy," Frank said. "On the square, we can take a break and get a Coke or some candy. Plus, we can all get there in a few minutes. If we have to walk all the way out to that old ball field, we won't get to play very long, and there's nothing out there." Frank also didn't want to fight off the Piper clan, who lived close to the field and would surely come running.

Tom took a deep breath and Frank knew that was his cue to shut up. But he wasn't finished. He had one last thing to try, and he knew that it would stop the garden club. He decided to write a letter. He went to the school library and found the address he needed. Then he wrote it—a beautiful one-page cry for help, help for the Courthouse Cubs' efforts to stop the garden club's azalea juggernaut. Finished, he put the letter in an envelope and borrowed a stamp from his Granny. He watched as mailman Comer Lee Barnett took the letter from his mailbox with the red flag turned up. The letter was on its way...

...to Richard Milhous Nixon, president, United States of America.

"I wrote the president," Frank told the other members of the Cubs. "I'm not wasting time talking to people around Acorn. Everyone is too scared of these old women and their flowers. President Nixon isn't afraid."

Jimmy said, "I don't think the president is going to care one way or the other." Frank was insistent. He told Janet about the letter, and she laughed. She laughed harder when she overheard him calling his Mema.

"I want to tell the garden club that I have written President Nixon and asked him to stop you," Frank told his grandmother. "I'm sorry that I had to get the United States of America involved, but you all left me no choice." He went on to tell her that a compromise could still be reached. The garden club could plant its azaleas at the library or the jail. The Cubs would even help plant the flowers in another place. Heck, the club could even tear down the health department and build a giant garden there.

"I'll pass this message along, honey," she said.

Frank was on a full-blown, cross-eyed, frenzied crusade. He had pushed all his chips to the middle of the table with his letter to the president. He was sure that he would get a telephone call or a letter from President Nixon, and he did.

Waiting and watching over the mailbox, Frank was not surprised when a large white envelope arrived addressed to him. The return address was The White House, Washington, DC. Frank ran into the house, waving the envelope, sure that inside was a letter telling the garden club to stop their antics. He sat down in his daddy's recliner and tore open the envelope.

Inside was an 8½ x 11 photograph of President Nixon and a letter thanking him for writing, wishing him the best, and inviting him to visit Washington, DC. There was no mention of the garden club or the Courthouse Cubs or baseball or a team of FBI agents on their way to Acorn to intervene.

That was the day Frank Wilcox lost a part of his innocence. Two years later, in eighth-grade mock elections, he cast his vote for Democrat George McGovern. Perhaps a new president would care more about baseball. McGovern lost to Nixon that November in a landslide.

The garden club went through with its plans and beautified the courthouse grounds. Before he graduated from junior high school, arsonists burned the old courthouse to the ground. Arson was a popular crime in Acorn County. The old courthouse was replaced by a more modern courthouse, and the space once used by the Cubs was turned into a parking lot. The Acorn Garden Club and the Azalea Garden Club worked together to beautify the new courthouse grounds. The fire, the construction, and the beautification ended baseball on the courthouse square.

A few decades later, Mr. King, who had so faithfully supported the Cubs, bought the boys new baseballs and watched them play from the front of his furniture store, died. Charlie Keller sent flowers to the funeral home. The card read, simply, "With sympathy, from The Courthouse Cubs."

THIRTY-THREE

THE SCOUT HIKE

Frank and Charlie lay in the weeds, hoping the full moon would not betray them to the cars that occasionally passed by on Georgia Highway 19 leading north out of Acorn. They were also afraid of the dog—a big German Shepherd named Midnight that was never on a leash. Midnight had reportedly bitten at least three faithful carriers of the US Postal Service. There would be no Boy Scout merit badge for the boys' mission, but there should have been some kind of survival badge.

Acorn's Boy Scout Troop 39 was legendary in North Georgia. Its membership always included dozens of boys, ages twelve to seventeen, and the troop was known for churning out Eagle Scouts and community leaders. It was sponsored by the Acorn United Methodist Church in partnership with the Acorn Kiwanis Club and the local Veterans of Foreign Wars (VFW) post. Many of Acorn's business leaders, farming leaders, and educators were volunteer merit badge counselors. Just working on merit badges introduced boys to a Who's Who in Acorn County leadership. Those earning scouting's highest honor, the Eagle Scout award, had their names engraved on a plaque hanging in the Acorn Town Hall. The troop met in a multiroom cinder-block building owned by the VFW. The VFW meeting hall was on the same property, but farther down an access road off Georgia Highway 19 north of town. The scouts' regular award ceremonies, known as Courts of Honor, were held in the sanctuary of the Methodist church.

Of the boys in Cub Scout Den 8, Frank and Charlie were the only two who had stayed with scouting long enough to join Troop 39. Most of their friends had traded scouting for school sports or for the high-school band. For Frank and Charlie, serving at the University of Georgia

243

football games had kept them interested in scouts until they were old enough to join.

Frank enjoyed the scout meetings and the military order of them, including salutes and terms such as "fall in" and "parade rest" and instruction on how to march in single lines. He liked the organization behind uniforms, earning ranks, and serving in leadership positions. He also liked the hikes and campouts, which included tips on survival, first aid, and plant identification. Scouting was never a formal military-minded organization, but founder Robert Baden-Powell had been a British lieutenant general, and many of the leadership and survival skills; outdoor activities; uniform attire; and emphasis on physical, mental, and spiritual development would certainly aid any boy wanting to one day join the US armed forces. That was one of the reasons the VFW had eagerly agreed to host the scouts on its property.

It was not easy for Frank to be a member of the troop, considering it met on Monday evenings and his family lived ten miles away on Brookwood Road—at the county's southern tip. He often spent Monday nights with his Mema, who lived in Acorn and who provided transportation to and from scouts and school. Sometimes Janet worked late at The Sewing Shop and then visited with her mama or even with Midge Keller, waiting on scouts to finish. On occasion, Frank went home with Charlie, who lived in town, and spent the night with his best friend. It took creativity and a lot of help for the Wilcox brothers to be active in Acorn activities while living so far from town.

Because of all the ride sharing, Janet had one serious and implicit rule: "Do not get in the car with a stranger. We will make sure you know who and when someone is picking you up and where you are going; do not get in the car with a stranger." When his parents spoke, Frank listened, specifically because Tom and Janet believed in Proverbs 13:24—from the King James translation of the Holy Bible: "He that spareth his rod hateth his son: but he that loveth him chasteneth him betimes." Spankings were not frequent, but the Wilcox brothers knew well the width and depth of their parents' love.

Janet's rule echoed in Frank's brain this particular Monday night at scouts. Frank could hear his mama's words so clearly it was as if she were whispering in his ear even though she wasn't anywhere around him. Just two hours earlier, Janet had dropped him off at the scout hut. She was going to a meeting at the church with Charlie's mom, Midge, and said, "I will be finished by nine, and I'll be back here to pick you up. Don't worry if I'm a little late, and don't get a ride with a stranger."

Charlie had gotten a different message from *his* mama. Charlie's next-door neighbor was attending scouts, and Midge thought it would be helpful and convenient for the neighbors to bring Charlie home from scouts, saving her a trip to the scout hut after the church meeting. When she called the neighbors, she told them to pick up Frank, too, and bring both the boys to her house. The boys could wait on their mamas to finish up at church. When Midge told Janet that the neighbor would fetch both boys from scouts, Janet thought it was a great idea.

Frank, unfortunately, did not get this new message from Janet and believed his mama would be at the scout meeting at 9:00 p.m. to take him home to Brookwood Road.

When the scout meeting was over, the boys all milled around outside the scout hut, tossing a football, waiting for transportation to arrive and take them home. Some of the older scouts could drive, and they left quickly.

"Charlie, Frank!" a voice shouted, and the two friends turned to look. It was Charlie's neighbor, David, whose brother had come to pick him up from the meeting. "You're supposed to ride home with us."

Charlie started a jog toward the car and then realized Frank was not with him. He turned around.

"Mama said I'm not supposed to ride with strangers," Frank said. To ride with strangers meant the rod would not be spared. "Besides, she told me she would be here at nine or just a little later."

Charlie stared at his friend, wondering if somehow he had just misheard Frank. "This is David, Frank," he said. "You know him. He lives next door to me. Come on, let's go."

But Frank was not budging. He knew David, all right, but he did not know David's brother. David's brother was driving. All Frank could imagine was that Janet would show up, be unable to find him, panic, and ultimately find him, and then she and Tom would demonstrate their King James love for him.

"I'm not going," he said. "Mama said she would be here."

David's brother got out of the car, somewhat disgusted, and said, "Your moms are at a meeting, and they called our house and told me to pick you up from scouts. You can come or not, but I'm leaving."

"Come on, Frank," Charlie said, now with urgency, taking a step toward the car.

Frank shook his head. "I can't," he said, and he turned his back on the car and picked up the football.

Charlie stood alone in the middle of the parking lot, unsure what had just happened. He watched his transportation leave the parking lot. He was in shock and pitifully said aloud to Frank, "What's wrong with you? You know David and his brother. That was our ride home. It's gone now. We're stuck here."

The scoutmaster walked outside and saw Charlie and Frank, who by now were alone in the parking lot. "Boys," he said, "I have to go. Can I take you somewhere?"

"My mama is coming to get us; she's just running late," Frank said. Charlie was sitting on a cinder block, his head in his hands, mumbling to himself like a boy on the verge of a nervous breakdown.

"OK," the scoutmaster said. "If you get worried, walk up to the VFW lodge, and they can let you use the telephone." With that, he got into his car and drove away. Now Frank and Charlie sat in the darkness of the scout hut parking lot with only the full moon's light saving them from the pitch-black darkness. Only an occasional car on the nearby highway broke the eerie silence within the moonlit darkness.

Charlie started walking up the road to the VFW building.

"Where are you going?" Frank asked him.

He turned around, flailing his hands, and shouted, "Where am I going? I am going to call my house because you let our ride leave without us. Didn't you hear him say our mamas told him to come get us?" Frank ran to him. Charlie's ranting made him laugh. They reached the VFW building at the top of the hill only to find it closed, dark, and empty.

"We came here once for an Easter egg hunt," Frank said, pointing to a large field. "There were hundreds of Easter eggs out there. We actually got here a little late, but, believe it or not, I found one of the prize eggs." He was going on and on about the Easter egg hunt when he looked at Charlie. Charlie was staring at him with a face of stone.

"How are we getting home, Frank?" Charlie asked.

Frank looked at his Caravelle watch. It was 9:20 p.m. His mama had never been this late before.

"Well, we can walk to your house," Frank said. "If mama is on her way, she will see us walking and can stop and pick us up."

Charlie started walking down the VFW driveway toward Highway 19. "Come on, because no one is coming, and the sooner we get to my house, the better."

At the highway, the two friends began walking along the highway right-of-way, which sloped down into a drainage ditch. Their only light was the light of the moon, and the grass was so tall it rustled against the shins of their Boy Scout pants. They had walked about ten yards when Frank said, "I think we're walking on the wrong side of the road. We should be walking so that we're facing traffic."

Charlie ignored him, and Frank didn't mention it again.

Occasionally a car or truck roared by, but no one ever stopped, and for that the boys were glad. The last thing they needed right now was an honest-to-goodness stranger offering them a ride. Down by the Acorn Water Works they walked, and past the Brooks brothers' garden store. Each place they passed brought up a story one of the boys told the other. As they neared Acorn, businesses gave way to houses.

Walking up a hill toward where two neighborhoods met, Charlie stopped and pulled Frank down into the drainage ditch. "We have to be careful of the dog up here," Charlie said, pointing to a big house on the right. "They've got a German Shepherd that's pretty mean. Its name is Midnight because it's black. You can't see it until it has already bit you. We have to be very careful and very quiet." It helped that Charlie lived in Acorn and knew important details like this.

They eased up toward the edge of the yard, still in the drainage ditch.

"We better crawl from here," Charlie said. He lay down in the grass of the ditch and started crawling. Frank was right behind him.

"I'm getting bit by some bugs," Frank whispered and got on all fours. Charlie looked back at Frank and did the same thing. Now, unfortunately, they looked like two dogs. Some dogs in the neighborhood saw the silhouettes and began barking, alerting Midnight, who also began barking. Midnight's bark was crystal clear among all the barking.

"If we run, we might die," Charlie said. "Crawl faster."

Frank dared a look into the big yard of the house, and it was unmistakable. Midnight stood like King of the Yard in the middle of the yard, barking, but not fiercely—just an occasional bark like a sentry.

"He's watching us," Frank said.

"How do you know it's a boy?" Charlie whispered back.

"I don't know. Who would name a girl dog Midnight?"

Charlie stopped and looked back. "There was a dancer at the fair's hoochie-coochie show named Blanche Midnight. I remember because she wore a black-and-purple costume."

Frank forgot all about the dog. "What? When did you see a dancer at the fair?"

"I wasn't in the show," Charlie said. "I was hanging around that tent, and there she was, standing outside, smoking a cigarette. She blew me a kiss."

The conversation had distracted the boys from crawling. It had also given Midnight time to investigate, and he or she was now much closer and barking louder. Several dogs were barking at these two strange objects crawling along the side of a state highway in the darkness of the night. The boys just kept quiet and continued crawling, and the dogs never did advance farther toward them.

When they finally cleared the yard, there was a store parking lot that was well lit. They walked through the parking lot, noticing the dogs had now stopped barking. Frank looked at his watch. There had been no sign of Janet anywhere.

"See that big pasture?" Charlie said, pointing across Highway 369, which intersected Highway 19. "We can save time by running across

Mr. Roy's pasture. We can come out of it past the high school, and then we will be pretty close to my house."

Mr. Roy Otwell Sr. owned the First Federal Bank and the Ford dealership, and he had an interest in several other businesses. He was also a powerful figure in the First Baptist Church. It was Mr. Roy who, at the conclusion of a worship service that included the Lord's Supper, invited the boys to come down front and finish off the small cups of Welch's grape juice. He even told them to grab a handful of the small crackers to eat on the way home from church. It was a practice that took the starch out of the preacher's careful sermon surrounding the body and blood of Jesus.

"Mr. Roy makes great lemonade," Frank said, thinking about the homemade lemonade Mr. Roy generally brought to every covered-dish luncheon at the church. Frank licked his lips, thinking about the sweet lemonade that was more sweet than sour. "You think he has any in his refrigerator? Do you think he's awake?"

"Forget the lemonade," Charlie said. "I've always heard Mr. Roy has a mean bull in that pasture and that it will charge people. Whistlin' Ben told me one day that that old bull stuck a horn in a Jeep tire."

"I've never heard that story," Frank said.

"Of course not," Charlie said. "You're too busy thinking about lemonade."

"Actually, I'm still thinking about Blanche Midnight," Frank said and laughed out loud.

"She really did blow me a kiss," Charlie said, chuckling.

They crossed the highway and mounted the fence. Charlie then looked at his friend, smirking. "Just to be clear, did anyone ever tell you not to climb a fence and run across a pasture in the middle of the night?"

"Nope," Frank said, and they hit the ground running. Charlie was much faster, but he slowed to a jog so he and Frank could run together. They saw no cows and certainly saw no bull. Their eyes were now adjusted to the moonlight, and they were surprised at how well they could see in the open space of the pasture. Mr. Roy's house was dark. At the other end of the pasture, they climbed the fence and landed in the

Tribble Gap Road right-of-way near Acorn County High School. They were just two twelve-year-olds on a late night run through Acorn.

They walked down Tribble Gap Road, turned onto Woodland Drive, and in minutes approached Charlie's house. A welcoming party was gathered outside.

"Lord, thank you; here they are," said Charlie's grandmother, who lived next door.

Midge Keller said, "Son, I told David's brother to bring you boys home, and he said you wouldn't come with him."

Charlie was a loyal friend, but only to a point. "I told Frank that we should go with them, but he wouldn't go," Charlie said. "I couldn't leave him there by himself."

"My mama told me not to ride with strangers," Frank said, staring at his mama.

Janet was silent—done in by her own rules. "We have to get home. It will be eleven o'clock before you get in the bed, Frank." The adults, including Charlie's daddy, all stood around saying their goodbyes, laughing about the confusion and giving sighs of relief for the safe resolution of the evening's chaos.

As Janet and Frank turned toward their car, Frank asked, "I have a question. Does Mr. Roy really have a bull? We kind of hoped to see it."

Charlie was now standing in his socks, holding up one of his shoes. "I can testify that Mr. Roy has cows," he said. He flung his shoe under the carport. Frank laughed out loud as he climbed into the car.

THIRTY-FOUR

JOEY HEATHERTON

The Marcinko's Rexall Drugstore was right across the street from The Sewing Shop in downtown Acorn. Crossing Main Street, the Wilcox brothers often entered the drugstore from its back entrance, where the greeting cards and wrapping paper were on display. A few noisy, un-carpeted steps led down to the larger drugstore, where customers had prescriptions filled and shopped for medical supplies, over-the-counter drugs, gift items, candy, comic books, and magazines. There was even a soda fountain.

Dr. Marcinko, while filling prescriptions, could see the entire store from a lofty place above the floor. While Frank bought most of his comics from Jackson's 5&10, he loved visiting the Rexall for a sports magazine, M&M's, a cold Coca-Cola, and Valentine's candy for the girls at school. His first-grade love, Mayvin, had received two small boxes of candy because he couldn't make up his mind between a red or pink box. Frank loved Dr. Marcinko, whose warm greeting always included his first name.

"How's Frank today?" came the voice from where the prescriptions were filled. Frank always waved back and said, "I'm great today. How are you, Doc?" Sometimes the friendly druggist took the time to come down and visit, asking about school, about girls, and about his plans for the future. On these occasions, Frank got his candy and drink and sat down on a stool at the counter to visit.

It was Charlie who had first introduced Frank to the sports maga-zines, giving him a subscription to *Sports Illustrated* for his birthday and then pointing out the magazines at the Rexall. The *Sports Illustrated* swimsuit issue had caused quite a stir, and before Frank could fully en-joy it, his copy of the magazine disappeared, only to resurface months later in Tom's white panel van. Anytime Frank and Charlie were to-gether, they bounced into the Rexall and looked through the sports magazines, especially those that predicted the upcoming college foot-ball season or had stories about their sports heroes. More than once the boys tried to steal a glance at a magazine for men but almost always heard a coughed warning from one of the ladies working in the store. A cough was a gentle reminder that they were being watched. It was out of these adolescent, hormone-driven, magazine-looking times that the boys were introduced to Joey Heatherton.

Joey Heatherton, Goddess.

As seventh graders, the boys were figuring out the birds and the bees. Frank had received "The Knowledge" from his Papa R. C. Any further doubts Frank had about sex were cleared up by an older girl, Francine, who sometimes walked to town with Frank and Charlie after school. Nothing scandalous happened with Francine; she just realized the two boys were using the wrong slang when describing genitalia and com-pletely cleared it up with a vocabulary lesson. Francine was a walking, talking sexual encyclopedia, and her educational lessons were dispersed in several two-tenths-of-a-mile walks from the Old King Cole Bakery to Acorn's Main Street. When Francine began talking, Frank wolfed down his chocolate-covered donut and took out a pencil and piece of paper.

"Are you taking notes?" Charlie asked him.

"We can't run the risk of getting this wrong," Frank said. They weren't going to get it wrong because the seeds of Francine's educa-tional talks were reinforced on Troop 39 campouts when some of the older boys smuggled their daddies' *Playboy* and *Penthouse* magazines. Sometimes those campouts included so much education about The Knowledge that Frank thought the Boy Scouts of America should have dreamed up a merit badge to go along with it.

But for all the information provided by Francine, the boys of Troop 39, and the *Sports Illustrated* swimsuit issue, nothing prepared Frank and Charlie for Joey Heatherton. She became the most popular woman at Acorn Junior High School.

Davenie Johanna "Joey" Heatherton was an actress, dancer, singer, and star of stage and screen. In the 1960s, she was all over television and had some fame joining Bob Hope's United Service Organization (USO) trips to visit US troops overseas. She also appeared on Hope's television Christmas specials. Joey Heatherton was known for her sex appeal, her provocative clothing, and her sultry looks on screen and in print.

In 1969, she married NFL wide receiver Lance Rentzel. While the marriage lasted only three years, Joey's connection to the NFL opened the door for photographs of the bombshell to appear in popular sporting magazines. And those magazines could be innocently found on the shelves of the Rexall, where Frank and Charlie visited.

After discovering that issue of the sports magazine, the boys had to own a copy. Within days, they had each scraped together enough money for a purchase. Walking into town from school, they turned down Main Street, passed the Ford dealership and Jack's Restaurant, and walked into the Rexall.

"Hello, Frank and Charlie!" Dr. Marcinko called out unseen, and the boys waved in the direction of the voice. "How was school today?"

"It was fine," Frank said, walking down the steps and over to the aisle of candy, where he chose a package of plain M&M's and a box of Junior Mints. Charlie passed on the candy because he wasn't a big fan of chocolate—something that Frank never understood. Frank put his dime into the Coca-Cola machine and pulled out a glass bottle of his favorite soft drink. Charlie wandered over to the magazines, took a copy of *SPORTS!* for himself and another for Frank, and walked back over to where his friend sat at the counter. He held the magazines as if they were precious commodities. The boys each put a dollar on the counter, and Dr. Marcinko held up the magazines and looked at the covers.

"Looks like a good football story in there," he said, sliding each magazine into its own brown paper bag that fit the magazine perfectly. Boston Patriot quarterback Jim Plunkett, the number-one NFL draft pick, was on the cover. The boys thanked the pharmacist and walked out of the front door onto Dahlonega Highway, around the corner from The Sewing Shop. They crossed two streets and reached the Courthouse Square, where they sat down on the nearest bench. The magazine viewing began.

It was not an obscene photograph. It was just the look, the slightly messed-up blond hair, and the sweater. The sweater was a significant detail. The sweater left everything to the imagination, and for two seventh-grade boys on a courthouse bench, imaginations were running wild.

"She's beautiful," Charlie said.

Those words were more than Frank could muster. He just stared at the photograph.

Charlie carefully replaced the magazine in the paper bag.

"Do we take these to school?" Frank asked.

"Why not?" Charlie said. "We have a responsibility to show others."

Frank opted not to take his magazine to school, but Charlie had no such reservations. If Charlie weren't already one of the most popular boys at Acorn Junior High School—and he was—his popularity soared on the stock of the black-and-white sweater of superstar Joey Heatherton. While teachers thought boys were just reading a *SPORTS!* magazine with quarterback Jim Plunkett on the cover, all eyes were on Joey Heatherton—page 25.

At the Rexall, the magazine business suddenly boomed. Dr. Marcinko had never seen anything like this. He sold out of the sports magazines and reordered more of them, and then he sold out again. A big reason behind the sales at the Rexall was its proximity to the school, and Charlie kept telling everyone that was where the magazine could be found. Fearing a complete market meltdown, Frank bought two additional copies himself, carefully removing Miss Heatherton's photograph from one and pinning it to a bulletin board in the room he shared with Jack.

"Why do we have this woman's picture on our bulletin board?" Jack asked. "Do we know her?"

Frank tried to explain the woman's beauty to his younger brother, but Jack wasn't yet up to speed on The Knowledge, and neither was he prepared for Francine's wisdom. Embarrassed over the photograph in his bedroom, Jack explained it to his sleepover friends.

"Here is a woman's picture that Frank cut out of a magazine," he said, giving friends a tour of his home. "We have no idea who this woman is or why Frank has pinned her picture to the bulletin board."

The sporting magazines began showing up at the junior high, pulled from within composition notebooks throughout the seventh grade. Boys everywhere were showing their copies or sharing them with others during class. Some copies were used to sweeten baseball card trades or to trade for pocketknives.

Into the third week of the frenzy, Frank walked home from school, stopped by The Sewing Shop, and then crossed the street to the Rexall for his afternoon snack. Dr. Marcinko greeted him, and Frank returned the greeting while hopping down the few steps toward the candy and Coca-Cola machine. Dr. Marcinko walked down from his perch and came around the counter.

"Did you have a good day at school today?" the druggist asked him.

"Yes, sir," Frank said, putting his dime in the drink machine. "I had an English test and did pretty well on it."

"Frank, can I ask you a question?"

Drink in hand, Frank sat down at the counter and turned to face the kind druggist. The look on Dr. Marcinko's face gave him pause.

"I'm fascinated. I don't follow all the sports today, but what is it about this magazine that is so popular?" He handed Frank a copy of the *SPORTS!* magazine with Jim Plunkett's photograph on the cover. Frank took the magazine and stared at it. His heart started racing, and his face flushed. He slowly began turning the pages, and then Dr. Marcinko gently took it from him and laughed.

"It took me some time, but I finally figured it out," he said. "When I was a boy, the girl was Jean Arthur. She was an actress. She was the most beautiful thing I had ever seen; I once watched one of her movies four different times." He winked and started back behind the counter.

"It is a pretty sweater, isn't it?" he said without looking back at Frank.

"It sure is," Frank said. "It's about the prettiest sweater I've ever seen."

THIRTY-FIVE

MORNING DEVOTIONS

Mrs. Eunice Bright of the Pentecostal Holiness and Primitive Baptist's Bright clans had declared a holy war on the Vietnam War counterculture invading Acorn Junior High School. At an even six feet tall, she was just the force to bring the war. She had long, brunette hair always pulled up in a tight bun on top of her head. She always wore a knee-length dress and dark hose with her black flats. Her glasses were held to her face by a simple chain with a charm inscribed, "Jesus Loves Me."

Mrs. Bright, as the school librarian, had the opportunity to see every student at the school, and she was alarmed at the boys' lengthening hairstyles, the girls' shorter dresses, bold colors, elastic strings of beads being referred to as love beads, and patches on blue-jean jackets that called for peace and love.

More than once Frank Wilcox heard her say, "Students should show restraint in following the ways of the world. Where in Acorn are you all finding these beads and patches? Are you going into godless Atlanta for them?" She wasn't the only one who thought the good Lord had left Atlanta to the heathens. Frank's daddy, Tom, driving out of the city after a Saturday visit to Grant Park Zoo, said, "I can't wait to get away from these damn hippies down here."

Charged with selling fresh-popped popcorn each day at recess as a fund-raising activity for the library, Mrs. Bright began handing out gospel tracts drawn in a comic-book fashion that called people to repent and know Jesus or die and go to hell. The tracts were produced by Chick Publications, and one particular title, *This Is Your Life*, was especially scary, Frank thought. A poor man reflected on his life before a faceless portrayal of the Almighty cast him into the lake of fire. Later in the track, the man realized he was dreaming, accepted Jesus as his Savior, repented of his sins, and ultimately found glory in heaven.

Hoping to prevent the junior high school from becoming a new Sodom, Mrs. Bright recruited a handful of students to begin an early morning time of prayer in the library, hoping to bring revival to the school. While school-sponsored prayer had been ruled unconstitutional for a decade, only recently had the US Supreme Court's Lemon Test been in place to measure the constitutionality of religious activities. Mrs. Bright's morning devotions, before school, slid in under the wire of approval. She intentionally left the library door open so other students could hear singing, prayers, and a devotion provided by one of the students.

These were tender days for Frank Wilcox. His beloved Granny, Kathryn Wilcox, had recently died after a short but horrible fight with breast cancer that had spread to her bones. Her death had shaken Frank's world and put in motion events that would lead to his family's move from beloved Brookwood Road to a new Acorn subdivision. To cope with his Granny's death, the changes on the farm, and talk of the move, Frank had retreated into his faith life for comfort.

It had been five years since Frank had come under Holy Spirit conviction through the death of his grandfather Holmes, Papa Paul; the summer revival services at the Methodists' camp meeting; and his baptism by Preacher Acree at the First Baptist Church. The year before, Frank had spent ten dollars of his own money to purchase a King James Bible at Parson's Department Store on the square. He had even had his name imprinted in gold on the front cover. Inside, he had written Bible verses that brought him comfort.

Frank had grown fond of reading the daily *Open Windows* devotion series at bedtime. At the First Baptist Church, he had moved from the children's ministry to a new, growing youth ministry of several dozen Acorn teenagers. It was this transition that opened Frank's eyes to the world around him. Suddenly he was surrounded by older teenagers already embracing the new culture, its music and dress and style, yet they were maintaining their faith life, too. They weren't Atlanta hippies beating a fast trail to hell.

Frank had fallen in love with Mrs. Virginia Williams, his new pastor's wife, who was leading Bible studies and Sunday School classes for teenagers at the church. It was Mrs. Williams who had recruited Frank as a seventh grader to organize a churchwide talent show sponsored by the youth ministry. About ten talent acts, from within the church, signed on for the talent show, which featured a small concession stand that sold doughnuts from the Old King Cole bakery and soft drinks. Dr. A. Y. Howell, beloved Acorn dentist, served as the master of ceremonies after Atlanta weatherman Guy Sharpe turned down Frank's offer to serve. The Jaycee talent show had been enough Acorn for him.

Nervous about calling the famous weatherman, Frank had procrastinated making the invitation. Mrs. Williams forced Frank to call Guy Sharpe one Sunday evening after worship services, saying, "My goodness, Frank. Guy Sharpe stands at the toilet and goes to the bathroom just like you do. Call him." Frank never forgot that advice when faced with a difficult conversation. He just pictured people going to the bathroom.

Like many of his fellow students now becoming teenagers and preparing for high school, Frank was engaging the new culture. He was wearing love beads and peace emblems on chains around his neck, and he was wearing bright-colored purple-and-orange shoes while his hair grew below his ears. He was also maintaining his faith life, both at home with the *Open Windows* and with his youth group at church. The antiwar counterculture movement of peace and love was naturally pointing many students toward Christianity and its messages of peace and love found in Jesus. The Jesus Movement was an organic West Coast movement that spread across the country, allowing students to embrace the cultural shifts and the Christian faith at the same time.

It was driving Mrs. Eunice Bright out of her mind. In the world of Mrs. Eunice Bright, there was a spiritual order of proper dress codes—dresses for girls and military haircuts for boys—and proper vocabulary rather than slang. And the music of Karen and Richard Carpenter or Glen Campbell was at the far edge of allowances. For Mrs. Bright, there was no room for this new cultural upheaval in the life of a Jesus follower. She was not alone in her thinking, and many in the United States were wrestling over the clashing of worlds in the frenzied final years of the Vietnam War.

Mrs. Bright's morning devotions were her safe haven for students who thought as she did, and it was a cleansing place for students wanting to escape the growing cultural choke hold on the youth of the day. There were no copies of The Living Bible, Good News for Modern Man, or The Way Bible translations in her morning devotions. There was only the King James Version, and if it had been good enough for King James I of England in 1611, then, by golly, it was good enough for the teenagers of Acorn, Georgia, in 1972.

She had heard about the youth ministry going on at the First Baptist Church. She had heard about their music, guitars and drums in student-led worship, Bible studies as students flopped around on big pillows on the floor, and young people standing around in the church parking lot for hours after church services ended.

Frank loved his youth group, and he, Charlie, and Wendell were all involved together. They were the youngest in the group of older teenagers, but they loved it. They especially loved the older girls, and the older girls migrated toward the funny and charming Charlie Keller. That alone was a win by extension for Frank and Wendell. When the three boys learned of a youth ministry sleepover, including boys and girls under the same roof, they were among the first to sign up to attend.

It was at this sleepover that Frank had his first taco. As he was born on the hog farm of Brookwood Road, everything he ate came from a pig except for the occasional fried chicken leg or Saturday-evening rib eye. He had no idea what a taco was when it was first mentioned, and then he relied on his older friends to ensure he put a taco together correctly. Charlie and Wendell had never seen a taco themselves, so all three boys stumbled through the night, eating tacos; reading from The Living Bible; and singing Christian songs, such as Larry Norman's "I Wish We'd All Been Ready," that sounded more like folk music than those hymns from the Baptist Hymnal.

Life was filled with guns and war,
And all of us got trampled on the floor.
I wish we'd all been ready.
Children died; the days grew cold.

A piece of bread could buy a bag of gold.
I wish we'd all been ready.

There's no time to change your mind.
The Son has come, and you've been left behind.

Frank began attending the laid-back youth ministry gatherings on Sunday evenings at his church. He got his own blue-jean jacket and began having Janet sew on the patches of peace and love. One night at a youth gathering, Mrs. Williams asked the students to draw a picture of themselves. Frank watched as an older girl held up her self-portrait as an ugly witch and then began crying at how she was afraid people saw her that way. This led to all the students holding hands and praying together. Frank had never, ever imagined anything like this ever happening at church.

Many of the students at Mrs. Williams's youth gatherings didn't attend regular Sunday services at First Baptist Church, but most of them were involved in the church's youth choir, which swelled to more than a hundred teenagers. The choir was led by Church Minister of Music Ron McClure, who was also director of the county's state Department of Family and Children's Services office. Ron was also a volunteer basketball coach in the county's growing youth basketball program. He was constantly inviting young people to join the choir, and many did for the opportunity to sing the folk songs about Jesus. Over the years, Mr. McClure added musicians to the choir, and it was not unusual for rock-and-roll concerts to break out after choir practice or on choir trips. Frank was envious of the guitar players.

Frank couldn't sing a lick, but he loved the choir, and Mr. McClure joined with many other adults, including Mrs. Williams, to encourage him along in his walk with Jesus. Frank was on a course, like so many other Acorn students, to know Jesus more deeply and follow him more closely within the frame of their own culture and not the culture of their parents or grandparents.

Frank was on a collision course with Mrs. Eunice Bright, who was still obsessing over where these anti-American patches and love beads were coming from. Who was providing this paraphernalia to children at her school?

Lester Freemont was a United Methodist and enjoying his own personal revival through his church. Knowing the deep faith commitment of Lester's family, Mrs. Bright had targeted Lester to join the morning devotions and to be a leader within them. Lester, with a King James Bible tucked into his book satchel, was also unashamed to stand up and lead the devotions on occasion.

After joining the morning devotions, Lester had done the natural thing that evangelists had been doing for centuries: he invited his friends to join him. He invited Frank and Pete Yancey especially. Frank, in turn, invited Wendell and Charlie. All the boys planned to meet one Monday morning and attend the devotions together as a group, partly to support Lester and partly because they wanted to be about anything that was about Jesus and faith.

Lester was already in the library that Monday morning when his friends walked into the room. Frank wore a large metallic peace sign on a chain around his neck. He had worn the same chain for his school picture that year and had been disappointed to find the photographer—or editor—had cropped out the peace sign from the photograph. Charlie had on red, white, and blue socks and a buckskin vest with fringe around the edges. All the boys had hair growing over their ears.

No sooner were they in the library than Mrs. Bright rose to meet them or challenge them or throw them out or pray over them—her intentions were not immediately clear.

"Can I help you boys? The library is closed right now, and we are about to have our morning devotion time," she said.

Pete Yancey, who, like Lester, had not yet made the full peace, love, and happiness transition, said, "We are here for the morning devotion time."

Mrs. Bright smiled at him and frowned as his associates—Frank, Charlie, and Wendell—followed him to a rectangular table where a pretty girl from the Church of God sat in her skirt below the knees and brown flat shoes. She was a little nervous when the boys sat at her table and especially when Frank sat right beside her.

"I'm surprised at you," Mrs. Bright said softly to Frank. "Your grandmother is a respected teacher at this school, and you are surely an embarrassment wearing a chain around your neck."

Frank did not respond, remembering that Jesus had said to keep turning the other cheek for as long as it took.

The boys waved at their friend, Lester, who was regretting his evangelistic tendencies and the guilt by association surely coming his way. Mrs. Bright pulled up a seat next to the table of boys, making the girl from the Church of God even more nervous. She scooted away from Frank as if he had some kind of Old Testament leprosy.

Lester began the devotion time with prayer, and then he asked for prayer requests. Several of the students offered requests. Frank asked that the group pray for his family, especially after the death of his grandmother. Someone asked for prayer for an out-of-work uncle, and others wanted to pray for a boy a few years younger who had been diagnosed with a serious illness. A few people raised their hands when asked if they had tests that day. With eyes closed, one of the students prayed out loud.

Lester used a devotion from the United Methodist Youth Fellowship—MYF—and the boys listened intently to their friend. At the conclusion, just because he could, Lester called on Frank to pray, and, having trained under the eye of Mrs. Williams at his church, Frank launched into it but not before he saw Mrs. Bright lurch and struggle with her breathing.

"Lord," Frank said, "we thank you for this time together. Thank you for the message that Lester has brought to us. Thank you for teachers and friends here at school. Thank you for Mrs. Bright organizing these devotions."

Lester's invitation to his friends sparked others to invite friends, and in a few weeks, the group of student worshippers had grown from just a handful to almost two dozen. Much to Mrs. Bright's horror, her morning devotions began to look more and more like the youth gatherings at the First Baptist Church. One of the girls from the Pentecostal church even came one morning with a peace sticker on her math book, sending Mrs. Bright staggering back among the *World Book* encyclopedias.

"Where did you get that sticker?" she asked the turncoat in a pitiful way. "I fear it's the end of the world."

It was now time for Mrs. Bright to accept that "Jesus hippies"—who really were pretty tame by honest-to-goodness hippie standards—had taken over her morning devotion time. But she gave one last, hard push to convert all those attending the morning devotions. She started with a speech about the devotions being a "lamp unto the darkness in the culture of Acorn Junior High School." She began calling out students because of what they wore or the length of their hair. She hated the elastic strings of love beads. She hated the music, shifting from the Carpenters to Grand Funk Railroad and from Glen Campbell to The Doors. Three Dog Night's "Joy to the World" meant there was no going back to the simpler times before the 1969 Summer of Love.

Jeremiah was a bullfrog.
Was a good friend of mine.
I never understood a single word he said,
But I helped him a-drink his wine.
And he always had some mighty fine wine.

Singin' joy to the world.
All the boys and girls now.
Joy to the fishes in the deep blue sea;
Joy to you and me.

If I were the king of the world
Tell you what I'd do.
I'd throw away the cars and the bars and the war
Make sweet love to you.

Sing it now, joy to the world.
All the boys and girls.
Joy to the fishes in the deep blue sea;
Joy to you and me.

Mrs. Bright finally snapped the day Frank wore his blue-jean jacket with a brand-new patch sewn over the left front pocket. It was the flag of the United States of America except that the field of fifty stars was now a white peace sign on a field of blue.

Through tears, Mrs. Bright ordered Frank to remove his jacket.

"I mean it, Frank Wilcox," she said as her voice trembled. "I will not have that jacket worn in this library while we are worshipping Almighty God. Where in the world would you have gotten such a patch?"

The violent explosion caught Frank off guard. He stared in stunned silence.

"Take it off right now," she said. "I won't have it. And I ask you again. Where did you get such a wicked patch?" She wheeled around to all the students, watching wide-eyed. "Where are you all getting these beads and patches? Where? Where?"

Charlie tried distancing himself from his friend, whispering aloud, "The role of Satan is played by Frank Wilcox." In days past, the children's ministry at the First Baptist Church had acted out the life of Jesus, and Frank had been chosen to be Satan in the play. Not content with simply showing up in the desert to tempt Jesus, Frank kept appearing in all the other scenes of the play, too. At the conclusion, Dr. Howell had introduced the cast and said, "And the role of Satan was played by Frank Wilcox." The congregation erupted in laughter because of Dr. Howell's great wit.

Now, Mrs. Bright was waiting for an answer. She wanted to know what store sold this unpatriotic, un-Christian flag patch because she intended to visit that store immediately after school. Frank answered her question, and his answer might as well have been a nuclear bomb detonated right there in the Acorn Junior High School library.

"My mama sells all these patches and love beads in her store," Frank said. "It's The Sewing Shop on Main Street." Janet Wilcox was no naïve businesswoman. When she saw young people wanting beads and patches, she began selling them in her store.

The Sewing Shop, in the eyes of Mrs. Eunice Bright, was now a direct portal to the darkest corner of hell.

Frank took off his blue-jean jacket, and Mrs. Bright ordered him to Principal Shoemake's office, where Mrs. Bright ordered the principal to seize the coat and destroy it. Mr. Shoemake knew the Wilcox family from church, and he wasn't about to wade into this territory without help. He called Frank's Mema to the school office.

Frank watched the three adults wrestle over the culture of the day, Frank's jacket, constitutional First Amendment rights to free speech and how those applied to students in Georgia's public schools, and whether the morning devotions was really the best place to get tangled up in all of this.

"Are you behaving?" Frank's Mema turned sharply and asked him.

"Yes, ma'am. I enjoy the morning devotions," Frank said, and he was truthful. He and his friends did enjoy the devotion time.

"I can't believe your daughter is selling this," Mrs. Bright said, holding up the jacket. Though she had a good foot and a hundred pounds on his Mema, Frank thought his Mema might just whip the librarian right then and there.

"You hold your tongue, Eunice; I mean it," Carolyn Holmes said. "We are not going to talk about my family. We will take this directly to the school superintendent if you say one more ugly word."

Mrs. Bright fought back the tears. Her world was rocked. She just wanted children to know about Jesus, and she just wanted the America of her childhood to be the America of today. She hated change, and she hated where change was taking her against her wishes. She would have passed out cold had she known Frank's Mema, wife of a World War II navy veteran, had bought a copy of The Living Bible translation and was reading it.

"I won't wear the jacket to the morning devotions," Frank said, volunteering a quiet solution that seemed to make all the adults happy. Mr. Shoemake, exhausted, smiled at him weakly.

Within a year, most of the real counterculture apparel had disappeared, even if the length of hair, general fashion, and music had not. Frank and his friends stopped wearing the patchwork jackets altogether. A 1968 movie titled *Marijuana*, featuring pop musicians Sonny Bono and his wife, Cher, as antidrug proponents, was being shown to students in many science classes. Frank, Lester, Pete, Wendell, and Charlie all still continued attending the morning devotions, and most of the boys had taken a turn leading them. Frank even came to friendly terms with Mrs. Bright but refused to pass out her cartoon tracts.

Mrs. Bright realized that she couldn't change their positions on America culture, but she did get a group of her devotion students recognized in the school yearbook, and Lester, Frank, Wendell and Pete were all in that photograph. In the photograph, Mrs. Bright is smiling.

THIRTY-SIX

THE KILL SHOT

"It's a kill shot," the coach said, launching the basketball toward the goal.

"Why do you call it a kill shot?" Frank asked.

"Because it kills your opponent," he said. "It kills their spirit, and it kills them on the scoreboard."

Frank's Mema was excited that one of her former students was returning to teach and coach basketball at the junior high. A handful of her former students had returned to teach in Acorn schools, but this one—Wayne Johnson—had been one of her favorites.

Seventh grade was when Frank and his classmates could try out for the school's basketball teams: the Bullpups and the Lady Bullpups. A few of the seventh graders, such as Wendell, Pete, and Charlie, had played for the school's football team, which had had some success playing a handful of games against other junior high schools in adjacent counties. No one really paid much attention to the football teams of Acorn County because this was basketball country. And basketball was king. Acorn County had a history of producing great high-school teams, especially among the girls. That was why Mrs. Hicks, back in the fourth grade, had put such an emphasis on shooting foul shots. And when the town of Acorn started a recreational basketball program for young people, they turned out in droves to play on the color-coordinated boys' and girls' teams.

Frank had played one year of recreational basketball because Mr. McClure, his church's minister of music, was an organizer of the league and a coach and had pressured Frank to play. It was a bad decision all the way around. The game moved faster than Frank could move and think, and often he found himself on the court as a spectator, watching his teammates play.

"Why do you just stand there?" Jack asked him on the ride from a Saturday-morning game in the high-school gymnasium. "It's embarrassing."

"I'm trying to figure things out," Frank responded. "I see everyone running, but I want to understand why they are going where they are going and what they plan to do when they get there."

Jack stared at him in the backseat of the car. "No one knows what they are doing. Everyone is running around trying to get open, take a pass, and shoot a basket."

Mr. McClure moved Frank to the bench, and Frank was content to watch and study the game. Because the league rules required each player to play a minimum number of minutes, Frank was inserted into the game with specific instructions: "Go stand over there, take the pass, and shoot the ball." No matter what anyone else did on the court, Frank found his spot, took the pass, and launched a shot toward the goal. Frank's shots often came in like bombs that hit unsuspecting players on the head—sometimes players on his own team.

Mr. McClure taught the team to play HORSE—a rotating shooting game that eliminated those unable to make shots. Without all the running, passing, and hands in his face, Frank became as good as any player at HORSE.

"Is there a league where everyone just plays HORSE?" he asked his coach one day after practice.

Mr. McClure just looked at him and said, "There's something out there for you to do well, Frank. I'm determined to help you figure out what it is."

"It's not playing basketball, is it?" Frank asked.

"No, and to be honest, it's not music either," he said, and Frank was able to laugh along with him.

Even though he wasn't a basketball player, Frank did enjoy the solitary time he spent just shooting the ball. Often, waiting on his Mema to finish up a faculty meeting so he could ride home with her, Frank walked over to the empty school gymnasium and shot baskets all by himself.

That was how he got to know Coach Wayne Johnson.

It was a Wednesday, and the school campus was already quiet. Most of the students were gone or standing in front of the school waiting for a bus or another ride home. Frank walked up the old, crumbling steps to the side door of the gym and tugged it open. The old metal door scraped against the concrete steps as it opened. He walked inside. The lights were off, but there was enough light coming through the windows to see well enough. He spotted a basketball not packed away from the day's physical education classes.

Frank sat down on the first row of the bleachers and tossed the ball up in the air. Staring at the court, he thought about the new game learned in physical education—battle ball, which was really a form of dodge ball. Teams lined up on opposite ends of the court and then threw a volleyball from one end to the other. Anyone struck by the ball had to change teams. Ultimately, one end of the court had all the boys on it, trying to kill the last man standing on the weaker team.

His mind wandered. Frank also thought about how embarrassing it had been that first few days of physical education class, changing clothes in a hot, sweaty dressing room with a bunch of other boys. They had been instructed to replace their underwear with jockstraps, which would help protect their nuts during games of battle ball and other competitions. This change of clothing also kept their classroom clothes from smelling bad.

He snapped out of his daydream when Coach Wayne appeared in the gymnasium and called out to him.

"You play basketball?"

Frank looked around to see if other boys and girls had entered the gym behind him.

"You're holding a basketball, so I thought you might play the game," the young coach said. He was about six feet tall with jet-black hair matching a jet-black mustache. He was dressed for the gym.

"I've never really played," Frank said.

"Come on; let's see what you have."

Frank walked out onto the court, dribbled the basketball with his right hand, and shot a few shots. A couple fell in the basket. Coach Wayne rebounded and passed the ball back to him, and after a few minutes, Frank caught his rhythm and sank most of the shots he tried. The more shots he made, the more his confidence rose and the better he felt about this exhibition.

"You want to play a quick game of HORSE?" the coach asked. "I should be at the faculty meeting, but I hate those meetings. I can call this a student meeting."

"Sure, I can play HORSE," Frank said. And the game began.

It was a quick game. Frank was no match for the long-distance shooting of the coach and was amazed at the way he glided on the court before pulling up to make a shot.

Frank was down to HORS, missed his shot, and watched Coach Wayne take the ball to half court. He dribbled the ball twice and let it go toward the basket. It swished through, hitting nothing but net. Frank had never seen such a long, perfect shot.

"Kill shot," Coach Wayne called it. As Frank's countershot weakly sailed toward the goal, missing everything, he understood what kill shot meant. He was dead, and the game was lost.

"You should try out for the team," the coach said. "Tryouts are next week. I can't promise you'll make the team, but you should try out for it."

Frank was stunned. Apparently, this coach didn't know him. Frank loved sports, but he was in no way capable of playing on an organized school basketball team. Heck, he was a middling battle-ball player.

"Shoot as long as you want," Coach Wayne said. He jogged out of the gymnasium, leaving Frank holding the ball in the middle of the court. Frank continued to shoot around until his Mema came to get him.

That night, at the supper table, Frank could hold it in no longer. "The basketball coach at school told me to try out for the team next week."

It was such a stunning revelation that every head turned to look at Frank.

Jack laughed out loud. "Your school has started a HORSE team?"

"It's true," Frank said. "And, I'm going to do it."

On the goal in the backyard, rarely used, Frank practiced shooting baskets. He no longer needed his granny shot to occasionally make a basket. On the day of the tryout, Frank received skeptical well wishes from his parents. Jack was not confident about his brother's chances.

"Don't tell them you are my brother," Jack said. "When they all start running at you, don't throw the ball at them. That's called a turnover, and they have a chance to score."

Without exception, every boy trying out for the team was surprised to see Frank at the tryouts. These boys had grown up with him, after all, and every student knew the strengths and weaknesses of every other student. No one had ever accused Frank Wilcox of being athletic.

The tryout was generally simple. Coach Wayne wanted to watch the boys run, pass the basketball, and take some shots at the goal. He was going to cut the squad down and have another tryout among those remaining.

To everyone's amazement, Frank made it past the first cut. So had Lester, Pete, and Charlie. Jim Vinton and Steve Dickson had also made the cut. To no one's surprise, Mack Holloway had made the cut. Frank was beginning to realize he had no business being in this company, but he was glad to be here nonetheless.

Coach Wayne was in a bit of a pickle with regard to Frank. It was tough to give a first-round cut to a boy you had personally invited to be at the tryout. It was doubly sensitive when, after the invitation, you learned that this boy was the grandson of your favorite teacher while growing up.

The next round of tryouts was brutally embarrassing. If only Dr. James Naismith, back in 1891, had shaped basketball rules to be a simple game of HORSE rather than a running, passing, throwing, shooting game of nonstop action. Frank was drowning, and he finally just took a seat on the bleachers to watch his friends compete for the final spots on the Bullpups basketball team.

Coach Wayne saw him and walked over. "What are you doing?" he asked.

"Coach," Frank said, "I can't play basketball." He smiled and chuckled, slightly embarrassed that Coach Wayne was learning what everyone else in the gym already knew. "I enjoy watching it, and I enjoy learning about it. But I can't play it."

271

"Tell you what," the coach said. "Why don't you be a team manager? Come to practices, go to all the games, and sit on the bench. I'll teach you as we go, and you can keep stats for me. You'll be a part of the team, but you just won't play in the games. You will have to dress up as I do for the games—wear black pants and a white shirt with a red sweater. You can even practice some with the team if you want to do that."

Frank was speechless. He had never thought about the chance to be around sports but not actually play the sport. The possibilities were endless. He was disappointed for Charlie when he learned his friend had also been cut from the final roster, but he was excited that Charlie had been asked to serve as a manager too. Lester and Pete had both made the team, and Frank was glad his two friends were going to be there with him. Mack Holloway, Steve Dickson, and Jim Vinton were also on the team.

It was a great season. On a bus ride home from a game at Chestatee Elementary School—in the county's northeast corner—Frank held the hand of a cheerleader. Had she kissed him, it would have been perfectly fine, but he was content to just hold her hand. Not a word was exchanged. He had just sat beside her, reached over, and held her hand. She had let him. Frank's heart was still pounding when he went to sleep that night.

Frank also learned a good deal about basketball over that season. During halftime of one game, Mack Holloway asked him to get "the Jet." The Wilson Jet basketball was a top-end basketball used for school competition. Frank returned with a can of sticky spray ball control and suffered the ridicule of the entire team as he prepared to spray it on Mack's hands.

"You should have told me to go get the basketball with Jet printed on the side of it," he told his friend. "I thought you wanted the sticky spray before you started the second half."

During another game, Frank started gathering equipment before the game ended. An errant pass slammed him in the head and sent him falling into the first two rows of bleachers. With the entire gymnasium wondering if he had been knocked unconscious, Frank gathered himself, waved at the crowd and sat down at the scorer's table. Lester brought him a cup of water.

Coach Wayne gave Frank the game's scorebook and told him to keep track of who shot the ball and whether it was a made or missed shot. He quickly gave him instructions, and Frank finished the season as the team's statistician. Charlie was glad to be in full control of all the equipment; the rest of the team was glad Charlie was in charge of the equipment, too.

The season ended with the Bullpups facing their closest rival, the Sawnee Elementary Chiefs. Some of the boys on the Chiefs had attended Acorn Primary School but had transferred to Sawnee for grades six through eight. There were a lot of shared relationships between the two teams, and it was as heated a rivalry as there could be for a group of junior high boys.

At the close of the first half, Jim Vinton took the ball and fired a long shot toward the goal that gave the Bullpups a one-point lead.

The game went back and forth in the second half, both teams fighting to win, and, as time expired, the Bullpups had a one-point lead and the victory. As the bleachers began to empty onto the court and the Bullpups celebrated the exhausting win, a referee blew a whistle. Sawnee's best player, Donny Beckham, had the ball and had called a time-out just before the final buzzer.

The fans were moved back into their seats, and a few seconds were put back on the clock.

The Acorn fans shouted, "We've got spirit; yes we do. We've got spirit; how about you?"

And the Sawnee fans responded, "We've got spirit; yes we do. We've got spirit; how about you?"

Back and forth the fans went during the time-out. Some of the students began stomping on the old wooden bleachers, and there was an electricity pumping through that old gymnasium. It hardly seemed like the place, Frank thought, where he and his friends had physical education class every day.

"We've got more! We've got more!" the Sawnee fans shouted.

"Kiss my ass!" a fan shouted behind Frank, and he turned to see who it was. He recognized Van Piper's grandma sitting with about half her clan.

The teams were back on the court for the handful of seconds remaining. The ball was passed inbounds to Donny Beckham, and Sawnee's star dribbled a few steps to the half-court line. Donny was the only player on either team sporting a flattop haircut, flying in direct opposition to the longer hair being sported by most of the players. If Mrs. Eunice Bright had wanted a hero, Donny Beckham would have been her boy.

"Kill shot," Frank whispered to himself. "It's going to be a kill shot."

Donny launched the ball just before the buzzer sounded. The ball sailed and stripped the net. Sawnee had won the game by one point.

All hell broke loose.

The Sawnee fans now poured onto the court, and the upset Acorn fans rushed down to meet them. Thinking they had previously won and now losing in a matter of minutes was more than the Acorn faithful could stand. Someone threw a metal folding chair. It clanged and danced harmlessly on the floor. Several sheriff's deputies rushed into the crowd. Frank sat hypnotized by all of it, sitting at the scorer's table three rows above the fray. Coach Wayne and the Sawnee coach had both rushed their players off the court and into the dressing rooms. Frank and Charlie were left behind. So much for team camaraderie.

Charlie joined Frank at the scorer's table.

"I can't get the equipment because of the crowd," Charlie said.

"I think we better stay right here and watch this," Frank said.

They watched as the deputies removed some of the real troublemakers, and the crowd began to calm down and leave the gymnasium. Frank and Charlie waited until the players and coaches returned safely to the gym floor, and then the managers began collecting everything for Coach Wayne. Frank watched as Donny Beckham went to every one of the Bullpup players and congratulated each on a good game. Donny even jogged over to Coach Wayne, shook his hand, and congratulated the coach, too.

An exhausted Coach Wayne walked to the scorer's table and asked Frank for the scorebook. As Frank handed it over, Coach Wayne shook his head, looked at Frank, and said, "Kill shot, right?" Frank smirked and nodded, angry that his team had lost.

Later that night, as Frank dramatically described the game to his parents, Janet described Donny Beckham's actions after the game as "gracious in victory." She told Frank to be that kind of boy. A few years later, in high school, Donny Beckham joined Lester, Pete, and Wendell as one of Frank's very best friends.

THIRTY-SEVEN

FOCUS

It began with doodling on a piece of paper in seventh-grade study hall.

It ended with the school's first-ever school newspaper, *FOCUS*.

Frank had continued writing his fictional short stories, filing them away in notebooks at home. Most of the stories had a central theme: A group of friends—Western lawmen, outlaws, gangsters, neighbors—had some kind of big adventure that ended well for everyone.

One of the Civil War stories about Confederate soldiers breaking free of a Union stockade had earned Frank high praises from his daddy, Tom. "That's a really good story. You need to keep writing them," was just the encouragement Frank needed to throw himself into the stories—handwritten on ruled notebook paper and bound together with staples.

Frank also got encouragement from Mrs. Carolyn Hicks, who, to everyone's joy and surprise, had moved from the primary school's fourth grade to seventh grade at the junior high. Mrs. Hicks, always the encourager, immediately found Frank and invited him to read his stories to all of her classes. After each reading, she instructed her students to thank Frank by giving him an applause, and the students complied. If Frank had any lingering self-confidence issues from the basketball court, the baseball field, youth choir, or the honor roll, those issues were fading quickly.

Now he sat in seventh-grade study hall, doodling. This free hour was built into each day, and students could use it to study for a test, work on homework, read a library book, work on a class project, or, in the case of Frank Wilcox, doodle. Frank sometimes read a library book. Many of the girls in his class were reading a controversial book titled *Go Ask Alice*, about a teenage girl's drug use, sex, and involvement in the counterculture. Many of the boys were reading Dalton Trumbo's *Johnny Got His Gun*, a novel written after World War I about the horrors of war that was now gathering a new audience among those protesting America's involvement in Vietnam.

If he wasn't reading during study hall, Frank used the free hour to write his stories. While trying to come up with a story idea, he often drew stick figures on a piece of paper.

He looked up to see what his teacher, Mrs. Teresa Day, was doing. She was at her desk, helping a student. Mrs. Day was young, beautiful, and friendly. She was also Frank's English teacher, and she was happy with him reading and writing and doodling during this study period. She occasionally asked to read his stories, and she offered criticisms that Frank appreciated and thought made the stories better. In some ways, she was the first editor that he ever had, and she was a tough one.

Bored and doodling, Frank took out a piece of notebook paper and, with the straight edge of a textbook, drew a horizontal line about one inch from the top of the page. Starting with that line, he drew three vertical lines, creating three columns underneath the one-inch header. Across the top of the page he wrote, "SOUR NEWS." With pencil in hand, he then began making up little news stories and handwriting them in the columns, working from top to bottom in each column. Except for a little mention of the school's basketball teams, the rest of the stories were satire—much like those he had read in *Mad* magazines purchased at Jackson's 5 & 10. At the bottom of the last column, he had a postage-stamp-size space to fill, so he drew a little cartoon with his stick figures standing around a crashed airplane.

"You OK?" one of the figures asked the other.

"Yes," the other one said.

Frank was not going to be a cartoonist.

He had just finished *SOUR NEWS* when he snapped out of his creative fog. Mrs. Day was standing over him. He had been so focused that he had not watched her get up from her desk and move through the aisles of students.

"What is this?" she asked him.

"I'm just playing around," Frank said and, horrified, watched as his teacher took the paper and read through it.

"Why don't we have copies made of this, and you can sell them at recess?" she asked him. Frank stared at her as if she had lost her mind and was babbling like a crazy woman on the way to Milledgeville. "Stop staring at me." She laughed and swatted at him with his paper.

"No one wants to read that," he said and held out his hand for her to return it.

But she didn't. "I'm going to the office and get stencils for the mimeograph machine," she said. "Can you redraw this? If you can, we can have copies made of it." Before he could answer, she had disappeared from the room. The mimeograph was a low-budget duplicating machine in use by schools and churches. Copy was typed or written on thin paper stencils the size of normal 8½ x 11 paper. The stencils were then attached to the machine, and ink was forced through the stencils and onto the paper. The ink smell was unmistakable until it dried.

Many students enjoyed taking a big breath of newly printed papers on the office mimeograph. Every time he took a big deep breath, Frank thought of Sonny and Cher.

Mrs. Day returned with a handful of stencils.

"Tonight, I want you to take your *SOUR NEWS* and redraw it on this stencil. Use a ballpoint pen to make a good impression on the stencil. If you mess up, there are lots of extras here," she said. "Bring it back to me in the morning, and I'll make copies. You can sell them at recess and use the money to pay the school for the stencils."

Frank looked at her in shock. "No one will pay a dime for this," he said. "A real comic book only costs twenty cents."

"Well, you can't give them away," she said. "Never give away your creativity."

She turned and left him sitting there with a stack of mimeograph stencils on the top of his desk.

It took Frank four tries to get *SOUR NEWS* on the stencil just the way he wanted. But even then, the vertical lines separating columns weren't completely straight, and his handwriting wavered from cursive to noncursive, depending on the short story. But it was done, and he returned it to Mrs. Day the following morning. She looked it over, took it to the office, and returned with twenty freshly printed mimeograph copies.

"Bring me two dollars at study hall," she said, winking.

Just before recess, Frank caught Wendell Mann in the hallway. His friend with the ever-smile was always ready to help anyone, anywhere, and he was now enlisted to help sell the copies of *SOUR NEWS*.

"Give me those thangs," Wendell said. "I've always wanted to do this."

Joined by Pete Yancey, Frank laughed out loud as Wendell began waving the papers in the air, shouting, "Extra! Extra! Get your issue of *SOUR NEWS*! Stick man survives airplane crash! Only one dime!"

Frank watched in shock as students reached into pockets and purses and produced dimes. Within minutes, Wendell had sold all twenty copies, and he gave Frank two dollars in dimes.

"You are a born salesman," Frank whispered to him.

"Just can't worry about what people think or say," Wendell said. "Just got to wade out there and make it happen."

Mrs. Day took the dimes to repay the school office, and then she gave Frank a dollar. Frank gave Wendell fifty cents of his dollar, figuring his friend had done the hard work of selling the newspapers.

Mrs. Day said, "Frank, you should start a school newspaper. You could put out one issue every few weeks, but make it about eight pages. Find some friends to help you." She volunteered to be the project's adult sponsor.

Frank came up with the name, calling the newspaper *FOCUS*, which he thought would provide a good heading for each page. *FOCUS* on sports, *FOCUS* on news, and *FOCUS* on people. It was also going to take a lot of creative focus to write each newspaper issue.

He first went to Wendell, and his friend agreed to write a weather segment each month. It became a comical part of each issue, as Wendell took whatever the professional Atlanta weathermen predicted and went in an entirely different direction. When he predicted snow in sunny, late March, classmates howled with laughter...until it really did snow, making Wendell an instant celebrity.

"There's nothing to predicting the weather," he told a group of classmates one afternoon. "I just listen to what the pros are saying in Atlanta, walk outside, take a big breath of air, and then predict whatever strikes me."

Frank chose his friends Jim and Macy to write sports recaps. Both played on the school's basketball teams and could write from a player's perspective. When Frank became editor of the school's yearbook as an eighth grader, Jim was chosen as the coeditor.

Charlie had no interest in drawing cartoons for the newspaper, so Frank turned to Emmett Morgan, another friend from Den 8 and a member of his Sunday School class. Emmett's cartoons rivaled those in Frank's copies of *Mad* magazine, spoofing politics and school administrators.

He recruited other friends, both girls and boys, as writers and proofreaders, and some for their penmanship to write the news stories on the stencils. Once each week, the students met after school to plan and work on the next issue. On production day, they turned the stencils over to Mrs. Day, who had copies made in the office. *FOCUS* sold for a dime and generally sold out during recess and lunch. After the school was repaid for its expenses, Mrs. Day put the rest of the money in a bag from the First Federal Bank locked away in her desk.

It didn't take long before Mrs. Day realized she had created a monster.

Frank became obsessed with *FOCUS*. And as much as he understood the meaning of the word *taskmaster* or *slave driver*, he became one. Forgetting his own sloppy issue of *SOUR NEWS*, he tore up stencils with crooked lines and redrew pages at home. He fussed at longtime friends for being late with their stories. He rewrote some of the stories because he thought he could write them better.

When he showed up one afternoon for a meeting of the newspaper staff, he found only Wendell in the room.

"Where is everyone?" he asked in disgust.

"They hate you," his friend said, smiling slightly. "Well, maybe they don't hate you, but they don't like you, and they don't want to be on the newspaper staff anymore."

"Well, we don't need them," Frank said.

Wendell looked at him. "I'll do whatever you ask me to do, but you need to relax. We can't sell these if everyone in the school is mad at you, and I don't want everyone mad at me."

Frank breathed in until his lungs expanded, and then he released it in a long sigh.

"You aren't going to cry, are you?" Wendell asked.

Mrs. Day stepped into the room and saw both boys sitting there. Some of the other staff members had already complained to her, and it was she who had sent them home.

"Frank," she said, "you have to watch that temper. It is not the best way to make and keep friends." If he felt slapped by his friends not showing up at the weekly meeting, he felt slapped again by the words of one of his favorite teachers and encouragers. But he didn't protest. Deep, deep within, he knew there was a conflict between the boy who sat in the morning devotions and the boy who lost his cool over the organization of the school newspaper. He also knew that he had to apologize to his friends even before Mrs. Day made that suggestion.

The next day, he went about trying to make things right. One by one, he sought out his friends and offered an apology, and one by one they accepted his apology. After all, these were friends of the rare kind—the kind who had been alongside you for about as long as you could remember.

"I get so mad at you," his friend Sandra said, accepting his apology. "And then the very next day, I'm back to talking to you."

At the next meeting of the *FOCUS* staff, everyone returned, and Frank apologized again to the whole group.

"Forgiven is forgiven," Wendell said. "Let's move on."

Mrs. Day arranged for the *FOCUS* staff to walk down Elm Street and visit the offices of the *Acorn County News*. If the smell of mimeograph had been intoxicating to Frank Wilcox, the smell of newsprint was even more so. He breathed in deep and held it.

On the walk back to school, he asked Mrs. Day, "Do you think they would print stories if we sent them down there? I could deliver them after school on my way to Mama's store."

Mrs. Day encouraged him to do just that, and Frank did. On his mama's old manual Royal typewriter, Frank pecked out a summary of a Boy Scout camping weekend and took it to the newspaper office. The story appeared the next week in the pages of the *Acorn County News*.

FOCUS finished the year successfully, making a profit of twenty dollars after paying for all its supplies and stencils and copying for the year. The staff decided to use the proceeds to buy Mrs. Day a wall clock for her classroom. The rest of the money was used at the Dairy Queen when Mrs. Day walked there with the staff one day after school.

As the students ate sundaes, drank Mister Mistys and chocolate shakes, Mrs. Day whispered to Frank, "And you thought you were just doodling that day in study hall."

Frank smiled at her.

THIRTY-EIGHT

THE CAFETERIA BOYCOTT

Frank lay in bed at night watching a lot of old Audie Murphy and Randolph Scott Westerns on Channel 17 in Atlanta. He also read a lot of Western novels, finally getting permission from Janet to read adult-themed Westerns. Permission had been granted on the grounds that Jack was listening to Bill Cosby comedy albums, and some of Cosby's humor included a bad word here and there.

Frank was always fascinated by the Westerns that included lynch mobs and by how easily one small conflict could escalate into a situation that was quickly out of control. There was a point of no return in the sequence of boiling events that led to someone getting hurt or lynched. Tom likened it to an out-of-control fire.

"It just takes a spark out in the hot, dry pasture for things to go up in flames pretty quickly," Tom warned his sons about playing with matches.

In the cafeteria of Acorn Junior High School, seven words were spoken one day, and those seven words represented the lighting of a match that quickly became a symbolic brush fire.

"There is a bug in my lunch," Travis Jackson said, staring at his lunch plate.

"What?" Wendell Mann asked as students jumped from their seats and surrounded Travis, who was pointing at a serving of white rice and brown gravy on his lunch plate.

"It's a bug," Travis said. "There's a bug in my rice."

"I don't see a bug," Wendell said. "All I see is rice. Maybe it's crawled under the gravy." An investigation began as Travis pushed back from his plate, disgusted. Wendell took a fork and began stirring around in the rice and gravy.

"It's in there," Travis said. "There's a bug."

Several other students had gathered around, whispering and pointing at Travis's plate, with Wendell stirring around in the rice and gravy.

"I don't see any bugs," Wendell said. "If you aren't going to eat this, can I have it?"

Travis got up from the table and walked out of the cafeteria, leaving his plate. Wendell sat down and finished the boy's lunch, including the rice and gravy.

Lunchtime at Acorn Junior High School was going to hell in a handbasket.

Before Travis Jackson had called "bug" in his rice, students were already being exposed to a national counterculture that included protests over women's rights, civil rights, and sit-ins against the Vietnam War. These were the days of crusades and bra burnings, which Frank wanted to see but couldn't figure out where bra burnings were happening and how he could get to them.

Everyone, it seemed, was against something, and everyone wanted to take a stand.

Travis began bringing his lunch from home after that day with the rice and gravy, vowing never again to eat in the school cafeteria for fear of eating bugs. It was quite a turn for Travis, who had jumped from trees, drunk gasoline, jumped from a moving car, and pulled spaghetti through his nose. Apparently, eating bugs was where he drew a curious line in the sand.

Already, there were students who always brought their lunch from home. They carefully packed sandwiches in small plastic bags with a bag of chips, maybe a piece of fruit, and a cookie. They bought milk in the school cafeteria. Travis now joined them, and he made sure everyone knew why.

"You all can eat bugs if you want to eat them, but I'm not going to eat them," he said.

Students purchasing their lunch, like Frank, began to inspect their lunch before eating it.

A girl shrieked in the cafeteria that there was a small brown bug in her pinto beans and onions. Students rushed to her table with the same zeal as if she had said, "Wow, there's a silver dollar in my spaghetti!"

For some curious reason, Wendell Mann was always at the center of the investigation. He took a fork and began stirring around in the girl's beans and onions.

"I don't see a bug in here," he said. "What did it look like?"

"It was small and brown like a no-see-um," she said. "It was swimming in my beans."

Wendell had already finished his lunch and sat down in front of the girl's plate with a dozen or more other students gathered around him. He looked across the table at another girl and said, "Can I have your cornbread?" The girl nodded her head that he could.

Wendell devoured the cornbread, pinto beans, and onions. He was enjoying double lunches from all this alleged bug spotting.

Over the next several days, more and more students began bringing their lunches instead of purchasing them in the school cafeteria. Frank was amazed that while a handful of students claimed to see bugs in their lunch, no witness had come forward to say, "I see it in there, too." Yet more and more students were protesting the cafeteria lunches on a handful of alleged sightings and the frenzy surrounding it.

Teachers tried to turn back the tide, encouraging students to eat in the cafeteria and to stop seeing bugs that just weren't there. Teachers who had sometimes brought their own lunches were now encouraged to eat cafeteria food as an endorsement of the food being served. It was too late. Now, rather than seeing a few bugs, the protesters were focusing more on what some felt was poor food quality.

Frank tried to report about the growing cafeteria boycott in the pages of *FOCUS* and quickly learned what censorship was all about. Principal Shoemake and Mrs. Day told him that he could not write about the boycott or even mention it in the pages of the newspaper. Frank joined the revolution.

In truth, Frank had always been fascinated by the children who brought their lunch. His friend Pete brought his own lunch, and Frank liked the idea of choosing what he wanted rather than having others choose what he wanted. Now, with a revolution at hand, Frank asked Janet if he could take his lunch to school. Janet allowed him to make and pack his own lunch of a ham sandwich, chips, and a banana, but she refused to pack it for him. Frank had no problem with this; he easily made two Georgia Bulldog sandwiches.

Bugs and poor food be damned. Frank was in the boycott because the administration had told him he couldn't be in it. The administration wasn't finished. A note went home to students, calling on parents to force their children to eat in the cafeteria unless there was a medical reason not to do so.

Students began not eating at all. Class after class entered the cafeteria and sat at tables with no food. Frank was among them. He even drew a fist of protest on the cover of his notebook and put his notebook in front of his place at the table.

Carolyn Holmes was in a tough spot. Her grandson was in the middle of the protest, and the administration knew it. They called on her to intervene.

"I want you to consider buying your lunch in the cafeteria," his Mema told him one day after school. "There are no bugs in the school lunches."

"I know there are no bugs in the school lunches," Frank said. "I like the school lunches. But teachers shouldn't stop us from printing school news in *FOCUS*, and this is school news."

"It is hard to teach young people about the Constitution and then tell them it doesn't apply to them," she said. "I agree with you that this has probably been handled wrong by lots of people." Then she paused. "Tomorrow, when you go to the cafeteria, I want you to do something for me. I want you to look at the ladies who have prepared a good, hot lunch that no one is eating. I want you—just you—to do that for me. Look at those ladies."

The next day, Frank walked into the cafeteria without his lunch and sat down at one of the long tables. He sat beside Wendell Mann and across from Pete Yancey. He then did as his grandmother had asked and looked at the ladies in white cafeteria uniforms standing ready to serve prepared food that no one was eating. He wanted to turn away from them, but he could not. He could not take his eyes off them. Frank thought one of them might be crying.

Frank felt as if he had been stabbed in the chest.

"Do you have lunch money?" he asked Wendell, who said that he did have enough money for lunch. "Let's go." Frank stood and began walking toward the stack of trays at one end of the lunch line. He hoped Wendell was behind him, but he wasn't turning to look. He didn't want to turn and see the dozens of students who were now watching him break the strike.

Frank took a tray and immediately felt Wendell's big hands take a tray almost at the same time.

He and Wendell got through the line, and Wendell was beside himself. The meal of the day was country-fried steak, and one of the ladies had given Wendell *three pieces* and *two yeast rolls*.

At the end of the line, the boys paid for their lunches. Wendell nudged Frank, who followed his friend's eyes back down the line. A trickle of other students had started through the line.

As quickly as the cafeteria boycott had begun, it was over. Within a few days, most of those students who had traded a hot meal for a sack lunch had come back over the picket line to eat their hot lunches again. Order was restored.

Frank and Wendell were never heralded as cafeteria heroes, and neither of them wanted to be recognized that way. One afternoon, however, waiting on his Mema, Frank went into the cafeteria to sit at a long table and finish his homework. He waved at the cafeteria manager, and she waved back at him. Frank hoped she might bring him a piece of the day's chocolate cake, but she didn't.

Soon after, an issue of *FOCUS* included a story about the dedicated service of the cafeteria ladies, how menus were selected each day, and how mass quantities of food were actually prepared. Frank snuck in a mention of the boycott.

THIRTY-NINE

THE INVITATION

No act of kindness, no matter how small, is ever wasted.
—Aesop

Frank stood outside the school and stared at another report card dotted with As and Bs and one C, in science. He had long given up on having a report card with straight As. He had long given up on being in the honor-roll listings of the *Acorn County News*. He just shook his head while staring at the scorecard in front of him. He had given it a good try in science but had come up a few points short of a B, largely because of geology. He kicked a rock, and then he kicked another. Then he spat on the ground.

He had once been jealous of those who made the honor roll with every report card, but he had long gotten over those feelings. No good came from being jealous. He had even gotten past the hurt of not being invited to join the select Making Academic Studies Habitual (MASH) club in the sixth grade. When Lester, Charlie, and Pete went on to get invitations to join the Junior Beta Club in seventh grade, Frank made additional friends through a woodworking class and Boy Scouts. He drew closer to Wendell Mann, too, because Wendell also wasn't in the Junior Beta Club.

"Don't worry about it, Frank," Wendell said. "At least we don't have to dress up like girls or go to meetings or sell candy bars or candles." In an initiation into the Junior Beta Club, some cross-dressing occurred, proving, Frank thought, that perhaps the brightest in the school weren't really that bright at all. One boy had even worn a girl's dress for an extra day when the initiation didn't require it.

Frank was trying as hard as he could to put aside these feelings of academic segregation among good friends, but the Georgia Department of Education would not cooperate. Academic lines were being drawn as the state began leveling students based on their academics. Level-one students were those at the top of their academic game. Level-two students were those who made mostly Bs and an occasional C. Level-three students were those in the unofficial academic basement. What's more, students assigned to a level stayed with that level's students throughout the day. Leveling reminded Frank every day that most of his closest and oldest childhood friends were at level one, and he was a level-two student. Whoever had come up with this system, he thought, without ever getting to know him...well, they were assholes.

Mrs. Mary Daniel, the school's eighth-grade English teacher, was the benevolent queen of the eighth grade. She was the sponsor of the school yearbook, she was the faculty sponsor of the school's Junior Beta Club, and she was the head of the faculty for the eighth grade.

Mrs. Daniel was also an agent of inclusion. She had an eye for the student left out or left behind, and she had a mission to make sure students felt included. This kindness was likely born from a physical disability that had left her walking with a noticeable limp and sometimes a cane.

It was Mrs. Daniel who had Frank promoted into level-one English and social studies. The rest of his classes were level two classes, placing Frank in the awkward position of toggling throughout each day between two completely different groups of students. It drew undesired attention from all sides—this boy who slipped in and out of levels.

"Look at it this way," Janet said, to Frank's consternation. "You get to be friends every day with twice as many students."

When Frank rolled his eyes, Janet continued. "You want to have as many friends as possible, Frank. Why not expect the next person you meet to be the best friend you will ever have?"

Now that he was placed with the level-one students in English, Mrs. Daniel began pushing him. Because of his leadership with *FOCUS*, Mrs. Daniel asked Frank to serve as the yearbook editor, and she nudged him to write more stories and send them to the *Acorn County News* for publication.

One of his published stories featured the woodworking club he had joined through Industrial Arts. The club made and sold wooden toys under the business name Diversified Products. Frank had pounded out the story on his mama's manual typewriter and walked it to the newspaper office after school one day. He had even asked to be paid for it, recalling the words of Mrs. Day to "never give away creativity."

"I would also like for you to print the story near the front page so that it helps our club sell more toys," he told the editor of the newspaper, who began to laugh even as he was paying Frank two dollars for the story. Frank shook the editor's hand as he pocketed the money.

When the story appeared in the *Acorn County News*, it came with an editor's note at the conclusion: "We deal with many public relations people, but Frank Wilcox is the only one who can walk into our office and have his own way."

While Mrs. Daniel proudly cut out his newspaper stories and stapled them to a bulletin board with the work by other students, Frank was always aware that his classmates—according to the Georgia Department of Education—were bona fide level-one students. What's more, every one of them—every single one of them—was a member of the Junior Beta Club. He was the lone exception. He felt like a level-two spy among the level-one students.

To make things worse, the school year was winding down, and the Junior Beta Club was preparing for its end-of-year party. Frank pretended to be invisible when all around him there was excitement about the after-school party and picnic at Amicalola Falls State Park. Amicalola Falls was thirty miles north of Acorn, just inside the reserve known as the Chattahoochee National Forest. The state of Georgia had included the falls in its plan for statewide, state-maintained parks featuring picnic areas and playgrounds. A walking trail led to a platform halfway up the falls, which were the highest cascading waterfalls east of the Mississippi River. The falls were also seven miles from the southernmost end of the 2,200-mile Appalachian Trail, connecting Georgia to Maine.

Frank listened—tried not to listen—to the Junior Beta Club excitement around him. Awkwardly, someone would ask him if he was excited about the party and then recoil as if struck by lightning, re-membering that Frank wasn't in the Junior Beta Club despite being in level-one English. As the party drew closer, Frank tried to get out of Mrs. Daniel's classroom each day as fast as he could.

One day he bolted from class and stopped at a water fountain down the long main hallway of the school. He drank extra water on this daily stop because it was late in the day and temperatures were warming up in the old building, which had no air conditioning. He could hardly wait to get home and out of these blue denim pants. He planned to just sit around in his white underwear until Janet yelled at him to put on some shorts. The lukewarm water of the fountain wasn't particularly refreshing, but it was wet.

As he slurped water from the low pressure of the fountain, he no-ticed a figure stopping beside him. He released the water faucet, sighed, and stood up to see his friend Pete Yancey. He and Pete had always been friends but had gotten even closer in seventh and eighth grades, largely because they were in the same homeroom class. Homeroom was where students began each morning and where the school's ad-ministrative information—such as class photographs and fund-raising efforts—was handled. Homeroom was immune from leveling. Students were assigned to homerooms alphabetically, and it was tough to avoid a Wilcox and a Yancey being in the same homeroom. The boys sat beside each other and took that time every day to visit.

They had first met in kindergarten and then were in Cub Scout Den 8 together. It had been Pete who stood outside the bathroom door, in fifth grade, as Frank dug green beans from his pants. It had been Pete who had rescued him on his jump from the Twin Lakes diving board. When Pete was on the Bullpups basketball team, Frank had been a team manager. They had discovered a friendship despite living more than twenty miles apart—Frank lived at the southernmost end of Acorn County, and Pete lived at the northernmost end of the county.

Frank stepped back from the water fountain, letting Pete get a drink. Pete handed Frank his books to hold while he bent down for a drink of water. Standing and taking back his books, Pete Yancey then asked a question that forever changed his relationship with Frank

Wilcox. In that question, a deep and lifelong friendship was galvanized. Frank never forgot it.

"Do you want to come to the Junior Beta Club picnic?"

Frank stared at Pete, expressionless. His eyes looked into Pete's eyes, and Frank's brow furrowed as he processed what he had heard and what he had least expected anyone to say to him.

"I can't go," Frank said, aggravated. "I'm not in the Junior Beta Club."

Pete said, "Well, there are extra seats on the bus, and Mrs. Daniel said that we could invite a friend to go with us. I want you to go. Lester and I talked about it, and *we* want you to go. You are our friend. No man left behind."

Speechless, Frank said simply, "OK."

Pete told Frank to go see Mrs. Daniel, who would give him a permission slip for his parents to sign, and she would give him details about the trip, too.

"Bring your baseball glove," Pete said. "Bring a bathing suit, too, 'cause we might get in the river." Pete started to jog down the hall and then ran back toward Frank. "If you've still got that spider bathing suit, don't wear it." He grinned, and Frank laughed with him.

Frank was still in a bit of shock when Lester walked up to him.

"Did Pete talk to you?" Lester asked. "We want you to go with us on the Junior Beta Club picnic. No man left behind." Frank had always respected Lester, not just because he was the smartest boy he knew but because Lester was humble about it. Lester never drew attention to his academic prowess and was always eager to help others. More than once Lester had explained something in math that was difficult for Frank to understand. Frank also appreciated Lester's cautionary approach to things. Frank had a kinship with Lester, too, around faith, and it was Lester who had pushed Frank to lead an occasional morning devotion.

"Pete just told me," Frank said, feeling a big lump in his throat. These friends had no idea how much he needed this invitation to a party, to feel a part of something, to feel included, and how much he needed someone to say "no man left behind."

"Well, good," Lester said. "I think it'll be fun. Mrs. Daniel said she was going to bring some brownies." Lester knew how much Frank loved brownies.

Frank had fun on the bus ride to the waterfalls. The cheerleader whose hand he had held after a basketball game was also on the bus, and he noticed she was now sitting with Jim Vinton. He smiled when he saw they were not holding hands but figured they probably would be if the sun was setting on the ride home. Darkness had a big effect on the courage it took to hold hands on a school bus.

The picnic and party were a lot of fun. Someone had also invited Wendell; and Frank, Pete, Lester, and Wendell spent time hiking up the falls as far as they were allowed. All the students ate a grilled hot-dog supper, played softball, and even waded into the river. Surrounded by lifelong friends who cared about him, Frank never once thought about the party being exclusively planned for the Junior Beta Club. It didn't matter. It did occur to him, as he looked around at his friends, that things would change as they moved to high school. Things had to change as they got older.

It was at the picnic that Charlie Keller announced that he was having a sleepover following the upcoming eighth-grade graduation. This prompted a retelling of the night Lester had played possum while the boys of Den 8 confessed their individual love interests. That story prompted the telling of other stories from their days in primary school, and Charlie was at the forefront of the telling.

Frank stood on the fringe of the students with Lester, Pete, and Wendell.

"Thank you for inviting me, Pete," Frank said, trying not to make a big deal about it but wanting to make his point. "I'm glad I came."

"I'm glad you did, too," Pete said, never taking his eyes off the storytelling and laughing to himself. Charlie was funny. Pete put his arm across Frank's shoulder. "We are going to have fun in high school."

"I wonder what high school is going to be like," Frank said.

"I doubt you'll be in the Beta Club," Lester said, bringing laughter from all four of them. "Wendell probably won't, either."

"Don't want to be," Wendell said as the laughing continued. "I think I'll join Future Farmers of America."

"You live in town," Frank said. "You don't live on a farm."

"I know, but I like cows and chickens," Wendell said. "My grand-parents have farms."

There was more laughing.

"Maybe we can start our own club," Frank said.

"I won't be on a newspaper staff," Lester said, laughing again. "They say you are an ass."

"Me either," Pete said. "I'll buy and read it, but that's all. I'm going to play football." Wendell said he planned to play football, too. Frank was still wrestling with how in the hell he was going to get out of play-ing football. He had signed up because his friend Sandra had said, "All the boys play football." That night he looked in the bathroom mirror, stared at his adolescent weight gain, and said to himself, "Frank, you are an idiot."

Later, as the students were picking up trash and packing up the bus to leave, Mrs. Daniel called Frank over to where she was sitting with another adult chaperone.

"Frank," she whispered. "Would you be willing to be one of our speakers at graduation?"

The timid boy who had cringed at the thought of reading his stories in front of the fourth-grade class was gone now. The lazy boy who first rejected an invitation to usher at Georgia football games was gone, too.

Frank stared at her for a moment and then said, "Yes, yes, I will." She patted him on the hand and watched as he returned to his friends—the state of Georgia's academic levels had evaporated.

FORTY

GRADUATION

It was the last week of school—the last week of eighth grade and the last week before high school. Frank's Mema was in an after-school faculty meeting, and Frank walked through the buildings of the old school, thinking.

It was hot in the old buildings, and the heat caused the old wooden walls and floors to smell. There were fifty years of sweat, dirt, and polish in this old building. The smell of adolescence seemed to hang in the air despite open windows that tried to keep the stale air circulating. If school had a smell, this building had a school smell to it.

As he walked with his books, Frank also held a blue, semi-transparent plastic water gun in his hand. This last week of school, students had been allowed to bring water guns for use during recess or physical education, and the school property soon resembled the O. K. Corral. There were gunfights as students changed classes and during classes when teachers weren't looking. Van Piper had even dumped a trash can full of water down the stairwell onto unsuspecting students.

Principal Garland Shoemake realized that this was a fun idea gone wildly bad and tried to rein in the water pistols before the week was over, but finally, the teachers threw up their hands in surrender and brought their own water guns. Frank laughed at his Mema, who had three "loaded" guns on the top of her desk and wasn't afraid to use them. She had called more than one boy to her desk only to playfully shoot him in the face with a water gun.

There had been other times of play at the school that year. For a while, students became obsessed with yo-yos, especially the Duncan brand. Students brought them, traded them, and played with them so much that teachers began confiscating them. That led to a yo-yo underground, with students sneaking them around the school. Then there were the clackers—two small acrylic balls, each tied to the end of a single string. The two strings were joined together by a plastic ring that slipped over the ring finger. With the right rhythm, a skilled student could swing the balls so that they clacked together. When one of the Gainey sisters used a set of clackers to beat the hell out of another girl, the toy was banned from the school with the threat of expulsion.

Walking, Frank emptied his water gun against a wall and then put the empty gun in his back pocket, all the while knowing a little bit of water would leak into his pants. He actually hoped for the leak because it was so hot this late in the afternoon. He backed against a wall outside his Mema's classroom and slid down the wall until he sat on the floor.

Bored, Frank opened his English book and took out the two-page speech that Mrs. Daniel had written for him to read at graduation. When Mrs. Daniel had asked him to speak at graduation, she actually had asked him to read the speech that she had written for him. Frank went from being honored at the invitation to feeling like a trained monkey. He didn't like the prepared speech, which was more of a historical tribute to the old buildings and decades-old memories of the school.

When his Mema had questioned why Mrs. Daniel didn't let him write his own speech, Frank had decided to do that very thing. He would publicly practice and go along with Mrs. Daniel's speech, but he secretly began writing his own speech. Now, sitting in the hallway of the empty school building, he read and rewrote part of his speech.

A part of Frank's defiance was rooted in grasping for control because he felt so out of control. Change was drowning him. Construction was underway for his family's new home two miles outside of Acorn, and that meant moving away from the family farm on Brookwood Road—it was the only home he had ever known. He was wrought with sadness over it. The move was inevitable after his Granny's death the year before. She had been such an integral part of the farm's management that R.C. found it difficult to continue without her. He sold the farm and moved to Atlanta. Kathryn's death also caused Frank to step fully into adolescence—it was time to grow up and be more confident.

He was uncertain, too, about this move to high school. He had gotten comfortable with his friends of the past eight years and was now
going to be thrown together with students from all over Acorn County.

Tom and Janet were also talking about having another baby despite
the fact that Wayne, his youngest brother, was already ten. Frank was
aware that he would be in high school when this baby was born, and
that was going to change a lot of things at home.

Then there was Charlie. Frank couldn't remember a day of his life
without Charlie Keller. He could not remember a single major experience of his life without Charlie Keller beside him. Now, as budding
teenagers, they were drifting in different social directions. It was a
natural drifting brought about by adolescence and interests. Charlie
was going to be a high-school athlete; Frank was not. Charlie was much
more popular than Frank and enjoyed entertaining the crowds. Frank
was just more withdrawn and preferred a handful of close friends such
as Pete, Wendell, and Lester. Frank knew that he and Charlie couldn't
remain best friends simply because their mamas were best friends, and
he knew that high school was probably going to pull them apart.

All this change was maddening. Frank decided he was going to
make a statement with this speech. He couldn't control a lot of things
in his life right now, but he could control this speech. It was going to be
his speech, and it was going to be done his way, even if he had to shock
everyone on the night of graduation.

He heard his Mema call for him because she was his ride home
from school. He gathered up the speech and hid it away. No one in his
family knew about the speech. When practicing in front of Janet, Frank
used Mrs. Daniel's speech, but otherwise he wrote and practiced his
own speech in secret. Janet had no idea about the graduation anarchy
being planned by her eldest son.

But Janet did have an idea about graduation.

"I think you and Charlie should wear red bow ties," she said.

Frank looked at his mama as if she had two heads.

"No, Mama," he said. "I'll just wear a red church tie like everyone
else."

But Janet was on a mission, and that week she went shopping in Atlanta for a red clip-on bow tie that ended up being the size of a grown man's fist. It was huge. When Frank put the tie on his neck he felt like a clown.

Janet had bought one for Charlie, too.

"I think it will be cute if you two lifelong friends wear bow ties," she said. "I've already talked it over with Midge, and I'm going to give Charlie one of these ties."

Frank knew Charlie wasn't going to wear a bow tie. Charlie had recently turned down an opportunity to spend the night with him and had even been too busy to read and laugh over Frank's stories. No, Charlie wasn't wearing a bow tie just because Frank was going to wear one. Those days were over.

Frank tried appealing to Tom, hoping his daddy would tell Janet to forget the bow tie, but that idea took no roots.

"Just wear the damn tie," Tom said while trying to crank the family's lawn mower. It was not Frank's best decision to approach his frustrated daddy, and Tom was surely frustrated lately. All the emotion Frank felt about moving from Brookwood Road was amplified in Tom. It was Tom's mama who had died, and he was moving from the only home he could remember. On top of that, he and R. C. had parted ways on the farm, and it just about destroyed their relationship.

Frank moaned about the tie to Wendell, who tried to make his best friend feel better about it but also said, "I hope your mama doesn't mention it to my mama at church. I don't want to wear a bow tie."

That was when Frank decided to tell Wendell about the speeches.

"Can I tell you a secret?" Frank asked Wendell. "I'm dying to tell someone, but you have to promise to keep it a secret." Wendell pledged his loyalty, which Frank never had reason to question. "I'm writing my own speech. I don't want to read the speech that Mrs. Daniel has written."

"She's going to kill you," Wendell said. "She's going to kill you graveyard dead." Remembering that Frank had been elected Most Dependable of the eighth-grade class, Wendell said, "We should have elected you Most Likely to Be Killed by the Age of Fourteen." Wendell put his hands on his own throat, demonstrating how Mrs. Daniel would likely choke the life out of Frank.

Frank gave Wendell the speech written by Mrs. Daniel, and his friend read it quickly. He gave it back to Frank.

"It's pretty goofy," Wendell said. "But you might want to talk to her about using your own speech. She might not let you graduate. That would be double embarrassing if you gave the speech, sat down, and then Mr. Shoemake said, 'Sorry, you can't graduate. You should have used the right speech.'"

"Why would it be double embarrassing?" Frank asked.

Wendell smiled and said, "You are already going to be embarrassed by wearing that bow tie."

Frank had thought about all the bad things that could happen to him because of his speech, which was why he had planned to have both speeches with him when he took to the stage for graduation. He thought about seeking the counsel of the girls in his class, but the counsel about playing high school football had shaken his confidence in them as a group.

In the end, he decided the fewer people who knew about his plan, the better off everyone would be.

Graduation was planned for the Friday evening of the last day of the school year. Frank got up that warm morning, excited, and hummed as he walked into the kitchen for breakfast. Frank was a morning person, always the first out of bed and usually humming. Tom and Janet stood in the kitchen as he walked into the room, and Frank's eyes saw the wrapped gift on the table.

Janet picked up the gift and handed it to him. "Congratulations on your graduation, son," she said. "We wanted to give you something." Frank was shocked; he had no idea graduations came with unexpected gifts. He tore into the box and found a square, black RCA clock radio about half the size of a bread box.

"You are going to have your own room in the new house," Janet said. "And high-school boys need to take responsibility for getting themselves up in the morning and getting ready for school."

More change, Frank thought. He couldn't remember a day when he hadn't shared a room and a bed with Jack, and some years he'd shared a room with both Jack and Wayne. In the new house, the brothers would be separated in different rooms. As he brushed his teeth, squeezing the toothpaste through the small opening, he thought it was a perfect picture of his life right now: everything in his life was being squeezed forward.

Frank thanked his parents for the clock radio, unpacked it, and plugged it into the wall. The radio had dials for both AM and the popular FM stations, which opened up a lot of musical variety and possibilities from Atlanta. The clock did not have a traditional analog face but instead had small, numbered cards that flipped over to show the hour and minutes. It was different, and Frank liked it a lot. He tested the alarm and found it to be extremely loud.

Jack threw his hands over his ears and said, "It will be loud enough to wake me up, too. They can just get me a fishing rod when I graduate from junior high school. I won't need an alarm clock."

At Acorn Junior High School, education was the furthest thing from anyone's mind on that last day of school. Water gun fights broke out everywhere, and teachers simply ignored them. Some students had even brought water balloons, soaking classmates and teachers alike. One of the balloons was even hurled across the lunchroom, creating pandemonium. During the morning, the eighth graders were excused from class to the old gymnasium, where they practiced graduation. Frank even read Mrs. Daniel's speech aloud to his classmates, and Mrs. Daniel beamed at hearing her words about the history of the school buildings. He felt a little guilty, but not so much that he changed his mind about substituting the speech.

Several moms and faculty members treated the graduating class to a lunchtime cookout on the school property. Frank's Mema brought a chocolate layer cake, which caused Frank to stand near the dessert table for most of the cookout, assuring himself a piece of her cake. After the cookout, students went to their final two class periods of the day, and then everyone went home to prepare for the evening's graduation ceremony.

Frank was wearing the red bow tie when he arrived back at the school for graduation. He stepped from the back of the family's Ford station wagon and nervously approached his friends. In his front pockets, he had the two speeches. His heart was pounding, and it only increased when his friends saw him. Their eyes went directly to the bow tie, and Frank noticed the chuckling. He was sweating buckets in the late May heat.

Charlie was in the center of a group of boys, laughing and telling stories, and he was not wearing his red bow tie. He looked at Frank, raised his chin as a greeting, and smiled. Frank saluted him.

"Frank." Mrs. Daniel's voice snapped him out of a fog. "Please come with me to the back of the stage." Frank followed her, wishing he could just stay with his friends and be one of the guys. But this train was rolling, and it was rolling full steam down the tracks. Inside, Mrs. Daniel pointed him to his place on the stage.

As the ceremony began, Frank stood on the stage with the dignitaries, including Mrs. Daniel, and watched his friends walk into the gymnasium past adoring family and friends. Funeral-home fans were waving all through the crowd as people fanned for relief against the stale heat of the gym. Frank felt a horrible pain of unworthiness bubbling up like an old friend. He knew he was only in this chosen position because of Mrs. Daniel. Frank was completely confident that he was not the people's choice for this honor of representing his classmates, but he was going to embrace it.

That was when he noticed the big smile on Wendell's face. Frank laughed to himself. Wendell mouthed some words that Frank thought were "What are you going to do?" but later learned were "You are going to die." Wendell knew Frank pretty well, and Wendell knew which speech he was going to use.

Frank had his hands on his pockets, feeling the two speeches inside them. Then panic washed over him. Which pocket contained which speech? He couldn't be sure. His teeth began chattering inside his head, and his legs felt as if they had no feeling. He felt a wave of panic.

Which pocket? Which pocket?

Oh, crap; now I have to pee, he thought, quite sure the entire audience was focused on him and watching him squirm on the stage with these adults. Sweat was pouring off his forehead, and Pastor Roger Williams, beside him on stage, handed him a handkerchief and whispered, "Just remember that favorite Bible verse of yours." Frank remembered standing in Sunday-evening worship and reading Joshua 1:9: "Be strong and of a good courage; be not afraid, neither be thou dismayed: for the Lord thy God is with thee whithersoever thou goest." He could almost hear his beloved Granny, now in heaven, whispering words of strength and courage to him from her bed at Emory Hospital in Atlanta.

Mrs. Daniel took the podium.

"I want to welcome all of you to our graduation program tonight. On behalf of the eighth-grade faculty, we are so proud of these graduates, and we join with their families and friends in celebrating this accomplishment and the bold step ahead into high school.

"We are going to have a prayer by Roger Williams, pastor of the First Baptist Church, and then we will hear from one of our eighth graders, Frank Wilcox," she said. "Frank was editor of the school yearbook this year and was voted Most Dependable by his classmates."

Hoping to further encourage his young church member, Pastor Williams took the podium and said, "I am honored to be here tonight. I especially look forward to what Frank will share with us, and I'm sure we can *depend* on him to do a great job." He emphasized the word *depend*, heaving learned that Frank was named Most Dependable. There was a chuckle in the audience.

Frank forgot about having to pee. He now wanted to puke—right there in front of God, faculty, family, and friends. Frank's teeth were chattering as if he were standing naked on the North Pole.

Pastor Williams prayed and then sat down, and Frank saw that empty podium waiting on him. Frank stood and walked to it, reaching out to it for support in a gathering storm. He reached into his right pocket, determining that fate would now decide his speech. He unfolded the speech he had written and placed it on the podium. Time slowed down. He could feel his own pulse as his heart beat inside his chest. Everything was in slow motion. Was he passing out?

Frank looked up and saw her sitting in the back row of the auditorium. It was Mrs. Carolyn Hicks. She raised her hands and pretended to clap, and then she blew him a kiss—or maybe she pretended to shoot a foul shot. He wasn't completely sure, but he knew that she was cheering him on. So he focused his eyes on her and began his speech, speaking directly to one of his greatest encouragers of the past eight years.

Instead of a tribute to the old school buildings and to the memories of bygone decades, Frank talked about why he loved Acorn County and why he loved Acorn. He talked about why small-town friends are like an extended part of family and how important it was to see schoolteachers who were also church leaders and to see church leaders who worked in stores or were your dentist or doctor. He talked about how nice it was that the county librarian knew your name, even as a boy; how a store owner took time to teach you how to sell raffle tickets to adults; and how your friend who owned the drugstore always acted as if his day's highlight was when you walked into the store. He talked about how much he loved the Dairy Queen and how sometimes they started making him a chocolate shake before he even ordered it. They knew him that well.

Frank talked about how much he loved homemade chocolate pie at local restaurants. He talked about how, in small towns, people didn't care if boys played baseball on the courthouse square and broke a window or dinged a passing car with a foul ball. He reminded everyone that children in Acorn could run and play all over town without parents worrying. Where else could you go to the doctor and get stitches from a man who loved you, knew everyone in your family, and may have even brought you into the world?

Frank even said the grumpiest of people really didn't mean any harm, and they helped a boy learn lessons, too. Frank smiled at Charlie. He talked about community and how people looked after one another, cared for one another, and prayed for one another. He had seen it all firsthand through the deaths of two grandparents—people in Acorn turned out by the hundreds to say goodbye to a friend now in heaven and to hug one another. He talked about how lucky they were in Acorn to have a Fourth of July parade that brought everyone together during the summer, a countywide fair, beauty contests, a talent show, and a big lake where they could all easily swim and enjoy family and friends.

He talked about living on the farm, separated from his friends during the long summer, and how coming back to school in the fall was like a reunion with people he had loved for his whole life. He talked about the fun they had at school on the playgrounds and at lunchtime and on field trips to the circus. Frank looked at his daddy and smiled. He then looked at Van Piper and said something about learning the painful lessons of life, especially when it came to treating people kindly. He confessed that he was never spanked at school but that he had sure learned how to duck walk down the primary school's cafeteria ramp. Mrs. Hicks threw her head back and laughed when he said that.

He talked about how they had helped one another with homework—even though none of them had ever been able to help him enough to make the honor roll or join the Junior Beta Club. There was some laughter from the audience. He talked about sleepovers, and he talked about the morning devotions at school—smiling at Lester—and how fortunate they were to be able to pledge allegiance to the flag and gather before school to pray. He said he wasn't worried about high school because he would be going there with his friends, and they would take care of one another. He looked directly at Pete Yancey when he said that. No man left behind, he said.

Frank looked at Charlie and said some friends were just family and always would be, and that he was fortunate to have a friend like that—someone who was his brother even if they had different parents—someone who pushed him to be better and bolder than he wanted to be.

Frank's eyes found someone else in the crowd. He found Mrs. Teresa Day, and he looked at her with tears in his eyes as he thanked teachers who saw a student's skills and hobbies that went beyond textbooks. He talked about teachers who encouraged students to be who God made them to be and to do what God put them on earth to do. Frank also thanked his Mema for being just that kind of teacher. He looked back at Mrs. Hicks, who was now standing in the very back of the gym and giving him two thumbs up.

Mostly, Frank talked too long. His four-page speech was twice as long as Mrs. Daniel's tribute to the school's history. And while Frank wasn't really that eloquent in his speech delivery, his points were well taken, and he noticed that many of the heads were nodding in agreement as he talked. When he finished, a few people stood and clapped, and then everyone stood and clapped. He turned to Mrs. Daniel to say he was sorry but noticed there were tears in her eyes. As he walked to his seat, she took his arm and hugged him. Pastor Williams shook his hand, and Frank began to cry—not sobbing, but just releasing all the pent-up nervousness.

After all the students had marched onstage and received small diplomas that really meant nothing, Superintendent Lambert praised everyone in the class, and Pastor Williams closed the evening with a prayer. A reception of cake and punch followed in the school cafeteria. All of his friends were dividing up into groups for transportation to Charlie's house for a sleepover graduation party.

Frank stood next to his parents and whispered, "Can you take me to Charlie's by myself?"

"Don't you want to ride with your friends?" Janet asked him.

He shook his head no and said, "I need to walk down the hall and be by myself for a minute." He walked out of the cafeteria and down the main hallway of the school. He turned a dark corner and slid down the wall until he was sitting on the floor. He closed his eyes and breathed in the old, stale air of the school building. He was emotionally exhausted. He could hear the excitement of students and families coming all the way down from the cafeteria.

"Frank?" a voice called for him as he heard steps approaching.

He leaned over and awkwardly looked around the corner to see who was coming down the hall.

He recognized her and sprang to his feet.

"Hey," he said, taking a step toward her and giving her a hug as she stretched out her arms.

"It struck me this week that my very first students were graduating from junior high school," she said. "I thought it would be fun to come out and see how you all had changed." She stood back and looked him over. He was heavier than he had been in first grade, carrying a pudge around his middle and in his face. His Papa R. C. called it "loading up to shoot up."

"Thank you for coming," Frank said in the shadows of the hall.

"It was a fine speech," she said. "You sure aren't the shy little boy counting the minutes until your mama picked you up from school. You've grown up."

He shrugged, not really knowing what to say. He knew that shy boy was still in him somewhere.

"Do you have big plans for summer?" she asked him.

"I'm going to summer school and taking a typing class," he said. "My friend Lester is taking a class, too. We're doing that together. I want to do more writing, and I need to learn to type."

Miss Johnson was no longer Miss Johnson, but Frank didn't want to get into conversations about marriage with a grown woman he hadn't seen in seven years.

"That's so great," she said. "I'm proud of you. I'm proud of all of you. I saw Charlie Keller, and I could have picked him out of a crowd of a hundred people. He's still so funny."

Frank nodded his agreement. "He's the most popular boy in this school. Everyone loves him." Frank saw his parents enter the hallway from the cafeteria, and he escorted his first-grade teacher down to see them. Janet didn't recognize her right away, but after an introduction, they talked for several minutes.

"Frank," his former teacher said, "I am proud of you. Go do great things, and be kind to people." She hugged him again and walked away. Frank watched her go, thinking it was fitting that the teacher who had seen him on his first day of school was there on his last day of eighth grade. He looked around the empty hallways one more time and followed his parents outside. Acorn County High School awaited in the fall.

FORTY-ONE

POSTSCRIPT

The sun came up on Saturday morning following Friday evening's eighth-grade graduation from Acorn Junior High School. In Charlie Keller's basement, twenty boys groaned and stretched from a long night of card playing, music, telephone calls to girls, and too much Coca-Cola. Wendell Mann was particularly glad to see the sunrise, because he had almost died during the night—not so much from the bottle rocket exploding near his mouth but from the medical treatment received from a bunch of eighth-grade boys.

It was already late, following graduation, when the boys finally arrived at Charlie's home. After the ceremony, the boys had joined all their classmates and families for a cake-and-ice-cream reception in the school cafeteria. Then they piled into cars for a carpool to the Kellers' nearby home.

Where the bottle rockets came from was never really clear. Wendell had them but did not claim to have brought them. Fireworks were illegal in Georgia but were sold across the South Carolina state line, about two hours northeast along Interstate 85. Someone had gotten the fireworks, and one of the boys had packed them away for the sleepover. What better way to celebrate the end of eight years of school than by shooting illegal fireworks?

Secured away in the basement, away from Midge and Joel Keller, who were upstairs, the boys decided to sneak through the sliding glass basement doors and make their way to one of the Kellers' nearby pastures—far enough away to not be heard. Someone even had the great idea to leave a radio turned on in the basement to keep things downstairs from being too quiet and maybe drawing suspicion.

Charlie and Wendell led the mob of boys in a quiet jog away from the Kellers' home.

Frank and Lester Freemont stood outside and watched the boys disappear down the driveway and into the woods.

"Shooting fireworks is illegal," Lester said, and neither of the boys liked the idea of sneaking away to do something. "My dad would say, 'If you have to sneak around to do something, it's probably not something you should be doing.'" Frank agreed with him.

The mob should have known a bad wind was in the air. Before shooting the fireworks, the boys attempted to toilet paper an eighth-grade teacher's yard but were caught in the act and made to clean up the mess.

"We had better go after them, just to make sure this doesn't get out of hand," Frank said, wrongly believing that any of these boys would listen to him about anything. The bow tie had sealed the deal on that hope. He started walking down the driveway, toward the pasture, and Lester walked with him.

They had not reached the mob when they heard the first bottle rocket explode in the air. Bottle rockets were one of the simpler forms of skyrocket fireworks. A bottle rocket was a small rocket attached to a stabilizing stick. The stick was placed in a bottle, the fuse was lit, and the rocket shot into the air for a few feet before exploding with a pop in the air.

Frank and Lester continued walking, hearing another explosion and then a pause as they guessed another rocket was being set in a bottle. And then there was prolonged silence. Pete Yancey was the first to reach them, and he was running, panting.

"Wendell has blown up his face," he said. "A bottle rocket exploded near his face."

Frank started running toward the direction Pete had come from. Lester and Pete were soon running with him. Pete had decided to return to the scene. The trio met the pack of boys. Steve Dickson was the only boy big enough to help Wendell, who was one of the strongest boys of the whole bunch. Someone had taken off a sweaty T-shirt, and Wendell was holding it on his mouth.

"Blam blah bloom," Wendell babbled as he approached Frank. "I'b otay."

Frank could tell his friend was anything but OK. The T-shirt was soaked in blood, and in the moonlight, it looked as if Wendell's mouth stretched to his ear. Lester and Pete stepped in to help Steve Dickson stabilize Wendell for the hike back to the Kellers' basement.

"What happened?" Frank asked Jim Vinton.

"I'm not really sure," Jim said. "He was lighting the fuse, and we were all standing back. I guess it was a short fuse, or maybe he accidentally lit the rocket. But it just exploded while his head was still too close."

Frank looked at Pete Yancey, who nodded in agreement. "I was standing pretty far back from everyone else; I'm not really sure what happened, but that sounds right."

As quietly as possible, the boys got Wendell back to the Kellers' basement, and he crawled onto a sofa against one wall. He looked up into a sea of faces staring down at him with mixed reviews. Some of the expressions suggested he had lost half his face; some of the expressions had a twisted sense of excitement on them.

Charlie Keller appeared with several bath towels, and the boys took turns smearing Wendell's blood all over him as a means of trying to clean him up. One of the towels was dipped in water; another was dipped in Sprite because, as someone said, "It's almost water."

"We have to tell someone," Lester said, and both Pete and Frank agreed. "He needs to go to the hospital." Frank recalled the stitches he had gotten from the rock hitting the back of his head, and this was a lot worse than that. The side of Wendell's face was badly swelling.

But the mob rose up, and it was suggested that they wait to see if the bleeding would stop on its own. Nothing would kill a fun party like having to haul a participant off to the hospital for stitches—acquired by illegally shooting off bottle rockets after sneaking away from the house.

Then someone suggested aspirin as a solution. Charlie disappeared and returned with a familiar bottle of Bayer-brand aspirin. None of these just-graduated eighth graders realized that aspirin helped prevent blood clotting, and they proceeded to give Wendell a sizeable dose.

The rationale was that Wendell was in pain, and the more aspirin he took, the less pain he would endure. That was the logic among a group of boys—none of whom would ever be a medical doctor or a pharmacist.

Someone suggested alcohol. One of the boys produced a half-empty pint bottle of Jack Daniel's Tennessee whiskey. He had brought the bottle from his home and now said, "I've seen them give liquor to a dying man on *Gunsmoke*. I think it's supposed to be good for gunshots, and Wendell looks gunshot to me." Fortunately for Wendell, wiser heads prevailed and prevented anyone from pouring Tennessee whiskey on the ragged cut along the boy's jawline.

Charlie had found a Polaroid camera, wormed his way close to Wendell's face, and took a picture. He gave no reason for taking the picture, but someone in the crowd said, "Good idea, Charlie."

"Get him a blanket," came a suggestion, and the boys covered Wendell in blankets. "Sweating is good for him. It will keep him from getting a fever." Lester asked for the source of this medical information and learned that the boy's great-grandmother said it was the truth; she also bought warts for a quarter each. The art of wart buying, under a full moon, involved rubbing a person's warts with a quarter and expecting them to disappear within a week. Nothing said, "We care about our friend" like resorting to Old Granny's witchy wart-removing counsel.

Miraculously, Wendell did not die. However, he lay semi-conscious on the sofa, covered in blankets, filled with aspirin, threatened with Jack Daniel's and Sprite, while the party went on around him. Every now and again one of the boys walked over to check on him, patted him on the head, and offered him more aspirin. During a game of poker, four boys even dealt Wendell into the game and played his hand for him. The boys were all about camaraderie. Wendell was in and out of sleep— or consciousness—or both—as card games and conversations went on as if nothing had really happened.

Frank, Lester, and Pete joined the others in checking on Wendell, and finally Lester could stand it no more. He went upstairs and informed the Kellers that Wendell had blown up his mouth with a bottle rocket. Charlie's father descended the basement stairs in two leaps. The

Kellers took Wendell to the Acorn County Hospital emergency room, where he received stitches in his mouth and legitimate painkiller.

The boys were actually surprised when Wendell returned to the basement and then to the sofa. It turned out that Wendell's parents had left town for a business meeting in Augusta after the graduation exercises. The Kellers notified them of the accident and ensured them that Wendell was fine. To their credit, the Kellers offered Wendell a restful bedroom upstairs, but he mumbled about wanting to rejoin his friends. The Kellers figured that he had already survived the worst of it. If he wasn't dead already, he was going to survive. Hell, Wendell Mann just might be invincible.

Returned to the sofa, Wendell smiled a horrific grin at Frank, who sat on the sofa's arm.

"You are my best friend," Wendell slurred through hazy eyes while patting Frank on the arm.

Frank felt guilty that he had not spoken up earlier and appreciated the fact that Lester had done so. Lester and Pete sat on the floor in front of the sofa as Wendell drifted off into a painkiller-induced and much-needed sleep. Frank laughed at the retelling of the accident story now that everything was out in the open and Wendell was going to live. Frank, Pete, and Lester spent the rest of the night there around the sofa, making sure Wendell had what he needed. He slept through almost everything.

The next morning the exhausted freshly graduated eighth-grade boys made their way to cars arriving to take them home. It was the official beginning of summer vacation. Frank climbed in the backseat of his family's station wagon and lay across the bench-style seat. He was going to sleep all the way home to Brookwood Road.

The station wagon door opened. It was Pete Yancey.

"Call me over the summer," he said. "We'll get a few of us together and camp out in the woods behind my house." He shut the door and then opened it again. "I told Wendell not to bring any bottle rockets." He was gone, and Frank laughed to himself.

ACKNOWLEDGMENTS

It has been fifty years since my mama, Nancy Vaughan, walked me into the Cumming Elementary School on Elm Street in Cumming, Georgia, to the first-grade class taught by Miss Jeannette Johnson. I started elementary school during the 1965–1966 school year.

The elementary-school building on Elm Street still stands with some additions on the back side of the property. It is now used by the Forsyth County School System as the Almon C. Hill Educational Center. In late June 2015, gathering research for this book, I went back to the old school building, walked its hallways, stood in my former classrooms, and sat for a few minutes in the old lunchroom with its stage. I visited with a staff member working in the room that had once been the library. I was there for two hours and took photographs, and the memories came rushing back to me.

The building I refer to as Acorn Junior High School was built in 1923 as Cumming Public School, serving grades one through eleven. It was the first school in Forsyth County to offer a high school diploma. When I attended junior high school there, the building was referred to as Cumming Upper Elementary and served grades six through eight. High school students had moved on to a newer Forsyth County High School—now Forsyth Central High School—back toward Elm Street. My late daddy, Doug Vaughan, was in the new high school's first graduating class (1956). Today, the old 1920s building is owned by the City of Cumming and is The Cumming Playhouse. I'm so thankful that the building still stands. One of the reasons Mrs. Mary Daniel wanted me to read her historic speech at graduation was because the building was scheduled to be demolished, as a new middle school was being constructed. That demolition never happened. In 2000, the school building was named to The National Register of Historic Places. The old gymnasium no longer stands. (Source: Historical Society of Forsyth County).

The success of *Brookwood* Road, published in 2014, inspired me to write and publish this follow-up book of stories from elementary and junior high school. I want *Elm Street* to be a tribute to small town life, where everyone knows your name, and as a tribute to the lifelong friendships made from walking through school together year after year.

I grew up in Forsyth County, Georgia—about forty miles due north of Atlanta. During the time frame of this book—again, the 1960s and very early 1970s—the population of Forsyth County was 12,170 (1960) to 16,928 (1970). The population when I graduated high school in 1977 was about 25,000. Today, in 2016, the population of Forsyth County is more than 200,000. Forsyth County, Georgia, has become one of the fastest-growing counties in the United States (statistics from the US Census Bureau).

That emotional place of my childhood is gone, and many of the physical buildings are gone, too. I often think of the departed heroes of my childhood – the men and women I respected because of the way they led our community and nurtured along children like me. I wish I could go back to the county library and see Mrs. Potts or visit Doc Marcinko at the Rexall. Heaven is going to be quite a reunion.

I hope this project will in some way preserve the beauty of small-town life for my children and grandchildren, and for yours, too. Those of us walking the halls of Forsyth County schools and the streets of Cumming, Georgia, in the 1960s and 1970s had a great childhood. If you grew up in small-town America, I bet you have similar memories.

Please allow me to thank some very important people:

- My Vicki for her encouragement and support of my stories over the thirty years of our marriage. These books—and any future books—would not happen without her encouragement. I appreciate her patience when I had to shut the office door and just write, and I appreciate her willingness to stop and read when I needed someone to give me a straightforward opinion. She's my answered prayer; words can't adequately describe how much I love her. Love really does follow the laughter, and we laugh all the time.

- My mama for her support of this book series. She has been my lifelong encourager, critic, inquisitor, and champion, knowing which role she needed to play at just the right time. I can't imagine where I would be in this life without her influence on me as a boy and as a man. She introduced me to Jesus, and she taught me to love turnip greens, fried squash, chicken pie, chicken livers, and chocolate cake. She deeply loves Forsyth County, its people, and its places.

- My sons Andrew, Richard, and Matthew—and my daughter-in-law, Elizabeth—for reading *Brookwood Road* and for encouraging me in these projects. The boys have heard a lot of these stories as bedtime stories or as traveling stories. They understand the power of storytelling, especially when it comes to keeping memories alive.

- My son William, who is my silent partner in this book project. William is very important to my writing and editing process. As a professional stage actor currently living in Washington, DC, William understands the science of storytelling and bringing a story to life. William reviewed every chapter as I wrote it, providing brutally honest feedback toward a goal of making the stories better. He's also a great encourager. I completely rewrote about one-third of these chapters because of William's feedback. Finally, he read it all again and gave his approval. If you like my books, thank William—my Willie Bell—because he makes them better.

- My friend Christine Jeffcoat-Furem, who is the manager of the Humpus Bumpus Bookstore in Cumming. One of the joys of this project has been meeting new people along the way. I have been blessed by Christy's support and encouragement. She and the bookstore have really become hometown partners in the project, and I appreciate her very much. During this effort, she blessed my family by taking some old photographs of our *Brookwood Road* home and recreating it through hand-drawn artwork. It's beautiful and hangs in my office. She has a gift for memorializing people and places through art. Here is her website: www.jeffcoatart.com.

- My friend Gearguy. Gearguy has helped me more than you can ever imagine with book cover artwork, Facebook cover artwork, and marketing help. He could easily just take my orders for graphic design, but he goes beyond order-taking and suggests things that make the artwork much better. I appreciate him. You can find him at www.fiverr.com/gearguy.

- My childhood friends who, in ways big and small, have encouraged me. A Facebook discussion group helped fill in some blanks regarding the *Fractured Follies* presentation in fourth grade. A special thank-you to Lori Walraven Harrison, who lent me our first-grade yearbook from Cumming Elementary School. A special thank-you, too, to my lifelong friend Lynn Raines McClure and her husband Steve, for their encouragement and help with gathering old school photographs to jog my memory.

- My first friend, Richard Webb, who is the inspiration behind the character Charlie Keller. Richard and I lived so much of this book together, and the retelling of many of these stories is from our mutual retelling of them to each other for fifty years. On two separate occasions, I sat in Richard's office there in Cumming and went through the story lists that were important to our childhood. More than once I called him so he could tell me a story, comparing his memory of it to mine. He was the first person to read those first stories I wrote as a boy, and I will always love him. Today, it only takes a few minutes for him and me to close the gaps of time and distance and be transported back to our shared childhood.

I'm not going to tell you the inspiration behind all the other characters. I will tell you that some characters are composites of multiple people.

A writer must limit characters to help the reader, and I've done that through composites. The best way to help you understand composites is to recall the 2000 movie *The Patriot*, featuring Mel Gibson in the role of patriot Benjamin Martin. If you know Revolutionary War history, you will figure out that the movie character of Benjamin Martin is a composite of real-life patriot heroes Francis "The Swamp Fox" Marion; militia fighter Elijah Clarke; General Daniel Morgan, who was the hero of Cowpens; Andrew Pickens; and General Thomas Sumter.

I did choose to keep the real names of some teachers, school administrators, pastors, and business leaders, just as a tether to reality, but—and this is important—some of the stories involving them are composite stories, which was another tactic I used to manage the number of characters.

A writer always writes through the lens of his or her own life. I know others will remember a different perspective on a story or an event, and that's OK. They are looking at life through the lens of their own lives. I liken it to placing a can of Coca-Cola in the middle of a table with ten people standing or sitting around the table, each looking at the can. Depending on the place at the table and the viewpoint, the can of Coca-Cola—and its labeling—looks different to each person. But it's still the same can of Coca-Cola.

Thank you for stepping back in time with me. I hope you have enjoyed—and are enjoying—this project as much as I am. Yesterday is gone, but it sure is fun to step back in time and be there among dear friends and family.

God bless you and yours,
Scott Vaughan, 2016
www.elmstreetmemories.com
www.scottdvaughan.com

About the Author

Scott Douglas Vaughan is president of Scott Vaughan Communications, LLC, Lexington, South Carolina, a company that serves the strategic communication needs of North American churches and faith organizations. He majored in journalism and minored in sociology at the University of Georgia, going on to become a writer, editor, and newspaper publisher. Vaughan is a former member and award winner in both the Georgia and South Carolina press associations. He and his wife, Vicki, whom he married in 1986, have four grown sons: Andrew (married to Elizabeth), William, Richard, and, Matthew. *Elm Street* is Scott's second book and is inspired by his childhood experiences during elementary and junior high school in small-town North Georgia. He is an Eagle Scout, earning Boy Scout's highest honor through Troop 39, Cumming, Georgia.

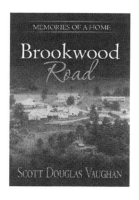

Also by Scott Douglas Vaughan:

Brookwood Road: Memories of a Home
Published 2014
www.brookwoodroad.com

Finalist, National Indie Excellence Awards, 2015
Readers' Favorite Book Awards, 2015

There are both deeds and misdeeds to be done as Frank Wilcox grows up with his brothers, Jack and Wayne, on a rural hog farm in the Deep South.

Frank, Jack, and Wayne are best friends as well as brothers, and their adventures include raising a pet raccoon, getting caught in a storm, and discovering a mysterious hideout. Frank discovers faith when a beloved member of the family dies, and his baseball confidence blooms when he receives an unexpected gift from his daddy.

Frank and his family leave Brookwood Road as he becomes a teenager, but his early years and the stories will be a part of him forever.

Brookwood Road has strong roots in the childhood memories of author Scott Douglas Vaughan, who promised his daddy that he would one day share the tales of life on the family farm. He does so in *Brookwood Road*.

Available at Amazon.com in paperback and Kindle formats.
Autographed and personalized copies are available by direct order from the author.

Made in the USA
Columbia, SC
15 January 2020

86649674R00191